Waltzing in the Dark

African American Vaudeville and Race Politics in the Swing Era

Brenda Dixon Gottschild

St. Martin's Press
New York

WALTZING IN THE DARK

ISBN 0-312-21418-9

Library of Congress Cataloging-in-Publication Data
applied for.

First edition: March 2000
10   9   8   7   6   5   4   3   2   1

*In acknowledgment and affirmation of Margot Webb
and the legions of African American swing era
artists whose names are lost to history*

and

*In celebration and thanksgiving
for my granddaughters, Sky and Sanji-Rei:
new life, new hope, new worlds*

History as "... a thin thread stretching over an ocean of the forgotten."
—Milan Kundera, *The Joke*

"I got a burnin' in my soul to recognize where I'm from...."
—Amel Larrieux, *You Will Rise*

Contents

Nine pages of photographs appear between pages 106 and 107.

Acknowledgments

With heartfelt gratitude and appreciation I thank the following people, all of whom supported me in this endeavor, believed in the necessity of the work, and kept the faith:

Mrs. Margot Webb, whose time, patience, and generosity in granting interviews and sharing her personal archive of clippings, photographs, contracts, letters, and programs made this work possible; Michael Flamini and Alan Bradshaw, my wonderful editors at St. Martin's Press, for their encouragement and forbearance (and thanks, Alan, for your gentle humor and sound advice); copyeditors Roberta Scheer and Meg Weaver for their skills and perspicacity; Lisa Rivero, who adroitly finessed the thankless task of indexing; Tricia Henry Young and Neil Hornick, for invaluable help and insightful criticism as manuscript readers; John Felder who, many years ago, introduced me to the living legacy of African American history; the Pennsylvania Council on the Arts, for a much-needed facilitation grant, with special thanks to Dance Program Director Charon Battles; the New York Public Library for the Performing Arts Dance Collection and Music Division help desk personnel; and Joselli Deans, Joan Huckstep, and Jonathan David Jackson, promising young scholars and doctoral candidates in the Dance Department at Temple University, whose savvy, verve, and enthusiasm are an inspiration to me—and, Joan, thanks for your excellent computer help!

Personal, loving thanks are due to my siblings, George, Christine, Ruth, and Ted, all of whom give me strength simply by being who they are and caring about me, the baby sister; my beloved daughter and son-in-law, Amel and LaRu Larrieux, whose passion for and dedication to their own work and interest in and respect for mine are blessed, joyous gifts; and my "main squeeze," my body-and-soulmate, Hellmut Gottschild—wise, witty, wonderful, my toughest critic and strongest advocate. Praise be to God, Ashe, and Amen.

Foreword

This work is about race and art, two contested constructs that are laden with connotations. They are as controversial as religion and politics, and all four concepts intersect and interfere with one another: we speak of the politics of race or art, of art or race as sacred, while race and religion may determine the trajectory of art or politics. Thanks to contemporary currents in cultural and ethnic studies, we begin to understand race as primarily a sociological construct—not a biological imperative—that is animated by issues of hybridity, marginalization, and postcolonial politics. And, thanks to performance studies, we can take heart in disrupting long held, European-based notions of art versus entertainment, high versus low. Although we may utilize revisionist intellectual tools to perceive these traditional constructs as mutable, labile, and slippery, we need to remember that race politics and cultural dogma determined, controlled, and restricted the world of black swing era vaudeville.

A good portion of the data appearing in this work were collected in archival research and interviews conducted from 1977 to 1980 for preparation of my doctoral dissertation. Upon recent reexamination I discovered that this work contained a wealth of material about a still-ignored area of American performance history. I was struck by its contemporaneity and immediacy. The early data have been revised and expanded in light of current research in the areas of cultural studies, performance studies, and race theory.

Following my initial meeting with Margot Webb at an African American theater archive exhibit over twenty years ago, a series of coincidences were revealed as our association progressed. Within the span of two generations, Webb's life and mine showed remarkable parallels. Both of us grew up in Harlem. While I was a toddler, Webb often visited relatives who lived a block away from the street where I grew up. The Harlem that flourished brightly in her prime still existed as a dim glow in my Harlem adolescence of the late 1950s and early 1960s. The social life of parades, fashion shows, clubs, dances, balls, and beauty contests were part of my youth, just as they had been part of hers. Both of us had been placed in "special progress" classes in mainly white, public junior high and high schools. We had attended the same high school and majored in the same subject—French—at a city college. We had both been seduced by ballet and aspired to dance in Europeanist genres (Webb was an adagio dancer and I a so-called modern dancer). Both of us had performed in Europe and entertained the idea of remaining abroad. Later, we gave up performing careers to become teachers and writers, wives and parents. As I complete this book, Webb is completing research on her family genealogy for publication. Often, in conversations with her, I experienced a distinct sense of *déjà vu* which made me aware of the legacy and continuity of African American culture in the Harlems of America. We shall see, in Margot Webb's career, the common events that link her to the African American gestalt of the swing era.

When I began research on "invisibilized" areas of African American endeavor and the interface between race politics and cultural formation in (African) American performance history some two decades ago, the mainstream community of dance scholars reacted as though I had gone off the deep end. Since that time such an approach has been validated by mainstream trends in cultural studies, and many dance scholars have picked up on these perspectives in their own research. My hope is that, at some point in time—maybe during my lifetime—the issues I pose will be obsolete, power and privilege will no longer be the property of the few, and what has been denied will be remembered and exalted.

Part I

"There are those in white society who think the black people are prone to violence. My own judgment is that their restraint and tolerance have been unbelievable."

—Jack Schiffman

Chapter One

The Race Trope in Swing Era Performance

Background and Premises

I enter a Manhattan subway station and board a crowded train. The stops, starts, and pulsating forward motion of the ride color the mood of the moment. In my mind's ear I hear Duke Ellington's *Take the "A" Train*. I see the song echoed in the body language of the passengers, its syncopation a counterpoint to their movements. I emerge from that underground cavern into the grating edginess, cacophony, and raw energy of the city—a typical day in New York. Going with the flow, I speed up, slow down, swerve or side-step, as needed, to get in the groove. It's a euphoric feeling to be part of it all and see the connections and beauty in it all: jazz is the rhythm of the city. Other times and other circumstances may conjure up Ella Fitzgerald's crooning or Billie Holiday's moaning. Better yet, I put my body on a dance floor, get the feet moving, riff to the steps of the Lindy Hop, and become a visual embodiment of the music myself.

The music and dance of the swing era have become part of New York, as much as skyscrapers and slums, Times Square and Harlem—and part of America. Their trademark is stamped on the art forms of every succeeding generation. They are in the air we breathe.

This book is a study of culture, with performance as the fulcrum. My focal point is the racial climate experienced by African American vaudevillians who worked during the swing era—roughly, the late 1920s through the 1940s.[1] I aim to uncover the specifics of "race etiquette"[2] as they affected the careers and lives of this significant cadre of Americans. My task is to be the notator, in words, for those who were "dancing in the dark."

By "dancing in the dark," to borrow a phrase from a popular song of the era, I mean many things: African Americans disguised themselves, were hardly ever allowed to be themselves, masked their blackness, wore their blackness as a disguise,[3] the mask (as it was since the days of minstrelsy) both a deception and a protection. These permutations were the function of a racial etiquette that affected black artistic existence and influenced the use and abuse of black artistic property. The disguise—shaped by dancing behind, under, through, and sometimes beyond the wall of segregation and discrimination—was a mask that rendered black endeavor invisible and put a cap on black achievement. But their loss was also white America's loss: they were prevented from performing in white venues, and the mainstream spectator was prevented from experiencing a vibrant, original cadre of talent—"and what does that mean in terms of what we got as real art?"[4] Despite these limitations, the work of these artists[5] still infused and influenced the shape and future of mainstream performance.

Some readers may ask: Why embark on such a study of that era at this time? What more is there to be said about race and racism in the United States? What are you uncovering? What is the significance of this? Hasn't this all been done? My response is that these facts need to be known and have not been acknowledged in a comprehensive manner. As much as we may think we know about American race history and theory, we remain in the dark on many specifics. And therein lies the problem. As Ralph Ellison observed: "what is commonly assumed to be past history is actually . . . a part of the living present. . . . Furtive, implacable and tricky, it inspirits both the observer and the scene observed, artifacts, manners and atmosphere and it speaks even when no one wills to listen." (xvi) Like the black body of Ellison's *Invisible Man*, black swing era history is a text of America's seen-yet-hidden legacy—a racialized ancestor whose many faceted story begs a listening ear—and it is crucial information if we are to understand American culture and heritage. "Invisibilized"[6] careers (as well as those of a handful of African American artists, like Duke Ellington and Louis Armstrong, who gained mainstream visibility) are at the center of this study and serve as a lens to examine the particular racial climate of the swing era and to help ascertain "what happens to a dream deferred," to borrow Langston Hughes's eloquent phrase.

Why do we need to know this? Just as Holocaust studies reveal aspects of that cataclysm that are only now seeing the light of day, so also it behooves us—poised at the threshold of the new millennium—to delve into the past and check out the specifics of our race etiquette in every conceivable walk of life, to acknowledge its ins and outs, to own up to "the sheer recalcitrance of racism in America." (Dyson 187) We are obliged to pay attention, to listen as the data demands a hearing and speaks for itself. What is amazing is the unimpeachable fact of the beauty, originality, innovation, creativity, and historical significance of African American cultural invention, with the swing era component as but one exquisite example. In the face of the American "racial mountain,"[7] the power of African American resilience, endurance, perseverance, vitality, and nobility can be acknowledged and, indeed, celebrated.

This study, then, is a continuation of the theory of invisibilization established in my previous work and here applied to the swing era. (Dixon Gottschild, 1998) This period demands—commands—attention because of the integral link between the black swing era aesthetic and global trends in modernism. This information is essential to our understanding of the history of culture and cultural formation in the United States.

Expectations and achievements are integrally connected. The progress of an individual or a community has been known to fluctuate according to presumptions and prejudices: great or meager assumptions tend to lead to the anticipated result. When the issue of racism is factored in, a complex and often crippling syndrome results. The African American experience is a history that is shaped by the presence of racial bias: insider forces, mores, and perspectives must compete with the values and privilege of the dominant outsider culture. In the race contest victories are limited, tempered by restrictions on achievements and reductions in expectations. (Actually, racism diminishes us all, but that is a topic for another book.) From the Broadway where it belonged, black swing era art was relegated to the back roads of American performance and positioned as raw material to be appropriated, watered down, and commodified for mainstream white consumption. The plight of the vaudeville artist demonstrates the racial etiquette of the era and is an example of how performance is a mirror and measure of society.

The career of one dance team, whose work was thwarted by the racial tenor of the times, serves as the barometer and tour guide on this excursion through the interfacing realms of African American vaudeville, swing era lifestyles, and pre–Civil Rights era discrimination. Known professionally as Norton and Margot, Harold Norton and Margot Webb embodied the contested narratives that framed and inflected African American performance in segregated America.[8] From a race studies perspective they are particularly interesting: on one hand, their atypical repertory posed special problems for them and set them apart, in a league all their own; on the other hand, the broad outlines of their career manifested the same issues and setbacks encountered by other black swing era artists. They were one of a handful of African American adagio teams[9] in dance history. Some tap dancers, exotic acts, and Lindy-Hoppers managed occasionally to make their way past the color barrier into the lucrative white entertainment venues. (And, although the team did not pass for white, Margot Webb's first name—already a modification of Marjorie, her given name—was sometimes advertised without the final *t* in order to suggest that she was Latina rather than black.) But, as for most of their vaudeville colleagues, there was no such opportunity for this team. Moreover, theirs was the same dilemma as that faced by conductor Dean Dixon or contralto Marian Anderson: they had embarked on a road posted, in effect, with "Whites Only" signs.

Whites could appropriate black performance styles, trends, and traits and offer them for praise and profit as their own in white performance venues, but the equation was not acceptable when it went the other way. The few slots open for African Americans in white show business called for stereotypes, whether of rhythm and speed, laxity and insouciance, servility, or sexual heat. (A topnotch African American tap dance act possibly could be booked on the Loew's circuit or at Radio City Music Hall; Stepin' Fetchit and the Aunt Jemima-esque Hattie McDaniel were big hits at the movies.)[10] But Norton and Margot were a ballet-trained adagio team who modeled their act after the most famous white swing era ballroom teams (like Veloz and Yolanda and the De Marcos)[11] to pursue a genre, formed and developed by whites, whose origins lay in the work of Vernon and Irene Castle,[12] the team that popularized this genteel style of ballroom dance in the 1910s. To top it off, Margot's solo specialty was a toe dance. Although they didn't have a chance on white circuits, the team was embraced by black audiences who welcomed these novelties in African American vaudeville and loved to see their own take on and master such traditionally white forms.

Actually, ballet was the team's basic orientation. However, with no appropriate venues open to them, Norton and Margot were concert dancers *manqués* who settled for careers on the vaudeville stage.[13] They were prototypes of the black vaudeville performer—the touring artist whose horizons were circumscribed by shoddy management, one-night stands, and the two-to-five-show-a-day format. Above all, there was racial discrimination. Indeed, these dancers, musicians, vocalists, comedians, acrobats, and specialty artists were "dancing in the dark," apart from the limelight of the big circuits.

Perhaps the African American in-group slang for blacks that was common currency during the swing era tells it all. Hipsters referred to one another as "spook" or "shade"—terms that were witty, ironic, sarcastic, and savvy in acknowledging marginalization. For example, in the swing era section of *The Autobiography of Malcolm X,* a shoeshiner at Boston's Roseland Ballroom tells Malcolm Little, who has been observing a white dance at the ballroom, "You ain't seen nothing tonight. You wait until you see a spooks' dance! Man, our own people carry *on!*" (X and Haley, 47)

The Waltz was Norton and Margot's favorite number and closely represented how they chose to see and model themselves. Bathed in an aura of fluid, ethereal romance, it was the dance most reminiscent of ballet adagio work and the lightest, whitest part of their repertory. To complete the disguise, Margot's looks (skin color, hair texture, facial features) were a natural white mask, so to speak, and she made the most of them with artfully appropriate make-up and coiffures. Modeling herself on Hollywood stars of the era, this beautiful young woman was once dubbed "the Marlene Dietrich of Harlem." And black audiences, from their own real-life experiences of masking and disguising, could appreciate the irony of this black team cloaked in a mantle of whiteness. Kept out of white venues yet wearing a mask of whiteness, they were waltzing in the dark.

Theorizing African American performance by definition involves theorizing race. The undergirding premise of this work is that, paralleling black life in the world at large, black performance careers were restricted and determined by the overweening condition and force of racial discrimination. This contention should be obvious and beyond debate. Using the career of Norton and Margot as a prototype, I aim to elucidate and document how this limitation was played out in a particular period of American history—the swing era. Basic to my assertion is the concept of African American venture and enterprise as a constellation of microcosms: black miniatures straddling fences to survive both within and beyond the white world, on the one hand, accepting the white status quo and trying to assimilate into it and, on the other hand, striving to maintain, preserve, and develop a separate identity.

Minstrelsy set the precedent. Ushering in a system of separate, unequal opportunity for black and white artists in the form of segregated minstrel troupes, it was the first and only legitimate, professional theater venue made available to African Americans up until the end of the nineteenth century.[14] This restriction meant that performers who really belonged on the concert stage began and ended up as minstrels, the only avenue open to them for a bona-fide, salaried stage career. An example is the career of concert artist Sissieretta Jones, nicknamed Black Patti because her vocal range paralleled that of Adelina Patti, a renowned coloratura soprano of the era. Had she been white, Jones might have performed on the same popular concert circuits as her eponym. Instead, she became the director of a minstrel troupe, Black Patti's Troubadours. Other concert performers on the minstrel stage included the Luca family of musicians and soprano Elizabeth Taylor Greenfield, known as the Black Swan or the African Nightingale (an allusion to soprano Jenny Lind, who was known as the Swedish Nightingale). Another example is Sam Lucas who, although he had hopes for a career as a dramatic actor, found profitable work only on the minstrel stage. (Toll, 217–19) The ironic as well as tragic result was that professional African American concert artists of the minstrel era were defined, by default, as black minstrels. It is worth noting that sobriquets like Black Swan and Black Patti reinforce the perception of black achievement as a microcosm or miniature of an original white model.

In addition, the black minstrel circuit in no way approximated the revenues of its white counterpart, so African American performers were expected to become accustomed to earning less than whites. In this regard the relationship between African American and European American performers is a microcosm of their relationship in the world at large, again allowing us to understand performance as a barometer of society. These patterns continued into the twentieth century and, by the time the swing era was in full tilt, most African American performers were confined to segregated black circuits drawing considerably smaller salaries than white performers of comparable talent. Many black artists made efforts to raise the ceiling and widen the doors. But this condition and its consequent secondary-citizen status were facts of American life.

A subsidiary premise concerns the African American community as a contested construct. There would be no discrete black community—no need for it—if racism did not permeate every aspect of American life. In spite of (and perhaps because of) pre–Civil Rights segregation and discrimination, the African American community was the bastion of black power and endeavor. Enforced racial separation and inequality not only had negative effects but also grounded and centered this community in positive ways. Notwithstanding fewer financial resources and limited services, the Harlems of America could boast their own infrastructures. There were organizations including black-owned and -operated newspapers, schools (mainly in the South), brotherhoods and sisterhoods (such as the Daughters of the Eastern Star and the Moors Science Temple of America), and churches; professionals including doctors, dentists, nurses, lawyers; artists; small, independently owned businesses including music and dance schools, taxi fleets, caterers, interior decorators, painters, carpenters, handymen, shoemakers, dressmakers, milliners, beauticians, printers, and more: individuals and institutions that provided for a community whose members could not obtain comparable services in white America.[15] It was this generic African American community that rallied behind the ranks of the swing era performers. The army of touring artists was regarded with great pride: they were cultural emissaries from a world beyond the community. In exchange for their talent, camaraderie, and news from faraway places, these communities embraced them, opening their homes to them, and providing them with support, protection, and approval in the form of food and housing, newspaper coverage, medical care, and black-world star status. Thus, the African American community, as a whole, can be construed as another microcosm, a black American satellite with its own values, mores, and resources—some reflecting, some rejecting those of the dominant culture. The main reason why African Americans artists could create such beauty in the face of such racial oppression was because of the strength, support, love, and encouragement imparted to them by the black community.

The profound impact of the dancing body and the dance world, premises central to this work, are unacknowledged factors in the development of American performance. Throughout performance history the pivotal role of dance has been trivialized while other performing arts (music, in particular) have been the focus of print documentation and scholarly attention. Although the swing era is famous for its composers and vocalists, dance—in a myriad of forms and styles—was at its core. Sometimes it was the dancers who taught musicians, particularly percussionists, how and what to play to accompany their ingenious improvisations. According to tap artist John Bubbles, "the dancers helped the drummers a lot, especially the white ones." Dancer Willie Covan said, "They could hear the dancers go off straight rhythm and doing syncopations [sic] and they began to put that into the music. . . ."[16] According to Duke Ellington:

> Some musicians are dancers, and Chick [Webb] was. You can dance with a lot of things besides your feet. Billy Strayhorn was another dancer—in his mind. He was a dance-writer. Chick Webb was a dance-drummer who painted pictures of dances with his drums. Way back, at the Cotton Club, we were always tailoring orchestrations to fit the dances. If you listen to the figures in some of Strayhorn's pieces, like "U.M.M.G.," those are dances—tap dances maybe—and you can't mistake what they essentially are. The reason why Chick Webb had such control, such command of his audiences at the Savoy Ballroom, was because he was always in communication with the dancers and felt it the way they did. (100)

This interdependent, cross-fertilizing relationship is an essential component in African and African American music and dance. By their performances across the nation, black artists brought an African American
presence and sensibility to white America.

Musical names associated with the era include bandleaders such as
Ovie Alston, Fats Waller, Louis Armstrong, Earl Hines, Count Basie,
Teddy Hill, and Chick Webb; arrangers such as Andy Razaf and Billy
Strayhorn; and vocalists such as Ella Fitzgerald, Alberta Hunter, Billie
Holiday, and Lena Horne. Most Americans are still unfamiliar with the
names of outstanding dancers of the era, which include tap artists such as
Charles "Honi" Coles and Charles "Cholly" Atkins, Pete Nugent, Buck
(Ford Lee Washington) and (John) Bubbles, Chuck Green, Teddy Hale,
Bunny Briggs, Baby Laurence; a host of Lindy-Hoppers, including
George "Shorty" Snowden, Norma Miller, Frankie Manning, and Leon
James; exotic or shake dancers such as Sahji (Madeleine Jackson) and
Tondelayo (Wilhelmina Reeves); modern interpretive dancers such as
Anise and Aland; and the ballroom team of Norton and Margot. Indeed,
these represent just a fraction of the gamut of dancers whose work was es-
sential to the "swing" in the swing era.

Whose Paradigm?

A theory of Africanist aesthetics is the final premise that drives this study.
It functions like a circumference: it is the enclosing boundary of this
work. Since the first Africans and Europeans set foot on these alien, new
world shores, their aesthetic (as well as political, social, and religious)
preferences have offered a study in contrasts. In an earlier book I discussed in great detail and with many cultural examples the signature
markers of Africanist (that is, African and African American) and Europeanist (that is, European and European American) standards of beauty,
right action, and good taste.[17] What follows is an extrapolation and dis-
tillation of those concepts as they relate to the swing era—since the swing
aesthetic is, indeed, a modern arm of the Africanist aesthetic. Translated
into era-specific attitudes, art forms, and lifestyles, these aesthetic principles became integral signifiers of modernism and were embraced by white

Americans as well as Europeans. They were manifested in the Negritude, New Negro, and Harlem Renaissance movements of the period, which were overlapping constructs and served as a rallying points for black pride and cultural hegemony. A culture that, heretofore, had been characterized as primitive, folk, vernacular—terminology that separated it from and subjugated it to Europeanist "art" culture—was extolled, although its creators, black people, remained outsiders.

The following Africanist aesthetic constructs are interrelated, interactive, and interdependent; in practice, they cannot possibly be manifested as separate entities.[18]

Embracing the Conflict

Unlike its Europeanist counterpart (epitomized in the harmony and resolution of the diatonic scale in music), the Africanist aesthetic takes delight in friction and dynamic tension. It can be understood as an encounter of opposites wherein expressions or practices that would be considered (in Europeanist terms) irregular or discordant are embraced rather than amended or erased. Embracing the conflict implies ironic reversals. For example, big-band brass and reed players intentionally made their instruments squawk and screech. The sounds that emerged were a brilliantly innovative reach toward new expressive horizons: sounds that would be characterized as ugly according to Europeanist aesthetics were seen as a new standard of excellence.

In the same vein, Louis Armstrong's rasping voice—and the many other jazz voices with unusual timbres—pushed the envelope of vocal expression in new directions. This kind of singing (that has its roots in the plantation field holler and, before that, in African expressive vocal styles) was privileged over the crystal clarity of the Europeanist choirboy sound. Yet, by Europeanist standards, its practitioners were simply poor singers. (It is at this site that issues of biased terminology arise: African American "art" songs—in this case, jazz vocalizing—are considered "folk" songs by Europeanist academic criteria. But those criteria are irrelevant, categorical errors in the Africanist perspective.) Indeed, rasping, gritty, husky, and swishing sounds (as in wire whisks on drums or the sound of an African instrument like the *chekere*) and atonal shadings produced by a feel for microtones were means of expression reflecting centuries-old Africanist values.

Embracing the conflict meant that, unlike Norton and Margot and their white ballroom counterparts, Lindy-Hoppers worked to attain more than just a smooth, flowing whole in their partnering. Various lifts and moves sometimes looked as though a dancing couple was engaged in combat: bodies might slam against one another, move in opposite directions, or move independently of each other. Yet, the total effect was not of a couple out of touch with each other but of two dancing bodies negotiating common ground and embracing the encounter of their difference.

Likewise, embracing the conflict means embracing life's comedy and tragedy in the same stroke, a basic characteristic of the musical form known as the blues. To reiterate, this premise and those following are overlapping, interconnected concepts.

High-Affect Juxtaposition

This principle deals with mood, attitude, or movement breaks that omit the transitions and connective links valued in the European academic aesthetic. Such an intense degree of contrast was read as disruption, in Europeanist terms, and wrought havoc upon concepts of continuity and resolution. For example, the Lindy-Hopper or rhythm tap dancer is allowed to insert anything, no holds barred, into her improvisations. Movements that are humorous, imitative, abstract, or sober may be juxtaposed, so that the concept of uniformity may be undermined—as long as one keeps the timing and preserves the rhythm. One might say that the level of free improvisation allowed in swing dancing paralleled the psychological concept of free association: the (black) dancing body was engaged in a nonlinear, non-narrative, movement experience. Aesthetic value was placed on "letting your hair down" (or, as a later generation put it, "letting it all hang out"). With right-brain creativity granted agency, left-brain logic took a back seat, and the intelligent, thinking body was allowed free rein to create and innovate. The emergent result was, quite often, a radical juxtaposition of effects.

The same holds true for swing music. This, by the way, is one of the reasons why the black swing aesthetic took hold as a vehicle for modernist expression: it disallowed those constricting conventions that defined a conservatory approach to performing arts and offered itself as an alternative. This new artistic approach gave validity to a broad, unexplored range of possible sounds and movements. Of course, all traditions use contrast as part of the shading and coloring that make art forms interesting and unique. But high-affect juxtaposition goes beyond the conventional, polite, acceptable range of contrast to that place of danger where the work may be characterized, from an outsider perspective, as poorly paced, naive, lowly, loud, flashy, or simply an example of bad taste. All these labels had been given to black swing culture by the dominant culture's pundits: when white dancers and musicians took up swing, generally they distilled and finessed it to a white-acceptable standard. But there were others who were smart enough to see that a new criterion was needed to judge these emergent forms. In the 1920s, critic Arnold Haskell credited African Americans with the ability to "blend the impossible and create beauty."(204)

Ephebism

This precept embodies the full force of individual and/or collective power, drive, attack, vitality, and flexibility. It manifests itself as a combined sensual, spiritual, and metaphorical intensity and energy wherein every note (stanza, movement, brush, or chisel stroke) is phrased with quintessential vitality, responding to rhythm and a sense of swing as inherent attributes. Ephebism is about fullness, going all the way, digging deep down into one's medium and reaching to its outer limits to the point that one is fully engaged in the lived experience of the art form, be it dance, music, painting, sculpture, or anything else. Experiencing the fullness of one's medium implies taking risks. Classical Europeanist aesthetic principles are, again, reversed: thus, energy takes the lead and primacy over form, and the living process shapes the product, rather than the other way around.

To translate these principles into swing aesthetics meant that body suppleness, vitality, and flexibility—the intelligence of the dancing body—were more important for dancers than demonstrating a predetermined movement technique such as the standardized ballet vocabulary. Rhythm, timing, vital flashes of innovation that might change with each performance—in other words, the overarching power of improvisation—were valued above set, formal, repeatable patterns. Ephebic energy is inexorably connected to timing and rhythm as principal values. This focal emphasis on rhythm, timing, percussive vitality, and luminous energy are rather muted values in academic Europeanist aesthetic practice.

Polyrhythm

This precept is most marked in African music and dance traditions and is translated in the African American experience as counterrhythms and cross-rhythms. The swing era shift from a two-beats-to-a-bar sensibility to four, eight, or even more beats predicated the shift to a landscape that offered a range of possibilities for interspersing, undergirding, overlaying, and cross-referencing improvised beats and rhythms.

The Aesthetic of the Cool

Just as these aesthetic principles are the circumference of this study, so this final principle is the embracing boundary and reference point for the four preceding precepts. Simultaneously predicated on visibility and masking, the cool is the dynamic tension that exists between the two; accordingly, those who manifest this precept have successfully accomplished a balancing act between semblance and secrecy. In academic circles this cool could easily be read as impoliteness. It goes beyond the Europeanist conventions of containment, aloofness, or detachment. It carries with it an attitude (in the African American sense of that word) of carelessness combined with a calculated sense of aesthetic clarity. The cool is manifested in the mien of the musician or dancer whose body and energy may be working ephebically hard, fast, and hot, but whose face remains as calm and detached as an ancestral mask. It may also be expressed in a dazzling smile that seems to come from nowhere to break, intercept, and disrupt the established mood by momentarily flashing its opposite and, thus, mediating a balance. Like the precepts of high-affect juxtaposition and embracing the conflict, the cool plays with the drama of opposites: hot is its indispensable complement, the two are flip sides of the same coin, and the one illuminates and contains the other. The cool aesthetic resides in embodying the paradoxes, from inside-out and outside-in.[19]

The zoot-suited "hep cat" was a swing era manifestation of cool. His costume may have seemed ridiculously ostentatious to pundits of the dominant culture. But it was a supreme balancing act to wear such an extreme outfit (billowing pants radically pegged at the ankles, long jacket with pinched waist, pointed-toed, thin-soled shoes, thick-linked, gold-plated chain and, to top it off, a wide-brimmed hat) and to saunter into a ballroom or club, affecting nonchalance: the outfit—hot; the attitude—cool. (See X and Haley, 52, 58) The extremes of the costume were so drastic that they went beyond the realm of the gaudy and came out as a new fashion statement, exemplifying Haskell's blend of the impossible to create beauty.

More to the point, swing music and dance were the essence of cool. Both integrated hot, energetic, vital rhythms into hip, innovative arrangements; both easily allowed improvisation and scored sections to democratically function as equal partners. Both were era-specific indicators of the brilliance, luminosity, flexibility, and flair, the humor, irony, and perseverance of African American aesthetics and the communities that had spawned them.

These principles were modified and finessed by Europeans and European Americans to fit their needs as they utilized the Africanist aesthetic in forms ranging from American ballet to mainstream popular music.

"It Don't Mean a Thing . . ."

What is swing?

From the Cotton Club's spring 1937 revue—its second Broadway production and the first in which all major music was created by blacks (African Americans Duke Ellington, Andy Razaf, John Redmond, and Afro-British Reginald Foresythe)—it was Duke Ellington's composition, *It Don't Mean a Thing if It Ain't Got That Swing*, that introduced the term "swing" in popular parlance. Swing became the *ne plus ultra*, the hot, sexy commodity of the era. There is a tinge of irony in the fact that swing was a hot ticket: the word itself had been used as a substitute for "hot"—as in "hot jazz"—by British Broadcasting Company announcers who, early on, associated the hot connotation with immorality. (Stearns, 197) Meanwhile, swing became such a marketable commodity in the States that, cashing in on the trend, Hollywood produced more than fifty movies containing the word "swing" in the title. (Miller, xxv–xxvi)[20]

As stated at the outset of this study, I calculate the swing era to run from the late 1920s through the 1940s. Some historical jazz writers take a harder line and date the era from 1935 to 1945, beginning definitively with the Benny Goodman band's booking at the Palomar Ballroom in Los Angeles. For example, Stearns asserts that "the Swing Era was born on the night of 21 August 1935." (211) However, contemporary scholarly methodology behooves us to look more closely at the roots and early examples of cultural constructs, particularly when the issue of cultural expropriation (from the African American community, in this case) and its attendant power politics are on the table. I give the era a looser, more general (or generous) chronology in order to acknowledge its black roots in the work of groups led by musicians like Fletcher Henderson, Bennie Moten, Sam Wooding, Louis Armstrong, Don Redman, and Duke Ellington (to name only a few) that certainly were "swinging" early on. This broader time line acknowledges that swing and swing bands led by black musicians existed prior to the 1935 Goodman engagement.[21] Important innovations by Louis Armstrong and Earl Hines as early as 1927 and 1928 were illustrative of concepts that would become inextricably linked to swing. In addition, these broader parameters embrace the substantial and significant overlap between Dixieland and swing on the early end, and bebop and swing in the post–World War II era.

Swing music, then, is jazz music that manifests an equal partnership between arranged orchestration and improvisation. Likewise, swing dance—epitomized by the Lindy Hop and rhythm tap genres—is performed to swing music and presents improvisation and arranged structures as equal partners. These are simple but workable definitions, and they need elucidation. Swing music and dance manifest a democratic play between rhythmic structures and rhythmic improvisation, "combining improvisation and arrangement in a single structure." (Ostransky, 246) Swing musicians attest to the fact that their potential for sublime improvisational achievement is determined by and dependent upon the groove and drive of their rhythmic base. (Goddard, 177) In fact, another simple, technical definition of swing is the change from "two-beat rhythms with accents on the upbeats [to] . . . four/four rhythms with accents on the downbeats." (Giddins, 13) The significant point in the doubling of beats in a bar is that this simple tactic expands the musician's or dancer's potential for improvising cross-rhythms. That is, if one begins to think and act with the number of units (beats per bar) increased, there is greater potential for inserting one's own counterrhythms over the basic beat. Then, if the performer takes the next step and begins to experience the eighth note as the underlying rhythmic unit, the trick can be taken to the complex rhythmic heights that are demonstrated in the best of swing music and dance.

The 2/4 beat was characteristic of New Orleans-based Dixieland music. This kind of beat is known as stop-time. The "oom-pah" tuba and the tinny, string sound of the banjo comprised the rhythm section of pre-swing bands, along with the piano. As swing dance historian Ernie Smith has pointed out, the tuba is a slow instrument: it would be well-nigh impossible to play a steady 4/4 beat on it for the length of a song. For dancers who followed the implications of the music, its sound encouraged the hopping, bouncy movements and verticality that characterized dances like the Charleston and the Black Bottom. The change to 4/4 time was predicated on a change in orchestral instrumentation. The tuba and banjo were replaced by the upright string bass, guitar, and the modern percussion battery (drum set and cymbals, drumsticks and wire whisks) which, along with the piano, produced a softer, shimmering, more flowing rhythm section—a swinging cadre. This new sound was conducive to developing complex, multirhythmic dances like the Lindy and rhythm tap dance. (Miller, xi-xxxvii) It was characterized by "first-rate improvisation against provocative riffs, and a vibrant, pulsating, rhythmic background." (Ostransky, 242–43) In addition, the size of the jazz band was expanded. Swing bands are called big bands because they grew from five or seven musicians to a total of twelve or fifteen.

Technically, swing also has a lot to do with timing and the perfect placement of notes in relation to rhythm. Another swing signature is the repetition device known as the riff, a musical motif that may be repeated up to twenty or thirty times in one number. This technique is an example of Africanist repetition utilized to create intensity and dramatic tension rather than boredom. "[I]t is truly an insensitive listener who is not able to understand what the jazzmen are driving at. Riffs at their best are driving, pushing, rocking forces that move the soloist to exceed his limitations. . . ."(ibid., 245) Performance critic Gilbert Seldes, writing in the 1930s, gave a good sense of the effect produced by the interplay of improvisation and riffing in a swing setting:

> The members of a good swing band instinctively improvise harmoniously. Individuals will no doubt remember a particular hot "lick" and repeat it on later occasions; there will always be tremendous pace, exciting rhythms and counterrhythms, and in most cases a frenzy of noise. I have heard a swing band rise step by step in speed and tone, repeating some thirty or forty bars of music until it seemed impossible to listen to it any longer. Yet that was only the beginning, and it was after the music had reached apparently its extreme limits that the really expert work began and the effects were multiplied by geometric progression; in this sort of thing the idea of a climax and a quiet ending [that is, Europeanist aesthetic principles] simply could not exist. When the leader was exhausted, he said "close," and abruptly a shattering silence followed. (ibid., 71)

Stearns described riffing as "a fine art which built up each number, chorus after chorus, in the manner of a *bolero*." (199)

The early contributions of trumpeter Louis Armstrong were quintessential in the development of swing. Beginning in the 1920s this great artist was working out the swing aesthetic at live performances with groups like the Fletcher Henderson orchestra (1923) and in recording sessions for Okeh Records in Chicago (1927–28) with the Louis Armstrong Hot Five and the Louis Armstrong Hot Seven. One of his solos on the Okeh recording of *Potato Head Blues* was described as "a triumph of subtle syncopation and rhythmic enlightenment; strong accents on weak beats and whole phrases placed *against* rather than *on* the pulse create delightful tension." His solo on *Struttin' With Some Barbecue* is "clearly breaking through the old formulas . . . a radiant experiment in the construction of long lines without sacrifice of melodic simplicity and rhythmic momentum." Armstrong's innovative phrasing and use of rhythm as melody presaged the advent of Charlie Parker nearly two decades later. Indeed, in the 1920s Armstrong was avant-garde, and swing was the shape of things to come. His ideas, worked out in solo improvisation, would be developed by bands like Bennie Moten's and Count Basie's in the early 1930s—before Benny Goodman's—to become the characteristic ensemble swing style.[22]

The "swing" in the swing era was as much indebted to dance as it was to music. Accomplished Lindy-Hoppers and rhythm tap artists worked like musicians, using the body like a finely-tuned instrument. These dancers had gained a sophisticated understanding of swing music and, specifically, the style and arrangements of the bands with whom they worked most frequently. They were dancer-choreographers and "used steps and dance patterns that not only reflected the music, but also provided counterpoint." (Miller, xiv) In this sense, the Lindy and rhythm tap, as performed by adept professionals, allowed the world to *see* swing as well as hear it.

Just as swing music was characterized by its riffs, the Lindy was known for the breakaway or swing out—where the partners literally swing away from each other, or the male swings his partner away from him, in what can lead to an improvisational time-out. In spite of its step patterns and it status as the dance to dance to swing music, the Lindy was not a matter of repetitive, learned step patterns; it was about merging movement with music and blurring the boundaries between them.

As Willie Covan stated, rhythm tap dancers were not simply inspired by swing music: they were, in many cases, the force and stimulus that pushed the music beyond its borders. Rhythm tap is all about using the body through the feet as a percussive instrument. These dancer-musicians could tap out rhythms that were beyond the range of band members. Several dancers assert that they taught rhythmic complexities to inexperienced drummers through their own dancing prowess. Rhythm tap dancers were, indeed, musicians of the highest order, and specific dancers worked for long periods with particular swing bands. Thus, Baby Laurence had worked with Count Basie; Bunny Briggs with Charlie Barnet, Count Basie, Earl Hines, and Duke Ellington; Jimmy Slyde with Ellington and Basie; Honi Coles with Cab Calloway; Teddy Hale with Louis Jordan. (Miller, xxxiv)

However, what constitutes swing is more complex than the simple increase in beats or rhythmic overlays and interplays. As with all art forms, there are definitions and then there is the *je ne sais quoi*, the ineffable, that makes something "what it is" rather than "what it ain't"—a truism expressed humorously by swing bandleader Jimmie Lunceford in his 1939 hit *It Ain't What You Do, It's the Way That You Do It*. Swing culture and the swing aesthetic are part of a rich lineage of Africanist cultural processes that intimate the power of repetitive human and natural rhythms balanced and offset by improvisation and spontaneity. Heartbeat, blood pulsing through human vessels, breath inspiration and expiration—as well as blood memories from slavery and from Mother Africa. Repetitive rhythms of field work, and the syncopated explosion of train wheels on railroad tracks. The rise and fall of ships on waves during Middle Passage. Skin-muscle-bloodstream memories and rhythms that are finally liberated and exorcised at the swing train station, figuratively speaking. Being inside this repetitive rhythmic imperative is what it means to be "in the groove." As Ellington's *Take the "A" Train* implied, the rhythm of the music and the rhythm of the subway train led to Harlem and good times—if not freedom. Jazz historian Robert O'Meally has pointed out that jazz music is fundamentally "good times" music for rites of communion, courtship, fertility; it is about communication, usually with a playful attitude toward the beat: sometimes the musician/dancer is ahead of it, sometimes behind it. (conversation with author, 9 April 1999) Swing music and dance reflect a particular style, attitude, spontaneity, and feel for improvisation at a level of expression that extends far beyond the realm of notated symbols, rehearsed steps, or set patterns.

Swing art forms intimated attitudes that did not emanate from European aesthetic principles. Swing posture—labeled "hep," "hip," "with it," "in the groove," and other evocative phrases—was an outpouring of African/African American manners, mores, and aesthetics that had to do with wearing a different mask: the mask of a cool and knowing irony, a humorous, street-smart cockiness that manifested discord (rather than diatonic harmony) and was proud of it. It was on display in African American music, dance, and lifestyles that became globally marketable in a century that was moving toward glorifying the antihero, a modernist move away from Victorian earnestness. The black swing aesthetic was in the right place at the right time.

The "Unit"

If there is one vaudeville institution that is emblematic of the race trope in swing era performance, it is the traveling "unit." The major employment vehicle for Norton and Margot, the unit brings to mind an unlikely historical antecedent. In medieval Europe, the Ship of Fools was a world unto itself. Separated and isolated from any particular community, it journeyed from port to port, its denizens[23] amusing the locals and then moving on. Likewise, these black performers moving across the country were separated and isolated from the worlds through which they traveled. Their ship was the unit. Though its walls were invisible and permeable, the unit functioned as an isolated bubble bounced about on the sea of white circumstance as it traveled from theater to theater across the nation. Its format followed the pattern of its predecessors in the black performing arena and dated back to old entertainment formulas and prescriptions that had been developed and modified, chronologically, through minstrelsy, pre–World War I vaudeville (like the famous *Darktown Follies* at the Lafayette theater in 1913), and the Theater Owner's Booking Association (TOBA) era.[24] The unit deserves special attention: it provides a wealth of information on African American vaudeville and race politics. It can be understood both as a metonym for the African American vaudeville performer who, likewise, was insulated and circumscribed within the parameters of racism, and as a microcosm of the African American community, an itinerant Harlem, so to speak. Whether confined to urban enclaves in cities like Chicago and Baltimore or living in rural Indiana or Oklahoma without the support of a centralized black community, African Americans welcomed the unit tours and relied on them for cultural reinforcement and group identity. The unit offered protection, support, and sustenance to its ensemble of performers. These artists learned the specifics of race etiquette the hard way: by raw experience on the road in America's heartland.

The unit was both secure and unstable: secure in that it imparted strength to its individuals as they encountered the alien world of middle America—the strength that only an institution can confer; unstable in its low salaries sometimes undelivered, meaningless contracts, and the inevitability of dealing with crafty agents, theater owners, and communities whose hostility could outmatch the unit's capacity for protection. Created by agencies and booking agents, units preserved the protocols that the entertainment industry dictated for contracts, salary guidelines, and internal structure. The formalities, however, were flexible. Since each act negotiated its terms individually with the theater owners or booking agents, the performers were free to leave if a better offer came their way. Contracts were usually for ten weeks of touring, and a unit existed for the length of one tour on one circuit.

The basic component of the traveling unit was the big band. The master of ceremonies introduced the program and was also a performer or musician in the show. Frequently it was the bandleader or a comedian-dancer who filled this slot. The entire cast joined in a big choreographed opening number and the grand finale, with the chorus line dancing as backup for the featured acts (although the unit tours going to the West did not include chorines). The opening number presented the theme of the show and often had a special song written for it, as did the finale. Themes frequently involved locations: the plantation, "down Mexico way," the South Seas, the Caribbean, Brazil, Americana. The opening was followed by a fast tap or novelty dance act. There was a range of eccentric acts in black (and white) swing era vaudeville. Performers such as the 300-pound Peters Sisters and the 250-pound vocalist Velma Middleton amazed audiences by their dancing agility; Middleton climaxed her routine by performing full splits. The team of Danny and Edith jumped rope while roller-skating. Dancer-skater Harold King concluded his act by skating, blindfolded, on a two-feet-square table. Physically challenged dancers like the one-armed, one-legged Crip Heard and wooden-legged Peg Leg Bates plied their disabilities as novelties.

This dance slot would be followed by a male or female vocalist, or sometimes both. When there were two, the singers customarily followed their solos with a duet or sang one later in the program. A comedian was usually next on the bill. A featured act (which might be a team like Norton and Margot) appeared just before the top billed act (usually a sensational tap team, like the Nicholas Brothers or the Berry Brothers, who had gained a high level of popularity and visibility in black show business), which was followed by the grand finale.

From featured acts to atmospheric background, dance inflected the entire show. According to Margot Webb, "There were always comics;

there were always tap dancers . . . and in all the years that I worked, there [was always a production number which] would either be a jungle type thing or a soft-shoe with the show girls parading around in the beautiful hats and gowns and the [chorus] girls dancing in front of them in shorter costumes. The same format existed for a very long time." (25 June 1980)[25]

Everyone joined in the finale. Each featured act performed a fast, eight-bar step to the same tune in front of the line of chorines, who were in front of the show girls, themselves in front of the band, and each act in the unit remained onstage after completing their bit. By the end of the finale, the stage was jumping with a full cast dancing and singing the same upbeat song. Finally, the entire cast joined together in a chorus to perform in unison some popular new dance step or an old favorite, such as the Shim-Sham, the Shorty George, or Trucking.[26]

Norton and Margot performed in unit tours on the East Coast black touring circuit that played the black theaters in New York (the Apollo), Washington, D.C. (the Howard), Philadelphia (the Lincoln and Fay's Theater), Baltimore (the Royale), and, occasionally, Chicago (the Regal). Performing with the units out West, they played in white vaudeville theaters that had booked African American shows in the movie-plus-stage-show format since the end of the 1920s. In other words, black touring units played in black houses located in black communities back East, and in white vaudeville theaters to white audiences out West. It was because of white vaudeville's decline that the latter opportunity became available.[27] In general a unit remained in each theater in each town for a week at a time. (Theater contracts specified one week with management's option for extension, depending upon a unit's success and the theater's booking schedule.) Occasionally they stayed for two or even three weeks, milking the maximum attendance potential of the local audience which was augmented by people attending from surrounding small towns. These venues did not book shows continuously and were often closed down for weeks at a time (which would have been unheard of during white vaudeville's heyday).

As a result of white vaudeville's slow death and dwindling number of performance venues, a white specialty act, such as an acrobatic or juggling team, might be booked independently and appear on the same bill as an African American touring unit. Generally, these acts did not mingle with the African Americans backstage, and they functioned as separate entities. Likewise, it was occasionally possible for a black vocalist or tap act to be booked independently on a touring white vaudeville package. Again, this was due not to mainstream initiatives toward affirmative action but to the shrinking waters of white vaudeville that caused white variety performers to jump ship. Here, too, blacks remained segregated from the white performers, onstage and backstage. But Norton and Margot were never booked on these circuits because of the too-white tenor of their act. When they worked independently, they were booked into African American units that were already on the road.

Units worked long spells on white and black theater circuits and offered continuous work for the most popular swing era performers. If an act was lucky, it could work from unit to unit for four to six months, possibly with no day off. Performers could also pick up extra work in white or black cabarets while on the road. White clubs followed the precedent set by New York's Cotton Club: all-black entertainment for an all-white clientele.

The unit's touring schedule in theaters was a lark, compared to the dreaded, fatiguing one-night stands that were common bookings for the bands. Norton and Margot refused to perform one-nighters; nor did they travel by bus. This meant that they missed out on work that might have been available to them as the featured specialty act on a band tour. (The one-nighters had no accompanying revue except, perhaps, a vocalist or a tap or novelty dance act.) The big bands went on many such tours out West and down South, playing in black theaters and white dance halls. According to bassist John Williams, who played in the bands of Louis Armstrong, Lucky Millinder, and Teddy Wilson, the bands played perhaps Friday through Sunday nights and filled in the rest of the week playing for dances at nearby towns until they moved on to the next region. (15 August 1980)

The musicians' life on the road was more grueling than that of featured acts, simply because musicians were in greater demand in a larger variety of venues, playing the theaters, nightclubs, ballrooms, after-hours clubs, and dance halls of the dance-hungry swing era. Big-name artists like Count Basie and Louis Armstrong virtually lived on the road. Williams recalled in the same interview that "We'd leave here [New York] in January, and it would probably be May or June before we came back." He described his longest string of one-night stands, in 1941, with the Louis Armstrong band: "We had thirty-one one-nighters—just dances. . . . [When] you finished the dance [any time between two and four in the morning], you'd come in the bus and change your clothes. Joe Glaser was traveling with us at that time [as road manager]. To make it in time for the job the next night, you'd probably get in town around eleven or twelve o'clock [noon]. So you'd go to the hotel, get some sleep, get up and play the dance, and do the same thing the next day. So for a month you lived in the bus."

Norton and Margot went on unit tours that originated in Chicago and went West in 1934, 1935, and 1937. The rules of Jim Crow prevailed and, in general, African Americans were not permitted in the audience at these white vaudeville theaters, not even when black units were performing. Occasionally theaters permitted blacks in the balcony but not in the orchestra. Light-skinned blacks might pass for white and thus gain general entry. In comparing Midwest and East Coast touring, Margot Webb states:

> If you started [a tour on the African American East Coast circuit] and you worked in January, you might work all through January and February. Now, you've completed the circuit—you're back to New York. Now, they wouldn't book you again right away, because everyone's seen your act—unless you change your act each time, and that would have been very difficult. It would mean paying for routines, for music, for everything, new gowns and all. . . . You'd have to find work in a club someplace else, and then work [this circuit] again, say, in the fall. . . . If you went [on the Midwest tour] from Chicago all through the Southwest, you could work every week, a week at each theater in each town, small or large. So you would have, maybe, twenty weeks straight without a break, without a day off, you see, because you worked every day. . . . And if you worked in a club, you could work a whole year if they liked you there. . . . (6 March 1978)

It was a matter of dollars and cents. There were no unions, no paid holidays or sick days, no medical coverage; and most performers did not have a personal agent or manager. In the most existential sense, it was the work that mattered, and the more work, the better, especially during the Depression. By the end of World War II, with the advent of the double feature, film-newsreel-cartoon format, the white vaudeville outlet had dried up as a source of employment for black entertainers, and only night-club work remained. Black artists had had their moment—or decade—of opportunity. They had filled those spaces vacated by whites who had moved on to other venues, and then it was over.

Simultaneously flexible and stable, the unit was a paradoxical construct of segregation, a miniature black community which, like the full-scale model, was independent of and yet utterly dependent upon the white world. Traveling across America, it reinforced the collective strength and group identity of its members, offering them a structure and protection against the alien mainstream society that provided their income but treated them like outsiders.

Playing the Race Card

In any given era one can investigate a society's performance culture and obtain a fairly accurate barometer of the state of affairs in the culture at large. By looking at dance, one can see reflected in specific genres the norms and mores of the society. Performance styles, forms, and trends that are in vogue reflect, inflect, or contest contemporary values and are so intimately enmeshed in social and cultural history that they can be read as a scan of a given era, a blueprint of the greater culture's power struc-ture. Take, for example the hierarchies that defined European ballet: the institutionalized ballet company, the classical repertory, and the technical lexicon of body positions. They are a map of a class system reflecting ab-solute monarchy, with Europe—and the European dancing body—at the center and on top of the world.[28] Other examples are the subtle grada-tions in performance prerogatives at a gathering of the Asante royal court in Ghana, or the Japanese etiquette of caste and power encoded in Kabuki. In each case the rules determining who, what, when, where, how, why, and how long one is allowed to dance reflect that culture's hierarchy of power and its understanding of what constitutes right or socially sanctioned behavior.[29]

In the case of African American vaudeville, race hegemony was a societal tool of power that commandeered African American performers as a cheap labor force whose fate was in the hands of a network of predominantly white owners, managers, and booking agents, and that affected the course and quality of their careers. Reflecting the relationship between blacks and whites in other areas of American life, the means of production of black vaudevillians—namely, black-based performance styles—was incorporated into the white mainstream without acknowledgment or compensation. This designation and displacement of privilege is a striking example of power politics at work on the cultural front that left the black vaudeville artist "dancing in the dark." The unit's day-to-day existence as it moved through white America is a case in point.

Given the grueling performance schedule when working the circuits out West, most of the time between unit shows was spent backstage, a situation that heightened the insular nature of the touring experience and deepened the chasm separating the unit from the white world across the footlights and outside the stage door. Life on the road was a daily routine of staying in the theater all day long—performing in four or five shows, sending out for food and necessities, living in a dressing gown between shows, preparing costumes for the next show—and returning, exhausted, to the hotel or rented room late in the evening, after the last show. Two obvious reasons for staying backstage were the relatively short amount of time between shows, sometimes less than an hour's free time in a five-a-day format, and the need to conserve energy for performance. As Webb explains, "In between, of course, most of the girls played cards. There was nothing much to do. . . . If you were in the theater, the time went very fast. . . . You'd do four or five shows a day, so you hardly had time to get your next outfit together. . . ." (6 March 1978) Webb added that there was no place to lie down or do a proper warm-up in the backstage area.[30] For all performers, black or white, the day-to-day reality of life on the road was no picnic. For African Americans, the issue was heightened: the third reason for staying backstage was the hostile racial tenor of the mid- and southwestern towns. African Americans were unwelcome in the white vicinity of the theaters; yet, black communities—due to the etiquette of segregation—were far removed from the central location of the theaters. Swing era performers like Margot Webb, born and raised in New York City, had to adjust to overt levels of racism and limits on performance potential that they could not have calculated before leaving the city. It is one thing to hear about segregation and something else to experience how it works. Realizing this, Norton and Margot refused to perform in the South to avoid what was assumed to be the most blatant and dangerous strains of this disease. (This was a wise decision, since Norton had a reputation as an outspoken man with a volatile temper.) Yet, they encountered deep discrimination in the Midwest. For example, Webb cites Elkhart, Indiana, as a low point in her travels, stating that it was impossible even to buy takeout food from white vendors in the neighborhood of the vaudeville house where they performed.[31] It was in instances like this that members of the African American community came to the rescue, acting as a buffer and lifesaver for the touring vaudevillian by opening their homes, pension-style, for room and board.

On the few occasions when they had a day off, black performers could run into trouble if they attempted to go to white theaters or restaurants. Webb recalls a rare nonworking day in Detroit when she and a friend, dressed with the impeccable care and style of swing era performers cultivating a successful image, were refused service in a restaurant. This was in the 1930s and they did not even consider lodging a formal complaint: they would be on the road again in a day or two. (6 March 1978)

In the world of performance and in the world at large, what is remarkable about the American race game is the regional nature of the way it was played and the variety of its intricate arrangements. Protocol and precedent changed from state to state, from nightclub to theater. Although some African Americans from New York and other northeastern urban centers may have believed that southern racism was the worst kind, there were others who appreciated the overt nature of the southern code: at least you knew where you stood. "Colored" and "white" signs may have affronted sensibilities, but they also obviated the embarrassment or potential danger of making a move that was destined for rejection, such as Webb's Detroit restaurant incident. In fact, midtown New York was as segregated as downtown Atlanta during the swing era, but the stakes were different. There was the illusion of freedom: one could sit wherever one chose on buses and subways, borrow books from the public library, or enjoy Central Park; and no one was lynched. Yet, the unwritten Yankee code was generally understood by the populace, black and white, and was entrenched and perpetuated by decades of conditioning on both sides. It was as effective a tool of segregation as the signs down South: "Blacks were permitted to attend downtown theaters in New York, although [i]t was an era when Negroes had trouble purchasing orchestra seats in theaters and meals in public restaurants . . . when indeed a Manhattan shadow of the Mason-Dixon line fell directly across the island at 110th Street." (Kellner, 195) Writer James Baldwin recalled that dividing line in an interview: "I was crossing Fifth Avenue and Forty-second Street on my way to the [main branch of the New York Public] Library and a cop—a traffic cop—said to me, a 13-year-old boy [in 1937], and I'll never forget this: 'Why don't you niggers stay uptown where you belong?'" ("I Remember Harlem")

In Washington, D.C., the nation's capital, African Americans were not allowed in white theaters. (Hughes and Meltzer, 288–89) As a general rule (excluding the few "Black and Tan" clubs, where the races mixed), neither in New York nor anywhere else could an African American attend a white nightclub despite the fact that some of these clubs presented only black performers. The most renowned offender in this category was the famous night spot in central Harlem, the Cotton Club, whose black entertainment for all-white audiences was its claim to "aristocracy."

African Americans were not employed by midtown Manhattan department stores, nor by white-owned stores on 125th Street, Harlem's main thoroughfare. As a result of a 1934 boycott of Blumstein's Department Store, the largest offender on the avenue, some African Americans were hired by that establishment. But it would take a riot in 1935 and another boycott in 1938, led by two ministers, one of them the Rev. Adam Clayton Powell, Jr., for the integration process to begin.[32] Before these organized civil protests blacks were refused service in white-owned restaurants in Harlem and, as in Washington, D.C., could buy clothes in major white-owned stores but were not allowed to try them on. Blacks could attend one Loew's theater in the Harlem community but were refused admission at another one that was designated for whites. ("I Remember Harlem") In order to shop downtown (and especially on Fifth

Avenue) blacks had to dress up to be served.[33] The community grapevine alerted residents as to which stores were favorable and which were off-limits in Harlem and greater Manhattan.

In 1935, after spending a successful decade in Paris and becoming the toast of the town there, Josephine Baker returned to New York and was refused accommodations at the St. Moritz Hotel. To add insult to injury, her Italian husband-manager and her French maid were told that they could remain—without Baker. (Baker and Chase, 191) In the 1940s Schrafft's, an ordinary, middle-class Manhattan restaurant, was notorious for refusing service to blacks: the staff waited on whites and ignored any blacks present. They didn't utter a racist word, but their message was clear. Banks and other commercial enterprises simply did not hire blacks. These conditions did not end with the close of the swing era: growing up in Harlem in the 1950s, I was aware that blacks could not "get a room at the Waldorf-Astoria"—a stock phrase in the black community at the time that served as a metaphor for all the accommodations even money could not buy if the customers were black.

Housing was segregated, although one black family might be tolerated in an otherwise white neighborhood. Frequently such a family was so light-skinned that their neighbors were unaware they were black. For example, Webb mentioned that part of her family had lived in Queens in an all-white neighborhood in the 1920s; however, their ethnicity was probably unknown in the community. (8 July 1998) Sections of suburbs where African Americans took up residence by the late 1940s and early 1950s (such as St. Albans, Queens, where a community of black professionals, performers, and athletes lived)[34] began as integrated communities but, due to white flight, became black suburban enclaves.

Other regional differences were so specific that, for example, African Americans were permitted to study at professional-level white ballet studios in New York but not in Philadelphia. The black dancer was not given any particular encouragement or professional opportunities in the New York classes but, simply, was allowed in the door. Light-skinned African Americans sometimes passed for white in order to avoid these restrictions. On the one hand, to pass looked like a denial of self and heritage; on the other hand, it was a way of plugging into the power and agency that was usurped by the dominant culture.

Performance management remained as racist as the banking profession. Power and profit rested in white hands. As it had been since the minstrel era, African Americans were virtually barred from this echelon of the entertainment profession. White agents, managers, and institutions, in an unwritten gentlemen's agreement, negotiated only with whites. Given this situation, blacks who had the opportunity to perform in Europe jumped at the chance. Norton and Margot toured Europe from June to December of 1937, experiencing a freedom and appreciation of their work that was unmatched in the states. Ironically, racism was their undoing, even in Europe: Hitler was the culprit. During an engagement at a posh club in Berlin, they received their walking papers from the Third Reich: no explanation, just a one-way boat ticket home.

End of an Era

With the growing momentum of World War II, the entertainment industry was shifting focus, and even African American vaudeville was on the wane. By the early 1940s the week-long bookings in white theaters had petered out as movies took precedence over live entertainment. This shift meant disaster for many swing era performers, particularly the dancers. Bands and vocalists survived, although the big band era was soon to give way to small combos, cool jazz, and intimate clubs. Quite literally, dancers were not given their space. Dance genres that required a lot of floor space were in trouble, and Norton and Margot's booking potential dropped accordingly. Lindy- hoppers also fell on hard times as ballrooms closed down nationwide. Tap dancers, whose space needs were minimal, could still be booked in the new small rooms and even in bars.

In time, every innovation becomes dated, and each generation reinvents itself. Just as the ragtime musicians established a style that was a reaction to the sweet, sentimental songs of yore, the small jazz group of the 1920s evolved into the large swing band. In turn, the post–World War II musicians formed small groups as an alternative to the big-band sound that, by then, had become hackneyed in its own way. Undoubtedly the swing era, characterized by arranged jazz music played by large bands with an orchestral sound, was on its way out by the mid-1940s. The switch from the hot big-band sound to that of the small, cool bebop combo was symbolic of a deeper shift in the American *zeitgeist*, black and white. Nevertheless, many elements in society had not changed.

It is ironic that, although one of the original impulses behind ragtime and jazz had been to crack the clownish minstrel stereotype, the singing, dancing, smiling—and, thus, ingratiating—image of African American bandleaders (such as Cab Calloway and Louis Armstrong) was ultimately seen as an updated version of the minstrel trope. But it was neither their doing nor their intention. The dull force of cultural bias was at work, razing the effect of individual achievement. To put it bluntly, every time a black person smiled, it was called a grin. The main obstacle was the continuing power of racism in American life: the situation had seen little improvement. (For example, lynchings proceeded with yearly regularity, and in 1937 the antilynching bill urged by the National Association for the Advancement of Colored People was killed by a Senate filibuster. [Bergman, 479]) Therefore, African American achievement was ushered into a dominant culture that remained shot through with racism and still perceived blacks through the minstrel lens. And therein lay the irony and the dilemma faced by the likes of Armstrong and Calloway: just about anything created by blacks was read and received as old stereotypes in new dress. Consciously or subliminally the progressive bebop musicians recognized this stalemate. Rather than trying to define themselves at the racist-ridden center established by the dominant culture, they established an alternative cultural force, or a center at the periphery.

In white post–World War II America, and for the first time in American history, there was a migration away from urban areas—not to the countryside but to newly formed suburbs. Along with this exodus, the advent of television made the exuberant night life of the swing era less special, less accessible, and less attractive to many Americans. The postwar mentality, marked by a return to the "normalcy" of family-centered activities, a near-paranoid anticommunist movement (spearheaded by Senator McCarthy and his House Un-American Activities Committee), and the threat of nuclear war contributed, psychologically, to the decline of swing era night life. Like Norton and Margot, many performers went from promising full-time careers with fairly decent salaries, to part-time bookings augmented by nonperformance day jobs, to no artistic work at all.

White vaudevillians had already begun to shift gears in the late 1920s. They had opportunities for gainful employment first in talking films and later in the burgeoning television industry, if not in other walks of life. With few exceptions there was little such opportunity for African Americans.[35] Had they been white, Norton and Margot might have weathered the changes by getting bit parts in movies or bookings on the exclusive Las Vegas–Hollywood–Miami–New York nightclub circuit. But the American workplace remained segregated in film media, live performance venues, and quotidian professions.

Norton and Margot's 1941 bookings at Dave's Café, a Chicago club, marked the end of their touring career together, although they made a final comeback in the New York area in 1946–47, after a five-year hiatus. But their cards were all played out, even though for a while they had persevered against the odds. Being African American, a ballet career had been out of reach for them, and even a ballroom dance career approximating the success and earning power of comparable white teams was beyond their grasp. Margot Webb, by now a wife and parent, returned to school, earned graduate degrees, and became an African American studies teacher and ballet coach for a new generation of aspiring dancers of color.

Is it irony or poetic justice that an oppressed people created two art forms, jazz and the Lindy Hop, that have come to represent freedom and democracy for twentieth-century cultures worldwide? Jazz music was the sound of liberation when Radio Free Europe broadcasts to Iron Curtain nations kept hope alive. The Lindy was danced in Nazi Germany at risk of concentration camp internment. In the sequestered space of the dance hall, Europeans and European Americans could indulge their fantasies and "go primitive" for the space of an evening. Indeed, the irony is how much of this swing era energy created by African Americans infused the society at large and permanently changed the American identity into a swinging quotient. This would be translated, in subsequent eras, into coolness, hipness, and other such indicators of the largely invisibilized black presence in American culture. Ineluctably this force created an image of America, Americans, and American life that is still a defining, prevailing notion. Loose-limbed, gum-chewing guys and gals (chicks, dolls, dames:

the jargon itself is fast, cool, angular—African American in flavor and accent)[36] who can dance crazy stuff like the Lindy, who are easygoing and have a sarcastic sense of humor—in other words, cool cats: this was the American image in the world between and after the two world wars. This is why and how the idea of "American boys" sprang up in Europe. (In the previous century, America and things American were generally seen as inferior imitations of European culture.) These American characteristics cut through the European gestalt of tragedy and nobility and offered, instead, attributes that were marked and sculpted by African American expressive culture. Even the sense of the performer/performance in everyday life was a part of this fresh, new image.

It is important to recognize that, beginning in the teens and twenties and continuing through the swing era, African American jazz music and popular dance genres were *major* elements in the modernist transformation of Europeanist pop and so-called high culture, inflecting them with innovations that revolutionized European aesthetic standards. Who was responsible for such important changes? We know some of the names of the major ragtime, blues, and jazz musicians; but for every name that is known, there are innumerable unknowns. Most of the dancers remain anonymous. Yet, white America and Europe reaped immeasurable benefits from these artists whose biographies are forgotten but whose output formed the basis for the Africanization of white culture on both sides of the Atlantic.[37] These hidden influences and presences have permanently changed the sound, character, and identity of American performance and, consequently, American life.

"Whenever we put life back into history it is the life of our questions to it."[38] My question to the historical information that I discovered is this: Especially because the swing era was a period of dense exchange between blacks and whites—an era characterized by the lingering spirit of the Harlem Renaissance and Negritude theory—how did black people and white people negotiate the ground between the (exoticizing) embrace of black creative endeavor and the perpetuation of racism as standard practice?

Taking up the themes introduced in this preliminary section, the chapters that follow may help provide clues to a response. Chapter 2 outlines Margot Webb's performing career and casts it in the context of the era. To further explore that context, I discuss selected aspects of Harlem, the black center of the swing era, in Chapter 3. Chapter 4 focuses on the issues of agents, managers, salaries, and, finally, appropriation of African American creativity by the dominant culture. The expatriate experience and how the race card was played at home and abroad is the subject for Chapter 5. Chapter 6 surveys the decline of the swing era, the demise of Norton and Webb's career, and the elements that contributed to both. The final chapter takes a wide-angle perspective to examine the connections between modernism and the black-originated swing aesthetic to conclude this discussion of race as performance politics—or performance as race politics.

Chapter Two

From Marjorie to Margot

Early Life and Influences

To begin this drama, a little background on the featured player is in order. Margot Webb, native New Yorker, was born Marjorie Smith on 18 March 1910. Both sides of her family were mulatto. Webb's light skin color played a large part in launching her career and in offering her certain advantages in the color-conscious world of African American society and the segregated domain of white America. Throughout her professional life, she had to balance this small advantage against the major "disadvantage" of being African American. Margot Webb personified the many ways that the black world touched, interfaced with, and frequently was repelled by the white world.

Long before she became a performer, show business was a component in Webb's life. All three of her maternal aunts were employed in the entertainment industry: Sarah (Sadie) Bush Tappan was a singer and dancer; Ethel Bush Allen was a dressmaker and had been employed by Fanny Brice and Broadway actress Edith Haller; Marion Bush Stubbs had been the personal maid for Ziegfeld Follies entertainer Delores and for actress Marion Davies. Grandmother Ada Lee Bush was employed in domestic work by wealthy New York families and for Broadway actress and author Jane Cowl. Webb remembers being taken to audition for a black child's part in a Nora Bayes production. Her father, George Mitchell Smith, was a classically trained violinist who also taught clarinet and saxophone. He traveled abroad with the James Reese Europe Fifteenth Regiment Band during World War I and remained abroad after the band's return, abandoning his African American family and living in either England or France. (Years later, through the show business grapevine, Webb learned that her father was alive in Europe, training musicians and probably performing. Senior musicians who were touring abroad with Webb in 1937 recognized her father one night in the audience in London. Apparently, Smith remained an anonymous spectator and made no attempt to make direct contact with his daughter.) Webb's mother, Gertrude Violet Fay Bush, was a pianist who worked the nightclub circuit.

Before Harlem became the largest definitive African American area of Manhattan (prior to the World War I migrations from the South to northern cities), blacks lived in small enclaves or were isolated and dispersed across the city. As Manhattan grew and expanded northward, so did its African American populace, always in search of decent housing. Webb's first two years were spent in cold-water flats in New York's immigrant neighborhoods. These were apartments in walk-up tenement buildings with no hot water, a bathtub in the kitchen, and a hallway toilet to be shared with another family. The Smith family nucleus was in one such neighborhood on West 16th Street but, in the extended family tradition that has acted as a safety net for African Americans, "home" included two other locations. Webb's maternal grandmother, Ada Lee Bush, lived on West 18th Street, and her father's mother lived on West 53rd Street, not far from an institution that played a large part in the family's life. This was the Church of St. Benedict the Moor, a Catholic parish with an African American congregation led by an Irish priest, Father O'Keefe, who baptized the Smith children.[1] For successive days or weeks on end, Marjorie and her brother, George, lived with one set of grandparents or the other while the parents worked.

As blacks began moving uptown and Harlem became a community, the Smith family joined the migration. Between 1912 and the 1930s they lived in several locations, including 124th Street, 132nd Street, and the Dunbar Apartments (a real estate venture sponsored by John D. Rockefeller, Jr. at 149th and 150th Streets). Some Harlem blocks were entirely black. In the beginning, most one-family brownstones remained white occupied, but apartment houses were vacated by whites as blacks moved in, although white flight had not yet reached major proportions. The Harlem community was becoming a rich cultural center, and at various times Webb's neighbors included Paul Robeson; the Harris sisters (Edna, who was in the original production of *Green Pastures,* and Vivian, who became a regular in comedy sketches at Harlem's Apollo theater); W.C. Handy and family; Gertrude Ayer, one of the first African American principals of a New York public school; and the family of Lester A. Walton, writer, diplomat, and ambassador to Liberia. It was Walton who, as a young drama critic for *The New York Age,* a black publication, dreamed of a black repertory theater producing original material and leased the Lafayette theater for this purpose. (Isaacs, 44) Yolanda Du Bois, daughter of W.E.B. Du Bois, was once Webb's counselor at a Young Women's Christian Association (YWCA) summer camp. The affiliated Harlem branches of the Christian associations exerted a strong social and cultural influence on the life of this community, offering a flourishing dance and drama curriculum as well as an athletic program and inexpensive housing for single men and women.

Harlem was full of paradoxes. Social and economic distinctions combined with skin-color discrimination to stratify the *haute bourgeoisie,* middle-class apartment dwellers, and tenement dwellers[2] into separate castes. Additional differentiations were forged between public and private school students. In spite of their dire financial circumstances, the Smith family had several assets that afforded them entry into Harlem's black middle class: they were light skinned; they had relatives beyond their immediate family who were in high places or were moneyed. (28 January 1999) Webb's maternal great-grandmother was Scotch-Irish.[3] Her uncle Julian Randall Stubbs (her Aunt Marian's husband), who "looked so Irish that his nickname was Pat," was Commissioner of Deeds for the city of Boston from 1909 through the 1920s. (The whites who hired him probably didn't realize he was black.) Webb and her peers, who attended Catholic primary schools on scholarship, did not associate with the public school crowd. She recalls, "It wasn't that you were snobs or anything, but you did get a better education [in Catholic schools]. Believe me, even then the public schools were not what they were cracked up to be. And, remember, we were in

a rowdy neighborhood [132nd Street and Lenox Avenue]; you didn't
associate with those people." (22 May 1980)

Class stratifications were evident from block to block. Although dominated by multiple-family tenement dwellings and smaller structures offering rented rooms with kitchenettes, a "rowdy" neighborhood might
also include privately owned single-family brownstones and a couple of
decent, high-rise apartment buildings, all sharing the same city blocks.
And some tenement dwellers, like the Smiths, saw themselves above and
apart from their immediate financial circumstances.

Because her maternal grandmother had been obliged to work, her
mother and aunts, through Catholic charities, had attended Catholic
boarding schools. In turn, Webb was sent to similar institutions for her
elementary school education while her mother worked for long spells
as a pianist playing in clubs across New York state. Later, Webb extended this tradition into the next generation by sending one of her
two daughters to Catholic schools.

From third through sixth grades, Webb attended the St. Frances
Academy in Baltimore, Maryland. The institution, that later became
the St. Frances-Charles Hall High School, was run by the Oblate Sisters of Providence, an order of nuns of color representing African diaspora peoples. In accordance with the dictates of segregation, these
Catholic schools were either all white or all black in staff and student
body. Some of Webb's cousins had attended the St. Frances Academy
before her. As one of the few schools in the country administered by
"colored" nuns, it was well known in black Catholic circles.[4] According to Webb: "They were black nuns, and I didn't know that they were
all black because they were all colors. There were blondes and there
were Cubans—lots of Cubans, even among the children. They weren't
Cuban-Americans. These were kids sent up by affluent families in
Cuba." (5 June 1980)

Conversely, Catholic primary schools in Harlem adhered to a different racial etiquette; in general, all students were black (even though
Harlem still had a mixed-race population), and all nuns were white. Prior
to boarding school, Webb attended one such school, St. Mark the Evan-
gelist, which was located on 138th Street. It was run by the Sisters of the
Blessed Sacrament, an all-white order (founded in 1891 by Sister Kather-

ine Drexel of the Bouvier family)[5] whose dedication and missions were primarily in Native American settlements.

Most of Webb's friends who went into show business were Catholic school alumnae and light skinned—an absolute prerequisite for the black female dancer's success in the swing era. Webb met Fredi Washington (and knew of her sister, Isabel) through this network. The Washington sisters,[6] who attended a convent school run by the Reverend Mother Katharine Biddle in Cornwell Heights, Pennsylvania (another school run by the Sisters of the Blessed Sacrament), described the Cornwell Heights school as an overbearing charity institution for nonwhite girls, which contrasts with Webb's more genteel description. This strange system of boarding school education and ecumenical outreach, although it would read as a charity handout in white middle-class circles, was a unique opportunity for a select group of black Catholic families who would not have been able to afford it otherwise.

One of Webb's earliest memories is of her father taking her to see a performance by Vernon and Irene Castle, the famous ballroom dance team, when she was 3 or 4 years old. Smith was a member of the James Reese Europe orchestra that accompanied the Castles on international tours, so he was actually introducing his daughter to his workplace. Although Webb attached no particular significance to this memory, the fact that she later became an adagio dancer, herself, renders it noteworthy. When the family lived on 132nd Street (they moved when Webb was 2 or 3), she was taken to vaudeville shows at the Lafayette, which was right around the corner. This early introduction to dance was reinforced by her education. Webb remembers that "Dancing was quite a thing in the Catholic schools. We had social dancing and an interpretive type of soft toe dancing. We had many programs throughout the year. I guess that's how they raised their money, as I look back on it. . . . From the age of six or seven I was always . . . on the stage, and we were always having some little programs. . . . In those days they didn't have any physical education programs [in Catholic girls' schools]. I guess dancing was about as close to it as we got." (5 June 1980)

The pervasive effect of the Denishawn style is evident in Webb's description of these early experiences. She was taught "Oriental" numbers, Egyptian dances, Gypsy routines with tambourines, scarf dances, Grecian dances—basically, all kinds of ethnic dances distilled into the catchall style popularized by Ruth St. Denis and Ted Shawn, modern dance forerunners who were influential choreographers and performers and opened their Denishawn schools across the nation. After completing the sixth grade at St. Frances Academy, Webb returned to New York, studied dance at the Harlem Branch YWCA with Vivian Roberts, a well-known dancer and teacher in the community, and enrolled in the 135th Street Library's drama program. (This branch of the New York Public Library is now the Schomburg Center for Research in Black Culture.) These acting and theater classes were run by Regina Andrews, a near-legendary inspirational figure for two generations of black artists, intellectuals, and ordinary Harlemites.

Webb's middle school years were spent at basically white junior high schools in Harlem. At this time, in both black and white public schools in New York, there were virtually no black teachers and, in compliance with the unwritten laws of northern discrimination, the public school system was de facto segregated. Webb and a handful of other black students attended white public schools on the basis of scholastic achievement and were placed in special progress classes. They were the privileged few who were allowed to attend academic high schools and receive a better education than the vocational track offered at the trade high schools that most blacks attended. (Stern, 201)

Webb's bona fide professional career didn't begin until 1932. However, amateur performances in school programs led fluidly and without interruption into semiprofessional and, ultimately, professional work. She found gigs through a network that dated back to her early adolescence. By the time she was thirteen and fourteen she was traveling to New Jersey on weekends and performing as a "pick" in the acts that preceded the main attractions at burlesque houses. (This was before burlesque found a new lease on life with the advent of striptease; in the early 1920s it was just another form of variety theater.) "Pick" is shortened from the pejorative "pickaninny," which may have been a modification of the Portugese or Spanish pequeño meaning little one, and referred to the black children— singers and dancers—who performed in backup and finale numbers for white vaudeville stars. (Stearns and Stearns, 80) According to Webb:

By word of mouth we'd hear that so-and-so needed some girls, and we'd just go [to audition. Usually the person working directly with them was a woman.] She'd teach you a few steps—all the same old stuff—fast, fast, the faster the better. All you had to do was be together and be fast. . . . We had to put on bandannas. There was always an opening scene where we were on the plantation. We'd sit on the edge of the stage and rock like idiots! They [the white audience] seemed to take it very seriously. With all these beautiful [read light-skinned] young girls singing *Swanee River* and rocking to the music—this was the plantation! Then, all of a sudden we'd get up and start dancing. There was no theme. We'd do a little tap, and maybe a little Russian thrown in. . . . We'd go from plantation to Russian to the time step.[7] We'd say we were sixteen. You weren't supposed to be working if you were younger than that.[8] The costume was always a little short, skimpy thing showing your legs—but not a nude-type affair. . . . (25 June 1980)

This stereotype of rhythm and speed was expected of black performers, regardless of the style and category of their work. Often, in later years, Norton and Margot were plagued by white audiences urging them to "get hot" when heat was neither their forte nor appropriate for their genre. Musicians like pianist Teddy Wilson had endured the same abuse and were told by club owners that their music was too sweet, too white. (Williams, 15 August 1980)

For Webb and her peers, in adolescence and as adults hitting their stride during the Depression, one of the main reasons for performing was to earn a living. Many of her friends were the children of professional performers, so this was a world that felt familiar and was accessible to them. Like Webb, they might have been raised by a grandparent or other relative. At a time when many Americans were indigent and higher education meant a high school education, it was common for adolescents to assume substantial responsibility in earning wages, either to augment the general family income or to defray personal expenses. It was with money earned from these early chorus line performances that Webb was able to study ballet with Louis Chalif, a Russian émigré and popular teacher of the era, at his 57th Street studio. (He instituted the Chalif Method, a technique used by ballet teachers and expounded upon in his five published textbooks.) Webb asserts that there was no particular attention or encouragement from these teachers since, as an African American (even a light-skinned one), there was no place to go professionally with ballet work.

After finishing high school she entered Hunter College. Majoring in French, she dropped out after her third year. The Depression was catching up with her family and a full-time student, even with a part-time salary, was an unaffordable luxury. Webb knew where to go to find work. She chose to enter show business rather than do housecleaning or other menial work. With the de facto segregation that virtually made New York a white city, blacks weren't hired as salesgirls, receptionists, waitresses, or bank trainees. Webb was lucky to have a relatively large earning capacity as a chorus girl. She states, "The salary given by the WPA was $22.50 [a week]. Everybody made that—Orson Welles, Romare Bearden, Langston Hughes[9]—whereas a chorus girl could make $75 a week." (25 June 1980) However, a chorine's salary could range from Webb's estimate to as low as $25 a week at a time when "salesclerks were earning between $5 and $10 weekly; topnotch New York stenographers, $16." (Haskins, 92) The advantages of the time step and "a little Russian thrown in" were obvious. Webb entered the professional world of entertainment as a chorus girl in shows choreographed and produced by black entrepreneurs such as Leonard Harper and Lew Crawford. Two of her earliest shows were Harper-Crawford collaborations in Brooklyn, New York. The names of the revues were typical: "The Hottest Colored Revue in Town," and "Second Edition of Sepia Rhythm." Skin color and hot tempos were prime components in the commodification of the black product.

In 1933, after about a year and a half of chorus work with an occasional solo in front of the line, Webb was in a Philadelphia show emceed by Ralph Cooper.[10] She was given a small specialty number: a fan dance. She knew nothing about this genre, whose success depended on skillful manipulation of handheld fans. Enter Harold Norton, a young dancer from the Midwest who had grown up in a show business family. When it came to dance, he seemed to know something about everything. Versatile and highly trained, he coached her and saved her act from total chagrin:

> I was toe dancing then, and he [Cooper] saw me practicing. He said, "We're going to put in a little novelty and let you do a toe dance with the

fans." I knew toe dancing, but I didn't have the slightest idea how to use the fans, and they're not easy [to manipulate]. They're great, big things. . . . They look very simple. I was flabbergasted! I couldn't get them to go: my wrists wouldn't go fast enough. I was so embarrassed because I had to take off everything and put on some kind of little, skin-tight thing the color of my skin which, of course in those days, was like going out on the stage nude. . . . [As for Norton,] I never saw a man who knew so much [about dancing]! He could do tap, soft-shoe, acrobatic, or trapeze work; he could do any style. He was raised in the vaudeville setup—like the Walendas[11]—trained from a child. He had done all those things. . . . He could do ballet; and then he did the interpretive work like the Spear Dance—he [choreographed] it for himself. . . . He helped me with the routine. He knew how to handle the fans front and back. . . . He rehearsed with me for a few days, and it was all right in the show—I was no Sally Rand [the white stage star who popularized the fan dance], but I looked good. And he was a great teacher. He taught [routines to] quite a lot of white dancers. (6 March 1978)

Cooper suggested that the two of them team up and work out some routines together. Visually they were a stunning pair. Good looks were enough to put over even a mediocre act, but this pair was formally trained and talented as well. Norton was the leader-teacher and proactive force in the team and continued in that role throughout their partnership. The team chose to use Norton's surname and Webb's given name. This was customary practice for swing era dance teams. For example, Veloz and Yolanda was the name of the white team Norton and Margot emulated.

Webb knows little about Norton's background or his present where-abouts, if he is still alive. Throughout their career he was reticent—if not secretive—about his past. The few details Webb gathered were communicated to her by his friends who came to see them perform. He told Webb that his parents were the dance team of Lopez and Lopez who had performed on the vaudeville stage when he was a child. However, he did not reveal why he had a different surname. Webb suggests that he may have been adopted or taken in by the Lopez family while retaining his birth name; or his mother (Mrs. Norton) may have remarried (Mr. Lopez); or Lopez and Lopez could have been merely a stage name. He claimed he was born in New Mexico and, at some point, went to school in New York state. He may have had a twin brother and a sister or step-sister. According to Webb, when they were preparing to go to Europe, he was unable to produce a birth certificate, and a woman identified as his half-sister had to sign for him to get a passport. In the mid-1940s, when his dance career was on the wane, he tried to become a New York police-man. Supposedly he then moved to Long Island and worked as a horse trainer. (8 July 1998; 2 June 1999)

Shall We Dance?

From accounts of people I interviewed—musicians, dancers, Norton and Webb's former students, and Harlem residents who saw them perform in the 1930s and 1940s—the excellence of Norton and Margot lay in the smooth, sustained effect of their work, supported by their strong founda-tion in ballet. For the color-conscious African American community, the light-skinned, wavy-haired couple convincingly pulled off the white ball-room repertory in appearance as well as performance. Norton was no-ticeably darker than Margot and looked Spanish, a connotation that allowed for a broader range of skin color than the white category. (See discussion in Chapter 5.) Ironically, had they been darker, they probably would not have been successful in the black entertainment world; con-versely, because they were doing a white dance genre but were not white (and refused to pass), they were rejected by white venues. Their reviews in both black and white news media described them as a sophisticated, el-egant "class act."[12]

The Norton-Webb style of dancing was not acrobatic. They were an adagio ballroom team whose aim was smoothness and visual beauty, a flowing totality rather than spectacular moments. Each ballroom team had its specialties; theirs were Waltz and sophisticated jazz interpreta-tions. Typical of ballroom style and nineteenth-century ballet partnering, Webb, as the woman, was the focus of their work, with Norton leading and exhibiting Webb in the lifts and spins that punctuate, highlight, and climax each ballroom number.

Audience response determined the routines that they used most fre-quently. Spectators identified artists with certain numbers, and they demanded repetition as much as critics demanded variety. Webb recalls that, touring with the singer George Dewey Washington, who was famous for his rendition of the song *Chloe,* the audiences everywhere requested this hit. Duke Ellington in his autobiography recalls the same phenomenon. On returning from a tour, his band was booked at the Apollo. The year was 1938, and Ellington's *I Let a Song Go Out of My Heart* was a hit. In preparing it for this live performance, he decided to try a new arrangement. The opening night audience response made it clear that they wanted to hear the version they had heard on the radio, and the new chart was removed after the first show in favor of the familiar old arrangement. (88) For Norton and Margot, this pattern meant that, for example, on returning to the Howard in Washington, D.C., where they might have performed six months earlier, they could be asked to repeat *Smoke Gets in Your Eyes* (a Waltz interpretation) or *Cavernism,* (a sophisticated jazz interpretation). Of course, this was a measure of their popularity. However, although their repertory was more extensive, they could spend the better part of a year performing the three best-liked numbers that people associated with them.

The team's performance style did not readily mesh with the jazz sound. Their romantic, fluid delivery stood in contrast to the more popular tap and Lindy genres. Swing music was so popular that one of their best-liked numbers was *Cavernism,* composed by James Mundy, arranger and tenor saxophonist with the Earl Hines band. It became one of their signature pieces beginning with their extensive run with the Hines orchestra at Chicago's Grand Terrace Café in the mid-1930s. But, aesthetically, they were more at home with the Waltz repertory, accompanied by a light-classic rendering of popular romantic ballads, preferably with strings. However, in the United States by the 1930s, many bands had ceased using stringed instruments. American audiences preferred the team's Bolero and sophisticated jazz repertory, whereas in Europe, Waltzes and specialties like the Tango were well appreciated, perhaps because they were still alive there as social dances. In addition, most European bands still used stringed instruments. With such a range of variables, the team had little guarantee that their musical arrangements would always sound the same. However, with certain topnotch bands, stylistic difference was welcomed. For example, in performing with the

Teddy Hill band on the European tour of the Cotton Club Revue (1937), Webb recalls the joy of dancing to the unique sound of this group and, particularly, to the improvised solos of one John Gillespie—a young musician whose work was so vertiginous, at times, that he acquired the nickname Dizzy. In such a case, cooperation and mutual admiration could result in an added eight bars of improvisation between dancers and musicians. Besides the few occasions when their music was accidentally shortened or lengthened, this was one of the rare circumstances in which the team improvised. (Due to the timing, balance, and synchronization necessary for executing the turns, lifts, and spins that are basic to this genre, ballroom dancing is an exact art.) Webb remembers that Gillespie "would go way off on his own. It wasn't in our arrangement at all, but he was always good. . . . That's why people started calling him Dizzy. . . . It gave you inspiration. . . . The audience would become attuned to what he was playing. . . . He improvised all the time. He had the music in front of him; he was playing his own version. . . . We were doing our same routine, but we would hear him . . . swinging out. He could tell [that we were attuned to him] by watching us. He was sort of fascinated by what we were doing, too. . . . It gave a little inspiration to your arrangement. (27 August 1980)

In other words, whether it was a European-inspired adagio or African American forms like the Lindy or rhythm tap dance, the dancers reinvigorated the musicians, and the bands kept the dancers dancing. As master tenor saxophonist Lester Young put it, "The rhythm of the dancers comes back to you when you're playing." (Stearns and Stearns, 325)

Ultimately, the success of a dance routine was inexorably linked to the performance and cooperation of the band. In nightclub work Norton and Webb rehearsed with the band a good two to three weeks before the opening of the show. The musicians became familiar with the team's arrangements and their movements. Cues in the music—drum rolls or, perhaps, an instrumental phrase or solo—were worked out to accompany lifts and spins.

The sequence of routines varied greatly and depended on the opening number. If they began with the Bolero, a forceful and rather dramatic number, they most likely would not perform an additional dance in that part of the program. If they began with a light number—a Waltz interpretation like *Smoke Gets in Your Eyes*—they would perform two more light dances in the same slot—perhaps additional Waltz interpretations like *Toujours L'Amour, Toujours, Charmaine*, or *The Song Is You*, or a sophisticated jazz interpretation like *Cavernism*, or a Rumba, concluding after three numbers. The Bolero and the Waltzes were feature acts that they usually performed while alone onstage. The Tango and Rumba, dances they choreographed to popular rhythms of the era, were built up as production numbers and backed by the chorus, who might do a popular dance like the Carioca or the Continental behind them. (Chorus numbers were staged by the choreographer of the entire production, not the team.) In this way, they were integrated into the larger production and were obliged to tailor these parts of their repertory to the overall concept.

Audience size and reaction affected their numbers in both subtle and obvious ways. If a theater audience was small or subdued, numbers could be shortened or even deleted. Sometimes the theater manager, producer, or dance captain made this decision. Often the entire show was shortened this way. It was frequently the 6 P.M. dinner-hour show that dragged. On a theater schedule of three to five shows a day, it was necessary to conserve energy wherever possible. The entire cast would give their all to the 8 P.M. evening show and the 2 P.M. matinee. On the other hand, if an audience was particularly enthusiastic, an extra eight bars of encore could be added to every act, and several more to the grand finale.

Besides the staples of their repertory, the team occasionally performed novelty dances that were presented as specialty numbers. One, not a favorite of Webb's, was an Apache which, like the Carioca, imitated stereotyped routines from popular white movies. The Apache genre came from French films with a low-life, urban bistro setting. No high spins or graceful air work was used. Instead, Webb was pulled, jerked, held by the shoulders, and thrown to the floor; she then slid across the stage. Norton wore a beret and tight-fitting shirt, while Margot wore the requisite short tight skirt with a split up the side and black silk stockings. It was not a number that stayed long in their repertory. It had been originally suggested to them by Leonard Harper, choreographer-director of the Grand Terrace floor show and one of a corps of uncredited black swing era choreographers.

When called upon to do a solo, Webb either performed a jazz toe dance or a Latin novelty number like La Conga, based on the popular conga rhythm of the era. For the toe dance she wore either a full-length satin skirt with side splits, a short, full skirt, or a sequined leotard. She choreographed a simple routine of elementary ballet work (*passés*—bent leg lifts; *bourrées*—small, quick steps done with the feet close together; and *chainé* turns—fast turns done by stepping from foot to foot) and set it to a swing version of some popular tune. The dance contained no jazz movements—that is, no body isolations or hip and pelvic articulations. The ballet footwork done on point to a fast, syncopated beat and spiced with quick turns seemed sensational.

Like most of their vaudeville colleagues, the team was multitalented, because having more than one ability offered greater job opportunities. But for them, dance was not a stepping stone to another career. Adagio dance was their special calling. They hadn't dared dream of a career as ballet dancers; yet, they studied ballet and utilized it as the fundamental orientation that inflected their style. Had they come along in the 1960s, they most likely would have been concert dancers working with a ballet-oriented modern dance company or perhaps with the Dance Theatre of Harlem. In any case, more options would have been open to them. During the course of their career, they took on other types of bookings in a futile attempt to survive between ballroom engagements. In spite of all these drawbacks, the team was well known in black entertainment venues for fifteen years, fulfilling "the fantasy, the aura of that particular period, which is still the kind of thing that draws young people into theater."[13] They were often compared to white box-office idols, and Margot was regarded as the black response to Hollywood's movie queens.

Between Two Eras

The team of Norton and Margot was created after vaudeville's heyday but before the demise of the Jim Crow era. New York's Palace Theatre relinquished its two-show-a-day format for the combination movie and stage show configuration in 1932. Radio and "talkies" pushed the white form over the hill, while black vaudeville moved into the vacated venues.

Because of the curiosity of adagio dancing by a black team, Norton and Margot could be booked regularly on black entertainment outlets that flourished as discrete microcosms in the pre–Civil Rights era. Another team, that of Thelma and Paul Meeres, had worked in the 1920s but had separated by the time Norton and Webb were performing. In any case, the Meeres's act was more novelty and ethnic in style than classic adagio dance. Then Fredi Washington and Al Moore had worked together for a short time, but both went on to other show business careers. With the exception of the teams of Anise and Aland and Ross and McCain, most black dance teams at that time focused on tap, novelty, exotic, acrobatic, or eccentric dance.

After meeting through the fan dance, both Norton and Webb continued their individual work in the Ralph Cooper revue with Norton as Spear Dance soloist[14] and Webb as chorus girl and fan dance specialty act. They began rehearsing together between shows, trying out the steps and partnering of ballroom work. Later in 1933, on their return to New York, they premiered as Norton and Margot at the Club Harlem, the former site of Connie's Inn (which by then had moved to midtown, under another name). According to Webb, the cabaret was owned by an African American who was a friend of Norton's. (9 June 1999)

In the beginning Norton hired other established, sophisticated choreographers to stage their routines. This often meant someone white. Their first choreographer was Jean De Meaux, who taught them the suave, downtown, adagio style. De Meaux also staged shows for Harlem night spots like Small's Paradise, the only lavish Harlem club, with a floor show and chorus line, that catered to a black clientele.

Musical arrangements cost from $50 to $75 apiece. The team's first arranger was Armand Lamet, whose work they used for their first bookings on the road. According to Webb, Lamet was especially adept at taking a song composed as a Waltz and transposing it from 3/4 to 4/4 time to give a unique touch to their Waltz interpretations. (This is one of the reasons why the result was termed a Waltz interpretation, rather than simply a Waltz: they teased the form.)[15] Webb asserts that a good arrangement had a potential performance life of two to three years. De Meaux and Lamet worked together with the team in rehearsal—De Meaux tailoring the movement to fit the best lines for their bodies, and Lamet setting the musical arrangements to the movement.[16] Once on tour, they made use of some of the fine black arrangers who were members of the bands that played for them. In Chicago both James Mundy and Wilbur de Paris of the Earl Hines band made arrangements for them. The team fared best with sophisticated bands like those of Hines, Noble Sissle, Ovie Alston, and Teddy Hill; all of these African American orchestras could interpret a variety of musical styles, including a traditional repertory of ballads and light classics as well as jazz and swing.

Costumes, musical arrangements, and photos took a big chunk out of their salary. In addition, travel expenses were not always included in their contracts. Whereas their average salary was $150 weekly (for the two of them), with a range between $100 and $175, the least expensive custom-made gown was usually $150, according to Webb. In the beginning they believed they had a chance to make it to the top and demand better salaries—and with good reason. They played to enthusiastic audiences and, from indications in the news media, they seemed to be headed for fame.

Interestingly, both the black and white press played up the fact that it was unusual for a black team to perform ballroom dance. In fact, newspaper advertisements for their first booking billed them as a "European Dance Team," which meant that they performed a white dance style. Rob Roy, a black reporter in Chicago, wrote that "For years now others have stolen our music and song. . . . Bands such as Paul Whiteman, Jan Garber, Casa Loma and others have visited our hot spots and departed with our tunes and swings but today the score is being evened, in dance if not in music. The adagio dance is not our dance—it comes from another people. However one must admit that Norton and Margot are a great improvement over any of the many teams [namely, whites] doing the dance in other sections." A white reporter in *Billboard,* the trade publication of the entertainment industry, recommended the team in the paper's "Possibilities" section in March 1938: "Margo and Norton—colored dance team, handsome in appearance and doing delicate, extremely graceful and accomplished work. Have a varied repertoire, running from typical Harlem swing stuff to languid tangos and waltzes . . . also rate a spot, with proper production, in a white revue." But what this journalist didn't bank on was the odds against a white revue hiring a light-skinned "colored" team who performed in a white style. The margin for confusion in such a blurring and crossing of the racial divide would have been too risky in the pre–Civil Rights era. (Paradoxically, it was partly due to their mask of whiteness that they were confined to dancing in the dark.)

The team was publicized in feature articles, reviews, gossip columns (Webb's photogenic face made her a perfect subject for such items), advertisements (Webb even did an endorsement for skin-lightener cream in a black magazine), and handbills. Although journalists commented favorably on the full range of their repertory, the average American nightclub customer or theatergoer—black or white—preferred the team's jazz numbers, liked their Latin numbers, but was cold to the Waltz interpretations. Yet, some black audiences were receptive: Webb cites the audiences at the Howard in Washington, D.C., a more bourgeois group than New York's Apollo clientele, and the audience at the black-owned Amytis Theatre in St. Louis (discussed in Chapter 5) as two exceptions.

Many of the social clubs, church congregations, and ladies' guilds that formed a basic integer in black community life hired celebrities like Norton and Webb to perform as guest stars, frequently at an annual dance or a debutantes' ball. Occasionally, Norton staged a routine for gowned or costumed amateurs with himself and Webb as the featured dancers. This same activity was expected of the white ballroom teams and dates back to the origins of ballroom dance as a diversion and art form of the *haute bourgeoisie*. In this era, the entertainment page and the society page stood next to each other in black newspapers, and the life of the two domains often intersected.

Norton and Margot's European sojourn was the highlight of their career. They were sure this was the opportunity they had been waiting for. Politically naive, they performed in Nazi Germany in 1937 and were scheduled for gigs in Scandinavia, Rumania, and Egypt, but these plans were abruptly curtailed by the momentum of war. Forced out of Germany, they returned to America in 1938 and, like many performers who spent time abroad, found that they had lost contacts. Bookings were even more difficult to arrange, despite their having been billed in the black press as internationally famous artists. To return her name to the public eye, Webb began a gossip column for the *Chicago Defender*'s New York office and was publicized for appearances in fashion shows, benefits, and other black society events. Whenever possible she also took on solo work in specialty routines or in a "one-gig" partnership—a one-engagement booking with another dance partner. For example, in 1941 she worked with specialty dancer Al Vigal performing an exotic routine at the Tic Toc Club in Montreal, Canada, and with Al Moore for ballroom work in New York. But there were fewer venues and fewer units going West. Even though critics acknowledged and praised their extraordinary work, Norton and Margot fell victim to the times.

Throughout their career the team worked without the benefit of a personal manager. This fact may have been an additional roadblock in advancing their career, but it was a luxury they couldn't afford. And they were not alone. Although bandleaders had managers, most small-time musicians and performers did not. Instead, the grapevine was their lifeline: they obtained bookings by word of mouth. As many times as the team seemed on the brink of success, circumstance worked against them. They were too late for the 1920s era of black Broadway musicals and too early for the post–Civil Rights era, when African Americans were able to secure employment in white venues.

At the end of their ballroom career, Margot was married in 1940 to William P. Webb, Jr., an athletic director for the Children's Aid Society and semiprofessional basketball and football player in the black leagues. As in her early years of growing up in an extended family, once again she lived with relatives. She and her husband and two daughters, both of whom were born in the early 1940s, lived in her mother-in-law's spacious apartment in central Harlem. Replicating her own childhood experience, Webb put her children in the care of their grandmother while she worked and attended college. She points out that it was due to lack of performance opportunities that she decided to return to college and begin teaching. Having completed her B.A. at Hunter College in 1940, Webb taught dance in after-school recreation centers while taking night courses to complete her master's degree in education at Columbia University Teachers College. (She earned the degree in 1948.) Occasionally she took on a weekend booking with Norton when he could secure one, but Webb's aspirations had shifted to family and education. The team's final bookings were in the one or two upscale black nightclubs that remained in Harlem after the war. They closed their career with a date in September 1947, at Harlem's Club Baron on a program led by singer Billy Daniels and musician-bandleader Valaida Snow.

John Williams, the Facey Sisters, Charles "Honi" Coles, and Norma Miller described the team as unique in style and exceptional in talent—"like nobody else."[17] Their repertory, stage presentation, and the critical response from the press were similar to those of Veloz and Yolanda, the famous white ballroom dancers of the era. Yet Norton and Margot, known and respected in African American show business and unique as virtually the only black ballroom team doing pure adagio work, had found no spiral of success and profit open to them. What set these two teams apart was racial discrimination. A Veloz and Yolanda review in a Cleveland, Ohio newspaper could be mistaken for a description of the work of Norton and Margot and points up the similarities: "Yolanda of the ink black hair and white shoulders, and Veloz, who can show off a woman to better advantage than any other dancer I know of, are appearing twice nightly in the Terrace Room of the Statler, surrounded by an aura of incredible polish and chic. Commencing with an interlude that might vaguely be described as a Waltz, they gradually drift into a Tango, eventually finish up with light specialty numbers." (French 1938) Minus the white shoulders (Webb's were tan) and ink black hair (Webb's was light brown), this could have been a description of a Norton and Margot performance. (And, according to Webb, Yolanda's physical appearance was situated in the border zone between black and white that included many light-skinned blacks.) Multiply this hotel supper club in a midwestern city by all the hotels, cabarets, and film-plus-vaudeville houses of the swing era, and the result is a measure of performance possibilities for the many white ballroom teams of the era—all off-limits for this African American team. Both teams had a repertory of Waltz interpretations, popular light specialties, and refined versions of Latin dances like the Rumba. Both teams created unique specialty numbers that no other team performed (Norton and Webb's sophisticated jazz performed to compositions such as Jimmy Mundy's *Cavernism;* Veloz and Yolanda's "Veolanda," a fast-footed variation done to a rumba beat), and both teams cultivated a refined image. But one team developed and thrived while the other atrophied.

In a *Variety* review of a Roxy Theater program in 1944, Veloz and Yolanda were headliners and Señor Wences, the ventriloquist, had second billing. Ironically, Norton and Margot had been on the same program with Wences years before—in 1937 at the London Palladium on the mammoth bill that included the Cotton Club Revue. (See Chapter 5.) Yet, they were never booked with stars like Wences in their homeland and never played a white circuit in the United States. Whereas Veloz and Yolanda's unique, individual touches worked in their favor, Norton and Margot's distinctiveness was their nemesis. As Webb ruefully points out, they would have been better off with a stereotyped repertory of exotic-erotic or percussive-rhythmic work.

At the height of their career, Veloz and Yolanda were soloists who offered entire evenings of ballroom dance as a concert form; at their height, Norton and Margot remained a small part of a vaudeville format, featured as a classy but eclectic specialty on traditional African American variety programs. The white entertainment world, generally derivative of and indebted to Africanist movement, form, music, and rhythm, remained closed to the team who adapted a white dance style and, ultimately, could not survive without exposure on white circuits. Although their situation was unique—particularly in light of their special repertory—it was also typical. They could touch the white entertainment world, interface with it, but not enter it.

This capsule version of Norton and Margot's career points to a larger story that deserves more investigation. It is about the place where they and many other African American performers began their careers— namely, Harlem. It may seem unfair to some readers that, once again, this black community is placed at the center of attention when African American communities nationwide—in Atlanta, Detroit, Chicago, Philadelphia, New Orleans, and elsewhere—were seats of significant and unique black achievement. Yet, like Manhattan itself, Harlem is one of a kind. Both Harlem and Manhattan reflected a cosmopolitanism and international flavor uncharacteristic of other American cities. Black artists flocked to Harlem, as did whites to Manhattan, to prove their mettle. For this reason Harlem is the focus of the next chapter.

Chapter Three

"You Didn't Go Downtown—
Everything Was Uptown":
Harlem, U.S.A.

Introduction

Margot Webb's early childhood living conditions on West 53rd Street, with numerous families housed in private dwellings intended as single-family units, were improvements over even more destitute conditions in older neighborhoods. Indeed, each move to a new neighborhood by African Americans in Manhattan was an effort to find better housing. Principally due to the ideals and savvy enterprise of a black real estate broker, Philip A. Payton, African Americans were allowed residency in Harlem in the 1910s and were offered "their first chance in their entire history in New York to live in modern apartment houses." (Johnson, 147) What was to happen to this community by the advent of the swing era was phenomenal and paradoxical: Harlem became both the magnet for whites seeking exotic pleasures and for blacks seeking freedom from white dominance. Although masses of African Americans migrated to northern cities like Chicago and Detroit, Harlem became the black capital and the black entertainment center of the nation, a microcosm of New York City itself. As Webb put it, "You didn't go downtown—everything was uptown." (8 July 1998)

Harlem nightclubs of the swing era were preceded by the social, gambling, honky-tonk and professional clubs (the latter were frequented by prize fighters, jockeys, and stage celebrities) of the turn of the century. The pre-Harlem social club was not primarily a place for entertainment; however, it could serve as an impromptu stage for visiting performers. In a segregated society, it was a substitute for the neighborhood tavern. Like their counterparts in subsequent eras, the clubs were often linked to the world of organized crime. At the close of the nineteenth century Manhattan's Tenderloin district—the brothel and graft area on the West Side, south of 42nd Street—had an African American neighborhood that housed several night spots, including Joe Stewart's Criterion, Ike Hines's Club, and Barron D. Wilkins's Little Savoy. From 1900 to about 1910 the new center of black life was West 53rd Street and its environs, near two black-run hotels, the Marshall and the Maceo. (The Marshall was a favored hangout of Bert Williams and George Walker, former minstrels and pioneer producers of black Broadway musicals at the turn of the century.) Well before the advent of black Harlem, white pleasure seekers had frequented black night spots in communities such as this. Whereas the rules of de facto segregation did not permit blacks in white establishments, whites had always taken part in black amusements and "it was no unusual thing for some among the biggest Broadway stars to run up there [to the Marshall Hotel] for an evening." (Johnson, 119)

By the time Ethel Waters was a young singer in New York (1919–21), Harlem had become the black center of Manhattan, and the 1920s saw the rise and glorification of its nightclubs. The most well-known spots included Barron's Exclusive Club (Wilkins had previously run the Little Savoy), Edmond's Cellar, Connor's Club, Connie's Inn, Ed Small's Paradise, and the Cotton Club. There were clubs on nearly every block in the many streets that comprised central Harlem. Small and large establishments survived through changes of ownership and name: Connie's Inn became the Club Harlem; the Cotton Club became the Plantation Club. To list all the Harlem night spots during the Prohibition, Depression, and swing eras would entail another research project; many are remembered only in the reveries of now forgotten troupers. In addition to legal, public facilities there were after-hours clubs and apartment-based rent parties that served the same function: the chance to earn a living while letting the good times roll. Small late night eateries (serving the popular specialty of the era, "yardbird and strings"—Harlem's nickname for chicken and spaghetti) also offered live entertainment. Rent parties were not held necessarily to raise the rent. As writers of the era pointed out, Harlem was besieged by whites, and the bohemian elements were in quest of the undiscovered, most authentic amusements. (Huggins, 74–82; Hughes, 1940, 370–77; Kellner, 199–200) The house parties, advertised on walls in apartment lobbies or in elevators, were a last bastion of black nightlife unencumbered by the white gaze.

This era saw an abundance of theaters in Harlem, including the Roosevelt, Douglas, West End, Hurtig and Seaman's Burlesque (which later became the Apollo, the most famous of black vaudeville houses), Keith's Alhambra, the Harlem Opera House, Loew's Seventh Avenue, Lincoln, and Lafayette. All featured live variety entertainment of some kind; some specialized in legitimate shows adapted from Broadway or a combination of a legitimate play plus variety acts. At least one African American felt that this outpouring of theatrical activity was a frenetic signal of a dearth of creativity. According to Theophilus Lewis, caustic critic for the *Messenger* from 1923 to 1927:[1] "What we call the Negro Theatre is an anemic sort of thing that does not reflect Negro life, Negro fancies or Negro ideas. It reflects the 100 percent American Theatre at its middling and cheapest." (Kornweibel, 116)

A third highly visible venue characterized swing era Harlem: the ballroom. The three most famous were the Savoy, the Renaissance, and the Alhambra. Besides the stellar attraction of the swing bands, the ballrooms' primary entertainment, social dancing, was democratically self-generated by the customers: anyone could participate. Frequently, a circle of spectators spontaneously gathered around a particularly excellent dancing couple, and the ballroom floor became an instant stage. These venues were the expanded, black sheep descendents of the tea dances that were held across America in white middle-class hotel ballrooms during the pre– and post–World War I era, with an important shift in emphasis. Instead of a genteel afternoon event, the swing era ballroom phenomenon was a no-holds-barred, late night frolic where class differences were left at the door. The ballroom was home to an

athletic, ecstatic, sweat-inducing phenomenon called the Lindy, a dance
that defined the swing era and its music as much as the Cakewalk had
been the keynote for ragtime music.

A brief examination of a leading example of each venue—nightclub,
theater, and ballroom—and the specific race etiquette that inflected (or
infected) it reveals how each one helped to make this city-within-a-city a
seductive attraction for both blacks and whites.

The Cotton Club

In cities from coast to coast, some of the biggest and best black night
spots, social clubs, and gambling houses, the products of a segregated society, were transformed into the extravagant, white-owned cotton clubs
and plantation clubs of the swing era that, ironically, reinforced segregation by catering to all-white audiences. New York's Cotton Club was the
most famous, and for almost two decades (1923–40) that name conjured
up images of a sophisticated high life that stood in sharp contrast to the
poverty and desperation of many Americans—and, certainly, most
African Americans—during those years. Run by gangster Owney Madden and his crime syndicate, the club's exotic decor was supplemented by
the presence of Madden's henchmen, some of them sporting flamboyant
names—like Big Frenchy DeMange whose duty it was to "spend time at
the club, giving the patrons the added kick of rubbing elbows with mob-
sters." (Haskins, 32) During Prohibition bootleg liquor was a major
source of profit for the club. The floor shows were modeled after the extravagant style of the Ziegfeld Follies although "the smaller scale of the
stage area and often three-sided audience perspective probably generated
a great sense of intimacy, three-dimensionality, and sensual heat."[2] Those
involved in organizing, producing, managing, and coordinating the productions—that is, all the people in power and control—were white. The
performers were black, and conditions for all but the top stars and the
musicians, protected by their union, were emblematic of the exploitation
experienced by nonunionized artists, black or white.

There were two revues a year: a fall show opening in September and a
spring show premiering in April. August and March were spent rehears-

ing the next package. In his autobiography bandleader Cab Calloway describes the club's decor when he auditioned his band in 1930:

> It was a huge room. The bandstand was a replica of a southern mansion with large white columns and a backdrop painted with weeping willows and slave quarters. The band played on the veranda of the mansion, and in front of the veranda, down a few steps, was the dance floor, which was also used for the shows. The waiters were dressed in red tuxedos, like butlers in a southern mansion, and the tables were covered with red-and-white-checked gingham tablecloths. There were huge cut-crystal chandeliers, and the whole set was like the sleepy-time-down-South during slavery. Even the name, Cotton Club, was supposed to convey the southern feeling. I suppose the idea was to make whites who came to the club feel like they were being catered to and entertained by black slaves. (88)

The plantation, the jungle, and other demeaning clichés still framed the landscape of African American entertainment. For example, Calloway recalls that the spring revue of 1930, the first season for his band, was titled "Brown Sugar—Sweet But Unrefined." (93)

This venue became the home of the black revue after it was no longer the rage on Broadway. Norton and Webb performed in clubs in the East and Midwest that imitated its lavish example. As in other areas of black vaudeville, the shows were carried by the extent and quality of the dancing. Two newspaper reviews for the fall 1937 season highlight this point. From the *New York Times*, 2 October 1937, "The Cotton Club specializes, and it is quite fitting, in dancing. There is a Mr. Dynamite Hooker in something called 'Black Magic,' the Messrs. Tip, Tap, and Toe, who are a spectacular lot on the head of a wooden drum, the Nicholas Brothers of stage renown, and a couple of more [*sic*]." These large drum heads were scenic props constructed for dancing, not actual drumming. Webb asserts that Norton originated the idea of dancing on the head of the drum (for his Spear Dance solo) and subsequently sold his drum prop to this tap team. Reviewing the same show, *New York Daily News* critic Dan Walker said: "Paradoxically, Robinson's absence [Bill "Bojangles" Robinson, the tap artist, was filming in Hollywood] makes one realize how many other superb dancers the show contains—the Three Choclateers, Freddy James, James Skelton and Tip, Tap and Toe. A dozen years ago, before colored revues had poured over Broadway like a hot chocolate sauce, any one of them would have been a dancing sensation." (26 September 1937) *New York Times* critic Jack Gould commented:

> Peg Leg Bates does tap dances which belie the fact that he lost a leg in an accident. . . . Aland and Anise . . . are back also with pleasing gracefulness, and in two youngsters, Rufus, 7 years old, and Richard, 5, Mr. Stark has found another pair of dancing youngsters who will probably be Cotton Club favorites. Others [dancing] in the show are . . . the Four Step Brothers, and the Three Choclateers. In keeping with its tradition, the Cotton Club is also introducing a dance, this one entitled "The Skrontch." (13 March 1938)[3]

With the exception of adagio team Anise and Aland all the dancers cited above were tap artists, either precision, acrobatic, eccentric, comic, or class acts. The variety of forms in this genre was dizzying.

Like the Savoy ballroom, the Cotton Club took pride in its status as the place of origin of new social dances. Truckin', the Susie-Q, Peckin', and the Skrontch were popularized as production numbers that subsequently caught on as ballroom dance fads. Conversely, steps like the Shorty George, conceived by Savoy Lindy-hopper George "Shorty" Snowden, traveled from the ballroom to the nightclub and vaudeville stage. The club also cashed in on current crazes from the white mainstream. Just as Margot Webb had been singled out from the chorus to do a fan dance, so also the revue that marked Lena Horne's debut featured this teenager as a fan dancer, with a costume consisting of three feathers. The product sold, in this case, was not the dancing but the exposed bodies. Lena Horne said, "I sensed that the white people in the audience saw nothing but my flesh, and its color, onstage." (Haskins, 95)

Besides the entertainment provided by specialty acts, chorus girls (generally twelve), show girls (generally eight),[4] and the opportunity for social dancing by the customers, the club also maintained a male chorus line. First appearing in the spring 1934 revue, the Cotton Club Boys—ten in all—initiated a male style of precision rhythm dancing done in unison that was difficult to imitate.

Backstage conditions for the performers were anything but rosy. Working in a club renowned for its menu of Mexican, Chinese, and southern dishes, these performers were not allowed meals or any other fringe benefits—not even leftovers, which were thrown away. There was only one ladies' room in the establishment and the "girls" were dissuaded from using it: the bathroom was for the patrons. (Haskins, 102) Their contracts stipulated deductions for lateness, missing rehearsals, and an extended list of minor infractions. There was no pay for rehearsals, which sometimes ran all night in preparation for a new revue. On a $25 weekly salary, the chorus lines performed three shows nightly—7:30 P.M., midnight, and 2:00 A.M.—seven days a week; they were not paid for additional performances that were added at management's discretion. Still, in the 1920s and during the Depression, many Americans, black or white, looked upon this opportunity as a blessing.

Although the male dancers were judged mainly on ability, the females were still chosen on the basis of skin color, and only the lightest females were accepted. This tyranny of hue was challenged by hoofer Lucille Wilson, who later became the second wife of Louis Armstrong. She was pretty, talented, and dark skinned. She won over management at her audition and was hired on a trial basis: she'd be out of a job if customers complained. There were no complaints, and she remained in the club's chorus line for eight years. Still, the color bar was the rule of thumb and prevailed until the black nationalist and Civil Rights movements of the 1960s.

Most of the chorines entered show business for the same reason as Margot Webb and Lena Horne had—it offered a viable salary for young, nubile, light-skinned black females during the Depression. Horne was escorted nightly to the club by her mother or stepfather. At sixteen she was performing, rather than attending high school, to augment the low family income during those lean years. She was able to audition in 1933 under the guidance of family friend Elida Webb (no relation to Margot Webb), a choreographer who had been a chorus girl in *Shuffle Along* and claims to have invented the Charleston. (Hatch-Billops interview, 7 March 1974). Elida Webb was one of the few black and female choreographers used at the club, quietly overstepping another barrier in the "whites only" policy. (Clarence Robinson had been the first black choreographer, creating and staging the spring 1931 revue.)

With the advent of radio the Cotton Club gained nationwide fame. In 1927 the Columbia Broadcasting System began to air the Ellington band live from the club; soon after, other Harlem cabarets were picked up by network radio. The Harlem sound reached across the nation, offering radio-listening tourists throughout America the chance to join the New York cognoscenti and the international set in going black.

The uptown Cotton Club changed with the times. In 1935 a race riot broke out in Harlem. It was inspired by the conflict between white-owned, overpriced, low-quality Harlem stores and a Depression-poor black population at the bottom rung of America's economic ladder. Coupled with the wane of the Harlem Renaissance, this added up to a sum that detracted from Harlem's pull as a place for whites to make merry. Moreover, many Harlem residents were becoming antipathetic to the well-off white element that continued to invade their neighborhood after hours. Profits were plummeting. In 1936 the Cotton Club moved from Harlem to Broadway and 48th Street.

After its move downtown, the old Cotton Club site was occupied by another cabaret of the same order, the Plantation Club. Norton and Margot performed at this venue in an extended engagement in 1938. The nightclubs where the team performed in other cities followed the same general pattern and policies as the Cotton Club—black entertainment for white clientele. The shows produced at these out-of-town spots, including the Cotton Club in Philadelphia and the Grand Terrace in Chicago, followed the example of the New York Cotton Club revues but on a less lavish scale. For better or worse, the New York Cotton Club was the epitome of its kind.

The Apollo

Long after the demise of the Harlem nightclubs, the Apollo theater continued the tradition of black vaudeville. Catering basically to a black audience, it also attracted a white clientele. It kept the variety format alive from the swing era into the fifties and sixties eras of rhythm and blues and cool jazz. Although backstage conditions and salaries were often deplorable, the Apollo remained one of the few sources of employment when most other vaudeville venues had folded. Moreover, it offered an ideological alternative for the Harlem community: audiences, artists, and technical crew were racially mixed, and the Apollo was a part of the com-

ONE WEEK ONLY
Beginning
FRIDAY, JUNE 20th

At The **125th STREET** **APOLLO**

AMERICA'S SMARTEST COLORED SHOWS!

125th St. near 8th Av. Telephone UNiversity 4-4490

NEW YORK'S GREATEST NIGHT CLUB REVUE—
ADDED STAR ATTRACTIONS

MIMO CLUB REVUE

NORTON & MARGO — EMORY EVANS

VELMA MIDDLETON

MOKE & POKE — LOLA PIERRE

S A H J I — MILLIE and BILLIE

"PIGMEAT" - PETE NUGENT

OVIE ALSTON AND HIS BAND

with ORLANDO ROBERSON

16 OF THE LOVELIEST BROWNSKIN DANCING GIRLS IN THE WORLD

WED. NIGHT Amateurs
Sat. Midnight Show

Apollo handbill for a unit show, 1941.

munity in a way that the posh nightclubs never were. In 1935, when 125th Street still had a white population and most businesses were owned and run by whites, the Apollo was one of the first enterprises on the street to employ African Americans.

A different class of whites came to this theater—bohemians and students (largely from nearby Columbia University and City College) rather than the celebrities, socialites, and politicians who frequented the extravagant night spots. According to Jack Schiffman, former owner of the Apollo and son of the first owner, Frank Schiffman, whites customarily formed upwards of half the audience at the Wednesday night amateur shows and the Saturday midnight show, particularly before the Civil Rights era when downtown houses like the Paramount, Capitol, and Strand did not feature black entertainers. (49–50) In the black world, the Apollo was seen as the theater of the people. It was not a magnet for the black bourgeoisie although they, too, attended.

The site that housed it had opened in 1913 as Hurtig and Seaman's New Music Hall, a variety house in the original Harlem neighborhood, a community that had started as an exclusive enclave for whites seeking to avoid association with the European immigrants who flooded downtown areas of Manhattan. But the area changed, and well-off whites moved elsewhere as immigrant whites and blacks moved in. By the midtwenties the site was a burlesque house catering to the ethnic white element. At that time, blacks were not allowed entry. In 1934–35 Frank Schiffman and Leo Brecher bought the theater from Sidney Cohen, who had been operating an African American vaudeville house on the site for about a year. It remained in the hands of the Schiffman and Brecher families until 1978. At that time a private group, the "253 Corporation," bought the building, marking the first time in the Apollo's history that it was owned by African Americans. (Bloom, 22)

A 1,600-seat house with two balconies and a combination movie-vaudeville format, the Apollo ran a continuous offering of four to five shows a day; a midnight show and extra daytime shows were added on weekends. The original price of admission was fifteen cents for daytime shows and a fifty-cents top for Wednesday and Saturday nights. For one ticket a patron could remain in the theater from 10 A.M. to midnight. The theater's strength and drawing power lay in repetition: when other outlets were gone, people returned to this venue season after season to see their favorites perform, often demanding a repeat of old routines. The Wednesday night amateur hour instituted by the theater became a tradition, and numerous artists who went on to major show business careers had their first exposure on these programs. Some swing era amateur night winners included Billie Holiday, Billy Eckstine, and Sarah Vaughan.

In contrast to the cabaret entertainment targeted for white clientele, comedy was a feature at the Apollo. In a performance environment geared to black audiences, the sharp-tongued, sexually explicit, race-conscious genre that is the bedrock of African American humor was a staple in the show format. Although this brand of humor was not overtly political (such as one finds in 1960s comedians like Dick Gregory and Godfrey Cambridge), it followed in the footsteps of those black minstrels who played on the fact that the black world is a world unto itself, a miniature America with its own criteria and mores that may be inscrutable to the white mainstream. Thus, much of the humor was in-group in nature. Swing era comics like Dusty Fletcher, Dewey "Pigmeat" Markham and Jackie "Moms" Mabley owed their stylistic origins to minstrels like Bert Williams. They were physical actors who worked in comedy skits and cultivated a specific character with a particular mode of dress. Markham originated routines that later were absorbed into the white mainstream and disseminated by mass media. He invented the "Here come de judge" routine, striding into "court" in huge pants held up by safety pins, enormous shoes, a baggy frock coat, and a run-down bowler or top hat. The routine was a travesty of justice. Other Markham skits harkened back to his roots in burlesque and minstrelsy. He always worked in blackface. Jackie Mabley's character was the female counterpart of Markham's: she dressed in ill-fitting clothes, sneakers, and a bizarre hat, with a toothless grin to complete the picture.

One of the highlights of comedy at the Apollo was improvisation, often involving the spectators. Performers ad-libbed, using backstage events, onstage musicians, and audience members to enhance the moment. In one of the gossip-review columns she wrote for the New York edition of the *Chicago Defender,* 23 July 1935, Margot Webb gave the example of a comedian named Sandy Burns who "embarrassed a young fellow in one of the upper boxes no end when he claimed that [it was his fault that] a fuse had blown out—and on top of that [he] said that the fellow took a dollar out of his pocket. . . . The audience went into hysterics, showing that audiences haven't changed much since the time of Nero. They still get the greatest kick out of the torture of others. . . ."

Apollo humor often seemed vulgar, stale, or corny to *Variety* reviewers; that Markham and Mabley were unfavorably received by them is a fine example of outsider incomprehension of the codes and mores of the in-group. Yet, these two were Apollo audience favorites. They used familiar aspects of family life and discord and were vociferously rewarded with the laughter of recognition. They addressed the ever-present specter of race prejudice in sardonic ways that struck the right chord with African American spectators. Their performances were geared for blacks, and particularly for this tough-to-please audience of working-class folks. Most important, they were fine artists and excellent performers, which is why they maintained long careers in show business. *Variety* (9 November 1938) marveled at the warm reception they received: "Jackie Mabley handles what little comedy there is, using [Willie] Bryant as a straight. Best is an old burley bit whose type goes over better with Apollo audiences than elsewhere, as a rule. They like the 'honeymoon' skit given 'em here." And again (15 May 1940): "What has long since been thought to have been eclipsed by a new era of show biz has a star-tling resurrection here this week at the Apollo. For fully twenty minutes toward the end of this 105-minute bill, Jackie Mabley, a femme charac-ter who might have been conceived in burlesque, tosses the darkest in-digo [that is, X-rated material] which she's presently masquerading as an act. . . ." And yet again (25 September 1946): "Pigmeat, standard comic at this house, is back again for the umpteenth time and regales the cus-tomers with stale gags and some dull repartee with [Willie Bryant] the emcee and bandleader. Though his material is creaky, it's nevertheless ef-fective with this audience. . . ."

These reviews belie the fact that Markham and Mabley were stars of the black entertainment world. The implication is that the Apollo audi-ence's preference in humor exhibited a lack of taste and sophistication. They failed to understand that repetition and recognition (of a black value system that ran counter to its white analogue, of the comic side of the tragedy of being black in America) were part of these comics' appeal. For the record, Markham and Mabley continued to delight black audi-ences well into the 1960s. Furthermore, the 1940 review registers a veiled complaint about the length of the Apollo show. In fact, the theater's pro-gram followed the old Theater Owner's Booking Association format: shows were generally from one-and-a-quarter to two hours long, with a preponderance of dance acts.

Clarence Robinson was the first choreographer hired by Schiffman and produced a new show every week. Leonard Harper and Leonard Reed were two other choreographers who staged Apollo shows. The *Variety* reviews outlined the structure and enumerated the acts presented at the theater. A review (11 September 1935) of a bill featuring the Louis Armstrong orchestra is typical in listing and evaluating the line-up of performers; it concludes:

> Works on the stage throughout fronted by specialists who include one of the best colored ballroom dance teams, Norton and Margo. Looking Spanishly without too much affectation, they're a graceful pair with competent routines of tango and modern terps. Four Step Bros. are legomaniacs. . . . "Pigmeat" Markham . . . ; Jimmy Baskette, okay straight; John Mason; and sixteen Clarence Robinson Girls . . . ; and Danny and Edith, tiptop rope dancers. . . .

Dancers like Margot Webb and Alice Whitman (of the famous Whitman sisters vaudeville act) appeared also as soloists, working in specialty numbers choreographed either by the choreographer or themselves. They and other "pretty girls" were also used in comedy skits, playing the female interest in walk-on roles. The theater also programmed tabloid versions of black Broadway shows,[5] as was the case with the 1940 Apollo version of the 1939 Broadway hit *Mamba's Daughters*. For the tab version of playwright Abram Hill's comedy *On Striver's Row*, the original play was revised and converted into a musical. Webb performed in it, creating the role of actress Lilly Livingston. However, she felt that it was yet another example of authentic African American achievement reduced to the song-and-dance, rhythmic commodity demanded by the powers-that-be of the white-run commercial entertainment industry. Despite her misgivings, the effort received good press in African American newspapers.[6] (In Abram Hill's parody of the black bourgeoisie, a working-class sweepstakes winner is manipulated by a bankrupt, upper-crust realtor into buying her way into Striver's Row—a metaphorical utopia of the African American upper middle class, which was also the most exclusive block of single-family brownstone dwellings in Harlem.) Besides tab shows, dramatic sketches were arranged for stars of the legitimate stage and screen.

For example, Louise Beavers, who played opposite Fredi Washington in the film *Imitation of Life*, appeared with Reginald Fenderson in a dramatic skit on the 14 June 1939 line-up. Both had just completed the film *Reform School*.

A typical Apollo finale, in which every act did a short bit, was an exuberant climax to an already fast-paced program. Gilbert Millstein, writing for the *New York World Telegram*, described it in 1947:

> The finale of the Apollo orchestras always leaves the cash-customers limp and feverish. Tiger Rag, perhaps, or Christopher Columbus [two fad dances of the era]. The trombones emit frenzied paeans, and the pianist bounces on his stool like a banker learning to ride horseback. Pigmeat weaves deftly in and out of the lines of girls. The tempo gets faster and more frantic—then it ceases for a second and starts in again slowly. The audience stamps its feet as the curtain drops, Pigmeat shuffling dreamily off the stage. They shout for him, but he doesn't go back for a bow. (23 January)

Although they may not qualify as ritual, Apollo shows offered a level of cultural ceremony that bound together the community of spectators in the kind of group experience that was later emulated by the big rock concerts beginning in the 1960s. Even after its golden age and well into the 1970s, the theater managed to keep abreast of the tempo of Harlem. By then, African Americans were free to go practically anywhere they wished in New York, and black performers were beginning to be booked in white venues. Blacks and whites flocked to Broadway theaters and East Side cabarets to see African American artists. Furthermore, the Civil Rights, Nation of Islam, and Black Pride movements combined to make 125th Street definitively Africanist in mood, which made most whites uncomfortable if not unwelcome.

Like other African American performers interviewed—and in stark contrast to the "home-away-from-home" description of the theater offered by its then-owner, Jack Schiffman, in his book on the Apollo—both Margot Webb and bassist John Williams stated that performers were exploited by the theater's low salaries and poor working conditions. According to Williams, musicians were paid considerably less in base salary and for extra shows at this venue than elsewhere and, since they never did fewer than five shows and sometimes were obliged to do six, there was really no breathing space in between. (15 August 1980) For many African American performers, success meant never having to return to this venue, particularly by the 1960s, when it was on its way to becoming a decaying, draughty shambles.

The Savoy: Home of the Lindy

Although the Apollo theater and the Cotton Club hold special sway in any discussion of swing era Harlem, the Savoy ballroom is in a league of its own. All three institutions were important sociocultural venues for the neighborhood, the city, the nation, and the international set. Yet, at the Savoy, race and class boundaries were blurred in ways that were un-dreamed of in other settings; and the black dancing body was its signifier, even when whites were the dancers. Like any ballroom, it differed from other performance environments in that the spectators were the perform-ers. Perhaps most importantly, the Savoy is where the Lindy Hop was born. This dance was all the rage across black and white America, as well as Europe, for nearly two decades. There were other ballrooms in Harlem, but, as Lindy-Hopper Norma Miller and historian Ernie Smith attested in a 1999 presentation, the Savoy was regarded as "the pinnacle. Folks used to say that the Alhambra was grade school, the Renaissance was high school, and the Savoy was college—and beyond!"

As a site where African American and white worlds touched and merged, momentarily, the Savoy ballroom in its heyday was inextricably linked to the Lindy Hop, a freewheeling dance distinguished by great feats of improvisation and athleticism. At other ballrooms in other parts of the nation, white dances and black dances took place on alternate nights, sometimes in the same facility, so as to enforce segregation and discourage interracial mixing. But not at the Savoy. The Lindy is a dance of liberation for at least two reasons: because of the freedom and innova-tion of its style, and because, at its Savoy birthplace, it served as a locus of pre–Civil Rights era integration and as a contact zone that ignored class distinctions. "Kitchen mechanics" (that is, domestic workers), defense workers, war wives, film and stage stars, the international jet set, wealthy white Americans—blacks and whites of all classes and castes gathered together in dance to soak up and bask in the spirit of the place.

In an era when such events were not conventional show business practice, the Savoy hosted transvestite or drag costume balls on a private rental basis. (Sunday nights attracted white stars in sports, entertainment, and politics, and Friday nights were generally reserved for private club and community events.) Josephine Baker attended one on Halloween 1935, soon after her return to New York, that featured "a contest for best costume, and black men wearing crinolines and Madame Pompadour wigs paraded in front of the judges." (Baker and Chase, 197)

The Savoy was home to two outstanding bands—the Chick Webb Orchestra and Al Cooper's Savoy Sultans. The groups took turns on the bandstand, providing continuous music all night. Count Basie called them "the *swingingest* bands" (Stearns and Stearns, 317), and journalist Otis Ferguson remarked that, when the place was in full swing, "the whole enclosure, with all its people, beats like a drum and rises in steady time, like a ground swell." (Gold, 50) It is fitting to describe this ballroom as a sacred space. It was a vessel for and generator of spirit just as much as any Harlem church. On its huge, block-long wooden floor social dancing reached ecstatic proportions. Cultural historian Bernice Reagon has aptly portrayed the spiritual dimension of social dancing as celebration and affirmation: "When black people go out on Friday or Saturday night they are . . . walking sacred territory. There is a way in which the only way you know who you are sometimes has to do with what you can do when you go home from work, change clothes, get with your partner and dance all night long."[7] This sense of spirit-union-communion is borne out by Lindy artist Frankie Manning's description of a typical night at the Savoy: "It seems like every single person on that floor is swinging. They're dancing, they're bobbing, I mean they're swinging so much even the floor seems like it's just bouncing with the beat of that music. . . . You feel so exhilarated—like you could just go out there and dance with anybody, you don't care who it is." Indeed, there was an inherent jubilation in the dance that was heightened by the aura and reputation of the locale.

Cultural critic and "Negrophile" Carl Van Vechten said that the Lindy was Dionysian, "a dance to do to honor wine-drinking, but it is not erotic.

Of all the dances originated by the American Negro, this the most nearly approaches the sensation of religious ecstasy. It could be danced, quite reasonably, and without alteration of tempo, to many passages in the *Sacre du Printemps* of Stravinsky, and the Lindy Hop would be as appropriate for the music . . . as the music would be appropriate for the Lindy Hop." Extending the idea that this dance is beyond the erotic is the statement made by renowned Lindy-Hopper Leon James: "I don't get no sexy eyeballs when I'm doing Lindy. I got too much work to do, man, keeping us going in timing, pacing, and beat."[8] Lindy artist Norma Miller described it as a "perfect attunement between dance movement and music," and Manning characterized it as "a love affair between you and your partner and the music." Dance historian Ernie Smith, who was seduced by the Lindy and the Savoy as a teenager, said "the kind of dancing that I was gravitating toward instinctually was being done in the black neighborhoods . . . effortless-looking dancing, mostly from the hips down."

The Lindy—at least the African American original style of the dance—was effortless looking, smooth, and swinging. It was the dance craze that swept America, black and white, rich and poor, from the Great Depression to well after World War II. At its Savoy home, it lured even more outsiders to Harlem, including those who couldn't afford to go to cabarets like the Cotton Club. According to Norma Miller, when the Savoy opened in 1926, it was a place that "belonged to black people. It was our ballroom that opened in Harlem—our social center, our community center. . . . Whites came to our ballroom. . . . There was a mixing and mingling of black and white at a social level that had never existed in America before." Indeed, by the early 1940s, one third of the patrons were white. (Gold, 52)

According to Smith, the freedom introduced into dance practice by the Lindy was perhaps its biggest attraction. But this freedom was tempered and qualified by the knowledge that someone else was brokering it for profit. As Norma Miller put it, "A lot of people wanted to do this dance. But . . . we had an edge and . . . that's the way we danced. . . . [We secretly vowed that] this will be something you will not do better than we, I don't care who you are. We wanted our tempos fast, and the white dancers didn't like that. . . . We didn't want them taking our dance—they had everything else."

What Miller and other Savoy Lindy-Hoppers effectuated was the protection device used by acts that played the Apollo: they densely packed their routines with speed and step clusters to prevent others from stealing them: "We sweated for that. We busted our butts to get it the way it was. . . . We created it. It came out of the blood and sweat of Harlem," said Miller. But, of course, others did take it away. White business interests wanted this market. For a while in 1943 the ballroom was actually closed down by order of New York's Mayor LaGuardia on a trumped-up morals charge. But the real reasons were, first, to thwart the sexually charged racial integration engendered on its premises[9] and, second, to lure the Savoy's sizable white clientele to downtown venues.

Furthermore, as was the case with swing music, styles of playing and dancing changed as these forms were appropriated by white practitioners and finessed to a white aesthetic standard. This meant that the grounded, from-the-hips, smooth style of dancing described by Smith became a bouncy, upright, jerky style taught at white dancing schools such as those run by Arthur Murray. The dance was even given a new name: the Jitterbug. Indeed, in spite of its origins, so eloquently expressed by Miller, the way it would be received in mainstream America reflected the racialized tenets of the day. As pointed out by Van Vechten in 1930, "Nearly all the dancing now to be seen in our musical shows is of Negro origin, but both critics and public are so ignorant of this fact that the production of a new Negro revue is an excuse for the revival of the hoary old lament that it is pity the Negro can't create anything for himself, that he is obliged to imitate the white man's revues. This, in brief, has been the history of the Cakewalk, the Bunny Hug, the Turkey Trot, the Charleston, and the Black Bottom. It will probably be the history of the Lindy Hop."

Just as Benny Goodman was believed to be the King of Swing, the Jitterbug was believed to be a dance invented by white teenagers—or so it seemed to the dominant culture. Six decades after Van Vechten's statement, Ernie Smith explained that the culprit responsible for the separation of black dance from black ownership is racism. He points out particularly that racism results in white people harboring bizarre beliefs about black talent, ideas, interests, intelligence, and potential, with dance a part of that pattern. He concludes by reaffirming his conviction that the Lindy Hop is a black dance, created by African Americans from their

African heritage and their experiences living in America. He contends that this legacy was expressed in the Lindy—thus making it a black dance even when whites perform it.

But the culprit—racism—caused the dominant culture to simultaneously accept and deny, approach and repel, African American expressive styles. Whites came to this black cultural wellspring, touched it, embraced it, and went away. This attract-repel relationship—institutionalized in American entertainment since the minstrel era—tainted the seemingly freewheeling contact represented by the Lindy at the Savoy. It infected every aspect of black-white social, cultural, and political discourse, while black expressive forms continued in their role as grist for the white entertainment mill.

Harlem Lifestyles: All the World's a Stage

"As far as we were concerned, Harlem was as close to Heaven as we were going to find on this earth," said Sadie and Bessie Delaney, middle-class black sisters who moved there from North Carolina in 1919. (Delany, Delany, and Hearth, 145)

With African Americans unwelcome in the city at large, Harlem, like black neighborhoods throughout the nation, was an American microcosm with a network of community services providing for the needs of its segregated populace. Still, Harlem was not a typical black community, just as New York is not a typical American city: both were symbolic meccas to Americans of particular persuasions. Writing in 1940, author Claude McKay described its uniqueness, stating that Harlem was "hectic and fluid . . . , lacking in the high seriousness" of black communities in Chicago, Durham, New Orleans, and Atlanta, which he characterized as "more sober and balanced." (15) For a people historically subject to racism and repression, Harlem represented the height of autonomy and self-determination:

> Encircled by millions of largely hostile white people, Negroes in Harlem nevertheless established a thriving and prosperous community within two square miles. The area presently contained every institution known to

modern living—hospitals, libraries, newspapers and magazines, hotels, restaurants and a shopping district, theaters and dance halls, even indeed a Y.M.C.A. and Y.W.C.A., all catering exclusively to Negroes. The community had its own Negro clergymen, doctors, pharmacists, lawyers, dentists and undertakers; besides all the multiple organizations, cults and rackets that make up a big city in America. . . . (Ottley, 1948, 243–44)

News of community happenings was disseminated by an extensive network of newspapers and periodicals. In a survey taken in 1940 of black communities across the nation it was found that "there were 210 Negro newspapers, mostly with local circulation, and 129 magazines." (Bergman, 488) Besides the more intellectual publications like *Crisis* (the official publication of the NAACP, originally edited by W. E. B. Du Bois) and the *Messenger*, major newspapers during the swing era included the *Norfolk Journal and Guide, Pittsburgh Courier, Chicago Defender, Afro-American, Amsterdam Star-News,* and *New York Age.* Such publications issued New York and Chicago editions as well as their home edition, and employed local and correspondent reporters. They served as the African American voice against discrimination and disseminated news of African diaspora peoples that was unavailable in white publications. Writer Arna Bontemps eloquently addressed the phenomenon by stating that "The justification of the Negro press, according to my argument, is that it fights for goals which if attained would liquidate itself." (Nichols, 30) These publications maintained sports, church, society, and theatrical sections, all of which dealt with community gossip and hearsay as well as facts. Then, as now, gossip columns were a major daily feature, offering inside tidbits and the latest rumors about stars who, in a small community like Harlem, might well be the reader's next-door neighbor.

Although many commercial enterprises were owned and run by whites, a substantial number of small businesses were black enterprises. (For example, Webb's gowns were made by African American designers.) The illegal numbers racket, owned by white gangsters with black runners who received the actual bets from customers, and race records, phonograph recordings by black artists targeted for black audiences, were thriving industries. Due to segregation in sports, there were black baseball, football, and basketball leagues. One of the best known and highest skilled of the basketball teams was the Rens, the team whose home was Harlem's Renaissance ballroom. Robert Douglas, first African American to be inducted into the Basketball Hall of Fame, was owner and coach of the Rens (1922–48) and managed the ballroom until 1971. In a 1975 *Long Island Newsday* piece written by Jane Gross, Douglas recalled the customary arrangement of teams playing in dance halls. "They'd stop dancing while you played. While the team rested, they danced some more, then after the game they danced some more." Big name bands booked at the Cotton Club and the Savoy also played for these dance-plus-sports events.

Another aspect of the Harlem lifestyle was musical training and dance lessons for children. If by 1940 most households were proud of having a radio in the living room (usually the large floor models designed after the Stromberg-Carlson example), the piano in the parlor was still a cultural status symbol. It was typical for the family member who had taken lessons to entertain guests with light classics or the popular boogie-woogie. Like many other performers cashing in on the community craving for culture, Norton and Margot opened a dance studio in central Harlem in 1936. In bourgeois style, their school was located on the first floor of a Striver's Row brownstone owned by Dr. Wiley Wilson, a prominent community physician. Here they taught children's classes as well as routines to nightclub performers. However, at the height of their performing career they were unable to successfully balance the two responsibilities. They closed the school in 1938.

There was also a black film industry. Small outfits, such as the black-owned Oscar Micheaux company and white-owned organizations with black producers and directors, made low-budget films, generally shooting in the metropolitan New York area. Webb appeared in walk-on parts in such films when dancing dates were scarce, but she contends that they were not shown in the North and were marketed for black audiences down South. She recalls working in one such film, *Sepia Cinderella,* starring singer Billy Daniels and Sheila Guyse.[10]

A large roller-skating rink where people glided to musical accompaniment was another popular community meeting place. Come summer, the community's swimming pool, the Lido, was a center for leisure as well as competitive finals. It was an important location for Webb because she was an avid swimmer, having learned the skill even before she studied dance.

According to Webb, the pool was a summer hangout for celebrities as well as ordinary Harlemites. Almost to silence the insult of segregated national competitions (particularly the Miss America pageant), the community held a plethora of such events. As a sideline, Webb trained beauty contestants, rehearsing them as though they were preparing for a show and chaperoning them when they visited Harlem clubs and businesses to drum up support. There were competitions to select queens of social clubs, fraternal orders, magazines, businesses, and even nightclubs—which were another fashionable venue for staging finals.

The Harlem community prided itself on its boldly stylish parades. These popular events were sure-fire hits that seldom failed to draw and please a crowd. Sponsored by local clubs or businesses, they usually took place on weekend afternoons. A favorite type was the military exhibition that included bugle-and-drum and rifle corps. Composed of community members ranging in age from children to senior citizens, they performed a dancing style of precision drill work that has become the refined specialty of black colleges and universities such as Grambling and Florida A & M. Two community institutions merged on the many occasions when beauty contest finalists, dressed in evening gowns or swimsuits, were exhibited in parade on elaborate floats. Both traditions enjoyed an enduring popularity in black communities nationwide and flourished until de jure segregation ended in the 1960s.

It is ironic that the advent of the Civil Rights era proved to be the undoing of Harlem and black communities nationwide. In the best of all possible worlds, integration would have made anachronisms of these ethnic enclaves. They had grown and prospered under the old hegemony of segregation. Surely, they were destined for obsolescence: once the goal of integration was achieved, blacks and whites would live in the same communities and share the same facilities. Part of this prediction came true and, indeed, with integration black sports teams and beauty contests died, along with hotels, theaters, small businesses—entire African American communities along with their infrastructures. But the other part of the equation was only partially realized. Over three decades after the end of the Civil Rights era, the dream of integration has yet to shatter the nightmare of American racism, and members of a huge African American underclass inhabit the decaying shambles that are the Harlems of America.

The irony and tragedy of the African American condition continues. By and large, blacks remain nominal presences in most areas of American public life, and even that limited representation faces the challenge of those who feel that equal opportunity is reverse racism.

In an era that preceded stage pornography (there was no African American burlesque tradition), the African American revue appealed to the audience's erotic needs by suggestive or explicit comedy and dance routines. Lena Horne and Margot Webb appeared almost nude in their respective fan dances. Though it would seem innocuous enough to an American audience at the turn of the millennium, it was highly titillating to the swing era spectator. According to writer Theophilus Lewis in 1926: "The best jazz bands of the land have been doing their stuff, adult humor has flowed freely and the general run of dancing has been so licentious [that] . . . in at least six out of the last ten shows at the Lafayette I have seen comely women do on the stage everything it is possible for one person to do in bed. . . ." And, again in 1927, Lewis observed, "Here in Harlem fifty cents purchases a two-hour revel in vice which formerly only bankers and Oriental potentates could afford to enjoy. Indeed, while he sits in his orchestra seat the tired tailor's helper is a banker, for he enjoys most of the sensations the plutocrat is able to buy. . . . While he observes the saturnalia he suffers only one disadvantage when compared with the sultan: he cannot touch the girls. . . ." The most risqué revues never left Harlem and were produced for uptown appetites. There were black producers staging shows of all kinds both in Harlem and midtown: Charlie Davis, Addison Carey, J. Leubrie Hill, Frank Montgomery, and Irvin C. Miller (of "Brown Skin Models" fame) were some of the best known.

In spite of the payoffs of performance, it was a hectic, fatiguing life for the swing era artist. Even those who were successful—particularly the big bands and their vocalists—kept on top by touring constantly and enduring the drudgery of the one-night stand. Since engagements were erratic, it was safest to accept every opportunity, and it was a common practice to hold two or three bookings simultaneously. A performer might work four shows in a theater during the day and then two more at a cabaret into the early morning hours. This was true for performers at the bottom rung of the salary ladder—chorus girls and teams like Norton and Webb—as well as for top stars. When he was over sixty years old, Bill Robinson had a sixteen-hour daily schedule during the two weeks before the spring 1939 Cotton Club revue opened, shuttling between *Hot Mikado* performances and all-night Cotton Club rehearsals. (Haskins, 143–44) In 1929 the Duke Ellington orchestra worked simultaneously in Ziegfeld's *Show Girl* and at the Cotton Club late in the evening. The cabaret bent its stringent performer rules when Broadway or Hollywood intervened. People like Ellington or Robinson could be excused from the early show for a more prestigious engagement—with a salary cut, of course. Later the Ellington band filled three simultaneous engagements: the Cotton Club, the Palace Theater, and the recording studio.

Comedy tap team Buck and Bubbles appeared at Harlem's Lafayette theater while performing in the *Ziegfeld Follies of 1931*. These two book-ings highlighted the variations in audience response. The active engage-ment of Harlem audiences often resulted in a more daring, if not more creative, performance:

> The contrast between the noisy informality of the Lafayette and the quiet solemnity of the *Follies* made a distinct difference. "I was doing the same steps in both places," says Bubbles, "but with a different feeling. Down-town, it was a battle between the acts; uptown, between the dancer and the audience. In Harlem the audience practically dared you to dance, and you had to swing. Downtown they just watched, and you couldn't fail. I danced loose and rhythmic uptown—flop and flang-flang; simple and distinct downtown." As in jazz the audience exerted a crucial influence. (Stearns and Stearns, 218)

It was an era of hard work tempered with some joy. Many African Americans believed they were on the brink of real change, and there were bursts of anticipation—euphoria, in fact—that Ellington touched on in his autobiography and that Harlem Renaissance writers, like Langston Hughes, expressed in their work. James Weldon Johnson, writer and ac-tivist, "was well aware of the exploitation and poverty that scarred the Harlem artistic and political community, but he still believed its progress to be more telling than its poverty." (Douglas, 89) Jazz was still young; its pioneers were at the beginning of their careers and sensed their creative powers and the influence they had on their audiences. Ellington, always diplomatic and deferential, acknowledged his indebtedness to the Harlem spirit: "Sometimes I wonder what my music would sound like today had I not been exposed to the sounds and overall climate created by all the wonderful, and very sensitive and soulful people who were the singers, dancers, musicians, and actors in Harlem when I first came there." (81)

For people like Ellington, Armstrong, and Robinson, who actually made it to the top, there was the unique satisfaction of being among the first African American artists to attain national acclaim. Yet, salaries varied on a broad scale in an era plagued by discrimination; exclusive hiring practices left many African Americans unemployed. Management, even of top performers, remained in the hands of whites, a practice that dated back to the minstrel era. These conditions left the African American performer at a disadvantage: from ownership of performance venues to the management and distribution of its artistic product, black means of production was firmly controlled by whites.

Harlem, bustling with activity: a mecca for musicians, poets, dancers, and visual artists. Nevertheless it was marooned, by segregation, on the isle of Manhattan which surrounded it, touched it, but repelled it. Occasionally, whites penetrated it. Occasionally, blacks made a sortie into white territory, but they were dancing in the dark. The conditions under which African American performers functioned prevailed in Harlem and from coast to coast. It took decades to realize that what was happening was a giant step in a new artistic direction that would permanently change American aesthetics.

Chapter Four

Who's Got His Own: Black Creativity as Commodity

Introduction

Fred Astaire—successful movie star and dance icon—is a household name: at least in part, his work is based on the black tap dance tradition and aesthetic that were developed by tap dancers whose names have been forgotten. Charles "Honi" Coles—tap genius and artist extraordinaire—was Astaire's contemporary but his career never reached Hollywood and his work is known by only a select circle of dance connoisseurs.[1] Paul Robeson—actor and activist—is also a household name: his first-choice career as a lawyer was thwarted, and his American acting career was limited to a repertory of stereotypes.[2] Three American lives. Their careers overlap in time, and all three worked during the swing era. The first two share the same medium, the second and third the same ethnicity. All were phenomenally talented. What separates the careers and choices of these three American men? White privilege versus black proscription—or, dancing in the spotlight versus dancing in the dark. Indeed, any number of other names could be substituted for these three to underline the dichotomy. In the performing arts, during the decades leading up to the Civil Rights era and beyond, racism stopped African American careers in their tracks, like the first runners in a relay race, with whites ready to pick up the baton and assume the victory.

An irony and offshoot of racism: besides the fact that Astaire's medium is based on a form of dance developed and evolved by African Americans (although his performance was a gentrified, finessed version of the original and, itself, became original by sheer force of distinctive personality and artistry), he was allowed to claim it as his own. Indeed, during the decades of his popularity Astaire and his ilk were the heirs apparent of tap dance, as far as mainstream America was concerned.[3] Conversely, Robeson was not permitted to practice law or to participate in American cinema in the leading roles his charismatic presence suggests that he deserved. Even for such a talented individual (a Phi Beta Kappa graduate from Rutgers University with a Columbia University law degree, fluent in several languages), a show business career with racially dictated parameters was one of the few avenues of endeavor available to him. It is open to speculation what Robeson might have achieved for America should his homeland have permitted him the careers in law and diplomacy that he was capable of pursuing.

To be clear, this is not an attack on the considerable artistry, talent, and achievement of Fred Astaire. But, to state an obvious point, it is not by chance or for lack of talent that Coles, his black counterpart, was barred from the possibility of national fame and fortune.

For Norton and Margot, racism meant not being able to work in the hotels and theaters in downtown Manhattan: their agents told them, flat out, that they could not get work as a ballroom team unless they passed for white. Although the team might befriend white dancers who came to see their act while they were touring, they were prohibited from visiting those same dancers at the white theaters where they performed. For many swing era performers these were the conditions that caused their routines to be stolen and incorporated into mainstream entertainment with a white stamp of ownership slapped on them. For example, the source of Donald O'Connor's backflips off the wall in the "Make 'em Laugh" sequence of the film *Singing in the Rain,* is purported to be the work of Harold Nicholas of the Nicholas Brothers.[4] Margot Webb recounted a similar example in the case of the tap team, Tip, Tap and Toe, who were booked with Norton and Margot at the Grand Terrace Café in Chicago and knew for certain that white dancers were attending their performances and eyeing their steps. She contends that at some point "teams like this finally got smart enough to at least charge them [white dancers] for teaching them the tap steps." In the same vein, Webb asserts that Benny Goodman had his band members come to the Grand Terrace and actually write down the Earl Hines music while it was being performed: "Yes—they were in the audience, sitting there, writing down the music." (8 July 1998)

Of course, plagiarism was and is rampant in the arts and is not limited to whites stealing from blacks. However, racial discrimination becomes the issue once we acknowledge the profit differential between black and white swing era performers on the one hand, and the American appetite for whites performing black stuff on the other hand. According to cultural critic Ann Douglas,

> *Amos 'n' Andy,* the most successful radio show in American entertainment history . . . starred the white vaudevillians Freeman Gosden and Charles Correll [and] was an updated minstrel show that apparently borrowed its style from *Shuffle Along's* black librettist-comedians, Flournoy Miller and Aubrey Lyles; Miller wrote some of its dialogue in the 1930s and after. . . . Negroes [sic] might not have their hands on the controls of media culture, but a significant portion of what [Constance] Rourke called "American Humor," some of what [H. L.] Mencken dubbed the "American Language," and almost all the new "jazz" music—in other words, *the mainstay content of the radio and record industries—were Negro in origin.* (1995, 106) (emphasis mine)

These examples, and the Astaire-Coles-Robeson analogy, point to widespread accepted practices of exploitation via discrimination in the entertainment industry. They lead into the meat of this chapter, which examines management and salary issues and the appropriation and commodification of African American performance styles in the mainstream marketplace.

Management

Norton and Margot were familiar figures on the cabaret scene in the Midwest, beginning with a long booking at Chicago's Grand Terrace

Café in 1934. They worked at the swank cabaret from April through December of that year and, again, from September to December of 1935. In 1941 Chicago once more became their base in an extended engagement at Dave's Café from October through December. On each occasion they secured additional bookings in the area to precede and follow these major engagements. When they left New York on a booking arranged through an established agency like Fally Marcus, one of the biggest vaudeville bookers, or the William Morris Agency, it was up to them to pick up local agents while on tour to continue working in the Midwest. Once the initial engagement had begun, regional agents came to the theaters and booked them on the spot. They played in nightclubs in such major cities as Detroit, Kansas City, Louisville, and St. Louis. In 1936, 1938, 1940, and 1941 they also toured and retoured on the African American East Coast circuit, both as a team and in solo work, and performed in white-clientele cabarets that were modeled after New York's Cotton Club.

The team performed on the same circuits and in the same vaudeville unit or cabaret format from 1933 to 1947, without the aid of a personal manager to work with them and develop their potential.[5] This choice was due partly to their suspicions about the notorious double-dealing and exploitative methods of white agents handling black vaudeville talent, and partly to expedience: a limited income made it seem more profitable, at least in the short run, to function as their own agents rather than incur management expenses. In summing up the team's outlook, Webb states:

> Say an agent took you into a theater and [the theater manager gave him] $5,000 for a show. Now, he could put ten or twenty people in that show, and maybe the payroll wouldn't come to more than $2,000. That would have meant that he had $3,000 in his pocket. There was no one to check on that. There were no laws regulating what he was to do with the money. And you never knew how much he was paid. . . . Now, say . . . he had eight chorus girls, and he gave them something like $75 a week apiece. . . . And then he'd give a singer so much, and . . . a team so much, and then he'd wind up with a good amount of money. . . . Now, that's plus a percentage, possibly, that you'd have to pay him for the job. . . . And then there were some who were unscrupulous who'd pocket that whole amount and leave town, leaving the performers stranded, with no salaries, saying that [the

theater] management didn't make enough money to pay them. . . . That
happened many times. (22 May 1980)

Indeed, getting stranded on the road with a promised salary undelivered, the result of employing a dishonest agent or manager, was one of the
many perils facing the swing era performer, black or white. And the team's
one try at personal management was a case in point. It was during their
Chicago period that they came in contact with one Joe Glaser. According
to Webb, "before he started booking acts he had been hanging around the
[Grand] Terrace. That's where he got the idea." (27 August 1980) According to composer-bandleader-pianist Earl Hines in the biography
written by Stanley Dance, "he was always around. He ran about town with
show people and had good ideas, and we listened to him." (1977, 50)[6] In
any case, like many entrepreneurial figures in the entertainment world,
Glaser and his friend Ed Fox, manager of the Grand Terrace, were associated with organized crime. According to lyricist-manager Charlie Carpenter, "Earl [Hines] and everybody used to call Ed Fox 'Pop' at that
time—Pop the Great White Father."(153) At Fox's urging Glaser was
slated to manage the team. Glaser booked them to go West, at better than
their usual rate, on a tour with bandleader Harriet Calloway's unit[7] for
January and February of 1935. Still, Webb recalls:

> Actually, one of the problems with Glaser was on the road. It might have
> been Louisville. He had this show out there and didn't want to pay cash.
> There were some young acts in the show, and he told them that the the-
> ater didn't pay him—which we knew was a lie. That was when Harold
> threatened to kill him, so we never worked for him again. We did get our
> money, but the others were stranded there. And this reminds me of my
> Aunt [Sadie], when she was traveling [when I was a child], she used to talk
> about her own people, African American managers, who'd leave people
> stranded in a strange town—you know, pocket the money—because there
> were no contracts that meant anything. . . . [Webb is referring to the The-
> ater Owners Booking Association days when small-time African Ameri-
> can agents booked black performers.] (8 July 1998)

On returning to Chicago, Norton complained to the police department about the criminal element behind Glaser's management. They

informed him that they could do nothing to help. The team resumed their run at the Grand Terrace and had no further interactions with Glaser. In the *Chicago Defender* of 30 March 1935, there is a photograph of Webb with a caption that reads, "Norton and Margot, who broke with Ed Fox, manager of Earl Hines, during the winter run at the Grand Terrace, returned to the organization this week and will complete the present tour." Webb characterized Fox as "low class—a very uncouth, uneducated man [who] cursed all the time but [was] very wealthy . . . and connected with gangsters." (27 August 1980) Fox and Glaser were buddies, two sides of one coin: Fox had released the team from their winter booking at his club so that Glaser could try out as their personal manager.

These two men were prototypes of management's role in the career of the black swing era performer. Simultaneously offering the potential for protection and extortion, their domain and power were extensive. Respected by some and detested by others, each successfully played both ends against the middle. Fox had Earl Hines under his contractual thumb for some time, and Glaser struck it rich for life when he became Louis Armstrong's manager.

Hines, by the mid-1930s, was bound to Fox in a contract that he had initially solicited but proved to be his nemesis. As Webb bluntly put it: "that's why he played the Terrace for all those years: he couldn't leave!" (8 July 1998) Like other bandleaders who preferred to concentrate on music and leave the business to a manager, he courted Fox, who was a considerable influence in Chicago's entertainment venues, but who "wouldn't give me more than a year's contract. It wasn't till the gangsters moved in that I got a lifetime contract at the club. Meanwhile, the radio was making us known around the country." Indeed, Margot recalled that in the 1930s the band was on Chicago radio nightly in live broadcasts from the club, and Hines became known as Fatha Hines. Hines's naiveté is evinced in soliciting a lifetime contract: only an inexperienced businessman would invite such a deal. Later, Hines detected Fox's true colors: "He sold us down the river, but when he sent us out [touring] we thought it was something new. We'd get a dinner on the train, and that was a big deal, but I was getting $150 a week and the boys [there were 11 band members in his 1932 orchestra] were making $75, $80, or $90. Fox was getting $3500 a week for the band when he was paying us that so he really made money." (Dance, 66–67) Hines learned that Fox was also creaming profits from the song-pluggers, unknown composers whose songs were played by the bands. Hines and the arranger received only a few dollars for playing a song, yet it was revealed that Fox received at least fifty dollars a song. By the end of the decade Hines finally succeeded in extricating himself from the contract by bringing legal suit against Fox.

According to bassist John Williams, Glaser graduated to cabaret and entertainment management from humble beginnings as manager of a chain of whorehouses for the crime syndicate on Chicago's South Side: "When Joe Glaser took you on, you stated your salary to him. If you couldn't get that much, then you took whatever you could settle for. If your salary was a hundred dollars a week, if you worked only one night on the road, you still got a hundred dollars a week." (15 August 1980)

This interesting arrangement was, obviously, a gamble. The odds were stacked in Glaser's favor if he was smart enough to manage promising artists whose salary potential would escalate. Apparently, he had a nose for success and, in a long career, was able to glean profits from many a swing era salary that he had under contract on this prix-fixe basis. However, unlike Fox, he was no dictator, according to Williams. In spite of any such arrangement, it was still possible to break a contract, particularly a short-term agreement. A musician could quit, or be fired, with two weeks' notice if the band was working and within twenty-four hours if it was unemployed. For a second-string musician who wanted to play it safe, a fixed salary might have seemed the lesser evil compared to no salary at all.

Thus, in spite of its notoriety, Glaser's deal with Louis Armstrong was not unusual and, according to Williams, was one of mutual consent. Rumor had it that he contracted the legendary trumpeter to a lifetime agreement at a fixed rate, regardless of the fact that Armstrong's earnings increased phenomenally during his long career. Everything beyond the fixed figure belonged to Glaser. Williams offers a more sanguine perspective:

Joe and Louis were, I'd say, like man and wife. He saved Louis's life in Chicago. People don't say anything about this, but Joe Glaser was just a poor guy running around Chicago with [Al] Capone when, already, Louis was a big thing. He [Armstrong] was playing in this club for one of the gangsters . . . [and] another club offered him more money. And you know how the gangsters were in those days . . . [they] ran Chicago. Capone and some of those guys were the big dogs. Anyway, they told Louis that if he left them to go into the other club they were going to kill him. . . . Well, Louis was very stubborn. He said something like, "This isn't slavery, I should be able to go where I want." So he quit. And by Joe being in [the mob]—well, they say Joe used to be Capone's flunky—he got wind of it, and he got Louis out of Chicago. That was the beginning of their friendship. But, now, about this money deal, I don't know. From what I saw when I was with the band, Louis had a regular salary—X amount of dollars was his salary every night that he played. Now, when all the expenses in the office were paid off, for the bands and the other celebrities they booked and after Joe Glaser got his percentage, what was left was split equally between the two of them—that's the story I got out of it. (15 August 1980)

According to saxophonist, clarinetist, and arranger Budd Johnson:

Of course, Louis was no businessman. . . . He trusted Joe implicitly. . . . Louis began saying, "I think I'm going to get with old Joe Glaser, because he ain't got nothin' and I can tell him what I want." Joe had been a hustler, a slickster, around Chicago, and he had just come out of prison. His family always had that place called the Sunset Café, and there was income for him from that. So he got hold of Louis, this jewel, and they started to make it big, and Joe became a multimillionaire. (Dance, 212)

Jack Schiffman, long-time owner of Harlem's Apollo theater, offers another version of the story: "Out of those early days came Glaser's shrewd and wildly profitable business arrangement with Louis Armstrong, which lasted until Glaser's death in 1969. According to the original contract, Joe paid Louis a salary of fifty thousand dollars. He also paid taxes and all of Armstrong's traveling expenses. The rest was his. Louis never complained. . . ." (164) Schiffman characterized Glaser as "the most successful independent booking agent in history. His stable of talent included Louis Armstrong, Lionel Hampton, Sugar Ray Robinson . . . and Noel Coward." (163) It is doubtful that Glaser contracted Coward or any other major white artist under the same conditions that he exacted from his black "stable." In fact, Coward's diary entries for 1954–55 show that he was very much in control in his negotiations with Glaser. Unlike the African American artists who were under the thumb of this shrewd operator, the Englishman clearly had the upper hand and regarded Glaser condescendingly:

> A character called Joe Glaser flew in from New York to sign me up for Las Vegas. A typical shrewd, decent, sharp agent type. The discussion was satisfactory financially, everything being contingent on whether or not I like Las Vegas. . . . The Gangsters who run the places [the swank Las Vegas casinos and hotels] are all urbane and charming. I had a feeling that if I opened a rival casino I would be battered to death with the utmost efficiency and despatch, but if I remained on my own ground as a most highly paid entertainer that I could trust them all the way. They are curious products of a most curious adolescent country. . . . Joe Glaser, whom I have taken a great shine to, never drinks, never smokes and adores his mother. He is now fifty-eight and, rather naturally, over the moon with delight at having got me under his wing. My name is big prestige stuff for a brisk little Jewish go-getter who hitherto has mainly booked coloured acts and promoted prize-fights.[8]

No matter that these "coloured acts" were some of the top names in swing music as well as trend-setters in modernizing the European orchestral sound: the politics of race dictated that Coward's contributions were privileged and valued over and above those of African American artists.

Irving Mills offers another object lesson in white management of black stars. A music publisher and entrepreneur, his ruse was to pay composers (including the young white Jimmy McHugh, one of the writers for the Cotton Club shows) for the tune, or even offer a weekly salary, but pocket the royalties, where the real profits lay. At various times he contracted the bands of Cab Calloway, Lucky Millinder,[9] and Duke Ellington. One day in 1943, when Ellington unexpectedly dropped by the William Morris Agency for a quick advance and, instead, was given his unopened mail by an office worker, he discovered that Mills, his former manager, had been holding back on his considerable recording royalties. The office assistant, Ellington notes,

> handed me about a dozen envelopes, which I proceeded to peel through casually until I came to one with a transparent window from RCA Victor. I

opened it and took a quick glance at the check inside. The figure $2,250 is what I thought I saw as I slid it back in the envelope. To myself I said, "Hey, if this is $2,250, I don't need to make this touch up here [the advance he had hoped for], but maybe my eyes deceived me, and it's really $22.50." So I pulled the check out again, and it said $22,500! . . . [By that time] I was already with the William Morris Agency. Irving Mills and I had come to the parting of the ways some years before. . . . We dissolved our business relationship agreeably . . . in spite of how much he had made on me. . . . (88–89)

These bandleader anecdotes are examples of major swindles,[10] but rip-offs worked at the most pedestrian levels and could be initiated by theater owners or road managers as well. Small-time performers like Norton and Webb and other dancers who were at the bottom of the entertainment hierarchy were easy targets for exploitation, as is shown in this story related by exotic dancer Tondelayo: "In Chicago they gave me bad money—you could see it was counterfeit—can you imagine that! We had to get rid of it. They said, 'Get rid of it the best way you can.' I couldn't say anything more: I had to take it." ("From Harlem to Broadway") Although such practices were commonplace, not every manager or agent was a crook. The Crackerjacks, one of the top-ranked acrobatic tap teams of the swing era, attribute their success to good management: "We found Morris Greenwald right at the start and stayed with him during our entire career. . . . Morris was a wonderful guy . . . and honest as the day is long." (Stearns and Stearns, 266)

Still, for better or worse, the African American entertainment industry was owned by white businessmen.[11]

Salaries

With the exception of headliners like Bill Robinson, Ethel Waters, and, later, Lena Horne, musicians had the highest potential earning power of swing era artists. In black and white show business, salaries varied immensely according to type of venue, geographical region, and popularity of the particular artist(s), although median salaries for black performers were lower than those for whites. Another element to be factored in was unionization or, rather, the lack of it: there were segregated unions for black and white musicians, and no unions for other performers. In the 1920s an ordinary musician hired on the touring TOBA circuit received $35 weekly plus a $5 meal ticket which, according to bassist John Williams, would buy food for almost the entire week. Frequently, meals on the road were prepared and served buffet style in the homes of African Americans where the performers could rent a room for about $4 per week. Instead of the meal ticket, "you could take three dollars and go to the store and get enough food for a whole week if you were cooking at home [that is, if a hot plate was provided with the room or if boarders were allowed kitchen privileges]." Williams had begun as a pit musician on the TOBA circuit and graduated from a $35 weekly salary to $75 by 1936 (playing with the Lucky Millinder band), and to $100 by the end of the decade. In the early 1940s, he earned $500 weekly with the Louis Armstrong small band. (15 August 1980)

Playing at Harlem's Lafayette theater in 1933, bandleader Willy Bryant received $45 a week and his sidemen drew a little less. Other musicians could be even less fortunate. In 1936 the young Count Basie and his band played at the Reno Club in Kansas City, characterized by Basie as "a cracker town": they played from nine P.M. until five or six o'clock the next morning for which the band members received $18 weekly and Basie $21. (Stearns, 212) This schedule was on a seven-day-a-week basis: it wasn't until 1939 that the musicians' union legislated one day off per week for its members. (Dixon-Stowell, 1981, 155) That same year, Basie left Kansas City, contracted to record a total of twenty-four sides for the Decca label at a flat rate of $750, no royalties included. Two of these sides, *One O'Clock Jump* and *Jumpin' at the Woodside*, became huge hits. (Ostransky, 241) In 1928 Cab Calloway was pleased that his salary had increased to $65. By the mid-1930s he was making $6,500, plus percentages. (Schiffman, 151–54) Yet, Chick Webb, the outstanding bandleader and master drummer, drew only $950 for himself and his entire band, the same salary drawn by the Fletcher Henderson band. For a week in 1932, rising star Duke Ellington and his band received $4,700. Yet exactly ten years earlier white bandleader Paul Whiteman was earning $7,500 weekly at the Hippodrome while grossing upwards of a million dollars annually. (Stearns and Stearns, 165)

There is an exemplary story of salaries and status tied up in vocalist Alberta Hunter's experience with Frank Schiffman, who in 1930 was managing the Lafayette Theater. He was reputed to hire artists at one salary and then cut it if audience reaction was poor on opening night. After Hunter's first performance (October 1930), her salary was cut from $250 to $150. (Taylor and Cook, 113) Although Hunter had made a splash performing in Europe (1927–29), her luck had been no better in Chicago. For the 1929–30 Christmas holiday season, Ed Fox had booked her at the Grand Terrace for $750 a week but cut that figure back to $200 because he didn't like her new continental style of delivery (which included singing some songs in French). Here, too, she took no action against the cut. (Dance, 65; Taylor and Cook, 110–11) These examples confirm Webb's contention that performer contracts meant nothing. The case of Ethel Waters was different: "She always demanded top pay, top *white* pay, for her services—in 1933, making $1,000 a week, she was, by her account, the highest paid female star on a Depression-depleted Broadway." [Author's emphasis] (Douglas, 338) Later in the decade she was able to command up to $2,500 weekly.

Dancers' salaries varied widely, with only Bill Robinson (and later the Nicholas Brothers) able to draw the top salary available to comparable white dancers. In 1934, Honi Coles played the Apollo for the first time at a weekly salary of $60, while the comedy tap team of Buck and Bubbles, having appeared in white vaudeville and on Broadway, commanded $750 weekly at the Harlem Opera House. The adolescent Nicholas Brothers could draw $450; by the end of the 1930s they were making $1,000 weekly. Bill Robinson drew $1,000 weekly at the Apollo until the late 1930s when Hollywood fame boosted his take to $3,500 for the fall 1937 Cotton Club revue, "the highest salary ever paid a black entertainer in a Broadway production, and more money than ever had been received by any individual for a night club appearance." (Haskins, 127) In comparison, the highest salaries paid to top white entertainers during vaudeville's golden age (the teens and early twenties) averaged—on a two-show-a-day schedule—$2,500 to $4,000 weekly. (The Apollo, black vaudeville houses, and the black touring unit operated on a five-a-day show schedule nationwide.) A novelty like Sarah Bernhardt had received

$7,000 weekly at the Palace, and the Marx Brothers $1,500 weekly on the Palace's vaudeville line-up as early as 1915.

This vast range represents the many strata and dimensions of show business. The $150 earned by Bessie Smith in 1934 (she had earned over ten times that amount a decade earlier) was the usual salary shared by the team of Norton and Margot and was, actually, the norm for black swing era troupers: "Harlem salaries for capable entertainers . . . ranged from $45 a week upwards. Any Harlem darling getting as much as $200 a week was in the rarefied financial stratum." (Sylvester, 50)

The number of dance teams of any ethnicity who have risen to stardom is nominal in comparison to the widespread popularity of singers and musicians. Dance forms a basic element of cabaret work and theater musicals, yet dancers are usually relegated to the background and are on the bottom rung of entertainment's economic ladder. Nevertheless, while Norton and Margot remained on a relatively fixed income during the swing era, comparable white dancers could spiral upward along the mainstream ladder of mobility, with salaries at least double the amount drawn by this black team, and twenty or more times that amount for celebrated stars like the De Marcos or Veloz and Yolanda. Although it was enriched immeasurably by African, African American, and Latino influences, adagio dance was looked upon as a white-owned form, and the message was clear: swing era whites preferred seeing whites or light-skinned Latinos— but, certainly, not African Americans—performing this genteel style.

Like most African American artists, Norton and Margot couldn't break the racial barrier and were never booked on major white vaudeville or cabaret circuits. (And, in truth, they were handicapped by the absence of a personal manager.) In contrast, as early as 1921 white ballroom dancer Tony De Marco and his first partner, Mabel Scott, received $300 weekly on the Pantages vaudeville circuit. By 1940 Tony and Renée De Marco drew $2,250 weekly. (Crichton) By 1938 Veloz and Yolanda earned $2,500 for a week's work at the Terrace Room of the Statler Hotel in Cleveland, Ohio. (Pullen) These differences go beyond issues of relative talent: the simple fact was that, due to discrimination, a black adagio team could neither command a top salary on the black circuits nor perform on white circuits. By 1948, the year after Norton and Margot gave up their performing career, the De Marcos were earning $3,500 weekly; they contended that their yearly salary was $100,000.

By the 1950s and 1960s, with the rise of Miami and Las Vegas resorts, salaries continued to accelerate by the thousands for white singers and musicians, black superstars (like Eartha Kitt, Nat "King" Cole, Diahann Carroll, and the Duke Ellington and Count Basie bands),[12] and a select group of white dancers who were featured in Hollywood films or Broadway musicals. Few opportunities emerged for most black dancers, for whom overworked and underpaid continued to be the rule of thumb. Exquisite artists like Honi Coles and Cholly Atkins were forced to break up their acts and turn to other pursuits—Coles became the stage manager at the Apollo, and Atkins began his highly successful second career as choreographer for the emerging Motown doo-wop[13] singing groups.

Although the Crackerjacks credit their success in part to Morris Greenwald, the top salary he could get for them at the Palace was $800; he told them that, were they white, he could have demanded $1,600: "he called us again and again to ask if we wanted to play the Palace—at half salary—but he never objected when we turned it down. The Palace had its policy, and we had ours." The Crackerjacks folded in 1952. (Stearns and Stearns, 266)

Cultural Exchange—or Rip-off?

Appropriation. What does it mean? Who does it and what are its consequences? When is it condoned and by whom? What does public domain really mean? These questions are crucial to the very sensitive issue of cultural exchange between blacks and whites in the United States. For the African American performer, the issue is highlighted and framed by the politics of race, the thorny reality that makes the landscape an uneven playing field. The force that separates free cultural exchange from cultural theft—or causes the one to become the other—is the unequal distribution of power. Who has the power in the American performance industry? Who holds the purse strings in terms of production and distribution of the cultural product? To reiterate the point made by numerous authors, the phenomenon of whites usurping the rhythm and style of an African

American genre is a continuing saga in the history of American performance. The pattern is highly pronounced in music and dance forms—
from ragtime, blues, and jazz through the rock, pop, and hiphop genres of
our present era. This assertion is not a personal bias or value judgment; it
is a fact that was openly affirmed by white swing era musicians such as
Benny Goodman and Bix Beiderbecke.

To be sure, cultural borrowing has been the name of the game since
blacks and whites met on these foreign, American shores several centuries
ago. Nineteenth-century minstrelsy formalized and standardized the rate
of exchange, gauging the public desire, black and white, for black performance genres, black stereotypes, and the simultaneous send-up and embrace of supposedly authentic black characteristics and lifestyles. In
addition, minstrelsy set the stage for blacks to "not have their hands on
the controls of media culture," to remain entertainers with whites holding the powerful means of production and distribution. Twentieth-century vaudeville evolved from minstrelsy and maintained many of its
inequalities, particularly in the realms of artistic management and cultural
appropriation. Black forms had become so popular, so Americanized in
the mind of the mainstream white consumer, that H. L. Mencken could
comment in 1927 that the only dances done at the "high-toned" social
events of the day were black in origin; and, indeed, in the 1920s the na-
tionalization of African American culture as a white American commodity "became something like a recognized phenomenon." (Douglas, 76–77)

Of course, black performers borrowed white forms, but not with the
freedom and success that whites enjoyed in borrowing from blacks. Norton and Margot are a prime example of this problem, along with those
African Americans who chose, against all odds, to sing opera, play European orchestral music, dance ballet, or act Shakespeare. Conversely,
whether it was called appropriation, translation, or transformation, it was
acceptable for whites to co-opt black aesthetic creations. During the
swing era not only were specific African American dances and music appropriated but a deeper, generic quality of swing became the cool, collective currency of contemporary American life, white and black.

It is noteworthy that in the early vaudeville period, an old tradition
from the plantation era became high fashion. Back in the antebellum
South, the musicians who played for the fancy white balls and cotillions

were by and large African American. Vernon and Irene Castle, the
pre–World War I ballroom dance team, revived this tradition by using the
African American James Reese Europe orchestra as their musical guides
in the United States and abroad. Through this mainstream connection
Europe's orchestra was instrumental in making African American music
the accepted accompaniment for the new dances. Irene Castle gave Europe full credit for creating the Fox Trot, one of the most popular dances
of the prewar era. (Stearns and Stearns, 98) Indeed, the period immediately preceding the swing era was a time of early jazz innovation that still
remains largely unacknowledged. Europe is also renowned as the conductor of the Fifteenth Regiment Band, the African American army unit
of trained professional musicians who performed across Europe during
World War I. This group spread the popularity of the new music abroad
and actually set the stage for the European success of African American
stars in the imminent jazz age of the 1920s.

Jazz was also disseminated by early recordings. The Original Dixieland Jazz Band—ironically, a group of all-white musicians—was the
first to record jazz music in 1917. It is worth pointing out that this distinction was not based on the creativity and talent of the group, but on
the racist rules of the times: before 1923 African American jazz bands
"were not allowed into the white-owned recording studios." (Greenberg,
4) Later the juke box, radio, and talkies became effective vehicles for
spreading the new sound. By the mid-1920s thousands of young hopefuls
were teaching themselves jazz by listening to their idols and playing or
singing along. Due to technological advances, authentic jazz became accessible to mainstream white America in a way that ragtime had never
been. Vocalist Bing Crosby described the technique: "We'd take a couple
of records in and play them and Al [Al Rinker, a member of the same amateur band, the Rhythm Boys][14] would memorize the piano chords while
I remembered the soloist's style and vocal tricks. . . ." (Stearns, 174) To
hear what Crosby meant, one has only to listen to the great Louis Armstrong's scat singing on *West End Blues* (Smithsonian Collection of Classic Jazz, 1987), recorded in 1928 for Okeh Records. Armstrong's early
"buh-buh-buh-buh" scat style was appropriated and transformed by
Crosby into his characteristic, crooning, ballad style.[15] At the same time
the Rhythm Kings, a group of white musicians from New Orleans, were

successful recording stars who unabashedly claimed that they aimed to imitate the black music they had heard back home. (Stearns, 175)

This new conduit for appropriation was not confined to American shores. English trumpeter Nat Gonella worked hard at becoming another Louis Armstrong. Faithfully studying the recordings in order to learn the Armstrong solos, he became a moderately adept imitator. Gonella freely acknowledged his appropriation, asserting that copying the great musician immeasurably improved his playing. He wittily concludes a backhanded homage to Armstrong by quipping that, "[s]hort of being a musical genius . . . the next best thing is to model oneself on the lines of someone who is." (Goddard, 180)

Yet, cultural exchange is a two-way street. Blacks copied as well. According to Marshall Stearns, bandleader Fletcher Henderson tried to imitate Paul Whiteman's plush arrangements because "it made money." (171) And bassist John Williams—who grew up in Memphis, Tennessee, and went on to play in the bands of Lucky Millinder, Louis Armstrong, and the small Teddy Wilson group—played in the 1920s with the Belton Society Syncopaters in Florida: "They were called 'The Duke Ellington of the South' because they had every arrangement that Duke was playing. . . ." (15 August 1980) Again, arrangements had been picked up from recordings.

Jazz continued its phenomenal ascendance through its connection to the dances of the twenties. White ballroom society orchestras were pressured by their younger clientele to take on the sound that accompanied dances like the Charleston and the Black Bottom. They acquiesced by hiring one or two jazz soloists. Bix Beiderbecke, the legendary white musician (who learned the black style by direct contact with black musicians and died at an early age) served this function with the Paul Whiteman band in 1927. (No white bands used black musicians at the time.) Whiteman was one of Duke Ellington's regular fans while Ellington's five-man group played at the Kentucky Club (1922–27), a popular after-hours hangout for Broadway stars. And, in another chapter of the same story, "Paul Whiteman and his arranger, Ferde Grofé, visited the Cotton Club nightly for more than a week, and finally admitted that they couldn't steal even two bars of the amazing [Ellington] music." (Stearns, 185)[16]

By 1934 Benny Goodman's repertory contained thirty-six Fletcher Henderson arrangements. Some of these had been used by Henderson three to five years earlier, but his band was invisible to mainstream white America while Goodman's was broadcasting every Saturday night from coast to coast. A 1934 Goodman version of a 1932 Henderson-arranged tune outsold the original by a thousand percent. This was partly due to poor management of Henderson's group, a fact that contributed to its demise. But it was also due to the discrimination that allowed the Goodman band primacy over black groups in order to fill white America's desire for white jazz bands. The culmination of this trend was spotlighted when Goodman was accorded the title "The King of Swing," which parallels Paul Whiteman's 1920s title, "The King of Jazz." Basie, Armstrong, and Ellington, rather than Goodman, supplied the depth, momentum, and innovative genius that undergirded the swing era, as well as the style that forecast the bop and cool jazz that followed in the mid-1940s.

White jazz musicians, once they became numerous and had somewhat mastered the black swing sound, had the privilege of their race, and black bands that had been booked for white events during the James Reese Europe era suddenly found that their professional horizons were narrowed. According to trumpeter Doc Cheatham, the "racial thing," to use his phrase, meant that black bands and individual musicians were frozen out of the lucrative white performance circuits in cities like New York and Chicago. He attributes the situation to the racial separation of the musicians' unions. The white union was in control of the downtown white venues and made sure to refer white musicians exclusively for this market. Coupling this discriminatory tactic with the practice of white musicians coming to Harlem or Chicago's South Side to listen to black musicians and steal their style, Cheatham paints a picture of insult added to injury. Such were the patterns for white musicians, while African American musicians were barred from entering white clubs as performers or audience: Cheatham recalls that "Harry James, he was always up in Harlem. Benny Goodman—all of them. All Paul Whiteman's musicians, all Ted Lewis's musicians." (Goddard, 294–95)

Besides Fletcher Henderson, other behind-the-scenes black arrangers of the era included James Mundy, William Grant Still, Sy Oliver, Margie Gibson, Benny Carter, Billy Strayhorn, Bill Grey, Elton Hill, Bill Moore,

Edwin Wilcox, Will Vodery (who was Ziegfeld's arranger from 1911 through 1932), and Don Redman (who played with Henderson and was responsible for many of the well-planned, synchronized Henderson arrangements). During his long career, Paul Whiteman used every available arranger. It was the arrangements of these artists, played on radios, phonographs, and in dance halls and cabarets nationwide that formed the foundation for swing music.

Recent research has attempted to advance the case that blacks and whites were equal innovators, partners, and players in the evolution of jazz.[17] However, ample evidence refutes that contention. More than some may be willing to admit, the world of jazz reflects not a utopian exception to the racial divide but, instead, another example of it.

Still, there was a level of worthy artistic exchange among white and black musicians. Goodman served the cause of integration by using the finest African American musicians in his band, a practice previously unheard of. He did so at the instigation of jazz aficionado, supporter, and writer John Hammond. In 1936, he employed pianist Teddy Wilson. Then, in 1938, Billie Holiday sang with the Artie Shaw group. Charlie Shavers played with Tommy Dorsey, and Gene Krupa hired Roy Eldridge. But problems arose around issues such as meals and accommodations, and Holiday ultimately left Shaw due to offstage segregationist tactics by hotel and restaurant owners over which the musicians had no control. Thus, the irony: this little step toward group integration brought about the segregation of individual black band members. In any case, the addition of black artists to white bands spread the new music rapidly. Of course, with the few exceptions that crossed over into white mainstream popularity (such as the Ellington, Hines, and Calloway groups), black bands did not have the power to disseminate their music as widely as the commercially successful white bands.

Similar examples of white power and privilege dictated theatrical practices as well. By 1930 the heyday of black Broadway was over, killed by the Depression and the ascendancy of white lyricists and composers who replaced the likes of Noble Sissle and Eubie Blake (the composers of *Shuffle Along*, the groundbreaking 1921 Broadway musical that paved the way for the African American musicals that followed). With the stock market crash of 1929, production money was understandably scarce. Less understandable was the calculated discriminatory tactic of using whites to compose African American musicals.

Most of the *Blackbirds* shows of white producer Lew Leslie used black casts (who were paid lower salaries than their white peers) with white choreographers and composers hired to create black dances and black music. As Doc Cheatham asserted, wherever a white could be substituted, an African American was out of a job. (This biased preference for whites over blacks may also have been the reason behind the use of near-white African American women for chorus lines and general stage exposure—the rationale being that the only black woman worth seeing on stage was a white one.) The major African American musicals from the 1930s through the 1950s were composed by whites: *Porgy and Bess* (1935, George Gershwin)[18]; *The Hot Mikado* (1939, after Gilbert and Sullivan); *Cabin in the Sky* (1940, Lynn Root, John La Touche, Vernon Duke); and *Carmen Jones* (1943, Robert Russell Bennett and Oscar Hammerstein, after Bizet). Problems with inequitable salaries and low cast budgets for black shows continued. Loften Mitchell recalling *Carmen Jones* wrote, "The show actually started offstage when Dick Campbell—acting as his wife's representative [his wife, Muriel Rahn, alternated the lead role with Muriel Smith]—openly fought Billy Rose about the salary scales Rose paid Negro actors. The result of the fight was that Muriel Rahn was the only cast member who earned as much as two hundred dollars weekly." (120)

As for dance, African American dance-directors were well known in the black entertainment world, staging shows in black theaters and nightclubs as well as in white show business. Yet, they were invisible men in the white world (and this was a male-dominated profession). They were not credited for their work but were looked upon as dispensable assistants to the white dance director. Coaching white chorus lines or featured soloists, they included Buddy Bradley, Charlie Davis, Willie Covan, Lawrence Dees, Herbie Harper, Charlie White, Frank Montgomery, Addison Carey, Sammy Dyer, Leonard Reed, Leonard Harper, Elida Webb (no relation to Margot Webb, and one of the few women in this group), John Bubbles (of the tap team Buck and Bubbles), and Clarence Robinson. About Robinson having choreographed the 1943 film, *Stormy Weather*, his wife, Hyacinth Curtis, said: "He was never given a contract for anything else. . . . If he had been white, I wouldn't be sitting here today, I'd be rich. Because any time you do a musical like that you don't look back anymore . . . you go on." ("From Harlem to Broadway") Both Robinson and Bradley choreographed abroad for London revues. Bradley remained in London where he finally found work and renown on a par with his white peers. He and his colleagues were responsible for taking the vernacular African American dance styles, as well as the rhythmically complex black tap forms, and transforming them into theatrical genres that could be performed by whites.

A *Dance Magazine* quote from September 1928 highlights another way in which black materials were appropriated: "Many teachers of tap and step dancing have been seen lately at the Liberty Theatre where *Blackbirds of 1928* holds forth. . . . Bill Robinson, America's best tap dancer . . . gives more than a normal course in this branch of dancing every evening."[19] In 1928 this major mainstream publication could dub Robinson "America's best tap dancer." This assessment predated the rise of Fred Astaire in the 1930s who, with his borrowing of black-based tap innovations, became the white-hope alternative to Robinson. John Bubbles actually coached Astaire in the 1930s: "I didn't mind—I got paid for it . . . but he wasn't very apt to catch the steps. . . . He wasn't very quick. So he brought his friend Marilyn Miller along too. She was really quick. So the way round it was, that I'd teach her, so she could teach him. . . ." (Goddard, 87)

But what was infuriating to black artists was the out-and-out stealing. It was not unusual for white producers or performers to scout black shows in the Harlems nationwide and lift entire routines. Singer Edith Wilson recalls this pattern, remarking that the way the African American performer retaliated was to continually change her act—a difficult task to be sure. (ibid.)

Nevertheless, it was not only through the white world that steps or routines were stolen or falsely credited. Lindy artist Shorty Snowden prided himself on his ability to incorporate into his dancing "anything that suggests a step." (Stearns and Stearns, 324) After seeing Paul Draper perform, he included some of the white tapster's ballet-influenced moves in his improvisations. According to Honi Coles, in recalling the adroitness of the Apollo chorines of 1934, "A dancing act could come into the Apollo with all original material and, when they left at the end of the week, the chorus lines would have stolen many of the outstanding things they did. . . . As a result most acts used to try and load their steps up to the point that they couldn't be stolen." (Schiffman, 64–65) These amazing chorus girls also helped nondancing director/producers like Irving C. Miller, Addison Carey, and Lew Leslie stage shows without lifting a leg. In such cases the director created the setting, theme and sequence, and the dancers or dance captain (leader of the chorus) worked out the actual steps. And, of course, their contributions went unacknowledged.[20]

Although the concept of precision dancing in unison with a sense of swing—what we call a chorus line—is an African American innovation, black chorus lines were organized after the white example of directors like Florenz Ziegfeld and Ned Wayburn and were divided by height. "Ponies" were five feet two inches or shorter. There were also separate lines for dancers of average height and for the tall ones. Like their white models, these black spectacles used some sensational theme as the organizing principle. For example the fall, 1937 Cotton Club revue was staged around its star, Bill Robinson. He introduced a new dance, the Bill Robinson Walk, in which fifty chorines accompanied him, wearing rubber Bojangles face masks and echoing and counterpointing his movements.[21]

As was the case with Paul Whiteman's gentrification of authentic early jazz, the Castles and subsequent adagio dancers, including Norton and Margot, were devotees of a genre that (with the exception of the Waltz) had appropriated original, erotic African or Afro-Latino dances and formalized them into stage standards acceptable to whites. For example the Rumba and, earlier, the Black Bottom and the Charleston were modified from their black grass-roots origins. In each case, dances that were done in an African "get-down" stance (knees bent, buttocks slightly angled back with concomitant pelvis retraction, upper body slightly tilted forward) with free-flowing articulation of the individual parts of the torso (chest, ribs, belly, pelvis, buttocks) were made more vertical (in a typically aligned-spine, Europeanist stance), with torso articulation modified into an acceptable standard for white tastes. Finally, these dances that probably originated as circle dances were made into Europeanist couple dances.

More than their musician colleagues, and in spite of the inspiration drawn from them directly and indirectly, African American dancers continued to decorate the background of American performance—dancing in the dark, shut out of the mainstream, and uncredited for their significant role in developing the American dance canon.

In concluding his book on the Apollo, the family business for two generations, Jack Schiffman wrote:

> White America has systematically stripped away their self-respect, replaced it with a self-contempt and self-doubt, and foisted upon them our image of them until they have almost accepted it as the truth. The beauty of the black man's saga in this country is that, despite his isolation from his homeland through slavery and his isolation from his self through our subtle brainwashing, he has managed to produce a culture as rich and vibrant as any that American society has brought forth. But it is to our lasting shame that we have skimmed the cream off this culture with little if any acknowledgment. There are those in white society who think the black people are prone to violence. My own judgment is that their restraint and tolerance have been unbelievable. (200–201)

According to musicologist Sigmund Spaeth, "What really matters is that Negro characteristics of rhythm, melody and harmony have become deeply imbedded in American music of all kinds and that these characteristics preserve their individuality in spite of repeated applications of sophisticated veneer, artificial sentimentality, insincerity and downright ignorance. *Any racial art that can stand such treatment must have a strong constitution and unlimited vitality.*" (26, emphasis mine)

These powerful quotes are keynotes of this chapter—indeed, of this book as a whole. They apply equally to music, dance, and American lifestyles. What occurred during the swing era was something irrevocable, as inexorable as technological advancement (that is, once you have electricity, you cannot do without it). The subliminal Africanist influences that had been under wraps for centuries were now out in the open and, for all intents and purposes, owned and managed by whites. The assimilation and commodification of African American culture by the dominant culture meant that whites were now swinging, jazzy, in the groove: whites were now black. However, this identity change was not a two-way street: blacks were not white. White success was regarded ruefully by blacks since it was gained, or so it seemed, at their expense. The American edifice remained a racialized pyramid with whites at the top and very little room up there for anyone else. What this race politic meant for African Americans performing at home and abroad is explored in the next chapter: what does it mean to be black? To be white? What is gained or lost in pledging allegiance to one identity or another?

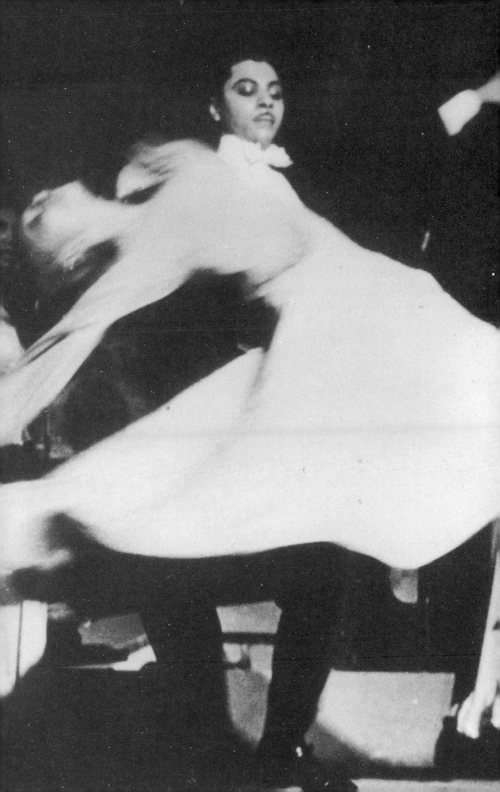

Waltz Interpretation

Previous page: *Waltz Interpretation*

All photos provided by Margot Webb from her private collection.

Studio Portrait, 1930s

Next page: *Bolero, 1941*

NORTON AND MARGOT CARRY ART TO EUROPE

The talented adagio dancing team of Norton and Margot, caught by a European cameraman, especially for The Courier, as they arrived in Europe, where they will be starred with the Cotton Club revue. The charming couple is among 62 performers who will endeavor to thrill the European theater- and nite-club public for 16 weeks. Just before sailing for the old country, the team did some splendid entertaining for Production Maestro Teddy Blackmon, who is keeping Western nite-lifers in the groove with his first-class revues.

Afro-American, *12 June 1937*

Previous page: *Toe Dance*

Right: *Club Sherbini, Berlin, 1937*

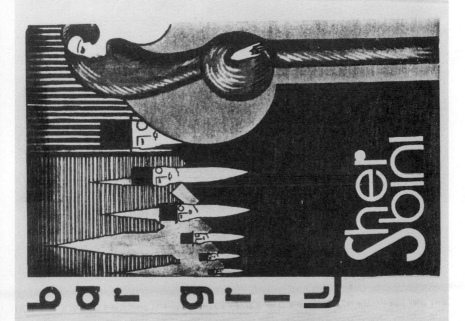

"La Conga," *1945*

Right: *Spear Dance*

Part II

"*There is many a white man less fortunate and less well equipped than I am. In truth, I have never been able to discover that there was anything disgraceful in being a colored man. But I have often found it inconvenient—in America.*"

—Bert Williams

Chapter Five

Color and Caste
in Black and White:
Performing at Home and Abroad

R ace, caste, and color undeniably affected the African American performer touring nationwide and in Europe during the swing era.
This chapter examines these issues in detail, picking up on the themes introduced in Chapter 1. Some historical background will help in understanding why black vaudevillians were confined to dancing in the shadow
of their white counterparts. With the previous century having witnessed
the abolition of slavery and two new amendments to the Constitution to
insure racial equality, how could the "racial mountain" endure as a firm
fixture in American life and even assert its dominion abroad?

Racism at Home

Dominant Group Racism

It is no coincidence that the first Jim Crow laws were enacted at the
same time as the first civil rights laws. The two opposing kinds of legislation illustrate white America's ambivalence in its ongoing attract-repel,
love-hate relationship with its black citizenry. On one side of the coin,

to satisfy the needs of white supremacy, state-by-state segregationist provisions—Jim Crow laws—were adopted by southern and southwestern states and the District of Columbia, beginning in 1875 with the state of Tennessee and continuing through 1916 with legislation enacted by Washington, D.C. (Bergman, 655; Franklin, 342, 486–87) These laws specified the racial segregation of particular facilities such as railroad coaches and other public transportation, schools, theaters, restaurants, parks, and more. In addition, the same states usually had laws designating intermarriage as a criminal offense.

On the flip side, the first federal Civil Rights Act was also legislated in 1875 but was repealed as an unconstitutional violation of states' rights in 1883, initiating an onslaught of abuse against African Americans that ranged from an officially sanctioned closed door policy in housing, education, employment, and leisure life to the horror of lynchings. By the twentieth century a complicated state-by-state process began in which civil rights laws were passed, mainly in northern states, with extensions or modifications added to them in later years. For example, the state of New York passed a new civil rights law in 1918 that was to extend "the equal accommodations privileges of earlier acts to include every conceivable type of public business, skating rinks, billiard parlors, bowling alleys, ice-cream parlors, etc." (Bergman, 387) Yet, discrimination continued in New York and other northern states, although it was not as drastic, violent, or severe as its southern counterpart. As late as 1935 the state of Pennsylvania passed a bill "prohibiting, under penalty, discrimination in a place of public accommodation against any person because of race, color, or creed." (Martin, 341) But bassist John Williams recalls that the letter of the law in accommodating African Americans was bent by simple tactics such as raising prices to discourage black patronage. A hot dog costing fifteen cents for whites could cost a quarter for blacks. (15 August 1980) And, of course, a hotel could claim that it was full when an African American inquired about a room.

In 1943 the New York City government approved a housing project, Stuyvesant Town–Peter Cooper Village, on lower First Avenue, to be constructed by the Metropolitan Life Insurance Company, whose board chairman stated: "Negroes and whites don't mix. Perhaps they will in a hundred years but they don't now. If we brought them into this development, it would be to the detriment of the city, too, because it would depress all the surrounding property." (Curtis, 206) Likewise, the Long Island suburb of Levittown, constructed in the late 1940s, was "symbolic of segregation in America" according to Eugene Burnett, an African American World War II veteran who was prohibited from living there because of his race. A clause from a 1948 Levittown lease states: "The tenant agrees not to permit the premises to be used or occupied by any person other than members of the Caucasian race. But the employment and maintenance of other than Caucasian domestic servants shall be permitted."[1]

African Americans in the military had experienced racism before, during, and after both world wars. Having fought the enemy with extreme bravery in World War I, the New York contingent of African American soldiers—the Fifteenth Regiment—had been dubbed "Harlem Hell Fighters" by the French who admired, respected, and heralded them; yet, the American government prohibited blacks from marching in the victory parade in Paris along the Champs Elysées. (Douglas, 87) For their exceptional valor in action this unit was further honored by the French who granted them the distinction of being the first Allied troops on enemy territory after the armistice. Sergeant Henry Johnson of the same regiment was "the first soldier of the entire American expeditionary forces to receive the Croix de Guerre with star and palm." (Johnson, 233–35) Despite these honors, white America was violently hostile to these returning heroes, greeting them with a red wave of bloodshed in the form of lynchings and riots.

The simultaneity of sanctioned public activities enforcing racism and legal action against it touches the heart of the American dilemma. As Margot Webb states, it was not laws that perpetuated discrimination, but "the attitude of people [that] kept blacks from achieving." (25 June 1980) American race etiquette varied, unaccountably, from place to place. Writer Mercer Cook, addressing the race problem, wrote in 1939:

> Negroes in New Orleans will tell you that Baton Rouge is more prejudiced; Jersey City is reputedly less prejudiced than Trenton; and I have heard it said that Savannah is in some respects less difficult than Atlanta. Occasionally there are differentiations within a single city: certain theaters will

admit Negroes, others will not; some hotels employ Negroes, others do not; street cars will carry Negro passengers, buses will not. These and other intricacies should suggest the danger of attempting to discuss the race question as a whole. (673)

And Langston Hughes compared his travels across the United States with a trip through the Soviet Union:

At St. Louis I went into the [railroad] station platform to buy a glass of milk. The clerk behind the counter said, "We don't serve niggers," and refused to sell me anything. As I grew older I learned to expect this often when traveling. So when I went South to lecture on my poetry at Negro universities, I carried my own food because I knew I could not go into the dining cars. Once from Washington to New Orleans, I lived all the way in the train on cold food. I remembered this miserable trip as I sat eating a hot dinner in the diner of the Moscow-Tashkent express. Traveling South from New York, at Washington, the capital of our country, the official Jim Crow begins. The conductor comes through the train and, if you are a Negro, touches you on the shoulder and says, "The last coach forward is the car for colored people." (1934, 162–63)

The language used here is telling: the "last coach forward" is a contradiction but, since it was the equivalent of riding at the back of the bus—and because African Americans could never be considered first—it was designated last rather than first. Commonly known as the "Jim Crow car," it was the first coach behind the engine, whose smoke and cinders made it the least desirable location. Such are the reversals and deceptions required by racism. Given the irony, ludicrousness, and tragedy that an African American was treated better in Soviet Russia than in his homeland, it is no wonder that those who had the opportunity went abroad, either permanently or for a sojourn. To counter this argument some critics might make the observation that, in "the absence of an African colonial history, blacks wouldn't have represented the same kind of 'threat' [in the U.S.S.R.] as they did in America. So, apart from the propaganda and 'novelty' factors, it was simply 'safer' for Russians to be welcoming."[2] Although this view may be historically correct from an outsider perspective, there is no denying the insider, gut-level reaction represented in the Hughes quote and based on his lived experience.

African Americans did not take this abuse lying down, but black protest could mean unemployment, harassment, torture, mutilation, or murder. As in previous decades, the black press of the swing era was flooded with articles, exhortations, campaigns, and general reports about racism's hazards and horrors. Particular attention was given to lynching. In September 1935, the NAACP's journal, *Crisis*, reported that African American actor Clarence Muse organized a Los Angeles benefit of white and black performers in support of the Costigan-Wagner antilynching bill that was then before Congress. However, claiming such laws would violate states' rights and using the filibuster tactic, the southern senatorial caucus killed every federal antilynching bill that was introduced. The number of lynchings that were recorded—which may not have been the total—varied in the 1920s from 63 in 1921 to 16 in 1927; in the 1930s from 24 in 1933 to 2 in 1939; between 1947 and 1962, 12 lynchings of African Americans were recorded. (Bergman, 401, 433, 463, 484, 514)

One sphere of discrimination most difficult to countenance was the flagrant flaunting of race prejudice in the nation's capital. Webb recalls Washington, D.C. as one of the most segregated cities on the East Coast, comparable in restrictions to midwestern cities like Elkhart, Indiana, and Omaha, Nebraska. The city representing the seat of American democracy refused to admit African Americans in public parks, restaurants, theaters, hotels, movie houses, and even prohibited blacks from the public sector of the House of Representatives restaurant. (Lautier, 125) Diplomat Ralph Bunche reportedly had once "refused a post as Under Secretary of State because he didn't wish to subject his family to the indignity of living in then-segregated Washington."[3]

For the 1933 performances of *Green Pastures*, the National Theater, then the capital's only legitimate venue, refused entry to African Americans; the major film distributors—Loew's, Metro-Goldwyn-Mayer, Warner Brothers—prohibited African Americans from attending their downtown venues. The city had an attitude that paralleled that of the English: indigenous peoples of African lineage were subjected to discrimination, while visiting black celebrities were treated as honorary whites—"Exceptions are made in the case of visiting rulers of foreign countries . . . and native colored Americans of distinction. . . ." (Lautier, 125) And, in turn, it was this same policy that made the English gracious and receptive to African Americans, in spite of their racism toward black Brits. The *Green Pastures* dilemma—with black Americans prohibited from attending a production performed by blacks whose subject matter was (supposedly) black life—preceded what became a long battle to desegregate American theaters and movie houses nationwide through a state-by-state approach.

This June 1932 item in *Crisis* emphasizes the degree of racial schizophrenia in the capital and the ludic dimensions of the etiquette of segregation:

> Mrs. Catherine A. Scott (white) of Washington, DC desires and prays for $20,000 from the Earle Theater from which she was ejected because the manager, James A. Campion (white), thought she was a "Negress." In her petition to the Court, Mrs. Scott claims that she and her daughter (also white) visited the Earle theater in January, paid for and obtained tickets for the balcony. As they ascended the stairs to the mezzanine, they were accosted by Mgr. Campion, who looked at them, at their ticket stubs, placed them (the ticket stubs) in an envelope, requested them to return to the box office to get their money refunded. Demanding an explanation, Mrs. Scott claims in the petition, "I was told that Negroes were not admitted to the Earle, and that as I was a Negress, I and my daughter could not enter."(193)

In his eagerness to enforce discrimination, the white theater manager overreacted. However, he had good reason to assume his assessment was correct: the practice of light-skinned blacks undermining segregation by passing for white was common in the capital, according to another article in the same issue of *Crisis:* "Naturally with its large mulatto contingent, there are numbers of colored people who simply go from time to time where they please and do not mention their descent—a matter which curiously irritates the White City."(187)[4]

The incidence of African Americans who appear to be white (and whites who are part black, whether they know it or not) points out the absurdity of race as a viable scientific or sociological construct and highlights the American quandary as to what constitutes race. This ambiguity gives credence to writer Claude McKay's implication that race, like creed, is really a state of mind, not a biological entity. McKay uses the example of blond, blue-eyed, white-skinned Walter White, who in 1940 was Secretary of the NAACP, to make his point:

> The White stories of passing . . . were delightful . . . [particularly] one illustrating the fingernail theory. White was traveling on a train on his way to investigate a lynching in the South. The cracker [*sic*] said, "There are many yaller niggers [sic] who look white, but I can tell them every time . . . by looking at their fingernails." And taking White's hand, he said, "Now if you had nigger blood, it would show here on your half-moons." That story excited me by its paradox as much as had the name and complexion of Walter White. It seemed altogether fantastic that whites in the South should call him a "nigger" and whites in the north, a Negro. When a white person speaks of Walter White as a Negro, I get a weird and impish feeling of the unreality of phenomena. And when a colored person refers to Walter White as colored . . . I feel that life is sublimely funny. . . . Walter White is Negroid simply because he closely identifies himself with the Negro group—just as a Teuton becomes a Moslem if he embraces Islam. White is whiter than many Europeans—even biologically. (1970, 110–11)

What McKay implies is as relevant as we begin the new millennium, as it was when he wrote it nearly seven decades ago. As Rinaldo Walcott says in his book *Black Like Who?*, "questions of blackness far exceed the categories of the biological and the ethnic."(xv)

Although white America couldn't figure out what constituted race, state legislatures were willing to introduce as many new laws as needed in frenetic, futile attempts to pin down a definition. Most often these mandates were clumsily, embarrassingly obtuse. A typical example was described in an article on Jim Crow laws in the April 1933 issue of *Crisis:* "The marriage laws of California forbid intermarriage of the yellow and white races. But a Filipino, though he be darker of skin, is not a Chinaman, and . . . may marry a white woman. The decision . . . was upheld by the Appellate Court. But members of the California State legislature have introduced a bill which will prohibit the reoccurrence of such miscegenation." (90–91)

Those who concocted such laws were driven to do so because evidence pointed to the bare facts: all across the nation whites and coloreds of every ethnicity were involved in closeted relationships. This white-black infatuation or obsession was not a topic for open discussion. When it was brought out for an airing, it shook the American imagination and grabbed popular attention. Not only was the 1934 film *Imitation of Life* a runaway hit, based on the already popular novel by Fannie Hurst (the story of a light-skinned black woman who rejects her heritage and passes for white); it was preceded (and followed in several stage and film versions) by the phenomenal success of *Show Boat*, the 1927 Jerome Kern and Oscar Hammerstein musical based on the Edna Ferber book of the same name. The love story of Bill and Julie is the tragic central theme. Julie, mulatto, is married to Bill and passing for white. At the climax of their tragic tale her true identity is unmasked. Just before the authorities break in to arrest her, Bill nicks her wrist, sucks the blood, and declares to his sympathetic but stunned friends who await the end with him, "Can anyone here deny that I have Negro blood in me?" By partaking of her blood, he fit the legal definition of Negro—that is, "having Negro blood"—and would, therefore, be legally allowed to remain married to her. (This matter of "black blood" was a serious and defining consideration in pre–Civil Rights era America and the reason why blood banks were carefully segregated.) The *Show Boat* and *Imitation of Life* stories may be difficult for subsequent generations to relate to, but they raised crucial issues for black and white Americans during the swing era.[5]

Actually, given the bleak racial outlook, passing was a fact of life for many black people. By no means unique to African Americans, it is a phenomenon common among underrepresented ethnicities living in a state of racial oppression. It is the ultimate assimilationist fantasy, the melting pot dream and the desire for upward mobility gone awry. Passing has occurred in India, South Africa, South America, and the Caribbean. Indeed, due to centuries of European antisemitism, Jewish people are familiar with the practice.[6] Passing can be unintentional. There are many Americans who are unaware of their African ancestry. And, of course black Americans, like those cited in the Washington, D.C., examples, may simply leave untampered the mainstream assumption that they are white. In each generation there have been blacks who leave behind family and community and deliberately assume a new identity in order to permanently pass into the white world. Add to these factors the long-range effect of generations of interracial mating and permanent passing. The result is that millions of Americans have some African ancestry, and almost all African Americans have some European ancestry.[7]

Blacks passed as whites in all classes and walks of life, but show business people were primary prospects. First, discrimination dictated that the black entertainment industry was populated by a large share of light-skinned blacks—the "passable" population—particularly women (since both white racism and in-group color prejudice privileged light-skinned female performers over darker ones); secondly, the itinerant life of the touring performer made it easy to explain away background and family history and claim a new identity; thirdly, the "for whites only" policy of many clubs where blacks performed put them in contact with potential white mates (in spite of prohibitions on such contact). Passing through intermarriage is cited particularly in the case of light-skinned female performers. For example, red-haired and freckled, the light-skinned African American singer Mildred Bailey (who was made famous by her hit, *Old Rocking Chair's Got Me*, recorded in 1932) married the likewise red-haired, but white, jazz musician Red Norvo (in 1933). When she was accompanied by her spouse in a city like Cincinnati, Ohio, she passed for white—or was considered an honorary white, by dint of her skin color and star status—and the couple was accommodated at the Gibson Hotel, the city's finest, and at good white restaurants.[8] White privilege could also be accorded to light-skinned bourgeois professionals, as illustrated by the following observation made by Sadie Delany, a white-looking educator, in her autobiography: "The other reason we did not have trouble on that trip through the South [in the 1930s] was that we were light. I was light, Mama was light, Hubert [her brother] was light. . . . People [that is, white people] knew we were Negroes, but they weren't as likely to bother you if you were lighter. I suppose if Bessie [the darker-skinned sister] had been with us we might have had a little trouble." (219) The unstated proviso in both cases was that no black-skinned friends or family members were to show up.

Those who passed permanently (leaving their heritage behind and taking up a new identity in a new locale) did so at a high psychological cost: the price of the ticket was the inner conflict inherent in the self-effacement and the underlying fear of exposure. Webb's bonds with the community were far too strong for her to pass into white society. She had no desire to permanently reject these connections, a prerequisite for forged entry into the white world. Furthermore, there was always the possibility that she would be recognized and exposed by a fellow African American in cities like Chicago or New York, where she was a familiar face in black show business—or simply exposed by a black person who detected her ruse (a fear that plagued blacks who were passing and put them on guard in the presence of other blacks). However, there were several times when the lack of work made passing the most viable, immediate alternative to unemployment.

Passing as Spanish, Webb taught dance and choreographed a show for children in July and August 1936, at a Jewish summer camp in New York state in the borscht belt, the Catskill area filled with holiday bungalows, camps, and resort hotels:

> I had to do it. There was no other way you could work. They wouldn't have a black counselor. . . . If you went to an interviewer and they thought you were black, you didn't have a job, period. I mean, that's the way it was. You knew that. So I took a chance on no one recognizing me or driving through the area. . . . When I first went up there, unfortunately, I ran right into a black man. . . . And I thought, "Oh, my Lord . . . Where does he work? Is he from Harlem?" Because he gave me "the look" [of recognition or acknowledgment of their shared heritage], but . . . he didn't do anything. He was a chauffeur. (19 November 1977)

It is interesting to note that what was required of Webb was simply stating that she was Latina. She was not obliged to feign an accent or give proof of her country of origin: "They just took me at face value. . . . In fact, I never thought about where I might have been from, now that you mention it. I used my first name with the *t* off . . . and a Spanish last name: they called me 'Mrs. Santana.'" (ibid.)

At another time when work was slow for the team of Norton and Margot, Webb auditioned for the all-white Aquacade of the 1939 World's Fair that was held in Flushing Meadows, New York. (She was an accomplished exhibition swimmer, having trained since childhood at

New York YWCAs.) She passed the initial audition and was scheduled for a call-back. However, she didn't return, fearing that somehow the black identity behind the white mask would be discovered.

A final example of Webb's passing occurred in 1941 in Montreal, Canada. She and her friend and colleague, Al Vigal, passed as French— from some unspecified Gallic colony—to perform as exotic dancers in a Montreal revue, *South Sea Magic*. One review described the show using the cliché-ridden vocabulary that approximated the predictably stale content: "Alvigal and Margo are supported by the chorus in another number in which he appears as a gentleman of color, attired in the huge hideous mask of a voodoo priest and little else. His thudding death-dance contrasts with Margo's Southern grace and wriggling flashing vitality, and is suitably backgrounded by the show girls gone native and grouped around an erupting volcano." (*Montreal Daily Herald*, 1 April 1941)

It is ironic that African Americans had to deny their heritage in order to perform such a routine as this. These examples of Webb's experiences as a non–African American show that the white producers, managers, and entrepreneurs of the swing era had one primary interest: maintaining the boundaries of racial etiquette in order to make a profit. To protect their earnings, creamed from black performers, they required only lip-service assurance that individuals were anything but African American. Webb's additional description of the Montreal booking further illustrates the seedy details involved in wearing the mask of whiteness. Vigal "wouldn't talk to anybody [he spoke only English], and then I would speak a little French. We had to be from the South Seas. . . . The agent [who hired us] told us they weren't going to hire blacks so we'd better be something else. 'It says here,' she observed, pointing to a clip from the Montreal paper, 'featuring a real South Sea Island dance team'" (8 July 1998).

As humiliating as it may seem, Webb and Vigal had accepted the booking. In vaudeville's waning years, engagements were few and far between, and this one paid well. This cabaret, the Tic Toc Club, unlike its swank Cotton Club counterparts across the border, did not employ African American performers. Hemmed in by the pretense and by a white backstage atmosphere that would have turned hostile should their true identity be revealed, they stayed to themselves. Irony was heaped upon irony: in Canada Webb and Vigal could not be hired as black Americans; yet, once they passed as French people of color, they were exposed to colonialist French racism towards a subject people, and they experienced a measure of discrimination equal to that experienced by African Americans working the white vaudeville circuits in the United States: "They were watching us all the time," Webb said. "Not only management, but [also] the people who worked in the show didn't want anything to do with us. They were very snooty, very cold. . . . We'd leave the club immediately and go to the black area [of Montreal, inhabited by Caribbean and African peoples] . . . where all the [black] show people would rent rooms when they were in town." (19 November 1977) Note that Webb and Vigal did not attempt to stay in Montreal at white accommodations. It is possible that the Canadian whites' stand-offishness was prompted by the fact that they had caught on to the team's masquerade but chose to treat them as pariahs rather than fire them.

In all walks of life the reason for passing was to gain equal opportunity for decent employment, housing, education, and a better overall standard of living. It is important to note that, on the whole, passing represents a rejection of roots due to necessity, not ideology. Whites tended to believe that blacks wanted to pass because they, like most whites, believed that being white was inherently superior to being black. By and large, whites were mistaken: blacks who chose to pass did not desire to be white for the sake of being white; rather, they "lusted for the life chances that whiteness once signified." (Chambers, 27) Indeed, the prevailing belief in the black community was reflected in this statement made by the master comedian Bert Williams: "People ask me if I would not give anything to be white. I answer . . . 'No!' How do I know what I might be if I were a white man. . . . There is many a white man less fortunate and less well equipped than I am. In truth, I have never been able to discover that there was anything disgraceful in being a colored man. But I have often found it inconvenient—in America." (Charters, 12) Claude McKay makes the same point. In writing about his white friends in 1937, his sentiments sound all too current:

> . . . [t]hey were not black like me. Not being black and unable to see deep
> into the profundity of blackness, some even thought that I might have pre-

ferred to be white like them. They couldn't imagine that I had no desire merely to exchange my black problem for their white problem. For all their knowledge and sophistication, they couldn't understand the instinctive and animal and purely physical pride of a black person resolute in being himself and yet living a simple civilized life like themselves. Because their education in their white world had trained them to see a person of color either as an inferior or as an exotic. (245)

For the African American vaudeville artist, issues of confusion and double or mistaken identity were not uncommon since the array of skin colors of black vaudevillians was a microcosm of the black world at large. The Whitman Sisters—Mabel, Essie, Alberta, and Alice—were, like today's Vanessa Williams, blond and green-eyed. Frequently they were mistaken for white, onstage or off. For Pete, Peaches, and Duke, a tap class act of the era, questions of racial identity sometimes made life difficult. According to Pete Nugent, "The first ten minutes of our act at a nightclub was a total loss. Our taps were drowned out by the buzz of people asking each other if we were white or colored." (Stearns and Stearns, 302) The question for Norton and Margot was an interesting one and highlights the awkwardness and naiveté of racial categories. Margot was light skinned with light brown hair. Norton was, as Margot describes him "a good brown-skinned color." He couldn't pass as European white, but could be seen as Latino. As mentioned earlier, the Latin label carried a different connotation in the swing era than it does today. Back then, performers in the United States who were Spanish- or French-speaking and claimed to be from another country were treated as honorary whites and were not subject to antiblack discrimination. Thus Norton, had he claimed that he was from Latin America, would have been allowed to perform in white venues, with Margot passing as white or Latina. The Latino specification served as a buffer or border ethnicity. This side issue complicates the race trope. According to Webb:

> They called Spanish "white" then; Spanish wasn't "black-and-Puerto Rican" or "black-and-South American." Today they lump the two groups together, but in those days if you spoke Spanish and were from any country speaking Spanish—you were considered white, whether you were dark-skinned or not. It was only after the Civil Rights era that Puerto Ricans and other

Spanish-speaking people decided to link up with African Americans in order to get some of the privileges and . . . benefits being given to blacks. . . . (17 April 1980)

Whether or not she was considered biologically white, the Latina performer of African descent was designated a foreigner, was accorded comparable status with whites, and was eligible for employment opportunities and public accommodations prohibited to African Americans.[9] The white-Spanish/black-Spanish issue underscores the tenuous nature of racial taxonomy and parallels the yellow-white-brown lunacy of the California intermarriage case cited earlier.

Black British pianist-composer-arranger Reginald Foresythe, who played with the Earl Hines orchestra in the early 1930s, offered a wonderful example of forcing the race card in one's favor. His father was English and his mother Caribbean. Playing with Hines at the all-white College Inn in Chicago, Foresythe went to the dining room for dinner. In response to being informed by the headwaiter that he couldn't be served, he angrily retorted: "'How dare you have the audacity to call me a Negro! Must I show you my passport? I am an Englishman, and I will go straightway to the embassy and cause this place more trouble than you can stand!' So here was the star he'd traveled around the world with as an accompanist [Earl Hines], eating in the kitchen, while they're serving Reggie in the dining room!" (Dance, 150) Dark-skinned Lavinia Williams, who had been a dancer in the original Katharine Dunham company, mentioned the same dilemma in describing the dance company's sojourn in Hollywood for the filming of the 1940 movie *Carnival in Rhythm:* "We were [passed off as] Brazilians. . . . [We were] anything but black Americans." (28 February 1981)

For many white-skinned African Americans—including Nugent, Ralph Cooper, Willie Bryant, and Fredi Washington—refusing to pass was a matter of principle and pride. In the 1920s, Washington had turned down an offer by a European millionaire to be her sponsor if only she would agree to pass for French. (Later she became famous for her role as the tragic light-skinned heroine in the original 1934 film version of *Imitation of Life.*) Reflecting on this period in her life some four decades later, Washington said:

Early in my career it was suggested that I might get further . . . by passing as French or something exotic. But there was no way I could do that, feeling the way I do. . . . I felt you do not have to be white to be good. I've spent most of my life trying to prove that to people who thought otherwise. . . . But to pass, for economic or other advantages, would have meant that I swallowed, whole hog, the idea of Black . . . inferiority. I did not think up this system, and I was not responsible for how I looked . . . I'm a Black woman and proud of it . . . and I will fight injustices and encourage others to fight them until the day I die or until there is nothing to fight against. (Darden, 105)

For those like Washington who refused to pass, neither social conviction, nor wealth, nor stardom could secure for them the mainstream respect and status that comparable achievements brought to whites.

Besides the blatant outrage of southern racism, there was a general if veiled atmosphere of discrimination in northern states. In the private sector celebrities like Cab Calloway and Adelaide Hall, along with ordinary African American citizens, were discriminated against in their attempts to purchase homes in white New York suburbs. (Both succeeded: in 1933 Hall won a legal battle for her home in Larchmont; and Calloway's first wife resisted racist hostility—including derogatory signs planted on their lawn—and bought a home in the Fieldston section of Riverdale in 1937.)[10] In addition, specific establishments in Harlem were segregated. During the swing era, there was still a sizable white population among Harlem's residents.[11] The main boulevard, 125th Street, was lined with white-owned businesses that refused to employ blacks until the success of the boycott organized by the Reverend Adam Clayton Powell, Jr., in August 1938. When the boycott forced the race card and white shopowners were obliged to integrate their staffs, they audaciously requested that light-skinned blacks be sent to fill the slots. This request was not honored. ("I Remember Harlem") The Apollo had been a segregated burlesque house in the 1920s; the major hotel, the Theresa, and largest restaurant, Frank's, refused to patronize blacks through the 1930s.

The climate of racism made possible the plagiarization, popularization, exploitation, and commodification of African American music, song, and dance by the white entertainment industry. Without debt or doubt, the dominant culture received these cultural gifts as theirs for the taking. But this coin was not two-sided: blacks were not supposed to take on white styles. On the New York stage, African Americans were subjected to "one of the curious factors in the problems of race . . . the paradox which makes it quite seemly for a white person to represent a Negro on the stage, but a violation of some inner code for a Negro to represent a white person." (Johnson 191)

The repertory prescribed for black artists in white venues was a reflection of dominant stereotypes. White critics were upset when companies like the Ethiopian Art Players in the 1920s presented Shakespeare or Wilde with black casts but were content when Broadway plays by white authors had the occasional black character played by a blacked-up white. Because white audiences would not sanction black appropriation of white styles, artists like Norton and Margot and the young Ethel Waters—who early on cultivated a white-influenced singing style that set her apart from her black contemporaries like Bessie Smith and Ma Rainey—developed their distinctiveness exclusively by performing for black audiences. (Douglas, 337–38) Waters succeeded in bridging the racial divide and later became a popular crossover star. Her innovations broadened the range of possibilities for black female vocalists. It is also important to note that African American interest in performing white styles is not automatically a rejection of black styles but an affirmation that blacks have as much right to appropriate the artistic property of the Other as do whites—and for blacks, whites are the Other.

Hollywood enforced a rigid discrimination policy and offered predictably sterile roles to blacks. Fredi Washington, after her success in *Imitation of Life,* was unable to gain a foothold in films. Thereafter, roles in the infrequent but occasional interracial scripts that called for light-skinned blacks were played by whites, particularly when the role in question was a romantic one. White America couldn't handle the idea of a black performer, light-skinned or otherwise, cast in an amorous relationship with a white.

So as not to confuse the issue and to make her position clear, Washington stated her racial allegiance as an African American in an article that appeared in the *Chicago Defender* on January 19, 1935 titled "'Part in *Imitation* is Not Real Me,' Says Fredi." Like many others, Washington was in a double bind: she wasn't cast in interracial love stories because she wasn't white; and she wasn't cast with black men (of course, there were no black love stories coming out of Hollywood, anyway) for fear audiences would mistake her for white. For this reason, when she played opposite Paul Robeson in *The Emperor Jones,* she was obliged to wear dark make-up. (Chambers, 27) Such was the irony of being black in Hollywood and on Broadway: if you weren't too dark, then you were too light.

Light-skinned bandleader-actor Willie Bryant encountered many of the same problems Washington faced. Local sheriffs in southern towns, uninterested in the fact that he was black, forced him to lead his band from a raised box placed on stage, since it was against the law for whites and blacks to share the same performing space. "You may be colored like you say," he was told, "but the audience doesn't know it." Like Washington, Bryant refused to pass and, like Washington, this immensely talented performer was offered stardom by a white entrepreneur if only he would. In 1940, during the run of *Mamba's Daughters,* the Broadway hit in which he costarred with Ethel Waters, a Hollywood producer propositioned him backstage. He recalls the producer telling him "We can't have Negro actors in the movies. But, hell, you don't look colored. I'll pay your expenses for three years while you hide out and lose your identity. When you come back, you're a white man and you sign a contract with me. . . ." (Churchill, 18)

Meanwhile, on the white side, it had become fashionable to have a perennial tan—a convention initiated by Cary Grant in the 1930s. (Douglas, 79) In a classic example of the black-white American dilemma, whites with tan(ned) skin were sought after in Hollywood, but blacks who were tan—or even white-skinned—were shunned. Actor Frank Silvera was one who managed to make good in Hollywood, although in a paradoxical way. It is characteristic of the American denial of blackness that he succeeded because, although he didn't pass, most white American moviegoers were unaware that he was black. According to Margot Webb, "That's why Frank Silvera made so much money—because he was really passing, in a way. He was always playing foreign people. He was either Jewish, Greek, Spanish—anything but black. No, he was never a black

American in the movies." (17 September 1980) And, as in other walks of life, Hollywood unknowingly opened its doors for some blacks who passed as white. Webb states, "We knew people who [went to Hollywood and] passed. . . . They never revealed their identity, not even with the black movement [of the 1960s]. They stayed in the white community. They were able to do that because they went when they were very young. They were unknown and just passed over." (24 April 1980)

In some instances blacks in Hollywood could be hired to do musical voiceovers for whites, because they weren't seen on screen; but a black dance team like Norton and Margot were never hired, as they might have been, as doubles in long shots for white stars shown dancing in movie musicals. (This was a lucrative source of income for white teams.)

African American actors who attempted to upset racial etiquette were summarily sent packing. The great American stage actor Charles Gilpin was fired from a 1927 Hollywood production of *Uncle Tom's Cabin* for refusing to play Tom in a sentimental, stereotypical manner. (Douglas, 87) And a disillusioned Paul Robeson gave up on Hollywood, hoping to have a stab at socially conscious, relevant roles in European films instead. (This was not to be: on the whole, even European productions stereotyped people of African lineage.) African American musicians, vocalists, and dancers were expected to tailor their image to fit the stereotype. Duke Ellington was subjected to Hollywood's racial straitjacket in 1930 when he appeared with his orchestra in a blackface Amos 'n' Andy movie, *Check and Double Check*—a film that belied his cosmopolitan, savvy presentation of self. Light-skinned members of the band were obliged to dark down in order to appear on camera. As one writer put it: "He didn't have much chance in the movies—he was suave, sophisticated, sexy, and smart, everything desired in a white performer but not in a black one." (Giddins, 116)

In 1943 white screenwriter Dalton Trumbo addressed the plight of African Americans in the film industry for *Crisis* magazine:

> In Hollywood the most gigantic milestones of our appeal to public patronage have been the anti-Negro pictures, *The Birth of a Nation* and *Gone With the Wind*. And in between the two, from 1915 to 1940, we have produced turgid floods of sickening and libelous treacle. We have

made tarts of the Negro's daughters, crap-shooters of his sons, obsequious Uncle Toms of his fathers, superstitious and grotesque crones of
his mothers, strutting peacocks of his successful men, psalm-singing
mountebanks of his priests and Barnum and Bailey sideshows of his religion. (366)

Trumbo continues by focusing on the status of African Americans in the
two world wars. Whereas American movies had an "invisible man" tradition with regard to blacks, Jean Renoir's film *Grand Illusion* shows a soldier
of African descent as part of a background scene—a small but significant
tribute to the part played by African Americans in World War I. In spite of
their enormous contribution in the war effort during World War II, no
Hollywood film recognized the role played by blacks in even a minor way.
For example, long shots of assembly lines never included blacks who, in real
life, made a significant contribution to the war industry. (367)[12] Trumbo
struck a sensitive chord: the entire issue of race and the world wars was another sore spot for Webb's generation.[13] Although blacks were required to
serve in the military, they were subjected to conditions of stark segregation.
A February 1942 article in *Crisis* titled "The Negro in the United States
Army" stated:

A seven-point statement of policy covering the service of Negroes in the
Army was issued by the War Department, through the White House, on
October 9, 1940. The statement aroused heated discussion, and its basic
point, the seventh, maintaining segregation of personnel on the basis of
color, was and still is resented. . . . Our radio technicians are being turned
down—yet the Army is begging for radio technicians. Our nurses and doctors are told they can minister only to Negroes. . . . The 1942 Negro resents
and rebels against 1842 regulations. These must be rooted out whether
they reside in the Mein Kampf of a Hitler, or in a memorandum in the ad-
jutant general's office of the American Army. (47)

Segregation of the military was sometimes manifested in particularly
humiliating ways. Lena Horne, who had been performing for the troops
under USO sponsorship, was officially censured and ultimately kicked
out of this American wartime institution after refusing to perform under
the following circumstance:

A USO-sponsored junket to Camp Robertson, Arkansas, stopped Lena in
her tracks. She was scheduled to give two performances, one for the white
officers and another for the black men. She was surprised at the second
performance, however, to see another sea of white faces. "Who are these
soldiers?" she asked. "They're not soldiers, they're German prisoners of
war," was the reply. "But where are the Negro soldiers?" Lena asked.
"They're sitting behind the German POWs," was the answer. To that
Lena . . . walked out. . . . (Buckley, 180)

One thing was certain: in spite of degree and variations, racism was a
theme that reverberated in every facet of American life, onstage and off.
One way to map racism in the performance milieu was to track the suc-
cession of African American firsts as racial barriers were crossed by individual artists who pioneered change. What follows is a sampling—only a
handful, but enough to demonstrate the pattern:

1914—"The first time a Negro orchestra had ever played in a first-class
theater, with the James Reese Europe band's booking at Hammerstein's
Victoria Theater, playing for Vernon and Irene Castle." (Charters, 127)

1930—The Duke Ellington Orchestra becomes the first African
American band to appear in a major Hollywood film, *Check and Double
Check.* (Calloway, 106)

1931—With an overflow crowd of African Americans having turned
out to see the Cab Calloway band at the Majestic Theater in Houston,
Texas, racial segregation in the theater was broken for the first time, and
blacks were allowed to sit in the mezzanine. (ibid., 139)

1932—Lucille Wilson becomes the first dark-skinned chorus girl at
the Cotton Club. (Haskins, 75, 76)

1936—Pianist Teddy Wilson becomes the first African American to
play in a white band, playing with the Benny Goodman band at Chicago's
Congress Hotel. (Hammond, 123)

Late 1930s—Bill Robinson becomes the first African American to
perform at a white Miami resort. (Calloway, 128)

None of these firsts led to permanent change; what these small inroads
meant was that, in isolated instances, whites were momentarily obliged to
let blacks penetrate their world. Innumerable examples such as these
arose in public and private interactions and venues, while the reins of con-

trol over the African American entertainment industry remained firmly
in white hands. The Sissle and Blake era of black musicals produced and
written by blacks was a short-lived phenomenon that spanned the 1920s.
Thereafter, mainstream swing era stage musicals about African Americans were written and produced by whites. An outstanding example is
Porgy and Bess—originally produced in 1935. To a cadre of African
American intellectuals and artists, this show represented a brand of paternalism that inspired deep resentment. The opinions expressed, below,
by Langston Hughes, voice the sentiments of this group:

> If it were not for the racial complications in American life, one might
> forego any further discussion of *Porgy and Bess,* and accept it simply as an
> excellent theater piece, and a helpful dinner basket. Unfortunately, its bas-
> ket has been a trap, a steel-toothed trap leaving its marks upon the wrists
> of the Negro people who reached therein to touch its fish. And the fish . . .
> themselves are tainted with racism. Art aside, it is an axiom in the Ameri-
> can theater that the cheapest shows to stage are Negro shows. Their cast
> budgets are always the lowest of any [here Hughes is referring to the fact
> that, in the same venues, black pay scales were lower than those for whites].
> If a Negro show is a hit, a great deal of money may be made. The bulk of
> this money does not go to Negroes. They are seldom if ever in the top ech-
> elons of management or production. Financially, the whites get the caviar,
> the Negroes get the porgies. A porgy is a fish, and *Porgy and Bess* concerns
> fishermen and their women. The character, Porgy, is a cripple, an almost
> emasculated man. His Bess is a whore. The denizens (as the critics term
> them) of Catfish Row are child-like ignorant blackamoors given to dice,
> razors, and singing at the drop of a hat. In other words, they are stereotypes
> in (to sensitive Negroes) the worst sense of the word. The long shadow of
> the blackface minstrel coarsens the charm of *Porgy* and darkens its grace
> notes. Those notes themselves are lifted from the Negro people. Borrowed
> is a more polite word; "derived from" an acceptable phrase. (1966, 843)

For the appropriation of the African American cultural product; for
the inequitable salaries paid black performers; for the racist glass ceiling
keeping blacks out of production and management; for the continued
misrepresentation and stereotypical depiction of African American
characters; for the pall of paternalism that cloaked the production—for

all these reasons Hughes was enraged. The irony of it all is that this folk opera became one of very few avenues of employment for African American opera singers—their "dinner basket"—at a time when white American opera companies would not have dreamed of hiring an African American.

In a more positive vein white musicologist Sigmund Spaeth voiced another view. First, he characterized Jerome Kern, George Gershwin, and Irving Berlin as having "assimilated Negro elements until they are able to imitate almost anything that is characteristic of the black man's music. . . ." Then, of *Porgy and Bess,* he said: "Here a white man, saturated with the atmosphere of Charleston's island jungles and Catfish Row, has produced authentic Negro spirituals, blues and jazz, but with the stamp of his own extraordinary individuality." (1938, 25)

Indeed, it seemed as though the African American cultural product was the rough- cut diamond waiting for the European American to refine it. For Hughes and those of like mind, it seemed as though Gershwin's "extraordinary individuality" was paid for at the expense of the African American world image: one of the worst effects of this show was that, in its extensive European tours from the 1930s through the 1950s, European audiences regarded the musical as a realistic depiction of typical African American life.[14] (By the 1960s, with extensive exposure to other images through the export of American television shows aired abroad, this work lost its hegemonic hold on the European psyche.) This convoluted circumstance in which a white man's creation is taken as the authentic portrait of African American life, can be called a case of mistaken identity; it is an ironic echo of the minstrel legacy when whites, nationwide and abroad, assumed that the minstrel stereotype was a realistic representation of African Americans, rather than a stage role. Stereotypes endure: we see them, alive and well, in the way in which African Americans have been received and perceived in American performance and American life. Perpetuation and proliferation of negative stereotypes provided psychological justification for negative and inferior treatment of African Americans in a mindset that seemed to say "if this is how they are, then they are getting the treatment they deserve."

Besides the predictably stock roles assigned to African Americans, another factor that contributed to the continuity of stereotypes was the perpetuation of blackface. Even after the minstrel show had long been re-placed by vaudeville, blacking up continued to be practiced in white and black vaudeville by both white and black entertainers. It is useful to recall that the very popular *Amos 'n' Andy* show originated in the 1920s and was performed originally by two white men in blackface. Later, when two black men took over these roles, they continued to perform their characters as the stereotypes that had been established by their white predecessors. This is the same route that minstrelsy had traveled: black men imitating whites imitating blacks. Until the practice was legally challenged in the 1960s, secondary schools, college programs, fraternity and sorority variety shows, and other amateur theatrical venues were additional outlets for blackface performance, which was deemed a harmless form of indigenous American humor. The list of Hollywood musicals that included blackface performance is extensive.[15] Even a performer as sophisticated as Cary Grant blacked up for a private event: in 1942, his thirty-eighth birthday was celebrated by a Hollywood bash at which Louis Armstrong and his orchestra provided music; the guests and Grant came in blackface. (Douglas, 79) Blackface was also an important export, with England taking a particular liking to it and tailoring it to British size by creating British minstrel groups and, like Americans, extending the practice to other venues after minstrelsy was dead.[16] It was only through concerted efforts spearheaded in the Civil Rights era that these practices were halted.

The advent of another Broadway hit, *Carmen Jones*, in 1943 continued the tradition of derogatory stereotypes of black characters. Addressing the folk opera based on Bizet's work, African American writer Loften Mitchell said, "For all of its success and acclaim, *Carmen Jones* troubles me. Actually, it seems that in the adaptation, the Negro stereotype is *sought*. [Author's emphasis] I feel this is more insidious than many other works that perpetuated the stereotype. *Green Pastures, Porgy*, and *Porgy and Bess* seem to me to be works created by people who didn't know anything about Negroes. *Carmen Jones* seems to be a work that deliberately used the stereotype to assure a measure of success." (120)

In addition to the issues blacks encountered in the broader, white community, a system of color-caste racism existed in African American circles. It ranged from an informed, ironic, savvy deployment of the light-skinned African American on the front lines of visibility to a vicious form of self-deprecation.

In-Group Racism

If, as asserted in Chapter 4, the dominant culture deemed the light-skinned black female as the only black woman worthy of being presented onstage, then why would the black community embrace this self-diminishing conceit? Even today, African Americans—women, in particular—struggle to come to terms with the black world's light-skinned/dark-skinned discrimination. According to one observer in the 1997 video documentary "Black Women On: The Light/Dark Thang," "When I think of the light/dark dynamic [in the African American community] I see a knife that someone else has plunged in our hearts that we twist, ourselves, and twist a little deeper each time we do something intentionally or unintentionally, consciously or unconsciously." This state of internal affairs, which has been called a form of "mental colonialism," has chipped away black self-esteem both from the outside-in and the inside-out. The following discussion does not offer solutions to color-caste discrimination but discusses origins, specific examples, and ramifications of this bizarre etiquette.

Along with historians and sociologists of African American culture, Margot Webb contends that this light-skinned hegemony originated in the simple fact that, early on, most of the people in the African American community who were well off were the light-skinned mulatto children or grandchildren of slave owners. Although born illicitly, they were the master's offspring, were accorded preferential treatment, and gained advantage over their kin. Before Emancipation many became part of free black society in the South; later many gravitated to Washington, D.C. When compared to the critical mass of dark-skinned African Americans, this black caste was economically well endowed and came to be considered the middle class of black culture. (This did not mean that it was impossible for dark-skinned blacks to make their way up the economic ladder. Indeed, they did, and when they succeeded—whether they were male or female—they frequently set out to acquire a light-skinned "trophy" spouse and bear light-skinned children.) However, their successes were paltry when compared to those of middle-class whites. As Webb dryly quipped, at one time (namely, from Reconstruction to the Civil Rights era of the 1960s) to be middle class in the black world meant simply to have a job. And if that employment placed the black worker in direct contact with well-off whites, then the black person saw, firsthand, what white privilege and power could buy. Almost invariably the best positions went to light-skinned blacks. Thus, in the eyes of some beholders, black success became inextricably linked to light skin color.

Black middle class jobs included such menial work as railroad porters (the Brotherhood of Sleeping Car Porters held a position of high esteem in the black community), valets, maids, or chauffeurs to wealthy whites, or dressers and tailors to white stars of stage and screen (like Webb's grandmother)—all of which, in the dominant culture, would have been categorized as ground-level working-class positions. Catering, another employment open to African Americans, was a highly respected pursuit in black circles. A good share of the outstanding catering families were white-skinned, including the Cuyjet family in Philadelphia and Webb's maternal great grandmother, "Grandmother Stewart," who owned a catering service and restaurant in Cape May, New Jersey.

In his autobiography the inimitable El-Hajj Malik El-Shabazz—the former Malcolm X—gave a sobering reality check on the real-world status of the black middle class in the Roxbury section of Boston, where he spent part of his youth. El-Shabazz, then known as Malcolm Little, worked as a soda jerk in the 1940s at a drugstore "on the Hill" (the Waumbeck and Humboldt Avenue Hill area of Roxbury, which he compares to Harlem's bourgeois Sugar Hill section):

This was the snooty-black neighborhood; they called themselves the "Four Hundred," and looked down their noses at the Negroes of the black ghetto. . . . These Negroes walked along the sidewalks looking haughty and dignified. . . . Under the pitiful misapprehension that it would make them "better," these Hill Negroes were breaking their backs trying to imitate white people. Any black family that had been around Boston long enough to own the home they lived in was considered among the Hill elite. . . . Usually it was the Southerners and the West Indians who not only managed to own the places where they lived, but also at least one other house which they rented as income property. The snooty New Englanders [Yankee-born blacks who looked down upon newly-arrived Southern blacks] usually owned less than they. (X and Haley, 40–41)

As for the nature of their employment in the real—read white—world, Little's customers lived a double identity. His account corroborates Webb's contention that simply having a steady job was a door-opener for joining the ranks of the black middle class: "People like the sleep-in maid for Beacon Hill white folks who used to come in with her 'ooh, my deah' manners. . . . Or the hospital cafeteria-line serving woman . . . telling the proprietor she was a 'dietitian'—both of them knowing she was lying." (59)[17]

According to Webb, Boston rivaled Washington, D.C. in the snobbishness and color-caste discrimination of its African American elite. Her Uncle Pat had married her mother's sister, Marian. The pattern was for light-skinned blacks to marry either other light-skinned blacks or, as Webb put it, for light-skinned black men to marry working-class white women. (28 January 1999). The implication, here, is that a well-heeled white woman would demean her status by marrying black, but a poor white female could be thus elevated from low status in the white world to middle-class status in the black world. What the black spouse hoped for from such a match were light-skinned offspring. Such is the folly of American race politics.

The preoccupation with skin color—and the advantages that light skin could mean for one's offspring—was so acute that color was an open measure of worth and was touted as such in conversation, in places of worship and social organizations (dark-skinned blacks were not allowed in certain black churches and clubs), in the entertainment industry, and in print media. Even as late as 1951 an *Ebony* magazine cover photo of Josephine Baker (wearing her usual whitening make-up), announcing an article about her return to the United States, carried a cover blurb about an article inside entitled "What Color Will Your Baby Be?" (May 1951) The concern with color implies the fear that a black-skinned child wouldn't have opportunities for advancement in American life. Indeed, African Americans were correct in that assessment, and it was not their doing— they didn't create the system. Nevertheless, in perpetuating the white-is-right standard, black people perpetuated their own devaluation. Black society structured itself in such a way as to proclaim, "if white means power, then white is preferred." However, the issue is not cut and dried—not black and white, if you will—and acquiescence to dominant culture values represents a sore spot for all cultural minorities.

In the performance arena, the original phenomenon of the light-skinned chorus girl was a necessity predicated by the system of white racism that valued white womanhood above all else and recognized beauty only in imitation of that standard. Accordingly, it was economic shrewdness that prompted Sam T. Jack to recruit a near-white chorus line for *The Creole Show* in 1890; but it was bad habit that dictated that, as Honi Coles explained, swing era chorus lines were "color-coded." Internalized racism ensures that the values encapsulated in this vernacular rhyme serve as an insidious, self-fulfilling prophecy:

> If you're white, you're right.
> If you're yellow, you're mellow.
> If you're brown, stay down [sometimes changed to "stick around"].
> But if you're black, stay back.[18]

In addressing the problem of internalized racism, Langston Hughes said: "But this is the mountain standing in the way of any true Negro art in America—this urge within the race toward whiteness, the desire to pour racial individuality into the mold of American standardization, and to be as little Negro and as much American as possible." (Sochen, 117)

A dark-skinned dancer like Ida Forsyne angrily explained her plight: "I couldn't get a job because I was black, and my own people discriminated against me." (Stearns and Stearns, 256) Webb asserts the truth of this statement, remarking that talented female dancers who studied in her classes at the YWCA knew they'd never have a dancing career simply because of their dark skin.

In-group racism could be as schizoid as its white counterpart. Ethel Waters recalls a "peculiar box-office rule" at Washington, D.C.'s Howard theater, one of the few African American venues in the capital: "For two evening performances and one matinee during the week they would sell tickets only to very light-colored Negroes. At those three performances you could see no black spots at all out front except when the lights were turned down." (105) Indeed, some light-skinned blacks regarded themselves—and were treated—as a separate caste who were apart from and superior to darker-skinned blacks. Of course, the problem was that those of blacker complexion might, literally, be their brothers, sisters, or parents, which was the theme of the controversial novel and film, *Imitation of Life*. Black families come in a variety of colors. Blood brothers and sisters may range in complexion so that one might pass for white while a sibling is clearly black Apparently, that was the case with white-looking author and *New York Times* book reviewer Anatole Broyard, whose black Creole heritage was not revealed until after his death. (Gates, 66)

Earl Hines describes in his biography how this in-group racism marred his childhood in Pennsylvania. His stepmother's father was white, and those mixed-blood relatives had often made him feel alienated and unwanted. However, once he became famous, they were ready to make him one of their own. But he would have none of it; to turn the tables on them, he showed up at one of their affairs with a young woman who had dark-colored skin and decidedly African facial features—an intentionally unacceptable gaffe. Hines cites another run-in with what he terms "blue vein society" when he and Louis Armstrong were prevented from playing with the Sammy Stewart band, which Hines contends was composed exclusively of light-skinned musicians. (Dance, 67–68) (This example is unusual: in general, male musicians weren't subjected to this black-on-black color tyranny.[19])

Without a doubt, there was a need for reaffirmation and celebration of blackness, and the significance of the era's Marcus Garvey black pride and power movement becomes clear. Theater critic Theophilus Lewis was so exhilarated to see a darker-than-usual line of chorus girls in one musical that he wrote a review titled "Blackbirds Are Turning Brown," which was subtitled "Substituting Ginger Chorus for High Yellow A Pleasing Novelty." (1930)

In a 1926 review—and with typical wit and irony—Lewis had expressed a wry outrage at color casting. His implication is clear: although African Americans may be guilty of in-group discrimination, the general practice of color-caste racism in show business was controlled and perpetuated by white producers like Lew Leslie:

The electric signs and billboards outside the Alhambra [a major Harlem vaudeville house in the 1920s] and the placards in the Harlem store windows read "Blackbirds of 1926." But "What's in a name?" Any show produced by Lew Leslie would be a specimen of nonpareil ineptitude no matter what it was called. . . . The majority of the musicians are brownskins and all the girls except two principals are biological whites. Such a vari-colored aggregation of entertainers, it seems to me, could be more appropriately called The Aigrettes of 1926; or the Golden Pheasants or the Cockatoos or the Flamingoes or even the Ornithorhynci of 1926. To call the show The Blackbirds merely for the sake of exploiting one threadbare song is as malappropriate as it would be to call it The Striped Back Apes because one of the blackface comedians remotely resembles one. . . . (May 1926).

Chorus lines and floor shows across the nation reflected this standard. Jazz historian and connoisseur Marshall Stearns described a typical Cotton Club floor show, commenting that it was an

incredible mishmash of talent and nonsense which might well fascinate both sociologists and psychiatrists. . . . [A] light-skinned and magnificently muscled Negro burst through a papier-mâché jungle onto the dance floor, clad in an aviator's helmet, goggles, and shorts. He had obviously been "forced down in darkest Africa," and in the center of the floor he came upon a "white" goddess clad in long golden tresses and being worshipped by a circle of cringing "blacks" . . . he rescued the blonde and they did an erotic dance. In the background . . . members of the [Duke] Ellington band growled, wheezed, and snorted obscenely. (183–84)

It is interesting to speculate whether the ambient sounds made by Ellington's musicians didn't also include an ironic commentary of distaste for the scenario. Let the reader recall that, with few exceptions, Cotton Club floor shows were staged by whites. As in Lewis's example of the color preferences in shows produced by Lew Leslie, what developed was a parasitic, dominant culture/minority culture perpetuation of the color-caste system, with black-skinned blacks symbolically cringing in worship of— and below—white-skinned blacks. For both blacks and whites, white meant power and, thus, was preferred. Josephine Baker was not alone in making herself up to be lighter than her true complexion throughout her career—it was a common practice with black female performers, light or dark, that persisted for many decades. (8 July 1998) The light-skinned but socially conscious Fredi Washington had come to Baker's aid during the 1921 Broadway run of *Shuffle Along,* the hit show that launched both of their careers. Baker's scene-stealing talent and dark complexion had made her an outcast with the mostly white-skinned chorines who, to retaliate, stole her make-up and dumped it. But Washington stood up for her and made the culprits return Baker's property. This was the beginning of a lifelong friendship. (Chambers, 27)

According to Webb, one of the few exceptions to the light-skinned chorus line convention were the shows produced by Larry Steele, an African American, in the 1940s. (8 July 1998) And the most renowned exception to the rule was the long-standing traveling show, known as the *Brown Skin Models,* produced by Irvin C. Miller, also African American. This revue toured the country from 1925 until the beginning of World War II. But these were exceptions. Onstage and off, as Webb recalled, "the color thing was simply accepted." (8 July 1998)

Touring Stateside

As discussed briefly in Chapter 1, racism on the road plagued the African American performer. The swing era version described here was simply a continuation of policies that had been in place since Reconstruction. In a letter written in 1922, Bert Williams said:

> I was thinking about all the honors that are showered on me in the theater, how everyone wished to shake my hand or get an autograph, a real hero you'd naturally think. However, when I reach a hotel, I am refused permission to ride on the passenger elevator, I cannot enter the dining room for my meals, and am Jim Crowed generally. But I am not complaining . . . I am just wondering. I would like to know when (my prediction) the ultimate changes come, if the new human beings will believe such persons as I am writing about actually lived? (Charters, 138)

In his biography Earl Hines addressed the insularity that resulted from racism on the road by admonishing his musicians to take with

them everything that they might conceivably need. On arriving in segregated southern towns, they headed straight for the black neighborhood, which would be centered in one section, frequently on the poorer
side of the railroad tracks. In order to avoid possible problems, they remained in the African American section until it was time to perform.
Then, en masse, the entourage left, by bus, for the white theater or ballroom where they were booked. They traveled together to and from the
white site: under conditions such as these, there was some safety in numbers. They were housed in the African American community by the
black middle class whose homes were spacious enough to accommodate
guests. (Dance, 81)

Racism was the primary seed of destruction in the career of Norton
and Margot. As discussed in earlier chapters, their style did not conform
to the African American stereotype, and there was no possibility of work
for them in white vaudeville, not even on the hotel circuit. Webb said, "It
was mostly Norton they objected to. [White] people objected to black
men being around white women. . . . It was this thing about the black
man—[they were always] so afraid that he might become interested in
some of the white women in a show—as if he cared!" (19 November
1977) In addition, the team had voluntarily reduced the potential scope
of their professional life by refusing to perform in the South under its
racially terrifying conditions.

Whereas Norton and Margot traveled by train (they refused to travel
by bus[20]), the bands frequently journeyed in a private bus with a white
road manager who represented the agency that booked the tour. He often
came in handy, serving as a passport for the purchase of goods and services in places that refused to do business with African Americans. Those
few who could afford it later traveled by private railroad coach. Always
the gentleman and diplomat, Duke Ellington stated the situation dis-
creetly: "In order to avoid problems, we used to charter two Pullman
sleeping cars and a seventy-foot baggage car. Everywhere we went in the
South, we lived in them."(85)

Although they did not perform down South, Webb's recollections of
other American cities are equally disheartening. According to her, "St. Louis
was impossible: they wouldn't take your bags in the railroad station. They
had white porters in those days, you know, and they had white firemen and

black firemen. If they had a fire [in a black neighborhood] a white fireman wouldn't put it out—you had to find a black fireman." (19 November 1977) In Louisville she performed with Norton in a nightclub where
the owner referred to the African American entertainers in the heinous,
albeit typical, manner that was acceptable in all too many Jim Crow era
white circles: "'Come on, you niggers! Time to go on; come on, my niggers!'—you know—all night long! You just had to close your ears because
you were getting paid. . . . He actually thought he was being affection-
ate!" (9 December 1977) In Philadelphia she and Norton experienced
many instances of racism, including the kind that still occurs in the year
2000 and is now known as racial profiling:

> In Philly we had very unfortunate experiences . . . we would drive home
> from the nightclub—we had a car that Norton and I shared. . . . Now, Nor-
> ton was a good brown complexion. . . . In those days the police would stop
> you [if your were African American] just for having a nice-looking car, and
> we were stopped several times, with comments like "Pull over, nigger," and
> they'd say "What are you doing with that white woman [Margot] in your
> car?"—just because we had a good-looking new car and because he was not
> white and we were coming from a white neighborhood. . . . (ibid.)

According to Webb, there were problems throughout the North with
hotel accommodations and restaurant service. Although the team never
performed in the Boston area, they had heard from colleagues that it was
"very racist up there." And Chicago was no picnic. A definitive racial barrier separated its North and South sides. The Grand Terrace was a Cotton Club-type establishment in the African American section of town,
with a hotel adjacent to it where the performers were lodged.[21] There was
also a favorite eating place, the Chicken Shack, owned by Ernie Henderson, an African American. (8 July 1998) Chicago's South Side was a
miniature Harlem, insulating and protecting its residents and visitors
from the rebuffs of the white world at large.

Because they could not be seen in white vaudeville theaters by black audiences across the nation (except by those who were light enough to pass),
the touring unit performers were sponsored individually at luncheons and
receptions in African American homes and churches in the black commu-

nities out West. Thus, even though they did not have the opportunity to see them perform, at least African Americans were able to meet and greet the vaudeville stars. (And the bands played, with a vocalist and perhaps a tap act, at dance halls that occasionally arranged a show for African Americans.) African American newspapers across the country were essential in alerting the community to the arrival of the touring units. Webb mentions one Lucille Schwartz as particularly effective in this advance-publicity capacity. She was based in St. Louis and was one of the vital links between the traveling performers and the city's black community. Ironically, Webb pointed out, Schwartz herself couldn't see the shows she wrote about because of her own brown skin color. (8 July 1998)

Eventually a select group of black St. Louisians did get an opportunity to see Norton and Margot perform as a solo act. In contrast to the many humiliating experiences related by Webb, the following story stands out as a uniquely gratifying exception. The one African American theater in the Midwest where the team performed was the Amytis Theater in St. Louis. According to Webb, this venue was part of a building complex owned by a wealthy African American woman who had seen the team in a unit revue in Chicago and booked them directly. Their contract, for the week beginning March 10, 1935, stipulated that they were to do "a performance of from ten to fifteen minutes each, and at least three performances or acts each day." (Webb collection) This time allotment would allow for up to three dances to be performed per show. The overall conditions and their featured status as the sole act on the program made this gig a welcome respite from the five-a-day vaudeville format. Room and board were provided by the theater, another unusual perk in the life of the swing era performer. The building that housed the theater also contained a recreation hall and hotel, making it somewhat of an African American resort in St. Louis. Each of the team's performances was structured as a cultural event that lasted over an hour. After their quarter-hour of dance, they attended a reception and coffee hour with audience members—described by Webb as the African American bourgeoisie of St. Louis. It seems apparent that the team had been chosen because they represented something akin to cultural uplift in the mind of the theater owner; she purposely did not engage any of the typical vaudeville acts in the unit. Webb said that they "Stayed in the building, and in between [performances] she had rooms with billiard tables and lounges—everything right there. . . . It was an elite group of people coming to her theater . . . and we would talk, and they'd ask us questions about show business, life on the road, our careers, and so on." (Dixon-Stowell, 1978, 26)

This resort-like haven for select African Americans served the same function as the special travel accommodations for the Duke Ellington band: insulation, separation, and salvation from the hostile world at large by the creation of a black microcosm. In both instances African Americans turned racism's disadvantage into a posture of privilege, relative and limited though it may have been. On the road and in white America, without the buffer provided by the large urban, East Coast black communities, such luxuries were actually necessities. And such a booking was, indeed, a rarity for the swing era trouper.

Since African American performers were not permitted to stay in white living accommodations near the white theaters where they performed, they were forced to find alternatives, although that might mean traveling some distance to the black community. Both bassist John Williams and Margot Webb mention that performers generally approached any African American they met—a redcap, cleaning lady, shoeshiner—and asked where the black section was located.

Williams recalled that he and guitarist Lawrence Lucy, both touring with Louis Armstrong, kept a book listing good people who had put them up in homes all over the nation, people with a reputation for "a good home, a clean house and good food." After the initial contact, the musicians telegrammed the homemakers in advance to advise of their arrival and to make arrangements for accommodations. These black private citizens knew the inconveniences and real dangers to African Americans traveling through white America, and they often provided services that afforded more than the basic necessities for physical comfort, such as sheltering a performer who became ill or incapacitated. Williams recounts a tale of particular domestic hospitality:

> Usually when we'd go to Knoxville, it would be our headquarters, and then we'd play out in the different little towns all around. Usually you'd be there a week or ten days. You'd get through, and the woman [of the house] would have washed your clothes—[it was] just the two of us [Williams and Lucy]

staying there. . . . [For breakfast there would be] anything you wanted—a big platter of eggs and bacon, hot biscuits, syrup. When you came home at night there was always something left on the table for you—cake, coffee, sandwiches. [At the end of the booking] you'd say, "How much do I owe you?" This would be for seven, eight, or ten days. [She'd say] "Oh, I guess, twelve dollars." You'd feel so ashamed, you'd have to give her more than that. [As a final touch, she would pack a home-cooked picnic lunch for them to take on the road.] (15 August 1980)

Even in those towns that had no black neighborhood there was usually, as Webb recollected, "just a very small section where a few blacks owned very nice homes. You know, in nearly every town in the country you'll find one or two blacks who have a nice home. Somehow, they manage to survive the prejudice and save their money and buy a home." (22 May 1980)

Both Williams and Ethel Waters (139) recount tales of having to reside in whorehouses because no other accommodations were made available to them. Williams's experience occurred while on tour with the Armstrong band in Montreal, Canada, the city where Webb and Al Vigal had experienced difficulties. According to Williams, reservations had been made in advance. Perhaps the Canadian hotelier thought that this was to be another white swing band. In any case, the entire Armstrong outfit arrived to find that the hotel suddenly "had no accommodations," a refrain commonly heard by blacks seeking rooms in white establishments. They were happy to find the brothel that ultimately put them up. (15 August 1980)

In the 1940s Waters, by then a star, had drafted her own pre-registration form which she sent to white establishments well in advance of her arrival:

It irked me that some of the hotels that couldn't find room for me were in towns where I'd been presented by the mayor with keys to the city. I figured out what to do about this one day when I was studying the set of rules pasted on the wall of a hotel room. Ever since, whenever I write for hotel reservations, I always enclose a set of rules I have made for the hotels. . . .

1. I don't like to mix with white people.
2. I don't want to eat in your restaurant.

3. I don't have guests in my room.
4. I am an isolationist and I will keep the key to my room with me. I don't like to walk across the lobby to get my key from the desk.
5. If you don't want colored people as guests, for Lord's sake don't write me that you're having some convention and, as a result, can't accommodate me. Just say you don't want colored people in your midst. I will understand. I may even sympathize with you because you are depriving yourself of so much good company. (261)

Down South the musicians encountered strict segregation. Williams recalls that in most Southern towns, "you played for the white one night and the black the next night. . . . Sometimes we would play a show for the white around 5 or 6 P.M. Then we'd go across the river—as we used to say—and play at a little theater for the colored. Dances were the same way. [In] some of the bigger cities like Birmingham, Atlanta, and Chattanooga, you'd play a concert in the municipal auditorium, and the house was divided [by a rope down the middle]—the whites would be on one side and the coloreds on the other." (15 August 1980)

From the distance of nearly seven decades, the southern etiquette of segregation seems no less humane than its western and midwestern counterparts. At least in the South African Americans had opportunities to see the performances, even if they were segregated. Nevertheless, in a world where racism was practiced in every walk of life and every region of the nation—even cosmopolitan New York City—the overt southern style grated upon the nerves of some northerners. (And, as the 1954 *Brown vs. Board of Education* decision would later confirm, separate services are, inherently, unequal.) Still, African Americans may have derived some special satisfaction in witnessing the achievements of their own in the company of their own rather than in the midst of a potentially hostile white audience, and rather than not seeing the traveling shows at all. In any case, the dollar prevailed—even over and above the rules of segregation—and whites and African Americans shared the same, though divided, space when the booking schedule did not permit a band to remain for two nights in the same town. Racism did prevail, however, in that the bands did not play at white theaters in the South, as they did in the Midwest and West. Southern bookings were in dance halls, cabarets, and the occasional black theater on "the other side of the tracks." The white theaters remained a whites-only bastion until the end of the Civil Rights era.

Back East the race game was as intense as in other areas of the country, but each region played it differently. Bassist John Williams cites an incident that occurred in the 1940s in midtown Manhattan with bandleader Lucky Millinder at a small bar on Seventh Avenue near the legendary Fifty-second Street jazz strip occupied by clubs and cabarets:

> Now, Lucky knew the owner. We went in—Charlie Shavers, Harry Edison, Lucky, and myself. We'd been rehearsing, so Lucky said, "C'mon, I'll take you by my friend's place, and we'll have a few drinks." We bought beers and were standing at the bar. The owner came up and told Lucky, "You and the boys come back and sit in the booth with me, and I'll tell you something." So we sat down. Lucky said, "What's your gripe now?" He said, "Lucky, I've got a four-thousand-dollar-a-week business here. Now, the drinks that you all have had are on me. Sit here and finish your drinks and leave. If my clientele come in and see you here, they won't keep coming." (15 August 1980)

The owner might have, indeed, been Millinder's friend and, alone, the bandleader may have dropped by for an occasional drink. That kind of freedom might have been unheard of down South or in the Midwest but, yes, it was conceivable in Manhattan. Yet, it was this very semblance of freedom that lulled black New Yorkers into the delusion that their city was a haven or refuge of sorts. In this one establishment Millinder may have had "honorary white" status as an individual, but he made a mistake in assuming that status extended to include his black colleagues. Even there, the sight of a group of African American men together in a white venue inspired as much apprehension in the swing era as it does today.

According to John Hammond, wealthy jazz critic and producer (born into the Vanderbilt family, he advocated for racially mixed bands in the swing era) conditions in New York were such that

> If you wanted to go out for dinner with black friends . . . you would have to telephone the restaurant in advance to check if it was okay. If a black worked in downtown Manhattan and wanted a haircut, he would have to go all the way back to Harlem to get one. No restaurants or bars would

admit blacks, outside their own neighborhoods. And it didn't do to get sick. Hospitals were rigidly segregated, even in Harlem. One time, I think in 1937, Jo Jones—playing with Count Basie's band—badly needed attention. He had a neurological disturbance and the sensible place to go was the Neurological Institute right up on 168th Street in Harlem. It was only because the resident psychiatrist happened to be a music fan and knew who Jones was that he let him in. Jones was thus the hospital's first black patient. (Palmer, 292)

Incidents of black performers (and average citizens) being refused even emergency treatment at white hospitals were not uncommon and include a host of examples. After their European tour Webb contracted pleurisy while performing in Philadelphia at a white club. Rushed to the nearest hospital—in the white neighborhood of the club—she was refused admission. According to her account, she was treated by an African American doctor and recovered in the home of a concerned private citizen in the African American community where she was bedridden for several weeks. (9 December 1977) This is one of the remarkable but not unusual examples of the way in which the black community served its traveling performers beyond the level of basic needs, sometimes making the crucial difference between disaster and demise.

Williams related another common situation for the African American artist: performing at a place where one was prohibited from using some or all of the facilities. This restriction was a major problem until the end of the Civil Rights era. Again, such circumstances indicate the eccentricity and specificity of race prejudice. As mentioned earlier—and as inconceivable as it seems today—the Cotton Club discouraged its black performers from using the bathrooms. Williams recalls that, performing with Millinder's band in 1936 at Palisades Amusement Park in New Jersey, the band was allowed to use all the facilities in the park except the swimming pool. (15 August 1980)[22] (Among ordinary citizens living in Harlem as late as the 1950s—including my own family—it was common knowledge that the Palisades facility was "prejudiced" and to be avoided in favor of the Coney Island Amusement Park.) In one of her "Harlem to Broadway" columns Webb relates the following restrictions imposed at a Long Beach, Long Island resort club:

Discriminating tactics . . . have the Cotton Club boys and girls very much
ill at ease. It's not exactly fun to sit around a club from seven until the wee
hours. According to one of the stars of the revue, the residents of the resort
complained to the chief of police about the members of the show walking
around the streets. Now, the street door is locked after the troupe arrives,
and no one is allowed to go out in the street. Besides, store owners do not
wish to serve any one from the show. Rather than refuse them directly, they
jack the prices up so terribly high that it amounts to the same thing. And
this is New York. As Jackie Mabley would say, "You could fool me, Mazie."
(*Chicago Defender*, 22 July 1938)

As with Lucky Millinder and his friends at a midtown Manhattan white
bar, here, too, a white milieu rejected the idea of a group of black people
penetrating their environment. Again and again, the message from whites
to blacks was "stay out of our sight, and do your dancing in the dark."

Those whites who acted in ways that countered the segregationist
rules of the day were subjected to harassment. On such example is Jewish entrepreneur Barney Josephson, a pioneer integrationist, who opened
the first white New York nightclub for a mixed clientele, the Café Society in Greenwich Village, in 1938. He encountered racial antagonism
from a constellation of white interests including police, licensing authorities, reporters, booking agents, and some of the white customers.
(Josephson had had definite political purposes in establishing his club's
policies. For example, when the young Billie Holiday was engaged there,
he insisted that she end her set with the haunting *Strange Fruit*—the tale
of a lynching—and not return afterward for encores.)[23]

After her experiences with racism, Webb felt that she could come to
terms with her father's desertion of his family, a situation that had
plagued her childhood with questions and doubts: "I'm putting it together
as a grown person; after I grew up I could see it. I couldn't see it when I
was little, of course, but I can see now why he . . . never came back
here. . . . Many of the musicians in that band went to Europe and never
came back." (9 December 1977) When the occasion presented itself, she
and Norton took off on a vaudeville unit tour to Europe, with high hopes
for better opportunities on stage and in life.

The European Experience

Background

Although the phenomenon of African American performers traveling abroad flourished in the twentieth century, the precedent was established in the previous century. The New York African American actor Ira Aldridge became a renowned tragedian and interpreter of Othello on the London stage after his English debut in 1826. After experiencing racial tensions in England he moved on, living in Russia and allegedly marrying a Swedish baroness. He is buried in Poland. Master Juba (born William Henry Lane, a free black, around 1825), a popular Jig dancer of his era, went to London with a white minstrel troupe in 1846 and continued performing there until his death in 1852. The Fisk Jubilee Singers performed Negro spirituals for Queen Victoria in 1875; concert artist Elizabeth Taylor Greenfield, known as the Black Swan, toured Europe in 1853–54; and Sissieretta Jones, known as Black Patti, toured abroad in the 1890s. And there were many more concert and vaudeville artists and black minstrel troupes who made the grand tour.

In 1903 Bert Williams's and George Walker's operetta *In Dahomey* ran for seven months in London and was also played in command performance for the ninth birthday of the Prince of Wales. In 1905 the Memphis Students Band toured Europe for a year.[24] In the teens Ida Forsyne toured Russia as a specialty dancer. During World War I the James Reese Europe Fifteenth Regiment band spread the new word of jazz across Europe. By the time Louis Armstrong was performing in Europe in 1932, the Duke of Windsor is reputed to have quipped, "I'd rather hear Louis Armstrong play *Tiger Rag* than wander into Westminster Abbey and find the lost chord." (Giddins, 83)

By the 1920s scores of African American performers gained fame in Europe, with the career of Florence Mills of *Shuffle Along* and *Blackbirds* as the shining example. When she was a child growing up in Washington, D.C., the delicate, waiflike Mills had appeared as a singing and dancing prodigy in the drawing rooms of European diplomats in the capital—a serendipitous foretaste of what was to come. In 1929 writer Claude McKay, a temporary expatriate, boasted that many of Harlem's best and brightest were in Paris. The cast of *Blackbirds of 1929* was there: Adelaide Hall had replaced Florence Mills (who, by then, had died from exhaustion and overwork) in the starring role. To the Parisian elite and its avant-garde artists the cast proved enchanting: both onstage and off they were the toast of the town. Other African American performers were also at work in theaters and cabarets. In addition, there were African American schoolteachers, nurses, and other professionals who took advantage of the option to travel abroad. (They may have taken inspiration from returning World War I veterans' tales of freedom for blacks in Paris and other European locales.) McKay also cites the African American communists who used Paris as the stopover en route to and from the U.S.S.R. There were also black students from London, Scotland, Berlin, and French universities who spent their holidays in the City of Light. Added to this lot were African American academics, professors and administrators from traditionally black colleges and universities. Finally, there were writers, painters, and poets, including Countee Cullen. (1970, 311–12) Indeed, one could say that the Harlem Renaissance was alive and well in the Paris of 1929.

According to Webb, light skin color for female performers was not as important an issue in Europe as in the United States. What was most important abroad was attitude, style, élan, and charisma. Actually, Florence Mills, Alberta Hunter, and Josephine Baker—all brown-skinned—became stars there at a time (the 1920s) when the white American entertainment industry was not yet ready for them.

Although many performers encountered racial bias (see Ottley, 1951, and Dunbar), just as many insisted that their continental sojourns were problem-free. Although she witnessed color discrimination against dark-skinned men seeking housing accommodations in London, Webb recalls no instances of racism in Europe aimed directly against her or Norton—except for the team's expulsion from Nazi Germany, a move that Webb interpreted as anti-American, rather than anti-African American. It is worth noting that, as African peoples from the United States, African Americans have enjoyed a freedom in Europe that differs markedly from the European attitude toward continental Africans. As Roi Ottley observed, "Negro Americans never upset the social, economic or religious equilibrium. For as Christians and Americans they are products of Western civilization—and, as such, different from Europeans only in the color of their skins. And because they are essentially a racially mixed people of brown complexions mostly, Europeans are not inclined to place them in the same racial group as black Africans." (1951, 6)

In many instances, consciously and unconsciously, Europeans tended to champion equality for African Americans while condoning their own discrimination against continental Africans (other than major dignitaries), Caribbean nationals, and naturalized (French, German, or British) citizens of African descent; similarly, white Americans bemoaned fascism and communism and encouraged world democracy, but discounted racial oppression at home.

Unlike African Americans, Afro-Europeans possessed low visibility. Compared to the total African American population, they were few in number. Not confined to the likes of a Harlem or any geographical area, they lived and married among the mainstream populace and were more readily assimilable than black people in the United States. They generally fell into three categories: those who came to the country to study or teach, usually at an institute of higher education; those who were imported as cheap labor; and expatriate performers (like Webb's father, George Mitchell Smith, and Josephine Baker). They represented a spectrum of social classes and African diasporic origins. In all categories, these "new people" eventually assimilated and passed into the nationality of their adopted country (unless they made a concerted effort to locate other peoples of African origin in order to live with and marry their own). In one or two generations of intermarriage with native-born citizens while living in France, Germany, or Great Britain—and lacking the identity and support of a defined black community—peoples of African descent became acculturated and voluntarily or inadvertently lost their Africanist heritage. This is the price paid for assimilation.[25]

The Unit Revisited

The vaudeville unit discussed earlier was the means by which Norton and Margot went to Europe, traveling with a unit tour headed by bandleader Teddy Hill. Billed as the *Cotton Club Revue,* the tour had been booked by the William Morris agency. The show followed the same formula as the revues back home: first a full-cast opening, followed by the individual numbers, the requisite plantation scene, and exotic scene (here represented by Norton's "Spear Dance" backed up by the chorus line), ending with a full-cast finale. The order of the acts was slightly modified after the London opening. See the sequence as it was listed in the London Palladium program for 23 August, 1937 on page 153. (Webb collection)

After a prelude by the Teddy Hill orchestra (one of the many fine African American bands of the era, with the young Dizzy Gillespie playing trumpet) the organizing theme of the revue—"Class"—is introduced, with vocalist Scott, tap artist Bailey, and the full chorus of "Copper Coloured Gals" augmented by the "classy" presence of Norton and Margot. This walk-on opener was staged by Clarence Robinson.

The Freddy and Ginger team is an example of African American appropriation from whites. Picking up on the mainstream popularity of Fred Astaire and Ginger Rogers, Freddy Heron was teamed up just for this unit tour with dancer Edna Mae Holly (who later married boxer Sugar Ray Robinson). They performed what was known as a military tap routine; both wore costumes that looked like military dress uniforms and tapped in regimental unison. However, their routine did not attempt to imitate the Astaire-Rogers style, and they borrowed only in name.

Tramp bands were a staple in African American vaudeville. Unlike the fancy dress of the other acts on this show—class acts, in other words—they dressed in overalls and plaid shirts and made music by playing on washboards, buckets, tubs, and a variety of found instruments.

Next, backed by the chorus, male vocalist Rollin Smith sang a song that fit neatly into the stereotype: a song about barbecue is as fitting as Bessie Smith's *Just Gimme a Pig's Foot and a Bottle of Beer.*

Note the essential role that dance played in the structure and organization of the show. The Copper Coloured Gals, although they never appeared alone, were key in opening the show and backing up most of the acts. Indeed, discounting the chorus line and the Teddy Hill Orchestra, seven of the numbers on the program were dance routines (Freddy and Ginger, Whyte's Hopping Maniacs, Norton's Spear Dance, Bill Bailey, Freddy and Bailey tapping together, Norton and Margot, and the Berry Brothers) as compared to three nondance numbers (the Tramp Band, Rollin Smith, and Alberta Hunter).

Cotton Club revue at London Palladium, 1937

Cotton Club of New York presents

9. THE COTTON CLUB REVUE[26]

Lyrics and Music by BENNY DAVIS and J. FRED COOTS
Production and Dances by CLARENCE ROBINSON
Orchestral Accompaniment conducted by
TEDDY HILL

"CLASS" JESSYE SCOTT, NORTON and MARGOT, BILL BAILEY
and THE COPPER COLOURED GALS

FREDDY and GINGER, The Astaire and Rogers of Harlem

THE TRAMP BAND

LUKE MARTIN, EDWARD PRICE, HARRY FOX,
WOODROW JOHNSON, GEORGE ALFONZO, ERNEST WILLIAMS

"BARBECUE," ROLLIN SMITH and
THE COPPER COLOURED GALS

WHYTE'S HOPPING MANIACS
NAOMI WALLER, MILDRED CRUSE, LUCILLE MIDDLETON
FRANK MANNINGS, BILLY WILLIAMS, JEROME WILLIAMS

ROLLIN SMITH, Vocalising

"JUNGLE" HAROLD NORTON and
THE COPPER COLOURED GALS

BILL BAILEY, Rhythm Tap Dancer

ALBERTA HUNTER, "September in the Rain"

"COPPER COLOURED GAL" FREDDY, BILL BAILEY and
THE COPPER COLOURED GALS

NORTON and MARGOT, "Poems of Dance"

THREE BERRY BROTHERS
The Last Word in Dancing Acrobatics

"THE WEDDING OF MR. and MRS. SWING"
ALBERTA HUNTER introduces:
The Bride..................MARGOT
The Groom...............HAROLD NORTON
The Deacon................ROLLIN SMITH
Bridesmaids, Guests, etc.

FINALE BY THE ENTIRE COMPANY

GOD SAVE THE KING

Whyte's Hopping Maniacs were a group of Lindy-Hoppers organized by Herbert White, head bouncer at Harlem's Savoy Ballroom. These dancing teenagers were popularizing the swing aesthetic by providing the visual counterpart to big band music. Their style was fast and furious and involved the difficult, time-sensitive air steps that characterize professional Lindy performance. (Frank Manning, listed on the Palladium program as Mannings, celebrated his eighty-fifth birthday in 1999, and has continued to perform and teach the Lindy in England and the United States since the swing revival of the early 1980s.)

Vocalist Smith reappears for another offering. Since the first song was upbeat and staged with the chorus backing him up, this number was probably a ballad with Smith appearing alone. The chorus is called upon, once more, to landscape Harold Norton's Spear Dance—here listed as "Jungle." (See Chapter 2, note 14, for a brief outline of this solo.)

A tap dance solo by popular rhythm tap artist, Bill Bailey, brother of vocalist Pearl Bailey, was next on the bill. Rhythm tap dance—a style in which the dancer acts as a percussionist, using his dancing feet as the instrument—needs to be heard as well as seen. Therefore, Bailey performed this as a solo without the chorus behind him. First developed by John Bubbles around 1922, rhythm tap represented a "switch in rhythmic accenting [that] may be described as the difference between Dixieland and the swing beat."[27] Then Alberta Hunter, in the "featured girl singer" slot, delivered her solo ballad.

Next, tappers Heron and Bailey teamed up with the chorus in an homage to the "Copper Coloured Gal."

The slot immediately preceding the most important act was occupied by Norton and Margot, who performed either two or, if an encore was called for, three dances from their repertory. They utilized their Waltz interpretations extensively in Europe, dancing to *Liebestraum, Smoke Gets In Your Eyes,* and *The Song Is You* at this point in the program.

The final slot—the place of honor—belonged to the incredibly agile Berry Brothers, three dancing acrobats whose timing and daring was legendary. Like their chief competitors, the Nicholas Brothers, they were a flash tap act. The flash acts combined straight acrobatics with jazz dance—spins, knee-drops, splits—all the while maintaining precise timing and tapping as the foundation of their routine. This combination of acrobatics and jazz, of hot and cool, usually left audiences screaming for more.[28]

The finale, "The Wedding of Mr. and Mrs. Swing," returns to the Class theme of the opening, with Norton and Margot as the classy couple and the entire cast taking on the role of guests at their wedding. Staged by Robinson, this was the opportunity for each act to come on-stage for an individual eight- or sixteen-bar finale and then, once everyone was on, to all end performing in unison some popular dance step of the moment or the tap dancers' "Shim Sham Finale." Asked about their roles as bride and groom, Webb explained that it was a matter of a fast, rhythmic entrance "down the aisle," with the "deacon" leading the service in a swinging, four-to-a-bar rhythm. They danced and sang their way through, with the other guests entering on cue, not missing a beat:

Deacon: Oh-Do-You-Take-This-Woman-To-Be-Your-Wife
Norton: I-Do-[Beat-Beat]-I-Do-[Beat-Beat]
Deacon: Oh-Do-You-Take-This-Man-To-Be-Your-Husband
Margot: I-Do-[Beat-Beat]-I-Do-[Beat-Beat](15 August 1980)

This full-cast finale exhibited the swinging, Lindy-friendly beat that characterized and named the era.

In London the revue was featured at the Palladium, the foremost variety house in England. In Paris it played at both the Théatre des Ambassadeurs and the Moulin Rouge. Although the show format remained basically the same, numbers could be modified, added, or replaced, as was the flexible custom of the unit when touring stateside. With European manners and mores less restricted than customs in the United States, choreographer Clarence Robinson enjoyed increased creative leeway. Dancer Edna Mae Holly, the female half of Freddy and Ginger, was given a special number that Robinson had included in the show specifically for the Paris performances. Webb recalls, "Over there—in Paris—you could dance topless. I remember Clarence taking her aside . . . and Edna Mae would do a little topless number . . . a shake dance. That was exotic to them, and she was brown, so that was exotic, too." (27 August 1980)

This unit, like the ones back home, existed for the length of one tour. After its bookings in London and Paris, the European *Cotton Club Revue* was disbanded. Following the run, Norton and Margot were booked as an independent act at both the Moulin Rouge and the Harlem Montmartre Club.

Paris: The French

In June of 1937 the *Cotton Club Revue* cast had set sail, from New York to Le Havre, for Paris. New York theater critic Richard Watts traveled overseas with the group and favorably reviewed them, mentioning an incident that occurred in passage which stands as an ironic comment on the contrast between the racist attitudes left behind in America and the relative freedom these artists were soon to enjoy in Europe:

> [T]he only thing I have seen [since arriving in Paris] has been the Cotton Club revue at the Moulin Rouge, and it is a pleasure to add that the visitors from Harlem are performing splendidly. I had a decided interest in the company, because I crossed in the Lafayette with them, found them delightful people, and felt indignantly aroused when I found that one charming Southern lady on the boat was taking around a petition, asking the captain to forbid a proposed performance on behalf of the seamen's fund, which the Cotton Club actors had volunteered to give. It seems that the lady felt that the color of the players made them unworthy to offer a show for charity. (*New York Herald Tribune*, 1 August 1937)

Webb recalls that the troupe, which was traveling second class, was invited to do one performance in first class.

Of all the European capitals, Paris was the most receptive to African Americans and, in general, to persons of African descent. The French tended to use color differences as a new text to be "integrated" into their aesthetic picture, albeit under their auspices and control. Color—or the variety and contrast of colors in black and white skin tones—became an artistic palette used as a unique performance value in the sophisticated French variety shows. Nudity was used in the same way, as an interesting addition to the creative possibilities of performance.

The following story was told to me about a Josephine Baker performance. It illustrates how the celebration of color and nudity could work together to create a new reading. It was in the 1930s. Baker, the reigning queen of Paris night life—and affectionately dubbed by the French "La Bakaire," was the central figure in yet another lavish floor show structured around her charismatic presence and butter-smooth, albeit lightened, brown skin. It was an Easter spectacle at the Folies Bergères. Baker's function in the opening number was simple: in show girl fashion, to parade down a long decorated staircase, pivot at the bottom, reascend, and exit. Surrounded by a French male chorus line and accompanied by the stately, churchlike tones of organ music, she, the "boys," and the stage set were a pristine picture in white—lily-white, literally, with Easter lilies and white feathers as part of the costuming and decor. Slowly, like a Madonna, with hands folded prayerlike at her breast, she paraded down the flight of stairs in an elaborately concocted, full-length white gown. She posed at the bottom, slowly turned, and ever so majestically ascended before her exit—treating the astonished, bedazzled, and delighted audience to a full view of her nakedness: for her gown was backless, from top to bottom.[29] (La Bakaire's derrière was a major part of her exotic-erotic attraction for the French. Baker's biography by one of her adopted children, Jean-Claude, opens with this paragraph: "What an ass! Excuse the expression, but that is the cry that greeted Josephine as she exploded onstage in 'La Danse Sauvage.' It gave all of Paris a hard-on." [Baker and Chase, 3])

This example of reverse stereotyping—namely, black is fabulous, instead of black is ugly—was received as a positive valence by many colonized people of color who welcomed even this backhanded embrace. It allowed Baker to attain stardom in France at a time when neither white nor black America would give her kind a chance. In the same spirit, even French chorus lines were occasionally integrated at a time when American show business wouldn't consider the use of anything but white chorines for white shows—and when black shows reproduced the color-coded chorus lines of light-skinned or near-white girls described earlier. The French even dared what was total taboo for white America: a stage picture of a black man surrounded by white females:

The French variety theater, with an eye on the box-office, makes a play on the Negro's color. Black girls are often spotted among the pink fleshy girls of the Casino de Paris. Back in the days when America was outraged by

Paul Robeson's kissing the hand of a white actress in a Eugene O'Neill play,
All God's Chillun Got Wings, Habib Benglia, a magnificent-looking black
Senegalese was, to the delight of French audiences, dancing at the Folies
Bergère in a g-string with white girls surrounding him. (Ottley, 1951, 73)

For Norton and Webb, as for many other African American performers, visual artists, and writers, Paris became their home base while they
were in Europe. Like most black performers they stayed in the Montmartre section of the city, the bohemian artists' haven where the hotels
were reasonably inexpensive. The difference in—and the joy of—performing abroad compared to working in the United States was that the
Europeans regarded the team's work as an art form in the same way that
they regarded jazz as serious music that deserved attention. For the first
time in their career, they played in clubs where there was a different kind
of white audience, one that did not subject them to cries of "Get hot!" and
other exhortations inappropriate to their style. The European audience,
accustomed to an older tradition of ballroom dancing stemming from the
Viennese Waltz tradition, was more receptive to the team's Waltz repertory and did not insist that they adhere to a jazz or exotic stereotype so
often required of them back home. This cultural cosmopolitanism meant
artistic freedom and encouragement for them. For the first time in their
career—and, unfortunately, it was to be the only time—the team had the
opportunity to play first-class vaudeville and variety circuits. Webb said:

> It was easier to work over there. In spite of the fact that you had to stay
> up late, you didn't work as hard, because here at places like the Apollo you
> did four or five shows a day on the black circuit in the East [whereas in
> London and Paris they played venues with a two-a-day format]. (27 Au-
> gust 1980)
>
> We spent the most time in France. London had very strict rules: you
> could only work for so long with your permit, then you had to go back
> to Paris. But you could work in and out of Paris. You kept an address
> [there]. . . . Alberta [Hunter] used to work up in the Scandinavian
> areas—Norway and such—but she still kept an address in London and
> in Paris; and that's why a lot of people stayed in Paris for years. You
> could live fairly well, but you really didn't make a lot of money [there].
> (6 August 1978)

The fact that French salaries were low was compensated for by the measure of exposure and potential for work elsewhere in Europe that could result from performing in Paris, the center of European art and culture.

Once the Cotton Club unit tour was completed and the team was performing independently, they were introduced to a new variety format. Unlike African American programs, it was, instead, the classic variety format, with each act self-sufficient and no overall theme or unifying motif. When booked on a program at the Moulin Rouge, they performed only one number.

As performers often do, Webb and Norton spent free time with other artists, particularly African Americans. Even without the unit, they continued the habit of isolation from the world at large. Perhaps it was their American conditioning in the separation of the races, or perhaps it was the language barrier. (Although Webb had majored in French at Hunter College in New York, she left school in her junior year 1932 and certainly did not speak French to any substantial extent during her vaudeville career.) Unlike her colleague Alberta Hunter, whose circle of friends in London included nonperforming English females, Webb struck up no close friendships with native Europeans, entertainers or otherwise, in Paris or elsewhere. But this reclusiveness was also characteristic of the way that the team of Norton and Margot moved through the world and envisioned itself—as a kind of self-enclosed unit-within-the-unit, set apart from the black world as well as the white. Webb did not drink, smoke, or live the high life frequently associated with the show business profile. (She was not alone: many dancers who needed to maintain precision in performance and overall body tone were non-drinkers. And many swing era performers were barely of legal age.) Her main contacts were with other female performers, like Alberta Hunter, whose lifestyles and tastes were similar. In fact, Webb and Hunter, who was a good deal older, complemented each other:

> Alberta wanted always to be around people she considered ladies and gentlemen. . . . She found such a protégée in Margot. . . . "She kept telling me that's what she liked about me, that I was a lady," said Margot. "I was too dumb to be anything else. I was very naive." (Taylor and Cook, 134)

Although Webb was aware that there were other people of color in Paris—Africans and Indians—she had no personal contact with them. Paris managed to have people of various ethnicities living throughout the city with little contact or conflict. Norton and Margot lived, performed, and traveled in circles where they rubbed shoulders with other expatriates, artists, and nightclub clientele of various ethnic and national persuasions. Audience members also included stars like Maurice Chevalier, the international clientele of Parisian night life (including wealthy East Indians and Arabs), and an array of African American performers, sports figures, and other notables including Josephine Baker, African American ballroom dancer Paul Meeres (living abroad at the time), Langston Hughes, and Jesse Owens.

Riding the euphoric wave of what was to be the only period of mainstream popularity in their career Norton and Margot, for this moment, were no longer dancing in the dark.

London: The British[30]

In London, the Cotton Club Revue played only at the Palladium—at that time, a venue representing the pinnacle of achievement for the vaudeville artist. "Played at the Palladium" was as strong an endorsement for future bookings in white show business as "formerly of the Cotton Club" was in African American circles. The show opened to a mixed press. Apparently, the stereotypical English aplomb was rattled by the stereotypical African American élan. One critic flaunted a condescending, though positive, attitude toward African American revues: "Either you like Negro revues or you loathe them. I like them, but seldom so well as the 'Cotton Club Revue' at the Palladium. It is not too long—eighty minutes—and not too noisy, except in brief passages. And it is chock-full of irresistibly rapid, accurate, and varied rhythm. The singing would be better if some of the words were audible. But the dancing is beyond criticism." ("J.G.," *Evening News,* 27 July 1937) A second reviewer gave an exotic-erotic spin, making a figurative meal of these black artists: "Heat, speed and rhythm are the elements from which these coloured boys and girls from Harlem construct a wild,

kaleidoscopic entertainment. Dancing—tap, ballroom, and acrobatic—
is the prime ingredient of the highly-flavoured dish. . . . The copper-
coloured chorus girls show their dark loveliness. . . ." (*News Chronicle*,
27 July 1937) A third review revealed racially biased innuendo and most
clearly demonstrates the aesthetic oppositions that were at play: "the
crude colour of the clothes (such as there are), the shattering sounds
and irresistible rhythms . . . the swagger of the Copper Coloured Gals
and other ladies . . . these things assault the nerves and leave the mind
(which had anyhow better be left at home) too numb for protest. . . .
The nearest we came to discovering any genuine inspiration was in
Harold Norton's dance, Jungle, though even that relied chiefly on noise
and vitality for its effect." He depicted Whyte's Hopping Maniacs as
being "too mildly described" by their name, saying that they carried
their frenetic energy "to a point where it becomes almost unbearable to
watch." The disgruntled reviewer concluded with one final swipe at the
African American performers, ending on a chauvinistic note by comparing the visitors with what he deemed to be the authentic article—
namely, the English variety show that shared the Palladium bill with the
Cotton Club Revue. He described the English section of the program as
"the best tradition of music hall"—which included Ted Ray, ventriloquist Señor Wences (popular in Great Britain and the United States
through the 1950s), exhibition roller skaters, and an adagio acrobatic
act as "all good," and said that "Gene Sheldon managed to pack into a
few minutes more drollery than was to be found in the whole of the rest
of the program." (*The London Times,* 27 July 1937)

Another reviewer presented a more balanced perspective, recognizing
that he saw a performance reflective of a different aesthetic outlook, and
thus praised the very speed and risk-taking that the previous reviewer had
belittled:

The whole show provides interesting comparisons between the methods of
coloured and white artistes, from the wild abandon of the Copper
Coloured Gals to the graceful dancing of a pair of greatly contrasted ballroom dancers [meaning Norton and Margot, here presented as the "white"
end of the spectrum, as far as the performance aesthetic is concerned].
Much of its appeal lies in the speed at which everything is presented. The

artistes include Jessye Scott, a light-hued soubrette and dancer; Harold Norton, whose "Jungle" drum dance was one of the finest bits of work of the whole piece . . . Whyte's Hopping Maniacs . . . whose dancing is about the fastest . . . yet seen here, for it appeared that at any moment any of the girls might get her neck broken in the frenzied gyrations. . . . [B]ut the artistes to whom the palm has to be awarded are Alberta Hunter, who is already a big enough favourite with London audiences . . . and Bill Bailey. . . . (*The Performer*, 29 July 1937)

Apparently, the English had not yet been introduced to the Savoy Ballroom style of the Lindy-hop, which was characterized by daring, acrobatic lifts and air work and had already become a popular standard across the United States. It is noteworthy that Hunter, hired to replace vocalist Vivian Eley, commanded the greatest praise. Since her expatriation to London in the 1920s, her song style had been inflected and transformed by French and English cabaret traditions to the extent that, when she returned to the United States, she was termed a *chanteuse*. That the reviewer singles her out as his favorite probably suggests his aesthetic ethnocentricity.

It is also worth pointing out that the English reviewers admired Norton's Spear Dance. Unlike what might be expected by its title, this piece was in no way suggestive of African movement motifs but, instead, was choreographed in the style of modern dancer-choreographer Ted Shawn. Singling out Norton's solo for special praise again suggests the English reviewers' favoritism for numbers that manifested Europeanist aesthetic penchants.

Contrary to the lukewarm press for the show as a whole, Webb's memory of the Palladium audiences' reception to the work of Norton and Margot, alone, is a glowing one:

> . . . the audience there was remarkable. When we opened there, it was really surprising to us when we did our first number—which happened to be *Smoke Gets in Your Eyes*, I believe. [a Waltz interpretation.] They just applauded and applauded. . . . [T]hey had never seen a nonwhite team dance like that. . . . They always expected . . . from a black show [everything else that was programmed on the Cotton Club bill]. But they didn't expect us. And we were a little worried about it. . . . I knew that Norton could do his

African dance and get . . . a lot of applause. . . . But if our first number
together hadn't gone over . . . we wouldn't have made it at all. But it was a
terrific success. (Dixon-Stowell, 1978, 23–24)

In this statement Webb corroborates the assertion about English aesthetic ethnocentrism. In these three examples—Norton's solo, the dancing of Norton and Margot, and Alberta Hunter's vocalizing—the English
reviewers seemed most content to see African American performers
adopting Europeanist aesthetic paradigms. Perhaps it was due to the
presence of a considerable number of African and Caribbean blacks living in Great Britain that accounted for this instance of the white British
(unlike the French) privileging black aesthetic assimilation over black ex-
oticism. Although the everyday contact afforded by living and working
with people of African lineage may not erase racism, it may serve to
dampen exotic stereotypes.

Still, the London reviews raise an important issue: the problem of
British prejudice against peoples of African lineage was both acknowledged and disputed during this era. British nationals of African ancestry
had clashed with whites in the race-labor riots of 1919 in London, Manchester, Hull, Cardiff, and Liverpool, riots sparked by job competition between white and black seamen and dock workers. Numerous other
writers have pointed to serious problems in the United Kingdom.[31] As
Roi Ottley stated, "one must understand that Britons have the same
racially split personality as our own Americans, who can wage war for
freedom abroad and deny it to black citizens at home." (1951, 40) According to African American anthropologist and historian J. A. Rogers,
the British passed their racial biases on to their new world colony, the
United States. (1940, 60) And Harold O. Lewis surmised that the British
are likely to reflect even more racism towards people of African ancestry
than white Americans because their discrimination may be reinforced by
an entrenched class system. (584) Still another author, Monroe N. Work,
addressed the issue of a British color-caste system: "[L]ight colored Negroes are accepted almost anywhere in England; the darker ones, including dark Hindus, are usually barred. . . . Men of color, business men from
the United States, the British colonies, students, and outstanding Indian
politicians have been barred from entering hotels." (349)

Such a system of color discrimination—regardless of ethnic background—is a far cry from the American system of racial categorization.
As discussed earlier, in the United States there was one set of rules for
treatment of African Americans, regardless of their skin color, and another separate code of conduct toward people of color from other world
cultures, also regardless of skin color. Conversely, according to the quote
above, all people of color—regardless of national origin—were accepted
or rejected by the British in proportion to the lightness or darkness of
their skin color—or the degree to which their complexion approximated
that of whites. In other words, the British system privileged color over
race, whereas the American system placed the race prejudice over and
above discrimination based on skin color.[32] Even today, the tendency in
the British press and British popular terminology is to categorize all people of color under the rubric of "black"—regardless of their ethnicity or
national origin and whether they are from Asia, the Indian subcontinent,
Africa, Australia, or the Americas. Such a generalization has never occurred in the United States. It is interesting to ponder the political implications of both systems, and which system of discrimination is less, or
more, inhumane.

Webb was aware of the British color bar as it affected the male performers in the *Cotton Club Revue*. Since there were no dark-skinned female performers—only "copper-colored gals"—the issue did not arise
among the women. The hotel where Webb stayed before moving into Alberta Hunter's home allowed the female performers to rent rooms but not
the men—many of whom were dark complexioned. Webb's observation is
corroborated, on another public front, by an incident experienced by the
renowned—and dark-skinned—Paul Robeson: he and his wife were refused service at London's swank Savoy Grill in the late 1920s. "For most
people of color England was hardly paradise." ("Paul Robeson")

African American bandleader Cab Calloway was impressed that the
red carpet was rolled out for him at the major, centrally located London
hotels. (1976, 137) But, in light of the foregoing, it is misleading for him
to extol the virtues of freedom for blacks in England: unlike Robeson and
the many other black-skinned male musicians, Calloway was white-
skinned and easily fit the British acceptance mode based on skin color.
Moreover, according to Webb, the establishment that refused to put up

the Cotton Club men was a small private hotel, the equivalent of an American bed-and-breakfast, in the Russell Square area of London. (22 May 1980) Like Calloway, the rebuffed men were also able to obtain lodgings in the main hotels in central London. The drawback was that these hotels were expensive. Another difference in American and British racial etiquette thus emerges: in the United States, discrimination would have kept the African Americans out of the public visibility of the expensive, central, downtown areas; in frugal England, the person of color was denied the bargain of reasonably priced accommodations. The specific eccentricities of racial injustice are predictably unpredictable.

In addition to the Savoy Grill incident, Paul Robeson had other problems in London. Like Ira Aldridge a century before him, he was the object of English outrage and disgust simply for playing the role of Othello—this time to white British Peggy Ashcroft's Desdemona. (Ottley, 1951, 26; "Paul Robeson") Many other performers were troubled by racism while in London: for example, when she was still a chorine in a Buddy Bradley London revue the dancer-actress Jeni LeGon reported her experiences with English racism in an article entitled "Jeni LeGon Likes London, But Not Its Race Prejudice." (*Norfolk Journal and Guide*, 1 February 1936)

With such a burden of evidence against it, London still presented itself as a refuge, with a strong body of testimony to support that contention. American-born black choreographer Buddy Bradley found the city a welcome change and an artistic haven after his experiences in New York. He had begun choreographing in London in 1933. (Stearns and Stearns, 160–69) As late as 1966 he remained an expatriate teacher and choreographer, happily redomiciled in a city where he was respected, acknowledged, and amply recompensed for his efforts. Like Bradley, Alberta Hunter and Adelaide Hall (of *Blackbirds* fame) stayed on as permanent expatriates; they may have encountered instances of British racism but, obviously, they deemed those rebuffs more tolerable than the American brand. Other lesser known performers made the same choice, when given the opportunity. Yet, most returned to the United States.

Bringing with them their swing music and Lindy-hopping—as interpreted by both blacks and whites—the American military had a substantial influence on British social life during World War II. The white military brought another significant import—namely, American racism which, as discussed above, was vastly different from the British brand. It was partly due to the ingrained American prejudices against interracial marriage that black GIs were prohibited from marrying their white British girlfriends. But this is not to let the British off the hook. As in the United States, the story was complex and many sided. On the one hand, "The private correspondence of the Foreign Secretary, Anthony Eden, shows how he tried to stop them [African American soldiers] coming, citing 'the unsuitability of the British climate.'" (Brooks) On the other hand, "British civilians displayed a disconcerting readiness to integrate the new [African American] arrivals in the social life of the country. . . . Sometimes they even preferred black troops to white: 'I don't mind the Yanks, but I don't care much for the white fellas they've brought with them,' one perverse countryman remarked." (Ziegler)

NAACP Field Secretary Walter White traveled to England during the war and reported, firsthand, on the openness and fraternity of the British, even in the face of the white American military's antiblack racism:

> One had told of the distinguished British family inviting a group of American soldiers to their home for dinner and dancing. Everything moved smoothly during the meal, but when one of the Negro soldiers danced with one of the English women, he had been assaulted by a Southern white soldier. A free-for-all followed in which the British took the side of the Negroes. And there was the story of the pub keeper who had posted a sign over his entrance reading "THE PLACE FOR THE EXCLUSIVE USE OF ENGLISHMEN AND AMERICAN NEGRO SOLDIERS." (Back, 190)

After living in the Russell Square boarding house at the beginning of the six-week Palladium run of the Cotton Club, Webb moved in with Alberta Hunter for the duration of the engagement. Then she and Norton returned to Paris for independent bookings at the Moulin Rouge and the Harlem Montmartre Club. They traveled South to the Italian Riviera for an engagement at the Casino Municipale in San Remo (September 1937). By October of 1937, they had traveled to Berlin to begin what appeared to be a successful, open-ended engagement at the Café Sherbini which, when it concluded, was to be followed by bookings throughout Europe and in Egypt (Cairo) through contacts that had been supplied by Hunter. However, two months into their run, the Berlin engagement came to an unanticipated abrupt end.

Berlin: The Germans

"During the Hitler years a subversive joke could be heard in Europe. Question: 'Who is the most desirable woman in Germany?' Answer: 'An Aryan grandmother.' An Aryan grandmother was one of the factors that determined whether a person was racially acceptable under the Nuremberg Laws." (Spiegl, 538)

The German love-hate attitude towards people of African descent was as eccentric and site-specific as in other European countries. The main difference was that racism was accorded legal status in Germany in 1935, the year the Nazis established a codified system of race laws forbidding citizenship, property ownership, and intermarriage to persons of Semitic origin, with additional regulations passed through 1943 that expanded these laws to include, among other categories, people of African descent. A decade before Norton and Margot were expelled, members of the cast of *Chocolate Kiddies* had experienced German racial erraticism firsthand. As was the case with the English, the Germans were willing to accord preferential treatment to African American vaudeville entertainers, but they were harshly biased against continental Africans:

> When *Chocolate Kiddies* had first played Berlin [1925], many Berliners had been hostile, not only because the actors were black, but because it was thought that they were blacks from French Colonial Africa.
>
> A year earlier, France had sent a regiment of tall, black Senegalese soldiers to Bavaria, hoping this would intimidate Germany into paying its war debt. . . . It had to be made clear to the public that the *Chocolate Kiddies* company was American, before tensions were dispelled. (Baker and Chase, 125)

Trumpeter Doc Cheatham was a member of the Sam Wooding band, the group that played for this show, one which had been written by the young, brilliant Duke Ellington in record time. (In his naiveté Ellington was paid, up front, for composing the show but received no royalties or further income, even though this hit ran for two years in Berlin). In a BBC radio interview Cheatham said that most people in Berlin were friendly but "there were some that gave us a little problem. One night a guy came out organizing in front of the theater. He said, 'Get these black people out of here—they used to cut off our noses and ears during the war!'" ("From Harlem to Broadway," 1995) Stories such as these circulated about Africans fighting against Germany during World War I. Even after *Kiddies* closed, Wooding's band remained popular in Berlin and played there regularly, from 1925 to 1931. They also toured Eastern Europe and Russia. In England in 1926 they were given a rather cool reception, while Germans remained loyal. However, jazz was shortly labeled degenerate, American recordings were destroyed, and no black musician would perform on a German stage for nearly two decades.

Josephine Baker was untouched by problems such as these as her experiences were in pre–Nazi Germany, when Berlin was an open city of freewheeling mores with regard to art, politics, sex, gender, drugs, alcohol: experimentation was invited and encouraged on all fronts. The early Baker was perfect for just such a moment in time. She was regarded simultaneously as a "figure of the contemporary German 'expressionism,' [and] of the German 'primitivism.'" (Baker and Chase, 126) The exotic-erotic trope was hard at work here, but Baker manipulated it to her advantage and seemed unperturbed—innocent yet savvy, sophisticated, and self-possessed even in the following situation on 13 February 1926:

> Count Harry Kessler, a publisher and art collector . . . recorded the fact that [Max] Reinhardt [the renowned German director] had called him at 1 A.M. . . . and invited him to come over. Kessler went and found Reinhardt "surrounded by half a dozen nude girls including Miss Baker also naked except for a pink gauze loincloth. . . . Miss Baker danced with extreme grotesque artistry and pure style, like an Egyptian or archaic figure. . . . She does it for hours without any sign of fatigue. . . . She does not even perspire. . . . An enchanting creature, yet almost without sexuality. With her one thinks of sexuality as little as at the sight of a beautiful feral beast." (ibid., 127)

To perform in a grotesque style is one facet of the theatrical technique known as alienation, which removes one from representational/emotional involvement with the performance/text. It was a modernist technique used in Brechtian theater to create distance/detachment from the subject and object of performance, rather than sentimental identification with them. The fact that Baker performed without becoming exhausted is another sign that she is not "throwing herself away" by her performance. Her sublime level of control was further indicated by the absence of sweat: she looked totally engaged—hot—but remained cool. In her intuitive application of avant-garde performance techniques, Baker was more modern than modernism itself.

On the one hand, for African Americans in the swing era, there was little day-to-day oppression in Nazi Germany. For Norton and Margot, Berlin offered the optimum in performing conditions—a reasonable number of shows per day, steady work, attentive audiences, a comfortable performance space, and a good salary. They would have been content to remain there indefinitely—unaware, as they were, of the political strife around them. On the other hand, Nazi race laws could be used to arbitrarily enforce segregation. As with other European nations, the pivotal point was the difference between Germany's treatment of visiting African American performers, continental Africans, and its own citizenry of African descent. There were an estimated two thousand blacks in Germany in 1933. (Lewis 1947, 578) This number increased following World War II as a consequence of "brown" war babies in Germany, as in other western European nations.

By 1933 Afro-Germans realized the potential danger of Nazi power and formed the League for the Defense of the Negro Race, an organization headquartered in Paris. Madeline Guber, an Afro-German born and raised in Berlin stated that "Because there were not so many of us . . . we had lived pretty well. But the Nazis brought their theories of racial superiority, and things became bad. We could not work in the factories. We were scorned as semi-apes. We were insulted on the streets." (Ottley 1951, 154) She stated that peoples of African descent were also forcibly sterilized, a fact borne out by other sources. (Lewis, 579)

As mentioned before, some of the German antiblack sentiment in the swing era was a direct result of the German experience in World War I:

"For the German people an awareness of the Negro came in even more intensified form as part of the anti-French propaganda during the occupation of the Rhineland by French colonial troops. Attacks against the Senegalese appeared in the German press, in songs, and even in texts used in some of the German schools." (Lewis, 578) The stage was set, therefore, for the Nazi ban on African performers in 1933, which preceded the anti-Semitic Nuremberg legislation in 1935. Germans also looked back to their historians, poets, and philosophers, pulled racist seeds from the writings of Nietzsche, Hegel, and Fichte, and used them for their own ends. The ban termed African art—along with many African-influenced modern works—as "degenerate, degrading, and in violation of German spirit." (ibid.)

Some Africans and African Americans were incarcerated in concentration camps—along with Jews, gypsies, and non-Jewish Germans who were homosexuals, communists, jazz buffs, avant-garde artists, or political protesters of Nazism. According to one concentration camp detainee, the treatment of prisoners of African lineage went through a schizoid about-face. At first they were subjected to extremes of cruelty—randomly murdered, denied food to the point of starvation, not allowed to talk with whites. For no apparent reason these policies were reversed, and the same prisoners became the object of special privileges, such as being given soap or being allowed an occasional bath. (It is probable that the Nazis hoped to turn one incarcerated group against another by selectively extending or denying basic needs.)

Ottley recounts the story of an expatriate African American musician who had given up American citizenship to become a French citizen. He was apprehended as an American during the Nazi occupation of Paris: "The German camp commander, quickly recognizing his musicianship, assigned him to conduct the camp's fifty-piece symphony orchestra made up of white prisoners." (1951, 163–64) The musician commented on the irony that he wouldn't have been allowed to conduct a white orchestra in America (or, for that matter, anywhere in Germany, except in a death camp).

The Nazis had a particularly perverse, ambivalent relationship to jazz. The Hitler Youth were adamantly, violently opposed to swing music and dance. These right-wing young people were instrumental in targeting their peers, known as Swing Youth, for official punishment. Swing music and the Lindy—known in Germany and England by its white American moniker, the Jitterbug—were considered morally degenerate, dangerous, and a cause of juvenile delinquency. The Hitler Youth acted as informers, infiltrating and reporting on swing dances and festivals. Between 1942 and 1944 an estimated 75 swing enthusiasts were confined in concentration camps by the SS. Yet, the SS indulged their own taste for swing by encouraging the creation of jazz groups in the camps with prisoners performing the taboo music for the officers.[33]

During their occupation of Paris, the Nazis, German and French, continued their inconsistent behavior towards blacks. On the one hand, they banned performers of African descent and destroyed a French monument to the Afro-French soldiers of World War I. On the other hand, they allowed Africans to continue to attend universities and to hold civil service positions, with Marshall Pétain naming an Afro-Frenchman, Henri Leméry, as minister of colonies. (Ottley 1951, 164) While some Nazis paraded their Afro-French mistresses through the city, they accused African American soldiers of sexual atrocities against German women. These fluctuations were attributed to Hitler's hatred of African peoples coupled with his desire to win them over— with an eye to eventual enslavement of Africa and its resources through neocolonialism.

Norton and Margot performed in Germany and were written about in the African American press as "the team who broke the Jim-Crow barrier of Hitler. . . . Working permits were obtained by Norton and Margot, along with an admonition to be careful of their behavior in the Nazi capital. Previously many Negro artists have been so careless . . . that the entire race has received a black eye, thus accounting for the ban against colored acts." (Afro-American, 18 November 1937) It is a sad statement about American political ignorance and African American lack of self-esteem that this black publication attributed to individual bad conduct a much more perverse scheme—namely, the German politics of ethnic cleansing, coupled with the concept of degenerate art, which discriminated against all art forms that were modern and/or non-Aryan. In the

Third Reich's attack on modernism all modern music forms were vilified. "Jazz was attacked and viciously parodied in so-called Degenerate Music exhibitions. One former jazz musician remembers that the Nazis prohibited all mutes,[34] which 'turned the noble sound of wind and brass instruments into a Jewish . . . howl.'"("Degenerate Art") In an irony of history that made strange bedfellows, jazz musicians were classified in the same category—that is, degenerate—as German avant-garde composers such as Hindemith, Berg, and Schoenberg. All were outlawed.

Yet, in the face of the startling upheaval taking place in world history, Americans, black and white, remained ignorant—sometimes willfully so—of the atrocities already set in motion by the Third Reich. Simply stated, Nazi Berlin was no longer the swinging city of the 1920s. If African American vaudevillians expected to be able to smoke marijuana (a common practice at the time) in Berlin in 1933—as they had in 1925—they were headed for big trouble.

It was only years later that Webb realized the racist underpinnings of the German experience. Her friend and coperformer, Valaida Snow, was one of the victims of Nazism and had been imprisoned in a concentration camp. Most probably she was handed over to the Germans through the Vichy network in Paris. Snow returned to the United States and performed in spite of physical and mental degeneration; she died in the 1950s. Webb recalls others who did not survive: "We have friends in Boston who have never been seen since. One [was an] artist that we knew up there in the Hemmings family [the Boston descendants of Sally Hemmings, slave mistress of Thomas Jefferson and mother of his mulatto offspring]. He got out, but his wife and family were left . . . when the Germans went through Paris. There were many blacks who were living in Paris who didn't get out." (22 May 1980) But when Norton and Margot arrived in 1937, these atrocities lay in the future, the Nazi terror had yet to apply its stranglehold across Europe, and the team looked forward to a period of steady work in Europe while reaping the benefits of expatriation.

In Germany the team performed only one or two numbers in the show at the Café Sherbini, a small but fashionable Berlin cabaret. Norton did not perform his well-liked Spear Dance because of the awkwardness in transporting the large drum, which he left in Paris to be sent back to the United States. Webb recollects that the Germans

Were very polite. We never had any problem there. I do remember that security men in plainclothes always followed us. I knew that. But, since we
didn't know what was happening anyway and weren't politically involved,
there was nothing they could find out . . . but they always followed us . . .
I guess when things got bad . . . they sent for us to get our passports in
order and leave.

    We were doing very nicely there working in a German club which had
only two acts there—us and a girl singer who was fair complexioned. . . . I
think she was passing—although she swore she was white, you know. But
in those days we ran into a lot of people in Europe who were passing. . . .
We went into restaurants where SS troops came in their uniforms. They
were parading all the time. . . . All we saw parading up and down the
streets were healthy, rosy-cheeked German kids. They were training them
from little kids, with uniforms and everything—great discipline. And the
men were great big buxom fellows. Whenever they came in to any club, we
stood up and said, "Heil, Hitler"—or else! We knew enough to do that—
yes. Everybody did. It was just a common thing, as we would say, "Hi,
everybody," you'd say, "Heil, Hitler." . . . (Dixon-Stowell, 1978, 28–32)

From the twenty-twenty vision of hindsight, their innocence may
seem inconceivable. But other young performers found themselves just as
blind to the truth. And, at this pre–World War II time, the true Nazi phi-
losophy and the plans for extermination were not blasted across the media
as public knowledge. The 1997 musical *Band in Berlin,* about the German
singing group, the Comedian Harmonists, makes the same point. As one
of the characters in this German-Jewish group says, "What to do? Everybody had to say 'Heil, Hitler' at one time or another. What did we know?
We were musicians, and we were young. . . ."(Feldman)

    Still, one can detect in Webb's statement that being shadowed by po-
lice and given officially ordered passage home were circumstances that
made the team feel important and protected—a sad comment on the fact
that they garnered no such consideration back home, neither in white nor
black circles. To be treated "politely" (and politeness was of utmost importance to Webb) in public and private venues, to perform at a lush
white club, to live well and have private bodyguards paid for by the government—that was the difference between dancing in the dark and dancing front and center. From a personal standpoint they had little to

complain about, and it was good while it lasted. Ironically, performance conditions were most favorable for the team in the one European nation that was as racially pathological as the United States. Here, again we see the basic paradox inherent in the German attitude toward African American performers manifested in the policy toward Norton and Margot, namely, an abrupt about-face from receptivity to rejection.

As the Sherbini engagement progressed, a series of incidents concerning the manager of the cabaret made Webb aware of problems for Jews in the city. "The manager or the owner of the club was Jewish [Webb wasn't clear if she held both titles] . . . She did get out. She married an Egyptian. The Egyptian students used to come to the club at night. They were all about our complexion, and she married one of them in order to get out, and we figured something was wrong then, because she was twice his age. . . ." (Dixon-Stowell, 1978, 29)

With almost no notice they were summarily delivered free boat tickets and orders to sail home from Hamburg in December 1937. What they were unaware of was the fact that in July 1937, when the Cotton Club Revue was playing at the Palladium in London, Hitler had opened in Munich the House of Culture and had initiated the pageant series titled "Two Thousand Years of German Culture"—which was to be an annual open-air spectacle with a cast of thousands to celebrate a mystical, mythological, and totally fabricated Aryan German heritage. He had also gathered together all the artworks deemed dangerous to be displayed in his infamous Degenerate Art Exhibit, which opened in Berlin the day following the opening of the House of Culture in Munich. ("Degenerate Art") Thus, Norton and Margot had arrived in Berlin soon after the Third Reich placed a national stranglehold on the arts. It is amazing that the team was invited at all. Surely it had to do with the fact that they were light-skinned (as Webb pointed out, their complexions resembled the Egyptians who attended the Sherbini) and that their performance was in a white genre. But then there came the moment when, like the Jews, it didn't matter if one was a well-heeled Egyptian or a suave, light-skinned African American dance team—all non-Aryans were given their walking papers.

There was no question of trying to eke out a living by remaining in Paris. That city was open and friendly, but its main function was as a *pied-*

à-terre before heading out for money-making bookings elsewhere. At the time they were forced out of Germany, Norton and Margot were working out the arrangements for engagements at the Kit Kat Club in Cairo, Egypt, the Thalia in Bucharest, Rumania, and the Ambassador's Cabaret of the Palace Hotel in Copenhagen, Denmark through Arena Tivoli, a Scandinavian vaudeville booking agency. To remain in Europe they needed these bookings immediately, but negotiations were not confirmed. Without secure bookings or a job in hand—and with Europe and the world embroiled in escalating global conflicts that caused even a dance team to be expelled from Germany—they returned home. With no social obligation or responsibility in Europe, their grasp on German reality minimal, and their connections to the daily life of Germans tenuous, they were even more insulated abroad than on the road in white America. They were strangers in a strange land. With their presence dispensable, their departure was inevitable.

Expatriates and Tourists

Perhaps for every African American artist the European experience raises the tempting proposition of expatriation. According to swing era vocalist Edith Wilson, it was a chance to travel and a temporary respite from (American) racism. (Goddard, 84) When asked her choice, Alberta Hunter put it bluntly: "Of course I prefer Europe. . . . What Negro with sense doesn't?" (Taylor and Cook, 114) Whether in Europe for a week, a month, a year, or permanently, the African American performer was sure to encounter a race-specific culture shock on returning to the States. For people like Hunter and Josephine Baker, there was an experience of deep disillusionment: after having expatriated during the 1920s, garnered fame and fortune on major, mainstream European circuits, and returned home in the 1930s to establish a career in America, they found that Americans, black and white, gave them a cool reception. They were treated as if the entertainment industry and the public were determined to make them pay dues for having left the American racial morass. It was as though they had been disloyal by allowing continental influences to alter their styles; that is, Hunter and Baker, like Norton and Margot, had adopted white stylistic codes that were atypical in black performance traditions. Neither was able to establish a career at home, and race played a big part in the problem. According to Hunter, "The white agents here . . . tell Negroes that a European reputation amounts to nothing but they will pay a white performer twice the salary he formerly received after he comes back from abroad. Many of these white performers I have myself seen hissed off the stage in Paris and London." (ibid.) Ultimately Baker and Hunter returned to their bases in Paris and London respectively (although, later in life, Hunter returned home and had a comeback career in the United States beginning in 1977).[35] The opportunities afforded them in Europe simply did not exist at home.

Other performers toured Europe but, despite Hunter's claim, did not expatriate. Take for example the one-legged tap dancer, Peg Leg Bates. Like most swing era performers, he began his professional career as a teenager, moving from minstrel shows to carnivals and then the Theater Owners' Booking Association black vaudeville circuit. He was spotted by Lew Leslie, in whose *Blackbirds of 1928* he performed on Broadway and then in Paris in 1929. He did not expatriate at that time. Unlike Hunter and Baker, Bates's act remained within the parameters of what was acceptable for blacks to perform, thus allowing him, like a few other top tap artists, to be booked on white American vaudeville circuits during the 1930s. He played at major white New York theaters such as the Paramount, the Roxy, and the Capital. In 1938, as the only African American performer in the show, he toured Australia. He did not expatriate at that time either. Indeed, with the exception of a small nucleus of individuals, African Americans traveling to Europe did not choose to remain abroad, even when given the economic and social opportunity.

Of the few who chose expatriation, numerous lesser-known figures settled in Europe around the same time as Hunter and Baker. Even earlier, concert vocalist Coretti Arle-Titz had lived and performed in both czarist Russia and the U.S.S.R., beginning in 1913. Interviewed for *Crisis* magazine in 1937, she had only words of love and praise for Bolshevik Russia, although she had felt the racism of the czarist regime. After a brief visit to the United States (she had returned only once), she was anxious to return to her Soviet home. During an interview by an African American who had met her in Russia she said, "I returned to America to see my mother, but my heart remained in Russia, where among the Russian masses I could forget that I am colored. I found America, with its oppression, frustration, Jim Crow and hypocrisy unbearable and soon returned to my beloved Russia." (Hall, 204)

What had worked for Arle-Titz might actually have been the sore spot for many African Americans: to expatriate might mean giving up one's identity, forgetting that one was "colored." Another unsavory aspect of expatriation was the singling out of the African American as an exotic-erotic—an otherworldly, somewhat alien object of the white gaze. Whether performers or private citizens, African Americans tell of being ogled on the street and in the theaters and public spaces of otherwise sophisticated, cosmopolitan centers. Thus, on the one hand, expatriation may be seen as the most liberating choice for the African American; on the other hand, if being freed of racial strife means having to give up identification with one's ethnic heritage in favor of the new order—even when one is still singled out and treated as Other—it may seem best to deal with life on the home battleground.

In Western Europe both transient and permanent expatriates were connected by a word-of-mouth network. Therefore, when Norton and Webb performed in Europe, other African Americans came to see them and were instrumental in helping them arrange other engagements and living accommodations. Alberta Hunter and vocalist Adelaide Hall were especially helpful to them. Then, there were African American meeting places in Paris and London, some of which were owned by blacks. (Although these were gathering places for African Americans, all ethnic groups were welcomed.) In Paris there was Bricktop's exclusive club, beginning in the 1920s—which was more a black-owned, aristocratic white club with black entertainment than an African American hangout. Louis Mitchell had a café and restaurant; Freddy Taylor, a former entertainer, owned a club on the Rue Notre Dame de Lorette. (Later, by the 1950s, musician Art Simmons's cabaret, The Living Room, on the Rue du Colisée, became a popular hangout.) Similar spots existed in other European cities, including Rome and Copenhagen. By 1934 the phenomenon of African Americans in Europe was so common that the *Chicago Defender* ran a column from Paris (1934 and 1935) to report expatriate news and gossip. It was titled "Montmartre" and was signed, "the Street-Wolf of Paris"; later it was called "Across the Pond," and the "Street-Wolf" signed his real name—Edgar A. Wiggins.

As in the experience of Coretti Arle-Titz, an interesting side trip in the expatriate and tourist experience was the seduction of Bolshevism and the possibility of traveling to or living in Soviet Russia. Not only did people like Paul Robeson and Langston Hughes journey to the Soviet Union, but also less well-known African Americans—students and professionals as well as artists—went alone or in groups. Communists courted African Americans in their effort to recruit oppressed minorities to the Bolshevik cause. In the spring of 1935 Norton and Webb had begun negotiations for performing in the U.S.S.R., even getting so far as to have a contract. The team had dreamed of the Soviet experience as an opportunity to perform in ways prohibited to them in America—or even in Western Europe. Webb said that the Bolshevik recruiters

> would come up to Harlem and try to get you to come to these affairs and to meet other Communists, and they [told us that they] would be very anxious to show America that they could show black ballet dancers—which was unheard of in those days—in their country. That would show America up. That was why we were so anxious to go over there and work with the Russians. I'm not thinking of the political side of it; I'm just thinking about the opportunity of dancing—and studying! We could have studied. Because we just stopped [studying in the United States]. After a while, you just say, "What do I need all this technique for?" (5 June 1980)

As Webb explained, the romance with Russia, for the African American performer, was not necessarily political but, more likely, aesthetic. In the 1930s there was as yet no American ballet tradition, and both the United States and Europe were awed by the legendary artistry of the Kirov and Bolshoi traditions. Anna Pavlova, Vaslav Nijinsky, and the Ballets Russes de Monte Carlo with its large contingent of Russian émigrés—all had performed in the United States; Norton's and Webb's ballet teachers were Russian émigrés. The team would have been part of a unit with their colleague Clarence Robinson as choreographer. However, like many Soviet offers, this one fell through, and these performers were lucky that they didn't wind up stranded in the U.S.S.R., which had happened to others. For example, a 1932 article in *Crisis* reported that a group of African Americans who went to Moscow to make a film on black life in

America and depended on their anticipated salaries in order to get by, found that "in the face of signed contracts calling for three months' work with a guarantee of return fare to America, [there was] issued from the Soviet Department of Education a curt, terse statement ordering all work on the picture to cease immediately." ("Black Is White Is Not," 1932) In any case, whether in the U.S.S.R. or Western Europe, it was the lure of a racist-free daily life and nondiscriminatory work opportunities that enticed African Americans to expatriate.

Trumpeter Arthur Briggs explained that, during the swing era, the expatriate colony of African Americans in Paris—visual artists, musicians and other performers, and boxers—were generally well-behaved. (Goddard, 284) The fact that he brings up the issue of behavior is interesting. Part of the African American expatriate's unwritten pact with the host country was to "become white" while, at the same time, remaining apart from the host culture: in it but not of it, in other words. In this black-but-white context, we can see that there were two Josephine Bakers with two careers. The first was the black Baker: outrageous, rubber-legged, mugging and screwing up her face, crossing her eyes—a marvelous clown. After lessons in diction, table manners, etiquette, and singing in French, German, and Spanish, what emerged was the second Baker—the white Josephine who by 1932 sported a blonde wig and sang *Si J'Étais Blanche* (If I Were White) at the Casino de Paris. This is a far cry from the "primitive" Baker who had emerged on the continent less than a decade earlier wearing only a girdle of bananas in the *Revue Nègre*. But such a metamorphosis was the requisite and formula for success for the expatriate artist who hoped to become a star. La Bakaire became an honorary French person and, in doing so, an honorary white. One savvy critic of the era, Nancy Cunard, stated the Baker issue in a way that still resonates today: "Aesthetically speaking it is also a perfect show-up of the ignorance and lack of taste of the critics in not seeing just what *was* so fine about this new star, and in chorusing their desire for it to be brought under the 'toning-down' process, brought into line with the revolting standard of so-called 'national taste.'" (329, author's emphasis) This "toning-down" was a requirement for the well-being and success of the African American expatriate performer, females in particular. It is a complex issue, for both Baker models were outstanding, unique, and in a class of their own.

The same holds true for Alberta Hunter: she was transformed from a
blues singer to a ballad interpreter. It is not that her artistry was lessened
by incorporating a Europeanist aesthetic in her presentation of self, but it
certainly was different. Individual female stars were required to undergo
a personality transformation in order to flesh out and provide a context
for their change in artistic style. Once this new text was adopted and per-
fected, it became one's new identity—the mask of whiteness, so to
speak—and the old persona was left behind. And, since cultural exchange
is always a two-way street, this move also brought some elements of the
Africanist aesthetic to white styles of singing and movement. Both
Hunter and Baker sang in French and English. Not a flamboyant personality like Baker, Hunter readily and happily settled into a comfortable
style of high-bourgeois English life:

> Alberta, with her very expensive flat shoes and equally dear tweed suits,
> looked right at home among all these proper Englishwomen. None of
> them was associated with the entertainment world, but they didn't seem
> the least stuffy. They sat on pillows on the floor and listened to poetry read-
> ings. Margot [Webb] at the time found their form of entertainment "very
> boring." But she was impressed that Alberta knew all these well-heeled
> people and was able to carry her own so well in conversation with them.
> (Taylor and Cook, 135)

Like so many issues in the black-white discourse, this one was not simply a matter of black and white—or good and bad.

Musicians underwent a European acculturation that was not nearly as
radical as the transformations experienced by the likes of Baker and
Hunter. For a musician (almost all were male), it was easy enough to tone
down his style as the need arose. After all, there were always jam sessions
or special settings where one could let go and groove. Unlike Baker,
Hunter, and other individual female stars, musicians were encouraged to
simultaneously keep alive old and new, black and white codes and could
be required to play in vastly different ways for different audiences. According to Arthur Briggs, the black jazz musician in Europe was required
to play in a subdued, softer style for engagements at smart spots like
Ciro's in London. On such bookings even the stars of African American

jazz—like saxophonist-clarenitist Sidney Bechet—were obliged to play quietly, if not softly. Musicians were able to accomplish this by playing in a lower register and/or using mutes. Briggs goes on to explain that the opposite was the case with most of the bookings he had on his return to the United States (with the Noble Sissle band). At home most people, white and black, preferred lots of loud sound to accompany their dancing. (Goddard, 284)

But it was impossible for a Baker or Hunter to reinvent their personas and their acts for American audiences, to have both a black and a white mask and, in effect, two separate identities, one American, one European. Still, had this been possible, they might then have switched codes on demand and performed successfully on both sides of the Atlantic as the musicians did.

As with in-group racism at home, we see African American expatriates contributing to the whitened prerequisites and formula for European success. Thus Bricktop, herself a legendary club owner and former entertainer, was quite strict about who and what was allowed in her club. Again, Arthur Briggs supplies some insights. He felt that working at Bricktop's was a difficult task. Her establishment catered to a select, largely aristocratic clientele. The bands had to do away with most of their self-chosen repertory and offer the patrons a diet of musical comedy selections. Briggs is careful to point out that, even so, these numbers were played by the bands in their own unique style and, indeed, they did swing—but quietly. He characterizes the result as "society music"; yet, the musicians were still able to play "some reasonable jazz." (Goddard, 286)

With such constrictions on their performance, it becomes clear why the after-hours jam session must have been an absolute necessity for the creative juices to stay alive and well overseas. Bricktop, herself, addressed her expectations, stating that places like hers catered to high society and royalty, that a Fats Waller type would be out of place in such surroundings: those people didn't frequent her club, and the "messiness" of jam sessions and grassroots swing culture was to be avoided, at all costs. (Goddard, 219)

For a musician like Briggs—as for Baker and Hunter during the swing era—the advantages of expatriation far outweighed its drawbacks. Like Margot Webb, he pointed out the relatively easy performance schedule in

Europe as compared to the States. Stateside, modesty was not a virtue.
Due to the large number of excellent black bands (with white groups getting the best gigs), competition was fierce among bands as well as with
musicians within one group. In Briggs's experience touring with the
Noble Sissle band, for example, he found that musicians would take long
solos if the audience was with them. Sissle encouraged this kind of improvisation and its concomitant competitiveness and lengthening of performance time. Such circumstances that might have been fun for novices
were devastating for old-timers. According to Briggs, "I reckoned much
more of that and my life would be considerably shortened. We'd play
sometimes from nine in the evening until five in the morning. Then
there'd be eight, ten, sometimes twelve hours in the bus to the next gig."
(Goddard, 285) Thus, when Sissle and the band returned to France,
Briggs quit and remained in Europe.

These considerations were not a matter of whim. Few nonperformers
realize the incredible toll that performing takes on the human body.
Trumpeter's lips split, bleed, and become hard as wood from overplaying
and can act as a conduit for mouth cancer. Vocalists overuse and misuse
their voices in efforts to reach past their own fatigue or the noise of nightclub or theater crowds. Dancers overwork their instrument and, like professional athletes, develop arthritis and bone deterioration at an early age.
A dear price is paid for the moments of success on stage.

However, there are other musicians who contend that they returned
to the United States for the very reasons that Briggs listed for staying
in Europe. According to pianist Elliot Carpenter, there was a great deal
of dissipation among his set of expatriate African American jazz
musicians—alcohol, sexual excesses, marijuana, and hard drugs. He
contends that he returned to the United States to save himself. He had
worked steadily on well-paying engagements at well-appointed venues,
including the Folies Bergères and aristocratic private parties (including
all of Elsa Maxwell's,[36] at one point). For this musician, home represented safety, sanity, salvation. (Goddard, 302–303)

One of the most eloquent statements about the African American expatriate experience was voiced by writer James Baldwin, whose in-depth
experiences living abroad lend substance to his reflections:

The danger of being an expatriate is that you are very likely to find yourself living, in effect, nowhere. I am not, for example, responsible for Turkish society, and I can have no effect on it. It is not here that my social obligations can be discharged. This means that, as time goes on, the expatriate may find that he has no real or relevant concerns, and no grasp of reality. He is living, really, on the hazards and energies of other people; he has ceased to pay his way. In my case, I've got no choice but to shuttle back and forth between the New World and the Old. I gain something from both places, after all, and possibly I am simply far too proud, consciously, to sidestep a danger [namely, the danger of being a black male in white America]. . . . (Dunbar, epigraph)

Whether in dynamic tension between two worlds—European and American, old and new—or insulated by the American racial tension between black and white, the black swing era performer was, like Baldwin, one who had "no choice but to shuttle back and forth" in a dance that ultimately rendered her or him ungrounded and insecure. What became of some of those careers and of the Harlem community that had been so significant to their development?

Part III

"I was never convinced that the melting pot was an appropriate metaphor for the way in which people ought to come together. . . . My ideal of a democratic community is a jazz band."

—Cornel West

Chapter Six

Coda to a Dream Deferred

Norton and Margot's career peaked with their European tour. All their efforts culminated at that pinnacle and gradually slid downhill thereafter. Retiring from show business in 1947, Margot Webb ended her career in a way that paralleled its beginnings. As an adolescent she had performed on weekends in New York area clubs and returned to school on Monday morning. In the end, she was attending graduate school during the day, teaching dance at Board of Education after-school recreation centers in the afternoons, and performing weekend gigs in order to resume her school schedule by Monday morning. But, of course, there was a difference: a good part of a lifetime had elapsed in the intervening years, and choices had to be made. She explained her choice to give up performing: "Actually, I couldn't just keep on without giving up the school job. I couldn't keep on indefinitely, because it limited you to places around New York . . . I couldn't go abroad; I couldn't go to California, or whatever. . . . No, you couldn't do that and keep the school job. So I had to decide one way or another." (17 September 1980) Webb had left college in favor of a performing career; this time, she left show business and opted for school and a teaching career.

The possibilities for the team's survival seemed bleak. By 1941, the white vaudeville theaters in the Midwest no longer booked African American unit tours; they had become double-feature movie houses. One slim employment possibility might have been the cabaret route in the Midwest; but even this option could have sustained them only sporadically for a year

or two more. Furthermore, that possibility would have meant life on the
road again and, unlike John Williams and many musicians, Webb could no
longer entertain the prospect of endless touring. Although a select group of
singers and musicians might garner extended bookings in white New York
area clubs and hotels (playing places like the Rainbow Room or downtown
hotels for year-long bookings, if they were lucky), an African American ballroom team performing in a white style would not be booked at such venues.

The need for floor space further limited the team's employment potential. The forties was an era of shrinking nightclubs, with large Cotton
Club type establishments giving way to small intimate rooms. According to Webb, "What we called the small clubs were small because we
couldn't work in them. They [African American club owners] would
have liked to have had us, but there was no space for us to dance. These
small clubs had a singer and a comedian [as well as a musical trio or
quartet—instead of a big swing band—and, occasionally, a tap dancer].
This type of entertainment could work the small clubs year in and year
out." (27 August 1980)

Facing a mere trickle of bookings, Norton and Webb dissolved their
partnership from 1942 to 1945. Despite fading prospects, they did stage
a comeback (in 1946) which was heralded by friends, fans, and colleagues who remembered their widespread appeal in an era that, chronologically, was just a few years behind them but, after the war, seemed
worlds away. Although it was the lure of dance that had brought them
back to show business, Norton and Webb were older (by then Webb was
37 years old) and had families. They also had acquired the educational
resources that could lead to second careers.

Given these limitations, the team's reunion lasted a little over a year.
Norton and Margot's final bookings were at Harlem's Club Baron in the
fall of 1946, followed by a few minor club dates on weekends that finally
brought their career to a definitive end in 1947. After they dissolved their
professional partnership, Webb lost contact with Norton. She and her
family moved from Harlem to the suburbs (St. Albans, a Queens, New
York, neighborhood) in 1950. By that time she lived in a different world.
As a junior high school teacher in Harlem—and like countless other upwardly mobile professionals in the 1950s—she commuted from suburbia
to her job in the city.

Indeed, the black bourgeoisie, again in search of better housing and in pursuit of the elusive American dream, began to move away from Harlem as soon as the opportunity presented itself. But the suburbs did not await them with open arms: they were middle class, but they were still black. Ironically, they found themselves in what eventually became segregated suburban enclaves in New Jersey, Connecticut, Long Island, and the borough of Queens: their goal had been integration, but whites fled as blacks moved in, everyone aiming toward upper middle-class status, higher salaries, and increased consumption in an ever-escalating standard of American living. The term "keeping up with the Joneses" must have been coined to characterize this postwar, middlebrow American *zeitgeist*.

Ironically, like many of the self-sufficient enterprises in Harlem and other African American communities, the black baseball and basketball teams were demolished by integration. As early as 1932, when the major leagues were still closed to African Americans, "winter baseball was integrated. Blacks, whites, and Latins played together for fantastic salaries (and fanatic fans) in Cuba, Puerto Rico, the Dominican Republic, and Mexico." (Buckley, 111) Then, with mainstream salaries and exposure a possibility by the end of the 1940s, black players opted to join white teams as the opportunity presented itself. White leagues began to accept individual black players but weren't interested in purchasing entire teams, so the black squads, like Robert Douglas's basketball team, the Rens, folded. By 1948 Douglas had lost his best players to integration and had no way of competing as an owner of a black team. A player who had received $1,000 a month from Douglas was now able to garner $5,000 with a white team. Douglas sums up by saying that "The same day that Jackie Robinson's team was winning the World Series, I was in Philadelphia trying to get my team into the [pro-basketball] league." (Gross)

The demise of these teams epitomizes the farce that masqueraded as integration: token individuals were supported, but black-owned businesses—athletic or other—were left to founder as their economic base was pulled out from under them. By the Civil Rights era, it also meant that, with more African American students accepted on a wider basis at white colleges, black schools, which, along with churches and social clubs, had been guardians and keepers of African American traditions, began their decline. Webb's outlook is a dire but noteworthy contribution to the discourse about the American racial divide: "in all the periods of integration, the blacks lose. . . . [W]hen they integrated the schools they didn't take the black principals and put them in the newly integrated schools. Two blacks and a hundred whites, you know—that's integration. So you get a white principal. So a lot of our [black] administrators lost their positions in education." (25 June 1980)

Lifestyles, show business, and Harlem were all changing during the 1940s. Since the 1920s Harlem had been the stage and site, the innovator and center of attraction, for American popular music, song, and dance and was dubbed the "Nightclub Capital of the World." But another world war and another Harlem race riot (1943) had shifted the tempo from hot to cool. Whites were less welcome uptown. Harlem's clubs were abandoned and its nightlife redirected to Broadway. According to some observers, the decline of Harlem's drawing power for white capital began in earnest with the Cotton Club's move downtown in 1936. Certainly, the white-owned and -operated Harlem entertainment industry was resented by black Harlem and was doomed by the advent of World War II. The community was concerned about the loss of Harlem's economic vitality and the part played by white entrepreneurs in this dilemma. Previous claims of white exploitation made by African Americans in show business dated back to labor disputes by Lafayette Theater stagehands in the 1920s, whose grievances concerned not only salary and working conditions, but also the accusation that "while the white promoters made money, they were doing very little to contribute to the development of black theatrical arts." (Huggins, 291) Webb's canny observations support this argument and reinforce her radical perspective on integration: "Most of the big clubs had closed [by the 1940s]. Some clubs moved downtown. After they got downtown, some of them tried integrating the shows, and some of them had possibly all-white shows. But they didn't have so many all-black shows. I guess they were calling it a 'period of integration'—which means, in all the periods of integration, the blacks lose out. It's the same as in the schools. We lose." (25 June 1980) Even as early as 1938 Webb wrote in her column, "Harlem to Broadway":

The Cotton Club is now presenting its revue at Long Beach six days weekly, omitting Monday night performances. Slow business is the reason. It is also rumored that the show may soon do without chorines and parade girls and use only acts. That is the policy employed by many cabaret owners these days. The chorines at the Plantation Club received a considerable cut in salary last week. The owners of the club may sell the place if they receive a high enough offer. Since the old Cotton Club lost its drawing power up at 142nd Street and Lenox Avenue the spot has never again reached its old popularity. . . .

There was a time when Harlem was a novelty and a "must" on all ofays' [read "whites'"] lists of places of importance in New York, but that day has past. What may be seen in Harlem may be seen anywhere in New York in downtown club shows and theaters. Everything the Race actors originated in the way of entertainment has been imitated and elaborated upon by ofays until we have very little left with which to capitalize on in our own vicinity. (Webb, 22 July 1938)

Webb's statement reflected widely held community sentiments. Harlemites were becoming hostile to both white clientele and white owners and managers, particularly after the 1943 riot.

The Cotton Club had moved to Broadway and 48th Street at a site which, from 1933 to 1934, had been occupied by the downtown Connie's Inn—a club which, itself, had moved from Harlem and was owned by Connie Immerman and his brother. The Immermans had named their new venue the Harlem Club. Feeling that the time was ripe for such a move, they had opened in midtown with an explicit policy of encouraging African Americans to join whites as customers. However, they were mistaken, and hostile repercussions forced them to close after a few months. (Haskins, 113) It is noteworthy that, in the following decade, entrepreneur Barney Josephson attempted a similar integrationist experiment in Manhattan's bohemian, liberal Greenwich Village area, instead of on Broadway. Nevertheless, even in that neighborhood, his Café Society cabaret was haunted by protest. The Harlem Club was replaced by the Ubangi Club which subsequently moved farther downtown into the location that later became Birdland. Then the Cotton Club moved in.

But the move from Harlem to Broadway was the beginning of a slow demise. By the fall of 1938 the Cotton Club had added a fourth show with "a cast of one hundred Negro performers, which goes on nightly . . . as an aid to the current effort to revive vaudeville." ("Cotton Club," 1938) In 1939 they were reduced to a six-day-a-week format, due to the ruling of the musicians' union requiring one day off per week for its members. (This move was probably welcomed by the owners, in light of the slow business addressed by Webb, above.) That year's fall show was produced without chorus girls and show girls and was more a variety hodgepodge than a synchronized revue. The overworking of a successful formula (and the white paying audiences had definite ideas about the kind of black entertainment they wanted to see), along with the changing tastes in entertainment caused the club's profits and morale to plummet by the end of 1939. The popularity of white swing bands among white people in white communities took former patrons away from black-centered entertainment, even after those black venues were moved to white areas of the city. Black shows simply were no longer the rage. The Cotton Club closed permanently on 1 June 1940.

In the years after World War II, lavish nightlife was no longer thriving on Broadway or other venues in mainstream America. In Robert Sylvester's opinion, the flight to suburbia was the culprit: "When you live an hour or more from Broadway [or Harlem, for black patrons] you simply can't stay up all night, get home and get back to work the next day in any kind of shape. So you go home earlier, or, more likely, you don't come to town at all." (293) This pattern—namely, moving from cities to suburbs—reversed the cycle that had prevailed in America for the previous century—namely, population shifts from rural to urban areas. Added to this trend was the overwhelming effect of television, creating conditions in which "the tired businessman doesn't even have to put his shoes on to see wonderful shows free in his own living room." (37) Early television was rife with variety shows, including the *Ed Sullivan Show, Your Show of Shows,* and the *Jack Benny Show,* all of which were able to draw the top names in vaudeville, nightclubs, and Hollywood to the new medium.

With the changes in urban population, social and leisure patterns, and overall lifestyle, the music—jazz music—changed concomitantly. The postwar period was the beginning of the cold war, an era of American retrenchment marked by fear of Communism, Eastern Europe, the

U.S.S.R., and the atomic bomb. The archsymbol of the era was Senator Joseph McCarthy with his House Un-American Activities Committee hearings—a performance in its own right that put the nation in a state of self-righteous panic. It was not a carefree, expansive era and, remarkably, jazz became cool in the context of an American landscape that was politically conservative.[1] The spectacle and extravagance that had characterized performance in the Depression era was replaced by the needs and demands of a generation who had matured in the belt-tightening years of a wartime economy. It was one thing for people not to have enough food—a fact of life for many Americans in the thirties; but wartime shortages that necessitated food rationing presaged a different world and an altered national mindset, one that might have made the spectacular seem out of place if not downright sinful. This wartime mentality segued into the postwar, upwardly mobile, suburban-oriented, family- and television-centered lifestyle of the 1950s, and live performance suffered accordingly.

The decline of nightlife was further abetted in the early 1940s by a legislated midnight curfew. With most draft-age men fighting in the war and those at home involved in war-related industry, provisions and services were limited. However, this change—with a night on the town forcibly ended at midnight instead of when "the milkman's on his way"— did not disappear with the end of the war and the lifting of the ban. For many, it marked another permanent change in American leisure patterns. Likewise, New York's twenty percent amusement tax was another wartime innovation that hung over into the postwar era: "For some reason, this tax was so rigid that it penalized a place with entertainment while exempting a place which offered only music. Thus the jazz joints merely dispensed with their dance floors and offered only music." (Sylvester, 296) This regulation affected large and small establishments. It meant that if a small club presented a vocalist with the music, then the amusement tax was in effect. However, the club could still be ahead of the game if hiring a singer attracted more customers; but if it were small in size, then there was no space for social dancing (which had been an important component of a night on the town in the prewar era). In a domino effect, the big swing era bands became superfluous without their complement of ballroom dancers; furthermore, they would have been an ear-shattering sound in the small clubs. The small jazz combo was perfect for this new intimate setting. This small club pattern had an obvious effect on both the dance habits of the American public and the careers of its dancers, be they Lindy-Hoppers or a ballroom team like Norton and Margot.

For white America—except for its teenagers, who continued to do a distilled version of the Lindy to the accompaniment of rock and roll music—the 1950s was a period of subdued social dance activity that went, hand in hand, with the conservative, stay-at-home tenor of the era. It is important to remember the tight grip that McCarthyism and anti-communist fervor held on the American psyche in that decade. The repressive spell was broken as new initiatives emerged, particularly the spread of the black Civil Rights movement (from its origins in the African American community to the white mainstream), and the Free Student movement (initiated in 1960 at the University of California, Berkeley, with the first student protest). Along with these early harbingers of a new era came the discotheque fever of the 1960s, ushering in a period that challenged the swing era for proliferation of dance fads and overall participation in dance as a social activity.

The wartime reduction in and restrictions on nightlife in general, the collapse of white-oriented Harlem nightlife, the fading popularity of the Lindy and swing music by the late 1940s—all contributed to the gradual demise of the Savoy ballroom. In the postwar era this hulking, square-block vault of space was an old dinosaur in a new world of compact "cool cats"—namely, the small clubs. In the early 1950s, when the Mambo and other Latino dances became the rage in Harlem, the ballroom accommodated this fad and hosted Latin bands. But its time had passed. It closed in 1958 and was torn down in 1959 to make way for a housing project and supermarket, facilities that still were too few and far between in Harlem.

With the end of the vaudeville touring units, the Apollo theater eventually was obliged to streamline its format accordingly. By the 1950s the chorus line was phased out and there were generally fewer dance acts on the program. The focus shifted to the featured act, usually a band or a vocalist. As a housewarmer, the featured band opened the program with one or two numbers. The musical introduction was followed by what is known as a "sight act"—namely, an acrobat or a fast tap dance act. Next came a singer, followed by a comedian. The rest of the show was given over to the featured act, which could be a band playing its most popular selections, a band with vocalist, a star-caliber vocalist, or a singing group. Generally there was only one dance act on a bill. (I personally recall this format when I was taken as a child to the Apollo. Singers like Nellie Lutcher or Dinah Washington were featured with musical accompaniment for up to an hour in this reduced variety schema.) Audiences attended performances to see the star rather than the show. With the ascendance of rhythm and blues in the 1950s, the male singing or doo-wop group (out of which evolved white imitations and, later white rock groups) became the centerpiece of the show.

Comedy changed too. The farcical actors with evocative names like Pigmeat Markham, Dusty Fletcher, and Moms Mabley were joined by the talkers—the stand-up comics, almost all male, who dressed in suits and didn't sing, dance, or pantomime. Fueled by the energy of the Civil Rights movement these humorists—including people like Nipsey Russell, Bill Cosby, Dick Gregory, and Godfrey Cambridge—broke the stereotype that had held sway since minstrelsy, paving the way for a new era in African American humor.

Unlike the Cotton Club and the Savoy, the Apollo theater had managed to stay afloat as a full-time, year-round presenter until the Schiffman-Brecher management closed it in 1975–76. It had changed pace with the community for four decades, but time finally won out. A 1,600-seat theater could barely compete with the "giant cold barns of Vegas or the mammoth amphitheatres of the road, where black performers now entertain an entire nation." (Hamill) As a result of civil rights advances there were increased performance opportunities for African American artists, and African American patrons could be accommodated practically anywhere they wished to go in New York by the end of the 1960s. Figuratively speaking, even the Waldorf Astoria was no longer off-limits. Like whites, African Americans flocked to Broadway and venues like Carnegie Hall for concerts by black artists. Besides, the Apollo was notorious for its decrepit backstage conditions and low salaries for all but the stars. For many African American artists, success meant never having to return to this ramshackle facility. Although it has occasionally been opened for use in the 1980s and 1990s, the theater was, effectively, a dead house after 1975. A made-for-television version of its famous amateur night contest, *Live at the Apollo,* was the 1990s copy of the Apollo's heyday.

In the minds of some observers the death of showman and figurehead Bill Robinson in 1949 (he had been the honorary mayor of Harlem for years) was the final stroke delivered on the swing era, at least in Harlem. In addition to the termination of careers like Norton's and Margot's, many highly successful careers went into major decline. Of 1947, the same year that Norton and Margot retired, Cab Calloway said, "The big band era came to an end for me in 1947, and the years after that were not easy to talk about. I went through some very rough times, I went from a guy whose gross was $200,000 a year to someone who couldn't get a booking. . . . I guess I became a little bitter, I saw Woody Herman and some of the other white bands still going strong, being booked in the big rooms, and the best I could do was some small hotel rooms and nightclubs." (184–85)

Here, again, we see race politics at work. African American musicians had originated and developed the swing sound, but white musicians had become its owners and inheritors. That was par for the course: whenever there were hard times or changing times for America in general, African Americans bore the severest brunt of the struggle. The Depression was hard on whites, and it was devastating for blacks; likewise, the swing era was over for many big bands, but it was the black bands that suffered most acutely. With very few exceptions, the big band engagements that were forthcoming were filled by white groups like the bands of Herman, the Dorsey Brothers, and Goodman—as well as countless white bands of lesser talent and renown—at hotels and resorts that basically were segregated venues and booked black musicians and bands rarely, if at all.

Calloway disbanded his group in 1947 and went into semiretirement, due to lack of work, until 1950 when he was offered the role of Sportin' Life in still another revival of *Porgy and Bess.* Hard times were everywhere. Ethel Waters recalled,

> that winter of 1948–49, I hit bottom. This time agents booked me into saloons without telling me what kind of places they were. It hurt. I don't think anyone who knows me would charge me with having an inflated idea

of my own importance. But I was Ethel Waters who had starred in Broadway revues, dramatic hits, and million-dollar Hollywood pictures. Yet there I was back to singing in saloons [which is how Waters had begun her career in Philadelphia in the 1910s]. I played the Click in Philadelphia and realized that the semi-innovations had just begun. They had a bar in the Click that ran the length of the block. There was a television set at each end. . . . When you come on, they don't turn those television sets off. They just turn them down enough so the customers can keep on watching Hopalong Cassidy, the wrestling matches, or the fights if they want to, or they can listen to you. (268)

Fredi Washington remembered, "There were months and years in between parts, and it's hard to build and polish a craft that way." (Darden, 109) Like Webb, who channeled her efforts into teaching young dancers, Washington continued working in the theater by coaching aspiring actors. She also helped organize the Negro Actors Guild and worked with the NAACP for desegregation of the arts.

For Webb, the transition from performer to ordinary citizen was eased by a busy schedule that had begun with teaching dance in after-school recreation centers and led to her becoming a full-time, public school physical education teacher by 1949. (At that time, there were no dance programs in the New York City public school system except as a supplement to the physical education curriculum.) Webb also set up her own Saturday dance program, first in the basement of her St. Albans home and, later, in a rented loft space on Second Avenue and Fourteenth Street in Manhattan. She taught ballet, toe, and modern dance to a group of her public school students. As an African American parent, she had a vested interest in the future of these young people of color.

Some performers were not as fortunate as those cited, and comebacks or alternative careers did not await them. Webb recalls seeing Aaron Palmer—father of dancer Pops Whitman, husband of Alice Whitman (of the Whitman Sisters), and a tap dancer himself (he was an early class dancer, much admired by his colleagues)—once in the late 1950s in the street. "He was like a bum, begging for quarters. This was right up on 126th Street, around the corner from the Apollo. When I saw this man dance, he was even better than Bojangles, I'd say. And he just went down. . . ." (27 August 1980)

Other tragedies included the untimely death of brilliant tap artist Teddy Hale who, like Palmer, was also a dancer's dancer. (Stearns and Stearns, 349) Having performed since he was a child in the early 1930s, he ended up as the janitor in a low-life club where he occasionally danced; he died in the 1950s. The great Ananias Berry, star of the Berry Brothers (and later the husband of Valaida Snow), died early of a drug overdose. There were numerous other people who, after spending a childhood and an entire lifetime in show business, had no place to go when the era that spawned and nurtured them was over: panhandling, unskilled manual labor, alcoholism, and drugs awaited them.

Some former chorus girls found an alternative glamorous employment as barmaids in the small local Harlem night spots that had replaced the clubs where they used to dance. The Cotton Club former chorines even organized a social club called The Ex-Glamour Girls which used to sponsor social events, including an annual dance.

This era also saw a major shift in Broadway musicals, from the tap-dance-centered variety format of the swing era to the ballet-oriented, dream-sequence, book musicals, beginning with *Oklahoma* in 1943. Basically, this was a shift from a black-centered aesthetic to a white one. Rather than study tap dance, young hopefuls whose sights were set on Broadway and Hollywood were more likely to pursue ballet and a white dance-studio style of jazz dance. Thus, tap dance experienced a triple whammy: vaudeville was dead, nightclubs were on the decline, and musical comedy was embracing new dance genres. Under pressure of no bookings, the tap team of Coles and Atkins broke up in the early 1950s. Both Charles "Honi" Coles and Cholly Atkins became teachers. Atkins coached at the Katharine Dunham school, and Coles opened a tap studio with another unemployed hoofer, Pete Nugent. After reuniting for Las Vegas bookings in shows starring people like Tony Martin and Pearl Bailey and then separating for long periods due to lack of work, Coles and Atkins were brought together again by an early wave of nostalgia to participate in a landmark history of tap dance concert at the 1962 Newport Jazz Festival. Apollo engagements followed once or twice a year through the mid-1960s, with an occasional spot on public or educational television. But, basically, their career as a team was over. Atkins became famous in his second career at Detroit's Motown Records as choreographer for

African American doo-wop singing groups. After serving as president of the Negro Actors Guild and working as production manager at the Apollo theater, Coles rode the wave of the tap dance revival until his death in 1992. His comeback had been astonishing, and he was featured in tap dance festivals and teaching seminars nationally and internationally. Coles was a key player in the tap dance revival—a movement that began in the 1960s, was in full bloom by the mid-1970s, and resulted in widespread regeneration of interest in this classic American dance genre.

Choreographer Clarence Robinson, who staged many of the shows that featured Norton and Margot, died in 1979. In his obituary in the *New York Amsterdam News,* he was credited with adding "glamour to 'colored' women before they were recognized as beautiful." (Rowe, 43) Willie Bryant, who succeeded Bill Robinson as honorary mayor of Harlem, became a disc jockey, first in Harlem and then in Hollywood. He died in 1964. Ralph Cooper, the versatile entertainer who first introduced Norton to Margot Webb, became a New York state official working in the Department of Human Rights through the 1970s. Dancer Howard "Stretch" Johnson, one of the original Cotton Club Boys, became an academic, teaching in the sociology department of the State University at New Paltz, New York. (This tall, lanky, rubber-legged dancer asserted that he invented a swing era fad dance called the Scrontch.)

A healthy number of swing era musicians were able to continue their careers well into the 1970s and 1980s. Bassist John Williams stated in 1980 that he was never out of work and had continued to play regularly since his career had begun in the 1930s. After working with the Lucky Millinder and Louis Armstrong bands, he joined Teddy Wilson's small combo in the early 1940s and continued in that group through the 1950s. He worked in the 1970s at Barney Josephson's Cookery Lafayette in Greenwich Village as part of a trio backing singers Alberta Hunter and Helen Humes. He also played major New York hotel engagements and still obtained occasional bookings in Europe.

Louis Armstrong, Count Basie, Dizzy Gillespie, Duke Ellington, and Cab Calloway continued to perform, with the first four developing into musical legends whose contributions to the canon of American classical music—namely, jazz—are formidable and well documented. Calloway's postwar career veered furthest away from his swing era profile. After his comeback in *Porgy and Bess,* he played in the African American Broadway version of *Hello, Dolly* with Pearl Bailey in 1967. (It is noteworthy that American racial etiquette required black versions of white musicals: integrated casting remained taboo on Broadway. This 1960s circumstance is a reminder of how little racial progress had been made in the realm of casting since the swing era had seen the production of the *Hot Mikado* and other all-black versions of white musicals, as well as all-black versions of *Macbeth* and other dramas.[2]) He made guest appearances with the Harlem Globetrotters and obtained other spot work on the resort nightclub circuit, working through the 1970s and sharing a December 1980 concert at the Brooklyn Academy of Music with the Count Basie Band (although, by then, he was in voluntary semiretirement). Also in 1980 he was featured in the film *The Blues Brothers.*

For those swing era seniors like Webb who are still alive, their show business careers may seem like a previous incarnation of themselves: so many significant periods of growth and evolution have followed that details recede in the past and wink in and out of focus. The near hits and many misses of Webb's faraway ballroom dance career parallel the off-center career of dark-skinned specialty dancer Ida Forsyne who, like Webb, was out of joint with her era (although for different reasons) and could not find steady work in her prime performing years. (Stearns and Stearns, 248–57) In a 1957 theatrical gossip column, hauntingly similar in overall tone to Webb's columns twenty years earlier, the team of Norton and Margot was mentioned as one of the all-time great dance teams in one writer's opinion—small credit for a dream deferred. (Burley)

For every human being the journey from childhood to adulthood is beset by unfulfilled achievements and thwarted expectations: that is part of the human condition. Add to this the issue of race prejudice, and the human comedy becomes a catastrophe. The tragedy, or outrage, of careers like Norton and Margot's and countless others is not that these people were necessarily better or more talented performers than their white cohorts but, simply, that they never had the chance to prove their mettle. Writer-activist Imamu Baraka expressed the rage produced by such exclusion in his play *The Slave* (1964), in which the fundamental need to have one's "turn" becomes the root of a revolution. Before murdering Easely, the white liberal, Walker, the black militant, says to him: "The point is that you had your chance, darling, now these other folks have theirs." (73) But, in reality, the revolution did not happen; Norton and Margot and their colleagues didn't get their rightful turn or equal shot at success.

Turning ninety in the year 2000, living in Miami, Florida, and recalling the years in show business, the life on the road, the small salaries and hard times, Webb states that she doesn't know how she survived. After spending many hours with her in interview and conversation, I conclude that she and her colleagues in black swing era America endured by the strength garnered and internalized from the African American communities that supported, sheltered, adored, and publicized its underpaid and invisibilized celebrities. This community included the black citizenry who fed and housed these performers through the Jim Crow era: the African American physician and Philadelphia family who sequestered Webb and nursed her back to health after a white hospital rejected her; the black newspaper reporters and photographers who spread the word that the units were coming to town; the old-timers who saw this cadre of young artists as the hope for the future; the young people who came to see these shows and embraced these artists as role models. This community and the institutions, ideals, and values it represented were why and how the African American vaudevillian managed to keep on keeping on. Out of this living experience, a rich, beautiful, complex legacy was produced under dire conditions of segregation. The positive side of dancing in the dark meant dancing to the black community.

The African American presence is basic to just about every aspect of American life. Black dance, music, and theatrical forms are fundamental threads in the fabric of the dominant culture, exerting a pervasive and profound influence. Although made invisible and considered nominal in some circles, this presence has been central to the development of supposedly "white" cultural formation and is manifested in ways and places where it is least expected. And, although its innovators have long since retired or passed away, initiatives rooted in African American vaudeville and the swing era have tailored and colored the American fabric in a broader and more sweeping way than has been acknowledged to date. An examination of the African American swing era legacy and its role in the cultural formation of modernism seems a proper conclusion to this study.

Chapter Seven

Legacy: All That Jazz

Prelude

What is to be learned from this study? Why dredge up this history? Haven't things gotten better? And hasn't this all been done before? These were questions that a white male friend and colleague raised during the proposal stage of this work.

As I see it, the nature of black-white relations in the United States (and in Europe) is such that a revisiting and revisioning of the racial state of affairs is a necessary agenda item for both blacks and whites of every generation. Although the deck has changed, the race card is still played on a daily basis in black-white interactions in every aspect of our lives. As long as this is the case and as long as there are untold stories, such as the foregoing accounts of Norton and Margot and a host of other invisibilized histories, then there is good reason for studies, like this one, to be written. Knowing full well that there are other peoples of color in the American race picture, I continue to speak in terms of black and white because, in the final analysis, the racial fault line is drawn along a black-white axis. Undeniably, the African-European paradigm is the bottom line of American culture, greeting, grounding, and orienting every newly arrived immigrant regardless of ethnicity or social, economic, political, or religious persuasion. Along with refugees from Europe and Latin America, Asian peoples from many cultures and nationalities are forced, gently or otherwise, to buy into this Afro-Euro polarity. As newcomers submitting to the process of Americanization, they are ineluctable heirs of both Africanisms and the anti-black racism that pervade American society.

Compared to the minstrel era, swing era vaudevillians seemed liberated, but they were well aware that their circumstances were warped by racism. Compared to the swing era, 1960s and '70s soul culture seemed liberated—especially in light of the civil rights advances achieved in those decades—but its practitioners realized that racism had gone underground and continued to plague them in covert ways. So, compared to the soul culture era, where is the African American performer today, the citizen of the hiphop nation? How much power or control does she have over the means of production and distribution of her artistry? Are African American artists marginalized? Is African American work regarded as art or as merely entertainment? Is the expressive output of the African American artist regarded as a reflection of black American culture, of the "Promethean energies of ordinary people,"[1] or as an exception to the rule of black underachievement? And has the deeply substantial legacy of the black artistic presence been fully acknowledged? These questions are posed speculatively and rhetorically in the context of this study.

This work can be regarded as an antidote to marginalization and a celebration of black centrality in the creation of the swing aesthetic. I concur with jazz researcher Jon Panish that, by and large, white Americans "still do not respect the integrity of African American culture. . . . Even those white Americans who were strongly attracted to African American culture were mostly unable or unwilling to recognize the subtle and profound ways in which that culture spun off different angles of vision on such cherished American ideals as individualism, freedom, and equality." (143) I might add that it is not only whites but also many black Americans, as well as other Americans of color, who are equally unaware of the Africanist presence and integrity in American culture.

Why write about all this? Because "Black American jazz dancing, dancing for social as well as performance purposes, for couples as well as for self-expression, is perhaps one of the great unrecognized art forms of the century." (Thompson) The expressive power of black dance—mainly subliminal, mainly unacknowledged—has been picked up by generations of European American dancers, both on the ballroom floor and the concert stage.

Marginalization—dancing in the dark—then and now: in the swing era the Lindy was appropriated and modified by whites and became the Jitterbug; in the last decade of the twentieth century, there is a Lindy revival but it is termed "swing dancing." Several young white undergraduates at Temple University—dance majors and avid swing dancers—were unaware of the black, pre–World War II roots of their new pastime until, as their professor, I pointed it out to them. Their suburban, middle-class crowd was "in the dark" as far as the Savoy and Whyte's Lindy-Hoppers were concerned. This is one of the social, cultural, and political problems in America: a lack of historicity and historical perspective, which makes it necessary to reexamine our collective past time and again. For some it will not be a second trip but a maiden voyage.

Following once again in America's footsteps (as they have since the minstrel era), England has bought into the Lindy revival.[2] Just as there are a new crop of swing dance clubs in Manhattan, so also London has its share. Those who are seriously engaged frequently dress in vintage garb: flouncy knee- or calf-length skirts and bobby socks for the women; suspenders, wide-legged pants (or even zoot suits) and wing-tip shoes for the men. There, too, the name associated with its African American roots, the Lindy, has been tossed aside in favor of swing dance. In both instances the word "swing" may be more related to its current usage, denoting looseness and a general, swinging attitude (indeed, I imagine there are swing evenings for swinging singles), than to the historical setting of the original Lindy and its swing era context.

Marginalization—dancing in the dark—then and now: in the swing era (with the exception of Bill Robinson) both male and female African American tap dancers served as backdrops for mainstream show business and Hollywood. In the tap dance revival of the 1960s and 1970s, young white females searched out aging black male hoofers, became their disciples, took up the form, and presented it anew. What is wrong with that picture? Conspicuously, the absence of the African American female tap artist. This incredible cadre of aging women hoofers, many of whom have passed away, had to wait until the 1990s for even the small-scale recognition that they are now receiving from an already marginalized group of academics interested in African American performance, women's studies, and cultural politics.[3]

What is maddening about these examples is that, in both the swing and tap revivals, black performance genres are accorded hierarchical, so-called art status worthy of the dominant culture's scholarship, preservation, and documentation only as whites begin to study and disseminate them. White academic attention promotes them from "folk-pop" to "art" status. This trend points up an interesting pattern: African Americans develop innovative forms of vernacular music and dance and then leave them behind, moving on to create new forms; whites adopt older African American forms and revise, codify, reconstruct, "academicize," and perform them. It is a bizarre, interdependent relationship predicated upon and determined by race etiquette and power politics but, ruefully, one for which we must be grateful: without it, the Lindy and tap dance would be dead, too great a loss to imagine.

In the beginning the swing aesthetic was the black creative innovation that expressed the African American spirit of the times: the Lindy and swing music were era-appropriate, time-specific means of communicating African American expressive culture from the mid-1920s through the late 1940s. But swing went further and became a liberating force for whites as well. Like old-time religion, it could inspire revelatory experiences, happenings beyond categorization of good or bad, turning points that brought with them a new take on basic assumptions:

> My first anxiety attack occurred during a Louis Armstrong concert. I was nineteen or twenty. Armstrong was going to improvise with his trumpet, to build a whole composition in which each note would be important and would contain within itself the essence of the whole.[4] I was not disappointed: the atmosphere warmed up very fast. The scaffolding and flying buttresses of the jazz instruments supported Armstrong's trumpet, creating spaces which were adequate enough for it to climb higher, establish itself, and take off again. The sounds of the trumpet sometimes piled up together, fusing a new musical base, a sort of matrix which gave birth to one precise, unique note, tracing a sound whose path was almost painful, so absolutely

necessary had its equilibrium and duration become; it tore at the nerves of those who followed it.

My heart began to accelerate, becoming more important than the music, shaking the bars of my rib cage, compressing my lungs so the air could no longer enter them. Gripped by panic at the idea of dying there in the middle of spasms, stomping feet, and the crowd howling, I ran into the street like someone possessed. (Marie Cardinal, quoted in Morrison, 2–3)

What the swing aesthetic accomplished, in one way or another, was revolutionary. It changed America's perception and presentation of self into the swinging standard that stuck: it is the jazz aesthetic that defines signature dimensions of the American experience and has, for decades, been a marketable commodity that the rest of the world has appropriated. Swing's melding of tight rhythmic structure and organization with improvisation as its equal partner is the fine combination that leads to sassy exuberance and ecstasy or—as in the quote, above—anxiety and madness. It is this ineffable quality that made jazz music and swing dancing the signatures of liberation for the anti-Hitler Swing Youth of Nazi Germany and those in captivity behind the Iron Curtain in cold war Eastern Europe. Jazz scholar Robert O'Meally characterizes jazz singing as "a song of the resilient individual self—the self that swings." (3 January 1999, 30) The same can be said of swing culture as a whole: the song, music, dance, and consequent lifestyle bespeak freedom in the deepest sense—freedom of the soul even when the body is enslaved. When Duke Ellington wrote *It Don't Mean a Thing If It Ain't Got That Swing* in the early 1930s, he coined a phrase that stood as a metaphor for liberation, then and now.

The following sections discuss the swing legacy as a primer in modernism and a paradigm of liberation for African American, European American, and European causes.

First Movement: Swing as Modernism

Modernism is defined, in part, by the full sweep of the Africanist aesthetic presence as it developed over centuries in Africa and the Americas and was assimilated by Europeans and Euro-Americans.[5] But, in the most immediate chronological sense, modernist developments were shaped, in part, by the swing aesthetic. This contention does not carry the implication that the Europeanist aesthetic is not the equal—and, frequently, the greater—partner in modernist cultural formation. However, that story with its many permutations has been well documented in the annals of mainstream academic thought and in the canons established by its intelligentsia. My task, here, is to tell the hidden part of the story and—as stated in Chapter 1—to be the notator, in words, for those who were dancing in the dark. Modernism imposes and implies the Africanist presence, if not the black body, as its silent signifier: an invisibilized text bound to a code of silence in a pact with the white anxiety that surrounds it. Accordingly, the Africanist presence as a driving force in modernism is manifested—or concealed, really—in the subliminal, underlying, deep structures of this movement. The black swing era aesthetic can be regarded as a racially charged site within whose confines some of the basic tenets of modernism were being worked out in performance.

But why shouldn't a black aesthetic be a basic, integrated (pun and irony acknowledged) aspect of modernism? Looking at African American culture, what we see are constellations of ideas, practices, means, and processes—tropes—that are frequently identical with what we know as the modernist impulse (and, later, will be essential in defining postmodernism). For example, Matisse calls a collection of beautiful, brightly colored collages "Jazz." His bold cutouts in primary colors create a new standard that parallels the bold blasts of Armstrong's trumpet notes that reorganized music, cutting and pasting it into a new norm, and interspersing it with a new color—namely, scatting—that was a bridge between the human voice and a musical instrument, between music and song, between language and nonsense. The sense of play, of parody, as well as spontaneity and improvisation, is essential to both swing era jazz and modern art. Call it the swing aesthetic. It certainly shaped the world view and the spirit of the times for the modern artist, not necessarily as a direct influence but more as a new wind in the atmosphere, taken in as easily as a breath—or gust—of fresh air. As one writer pointed out, "A majestic Armstrong transformation of a stupid song (like *Sweethearts on Parade*) is analogous to the modernist art of collage, assemblage and the metal and raw wood sculpture of Picasso. Vernacular, or demotic, modernism is the feat of creating more out of less or almost nothing at all." (Appel, 18) This is the site where, for many modernists, the swing era jazz aesthetic became a blueprint for found art, collage, and assemblage. The idea is that the newly created whole is equal to more than the sum of its parts: the musician is superior to the songs he may interpret; the assemblage is more than scraps and pieces of objects.

Black culture is appealing in its particularity but, at the same time, it has a universal appeal—which is why jazz music and dance stand as keynotes of modernity: they represent the wit, irony, parody, spontaneity, metacommentary, and self-reflexive turn that the twentieth-century world aspired to. Simultaneously cool and hot, distancing and inviting, black culture was, indeed, a twentieth-century universal. By the swing era, Europeans and Euro-Americans had appropriated jazz and the Lindy; by the end of the 1980s, kids in Afghanistan knew how to do the Moonwalk of African American performance artist Michael Jackson, and Germany could boast rap artists of both German and Turkish lineage. As Michael Dyson put it in *Race Rules,* "blackness . . . [is] itself a universally appealing identity . . . blackness has gathered into its own formation a wonderful variety of social and cultural elements that make it eclectic and ever evolving." (193) "Eclectic and ever evolving"—process-oriented, rather than fixated on the end product—as well as simultaneously forthright and subtle, and characterized by innuendo and double entendre—all these are signposts of the swing aesthetic that were melded into the modernist code. This aesthetic offered a near-revolutionary sense of aural and visual rhythmic precision to the Europeanist perspective. It "dramatically raised the standards of exactitude and variation in timing and motion. The white novelist Mary Austin, praising the impeccably crafted art of . . . Bill Robinson, in *The Nation,* remarked that 'the eye filmed and covered by 5,000 years of absorbed culture' is cleared by the 'rhythm' of Robinson's flying feet. . . . Bojangles represented 'the great desideratum of modern art.' Black art offered a way out of the misty and bogus realm of the Titaness." (Douglas, 93) Some of the most obvious, tangible links between swing culture and the modernist aesthetic include abstraction, atonality, dissonance, improvisation, a lack of sentimentality combined with a sense of irony and a wrenchingly definitive move away from the "bogus realm

of the Titaness"—meaning, with regard to music, the hegemonic grip of
the Germanic musical tradition that dominated orchestral works in Europe and Euro-America.

Indeed, the swing jazz aesthetic epitomized the modernist ethos. European and Euro-American composers of orchestral music jumped on the
bandwagon, importing and expropriating jazz principles in their work.
Meanwhile, a crop of white jazz musicians sprang up, having been nurtured on both sides of the Atlantic by the spread of the black sound on
phonograph records and in live performance.

In addition to the music itself, the black jazz musician brought a new
in-your-face, dramatic theatricality to the musical comedy stage and the
cabaret, a brashness of styling and self-presentation that was "shocking to
white [European] audiences, taught to admire refinement above everything else." (Goddard, 86) They gave it the fullness of Africanist expressive performance styles that do not separate movement and vocalizing
from music. Thus, the black swing musician played with his whole
body—or played his whole body as his musical instrument. Embodied in
the swing tradition of the dancing bandleader (like Cab Calloway) and
the singing musician (like Louis Armstrong), playing one's instrument or
leading the band involved body movement, perhaps even recognizable
dance steps, as well as singing, scatting, or rhythmic speech or chants (like
Dizzy Gillespie's famous *Salt Peanuts* verbal refrain in the song of the
same name—a bebop generation spin-off of this tradition).

As a result, what emerges is the view of jazz music and the swing jazz
aesthetic as exotic-erotic-primitive, a major focus in modernism. The
image of Josephine Baker—dancing in her fast, eclectic, rubber-legged
fashion, naked except for a belt of bananas around her waist, exuding a
strong sexuality all the while she is mugging and playing the clown—is
the quintessential signifier of the jazz aesthetic as primitive trope. Her
mixed-message persona—both sex kitten and slapstick comedienne—
disrupted established norms of either/or for females and invoked a new
aesthetic standard. Such an image played havoc with established European conventions of beauty and good taste. At this time in her career,
Baker was a sublime example of the trickster, that staple icon in African
aesthetics who takes on comically ironic, mocking, and self-mocking roles
and discards them just as easily. It is at this site—tricksterism—that the

swing aesthetic and modernism met and challenged the establishment canon.

But white musicians had some catching up to do. Indeed, the black swing sound was in the avant-garde of musical endeavor and, like all avant-garde arts, was misinterpreted. On one hand, jazz was appropriated by Europeans and Euro-Americans who displaced its black originators in live and recorded performance opportunities and renamed the legacy as their own. Yet, on the other hand, there was no way that the Eurocentric perspective could welcome and comprehend the long-range implication of the changes that were underway at the time: race politics stood in the way of this natural imperative. A French music critic, writing in 1930, characterized Louis Armstrong's music as "only a naive and impoverished anarchy allied to a puerile cult of dissonance," and one French composer wrote off the jazz principle of group improvisation by asserting that it was mathematically impossible because it would require superhuman intuition for four performers to figure out what their partners were about to play. (Goddard, 137) According to Marshall Stearns, the Fletcher Henderson band of 1926, which he termed "truly swinging," was admired but condescended to by white musicians who misconstrued its dissonance as "playing out of tune": "By [conventional] European standards the white jazzmen were right. But the ears of most [white] musicians are better educated today. What sounded rough and out-of-tune then sounds relaxed and swinging now. The [African American] jazzman's notion of the liberties that may be taken with the perfect pitch of European music has been steadily broadening toward a predictable goal—the freedom of the street-cry and the field-holler." (1970, 202)

African American jazz bands touring Europe had a substantial influence on pushing European music in a new direction. One of the most important early groups was the legendary Sam Wooding band. Invited for long residencies in Berlin from the mid-twenties through 1931, they played for the hit show *Chocolate Kiddies,* for two months in 1925. (See Chapter 5) This ensemble had a profound influence on the sound of German cabaret music, moving it toward the sardonic-ironic measure that is associated with the likes of Marlene Dietrich and Frederick Hollander (who wrote some of her most famous songs), Bertolt Brecht, and Kurt Weill (who wrote essays about jazz for a Berlin radio magazine in 1926 and was composing American-style songs). ("From Harlem to Broadway")

It is noteworthy that black swing era arts and modern art were, together, condemned by Hitler's Third Reich as degenerate art and music—*Entartete Kunst* and *Entartete Musik*. A generous sampling of works so designated was organized for public view as a sort of primer to educate German citizens on what to look out for. These 1937 exhibitions, mentioned in Chapter 5, contained works by modernist European masters of visual arts, serial music composers, and jazz musicians. In one regard the Nazis made a right connection: there was a link between European modern art and music and African American modern music and dance. A Nazi poster for the degenerate music exhibit tells it all: it is a cartoon depiction of a man in blackface, dressed in top hat and tails, playing a saxophone, with a large star of David in his lapel. Modernists, Jews, and Africans were all in the same boat: as drama critic and theorist Martin Esslin put it, "Blacks were just another version of Jews." ("Swingtime for Hitler") In addition to jazz music, the Lindy specifically was targeted as degenerate. The Nazi party line on the dance was that it was the obscene folly of an inferior, primitive race, characterized by "cannibalistic abdominal contortions." (Back, 183)[6]

The winds of German racism as the harbinger of artistic repression were blowing before the Nazis officially came to power in 1933. Esslin recounts a frightening anecdote that presages both trends in a single event:

> I still remember when I was about nine or ten years old, 1928–29, in Vienna at the Opera House there were tremendous riots because Ernst Krenek . . . a great follower and pupil of [serial composer Arnold] Schoenberg, had written the first serious opera, *Johnny Spiel Auf—Johnny's Serenade*—in which the hero, in fact, was a Negro saxophonist. He introduced saxophone into the Vienna Opera House and there were tremendous demonstrations—riots—that this holy temple of the German muses had been desecrated by *Negermusik*—Negro music. ("Swingtime for Hitler")

Although literature is not the focus of this book, a brief digression in that direction is apropos. Mary Austin's remark about the bogus realm points to the deep structural, subliminal ways in which the swing aesthetic worked its wonders in defining modern literature. Dating back to premodernism and the work of authors like Mark Twain and Herman Melville, the Africanist aesthetic legacy had been a submerged but significant force in American letters.[7] As infused as American culture is with Africanist presences, this is hardly surprising. And, with the perpetuation of racism to deny it, its invisibilization is also not surprising. In 1924 writer Carl Van Doren told an audience that the African American legacy held the unique capacity to bring "color, music, gusto, the free expression of gay or desperate moods" to a flagging American literary tradition. (Douglas, 81) Even though, seven decades later, we discern the primitive trope in this statement, Van Doren was correct in his assessment. The particular interplay of emotion, spontaneity, energy, speed, rhythm, timing, parody, irony, innuendo, improvisation—and tricksterism—that are essential components in Africanist aesthetics were what was needed to modernize American literature.

It has been pointed out that Ernest Hemingway sought out and soaked up jazz and the blues in Chicago cabarets in the early 1920s, reflecting them in his uniquely American style. African Americans are frequent presences and resonances, particularly in his early work. (Douglas, 111; Morrison, 63–91) T. S. Eliot's *The Waste Land* was regarded by some as a kind of jazz, and minstrel and music hall presences are said to constitute a major, although invisibilized, component in his poetry. (Douglas, 113) Clearly, any writer worth his salt would be out of the modernist trajectory had he not been influenced by Africanist resonances—whether it was Lawrence Durrell, playing jazz piano in the Soho sector of London as a young man, or Kingsley Amis, Norman Mailer, and a host of others soaking up jazz culture and allowing it to draw them in and inflect, if not transform, their perspectives. A generation of white artists imbibed the swing aesthetic in the artistic haunts they frequented and from the world at large. But the race card stood in the way of open acknowledgment and celebration of the black presence: black influences in white literature, as well as literature by blacks, suffered a long history of repression, denial, and obscurity. From the Negritude and Harlem Renaissance movements emerged a cadre of talented writers, including Claude McKay, Countee Cullen, Nella Larsen, Langston Hughes, Jean Toomer, Wallace Thurman, and Zora Neale Hurston, who made major contributions to modern American literature. However, unlike the works of their white counterparts, this oeuvre was allowed to go out of print, languishing in the dark until recently rediscovered.

Returning to swing era dance, the Lindy stands as a signifier of modernism and the modernist impulse. Like modern art, it features a strong emphasis on the individual imperative. Out of the rhythmic base of its set structure, the dance was defined by the distinctive talents and expertise of its practitioners in the art of instantaneous improvisation. A good Lindy-Hopper could "quote" movements from everything and anything—from old fad dances to moves seen in church or gestures glimpsed while walking down the street. According to El Hajj Malik El-Shabazz, who worked in Boston's Roseland Ballroom in the early 1940s, "The white people danced as though somebody had trained them—left, one, two; right, three, four—the same steps and patterns over and over. . . . But those Negroes—nobody in the world could have choreographed the way they did whatever they felt. . . . (X and Haley, 50) Later, when he was still Malcolm Little and had moved to Harlem, El-Shabazz himself became an adroit Lindy-Hopper at the Savoy. One dance researcher, in examining El-Shabazz's relationship to the Lindy, pointed out that he "evidently understood its capacity to absorb into its vocabulary virtually any other dance movement from any culture." (Monaghan, 2)

The implications of this dance and its replication of innovations achieved by swing music render it deserving of the title "modern dance"— a name that has been reserved for a genre of concert dance (itself indebted to, but in denial of, Africanist roots) practiced in the thirties, forties, and fifties almost exclusively by Europeans and European Americans. Thus, the modern dance canon needs revision and expansion so that Lindy Hop choreographers and dancers like Frank Manning, Leon James, and Norma Miller are cited in the same breath with "modern" dancers like Martha Graham, Helen Tamiris, Doris Humphrey, Charles Weidman, and Mary Wigman; and the rhythm tap innovators led by John Bubbles belong in the picture as well. Modern dance forms were generated in ballrooms, nightclubs, and on the musical comedy stage, as well as on the concert stage. In spite of differences in means, forms, and aesthetic premises, all of it is art, and all of it is modern. We need to do away with the labels that separate popular and so-called art culture. In the case of the Lindy and so-called modern dance, these labels serve the function of racism by separating the realms of endeavor that have traditionally been reserved for blacks—that is, vernacular or pop culture—from those that are the exclusive property of whites—namely, the world of "art." These labels reify a cultural trope that privileges white forms over and above black forms. Nevertheless, the Lindy bridged these hierarchical divisions in the same way that swing music achieved this end. As one writer pointed out in speaking of Duke Ellington's oeuvre, this music legend, "like the other great figures of American modernism, be they Buster Keaton or Ernest Hemingway, had found a way to be both popular and intelligent." (Watrous, 33) The same could be said of the Lindy and the sophisticated, rhythmically complex form of tap dance that was popularized and made accessible by the likes of Baby Laurence, Bunny Briggs, Pete Nugent, Coles and Atkins, and the great John Bubbles. Both rhythm tap dance—with its cool energy, indirect approach to the audience, and attention to the task with the artist as skilled technician—and the Lindy—with its radical partnering and acrobatic moves—offered subliminal prototypes for European American "modern" dance as well as for postmodern dance and contact improvisation.[8]

One concert dance heir of the swing aesthetic whose output is of particular interest in this regard is white female choreographer Twyla Tharp. She received training in music and a variety of dance styles, including tap. The full sweep of her work—even after she disbanded her own company in the 1980s to choreograph for the American Ballet Theater and do freelance work—mirrors the swing aesthetic, both patently and as a driving, subliminal force. Some of her works (including *Eight Jelly Rolls*, 1971 and *The Bix Pieces*, 1972) used scores of swing and preswing music. In other works it is the sense of dynamic attack in movement and rhythm, radical shifts and displacements of body weight, sexual equality in partnering (a common Lindy practice appropriated by postmodern dancers since the 1960s), and parodic sensual humor (like Josephine Baker, sexy, silly, and savvy all at the same time) that reveal her identity as a child of swing. From the 1970s (with works like *Deuce Coupe* and *As Time Goes By*, both choreographed in 1973 for the City Center Joffrey Ballet) through the present, Tharp imported this aesthetic into the ballet world, extending the swing aesthetic in ways that left even George Balanchine[9] behind.

She stretched, pushed, and extended ballet to render it ever more accommodating to the undergirding force of the African American swing presence.

If swing music can be defined as a democratic equation of tight rhythmic structure and organization balanced against improvisation as its equal partner—or improvisation within an arranged rhythmic structure—then, metaphorically speaking, Duke Ellington and Louis Armstrong can be seen as representatives of the two sides of the swing coin: Ellington the composer-arranger and Armstrong the improviser. Ellington, in his symphonic works, took the traditional Europeanist form of orchestral music just about as far as it could go while still respecting its definitions. (Other composers—including serialists Arnold Schoenberg and Alban Berg, electronic composers like Karl-Heinz Stockhausen, creators of musique concrète like John Cage, and postmodernists like Steve Reich and Philip Glass—basically abandoned the canon.) Ellington was a jazz composer, unlike Gershwin who was "a composer who borrowed from jazz" (Giddins, 109–110) He bridged the gap between those old hierarchies, popular and "art" music and, in the process, blackened the white aesthetic in orchestral music. In a series of articles run by the *New York Times* on the occasion of Ellington's one hundredth birthday (17 January 1999), Robert O'Meally observed, "Rather than squeezing home-grown forms like the blues and the 32-bar song into European symphonic frames, he used these vernacular forms to build a series of works composed of related movements. Duke created uniquely Ellingtonian music that worked equally on the concert stage and in the dance hall." (33)

Similarly, Wynton Marsalis remarked that "Armstrong took the blues sound and applied it to harmonic progressions from the classical tradition of Europe, making it possible to play the most non-American material with soul and feeling." (1) Armstrong's influence was a radical, subversive one that changed the shape of jazz to come—not only the music, but also the jazz persona. If Ellington's presentation of self was the handsome, sexy, man about town, then Armstrong's was that of the trickster. A trickster is more than just a comedian. In traditional African culture he is the guardian of the crossroads, that important site where vertical and horizontal energies of past, present, and future converge and converse. The trickster is a seer—providing glimpses, inklings, of the future—as well as a voice for his constituency. Armstrong's scatting, for example, is a lot more than nonsense. To the untrained ear, it might sound like a decorative means of filling in empty spaces. However, scatting is undergirding—not overlay—and it can serve to play up the bass rhythm, emphasize meaning, underscore emotion, or even create new meaning. The fact that scatting has become a basic tool in the jazz vocalist's palette is due to Armstrong's innovative adaptation of this old Africanist technique. As one writer in a 1930 issue of the English music magazine *Melody Maker* pointed out, Armstrong was a master of innovative self-expression, finding "unorthodox," eye-opening, highly original ways of making music speak. (Major Stone, quoted in Goddard, 180). He possessed an inimitably glorious talent for presenting himself as the music and the music as himself, seamlessly and masterfully fusing the language of swing with his own personal vocabulary.

This unorthodox individuality was a quality that was lusted after by European modernist composers and visual artists. That is why, in 1919, orchestral conductor Ernst Ansermet had presaged that African American music might be the "highway the whole world will swing along tomorrow." (Giddins, 84) The following quote, from *Melody Maker* critic Spike Hughes, after Armstrong's European debut at the London Palladium, pinpoints a constellation of ideas that were central to modern European orchestral music, ideas that the reviewer, who had previously known Armstrong's music only through recordings, had seen realized in Armstrong's performance:

I had never realized the extreme economy of means by which Armstrong achieves his effects, and the light and shade he uses to build his climaxes.

This instinctive building of climaxes reveals the true artist; never in my experience have I known Armstrong to defer or anticipate the last note of a number or allow a bar to go on for too long. You know that when he has finished playing there could never have been a second's more music and that the last word on the subject has been said. (Goddard, 181)

In other words, Armstrong's playing fit the purpose and needs of the music: form followed function and, to borrow modernist architect Walter Gropius's phrase, less was more. Thus, Armstrong incarnated two of the basic principles of Bauhaus aesthetics.[10] At that point he "was the only figure in musical history—high or low, Western or other—whose singing was as influential as his musicianship, proving twice over that improvisation can yield not just the authority but the perfection of composition." Indeed, Armstrong's innovations in sound and style expanded the range and potential for the trumpet in symphony orchestras as well as in jazz. "Philharmonic orchestras that once favored concision now used a heavier vibrato (the conductor Maurice Peress recalled that when he studied trumpet his teacher made the students listen to Armstrong records)." (Giddins, 85, 87)

Armstrong accomplished his feats by superseding the reigning Europeanist aesthetic canon. In this sense one is tempted to compare him to 1990s hiphop artists who also have redefined and reshaped the meaning of art and artists, particularly in their talking-singing style, polyrhythmic complexity, and tricksterish self-presentation. Actually, were it not for Armstrong, the hiphop persona might look quite different. It was Armstrong who helped to upend old minstrel stereotypes by daring to be a "sexy, stylish, African American black joker-artist whose music's undeniable splendor projects an equally undeniable spirit of freedom." (Giddins, 87–88) Thus, Armstrong's modernist, swing jazz aesthetic was a harbinger of both postmodern music that jolts and jokes with the text and postmodern performance aesthetics—epitomized in hiphop forms—that recognizes the performer as the performance. Listening to his 1950s hit *Mack The Knife* brings into clear focus much of what is stated. Indeed, Europe was seduced by Armstrong: jazz epitomized the existentialism that post–World War I European modernists advocated and espoused. With a host of other jazz artists, he had been born and bred in the outsider, outlaw life that formed the content of works by composer Kurt Weill, writer Bertolt Brecht, and an entire school of modern endeavor. Armstrong the modernist is also the subversive, disrupting established codes and standing at the crossroads, pointing the way to liberation.

Second Movement: Swing as
Subversive, Disruptive, Liberationist

Ask the Lindy-Hoppers who lived in the "'hood," worked as "kitchen me-chanics" during the day and, come dark, took on a new identity at the ballroom. Ask the vaudeville-unit trouper doing five shows a day and one-night stands but refusing to throw in the towel. Ask the white Amer-ican swing era youth whose indigenous habitat was Wonder-Bread-squeaky-clean but who (like historian Ernie Smith, growing up white and working class in Pittsburgh)[11] lusted after the black style of dance and music that, to her, was the heart of swing. Ask the European royalty whose background and upbringing stood in stark contrast to the swing culture they sought out from dusk to dawn. Ask the Russians, Hungari-ans, and East Germans living behind the Iron Curtain, their comings and goings rigorously monitored, who looked to the sound of Willis Conover and Radio Free Europe for the freedom offered by the swinging sound of jazz. Ask the Swing Youth of Nazi Germany, who pitted themselves in direct opposition to the Hitler Youth movement by dancing the Lindy, listening to jazz, and dressing like hep cats—all of which marked them as "degenerate." Ask, and all speak out, proclaiming swing as the sound of democracy and the legacy of freedom.

Swing culture provided each of these constituencies with an aesthetic of liberation: the cool, easy, laid back, improvisational nature of swing arts intimated the same values in lifestyle and world view, socially and politi-cally. In other words, the aesthetic of swing translated into a politic of swing. For African Americans, this conversion was partly necessitated by racism: politics was translated into cultural activity, since segregation barred blacks from mainstream political participation. Swing culture could exert a subversive political power in many ways. An issue that most infuriated white racists was the crossing of racial boundaries at swing events. Even though blacks and whites were separated by segregated seat-ing arrangements or separate theaters and ballrooms, it was inevitable that slippage occurred along the margins of the racial taboo—especially given the volatile, ecstatic, and community-making swing events that brought different people together. It was impossible, given this exuberant, climactic gestalt, for audiences in their enthusiasm to rigorously observe segregation's artificial boundaries. There, at the periphery, in the few places (almost always in the black community) where blacks and whites could publicly meet and mingle, age-old boundaries were blurred, and racial taboos were broken on the backside of the dominant culture: spontaneous integration was a common occurrence.

It was the physical body of swing culture as personified in the black dancing body that was feared. This black swing body insinuated a flexibility that translated as moral looseness, a freewheeling attitude that translated as radicalism, and a confident presentation of self (this dance cannot be done in a shy manner) that challenged racist tenets of black inferiority. The next step was logical (and had occurred, generation after generation, since the minstrel era): in spite of racial taboos, the white population, particularly white youth, was fascinated by and drawn to the black dancing body. And there lay the deep-seated threat posed to a racist dominant culture by swing music and dance: it intimated miscegenation, the union of black and white bodies, not only on the ballroom floor but, ultimately, in bed. Thus the Lindy itself held the potential to undermine and subvert racism: the dance's smooth integration of music and dance symbolized the integration of blacks and whites.

Since whites could travel anywhere they wanted, many came to the Savoy ballroom in Harlem, the segregated Roseland ballroom in Boston (not only on white nights, but to crash the dance events set aside for blacks), and to ballrooms nationwide and abroad that were frequented by black performers and patrons. Themselves subject to racism on a daily basis, African American swing era performers were well aware of these integrative transgressions and the consequences they could give rise to in a hostile dominant culture. Lindy artist Norma Miller and swing composer-musician Earl Hines both described swing era performers as freedom fighters. Long before the Civil Rights movement there they were, on the road in small-town white America, playing to all-white audiences, revealing and spreading the black aesthetic and changing mainstream performance perspectives in the process. The irony: an oppressed people's artistry became the keynote of freedom for a dominant culture that segregated the dancer from the dance, that loved the message but denied and discriminated against the messenger.

The black-white racial divide was also subverted by those light-skinned blacks who passed and, thus, gained entry to Cotton Club-type venues and other whites-only accommodations. Blacks passed as white in order to see an all-black show targeted for a whites-only audience: such convolutions are characteristic of American race politics. This racial etiquette invited—if not demanded—tricksterism, and tricksterism is deeply implied on the black side of the American racial equation.

Because overt protest on the whole was too risky, African Americans were obliged to tolerate racial oppression for reasons of survival. However, they did not readily accept this situation. They developed intricate systems of subversion: coded languages, songs with double meanings, messages transmitted through drums (which is why American plantation owners outlawed the drum early on). Subversion was an essential and necessary tactic: it was the price of the ticket for Middle Passage and the injustices that ensued, generation after generation. Each era of African Americans developed their own codes that were appropriate to their epoch, their communities, and the larger context of the dominant culture. So, for example, enslaved African Americans hoping to follow the Underground Railroad (a wonderful code name, in itself) to freedom sang spirituals that carried hidden messages. The white slave owner had no idea that *Follow the Drinking Gourd* was not simply a mournful black spiritual but a signal that the Big Dipper constellation could be seen in the northern sky that night to guide a group of African Americans to freedom. Reconstruction work songs and chain gang chants (such as the *Boll Weevil* song) were embedded with coded insults about unscrupulous white bosses. These are just two examples of a practice that actually predates African enslavement and is rooted in African conventions of socially sanctioned ritual abuse in the form of insult songs and indirect or coded ways of delivering social and political criticism. It is an excellent example of the way in which traditional African practices were tailored and reshaped by African Americans to meet their survival needs in a hostile new world.

Accordingly, African American culture has always been subversive and improvisatory, by force of circumstance, with its members adept at code-switching—both in verbal and body language—as the need arises. In the performance realm these practices are part of the "long, irreverent history of black performers signifying attitudes that went over the heads of white audiences." (Giddins, 24) By the time the swing era was in full tilt, blacks had developed elaborate, site-specific, era- and occasion-specific ways of signifying, playing the trickster, and subverting the master.

Cab Calloway's *Hepster's Dictionary* brought some of the swing era linguistic code to light in a pocket volume that was circulated among whites who wanted to be "hep" (an early version of "hip").[12] On examination of the miniature lexicon, it becomes evident that African American adjustments to standard English practiced back in the 1930s became common usage in late twentieth-century white America. Terms such as chick, corny, collar, reefer and weed, and too much are African Americanisms that have become part of current usage by blacks and whites, here and abroad. Then, there are terms that were not exported or appropriated, particularly the more obscure terms for sexuality, as well as the many coded ways of referring to white people. "Ofay" was one of a host of words denoting a white person. A rather innocent-sounding phrase, "the boy in the boat," was one of many that signified women's genitals. (Giddins, 144) Coded words or phrases such as these appeared in song lyrics and in hepster discourse, thus offering a range of meanings to swing era listeners, depending on how intimate their knowledge of black culture was. Such coding is common among disenfranchised peoples living under the thumb of an alien culture. What is unique about African American slang is that, from the swing era to the present, it has been exported, along with African American culture, as a hip commodity for global consumption.

For a sublime example of coded subversion swing era style, turn again to Louis Armstrong. This particular example, recounted by jazz writer Gary Giddins deserves repeating: it involves recordings Armstrong made with the Mills Brothers singing group between 1937 and 1940. Several old minstrel songs, part of the vocal group's repertory of sentimental American songs (and one of the reasons why they were well liked in white circles—probably they were the first black singing group with crossover popularity) were included in the sessions: James Bland's *Carry Me Back to Old Virginny*, Benjamin Hanby's *Darling Nellie Gray*, and Stephen Foster's *The Old Folks at Home*. In his inimitable style—rasping voice, scatting, and injection of improvised comments—Armstrong deconstructs and revises the songs' messages, particularly in the Foster tune. On the lines that turn on the freed black's longing to return to plantation life, Armstrong launches into an overblown "darkie" caricature, parodying the lines by rendering them as if he were a sanctified, emotional preacher. At the end he adds two lines of his own, and thereby hangs the tale: letting go of the preacher character, he returns to himself and says, with irony, "Well, looka here, we are far away from home," mocking Foster's sentiments, followed by "Yeah, man," in a rasping, menacing tone. (23–27)

In Bland's *Carry Me Back to Old Virginny* (by the way, Bland was African American, a fact unknown by many white supremacists who looked upon this song and others in Bland's prolific output—such as *In the Evening by the Moonlight* and *Oh Dem Golden Slippers*—as part of their heritage), the Mills Brothers begin by singing the song straight. Then, Armstrong enters by scatting and upping the tempo to double time, already changing the character and intention of the message. Next, words that are written in that fake but commonplace Uncle Remus-type dialect are enunciated with clarity: Armstrong changes a phrase like "ole massa" to "old master"—effectively stripping the phrase of its intended obsequiousness. Finally, his trumpet playing comes across as an unmistakable call to freedom rather than a yearning to return to plantation life. It is most probable that swing era whites listening to these renditions would not have a clue as to Armstrong's signifying. This was his ironic, metaphorical wink at and homage to his African American listeners who could understand, from experience, the subversion and survival strategy.[13] In a more straightforward political stance, Armstrong had chided the Eisenhower administration during the school integration crisis in Little Rock, Arkansas, in the 1950s, refusing to tour abroad as a United States cultural ambassador until the government took action. (Giddins, 102)

In his American masterpiece *Invisible Man*, Ralph Ellison utilizes Armstrong as a trope of subversive invisibility:

I'd like to hear five recordings of Louis Armstrong playing and singing *What Did I Do to Be So Black and Blue*—all at the same time. . . . Louis bends that military instrument into a beam of lyrical sound. Perhaps I like Louis Armstrong because he's made poetry out of being invisible. . . . And my own grasp of invisibility aids me to understand his music. . . . Invisibility, let me explain, gives one a slightly different sense of time, you're never quite on the beat. Sometimes you're ahead and sometimes behind. Instead of the swift and imperceptible flowing of time, you are aware of its nodes, those points where time stands still or from which it leaps ahead. And you slip into the breaks and look around. That's what you hear vaguely in Louis' music. (8)

This sublime description gives a sense of Armstrong's profound influence on the aural potential of the twentieth-century ear, and not only the ear of the invisible man. Armstrong and the jazz aesthetic he represented opened up new avenues for artists and ordinary people of all ethnicities and walks of life. His sound—and the sound of bandleaders like Henderson, Wooding, Basie, Ellington, and their exceptional musicians—changed the way we perceive and experience the world. This influence was so profound as to subvert what went before it and to stand, alone, as a trope of freedom—or of subversion when freedom was disallowed: "We are so accustomed to hearing jazz and American-influenced popular music—the sound of the twentieth century—that our ears cannot imagine a world of sound without the freedom of syncopated jazz." (O'Connor, 20)

Duke Ellington played a significant role in the dissemination of swing as a signifier of liberation. Not so much trickster or subversive, Ellington composed orchestral suites throughout his career that demonstrated pride in black culture and heralded the black experience, channeled through his music, as the sound of freedom. Whereas Armstrong injected revisionist texts into the racialized American song of an earlier era, Ellington forthrightly proclaimed "the character and mood and feeling of my people" (Watrous, 33) as a valid landscape for his symphonic compositions such as *Black, Brown and Beige* (1943), *New World A-Coming* (1943), *Deep South Suite* (1946), and even pieces as late as *The River* (1970): "Blurring the boundaries of high and low art became his way of protesting segregation and discrimination in society at large." (Tucker, 32)

Ellington's profound influence on orchestral music, particularly the relationship between jazz and symphonic composition, once "condescended to or totally ignored," today is understood as "amazingly relevant" (Ratliff, 31), thanks in part to the efforts of composer-trumpeter Wynton Marsalis, artistic director of Jazz at Lincoln Center. According to Marsalis:

Duke understood that music could be called upon to evoke diverse aspects of our national character, and he drew on the musical personalities of his band members to create a particular American tapestry of mood and style. So the alto saxophonist Johnny Hodges, with his urbane nonchalance, could be a city slicker or a crooner. The big-toned trumpeter Cootie Williams from Alabama could be a country boy or a preacher or even Paul Bunyan. And the gruff but sensitive tenor saxophonist Ben Webster could be a boisterous brawler or a lyrical poet. Duke felt that such characters were variations on figures from a mythic past, which came mainly from two places: the long suffering of slavery and the so-what-if-it-hurts jubilation of New Orleans. (31)

In other words, Ellington fused African American and European American mythologies and musical traditions in a mix that flowed as naturally and easily as contacts between blacks and whites might have if racism didn't exist. This does not mean that he honeyed over the real-life suffering of the black experience; instead, his work presented that experience as quintessentially American. Thus, Marsalis can justifiably assert that "His was a distinctly democratic vision of music in the service of the whole band's sound and, more than any other composer, he codified the sound of America in the 20th century." (1) And, I would like to add, Ellington not only "codified the sound of America in the 20th century" but he created it in the service of democracy and freedom for African Americans and, by extension, for all peoples.

One of the most poignant examples of swing as both subversive and liberationist was a movement that arose in Nazi Germany. Its young adherents were dubbed Swing Youth—*Swingjugend* in contradistinction to *Hitlerjugend*—and were centered in Hamburg.[14] In this instance, the Lindy served as an antidote to fascism, its free-spirited, improvisational gestalt embodying ideals that countered everything Nationalist Socialism stood for:

In October 1935, taking their place alongside the Nuremberg Laws which set Germany apart from the rest of the civilised world, came the edicts enacted by *gauleiters*[15] from Saxony to the Sudetenland, banning "swing and hot music" on the radio, proscribing all syncopated music, the use of wah-wahs, mutes and saxophones and any elements of hot music. . . . Huge signs in Gothic script saying *Swingtanz Verboten* (Swing-dance Forbidden) were hung at the doors of dance-halls. (Ackerman, 20)

For the Nazis, the prohibitions were absolutely necessary: like Great Britain and the United States, Germany was enthralled by the swing aesthetic as rendered by both black and white artists. Although British and Euro-American racists may have detested the Lindy's potential for integration, the Germans pathologically equated swing culture's ability to erase difference with a fall from Aryan grace into the muddied waters of miscegenation. But their vehemence did not stamp out the movement until they sent *Swingjugend* to concentration camps. As is the case with African-based vernacular dance since plantation days, the Lindy embodied, like its African American creators, the transcendence of slavery, oppression, and repression. Likewise, it served the same function for German youth: "In those sounds and motions they discovered a living response to the terrorising racism that lurked in the shadow of modernity and which found its expression within the Third Reich." (Back, 194–95)

The Nazis launched a forceful counterattack on Swing Youth as well as on all manifestations of swing in German society. But, because swing rivaled Nazism in popularity—at least among particular segments of the population, with even some Nazis among its enthusiasts—the German officials had to wager a compromise. For Germans who insisted on listening to swing, they could have it but with German propaganda as its content. The Nazis actually set up a committee of experts, under Goebbels's cultural oversight, to discriminate between *Negerjazz* and acceptable German music. German dance bands were encouraged to play "in the sanctioned mode (no plucking of the double bass, no scat vocals, favoring the use of 'German instruments.')" (Ackerman, 20) The attack went so far as to encompass an all-out propaganda campaign via German radio aimed, specifically, to be airwaved back to British and American troops to undermine their morale. In a corruption of Brechtian irony, the German radio station broadcast parodies of popular British and American songs. The first verse could be sung straight, followed by anti-British or antisemitic inserts. For example, the Cole Porter song *You're The Top* (introduced in the 1934 Broadway musical *Anything Goes*), had these new lyrics inserted:

You're the top, you're a German flyer
You're the top, You're machine-gun fire
You're a U-boat cap with a lot of pep, you're grand
You're a German blitz, the Paris Ritz, an Army band. ("Swingtime
    for Hitler")

There were versions such as this of many popular American and British songs. Some were directly antisemitic; others parodied Allied figures like Winston Churchill. These programs were broadcast daily. Specialists in Goebbels's propaganda ministry researched the songs and wrote the words; they were the only Germans officially allowed to listen to Anglo-American music, and solely for this reason. The renditions were musically smooth, since the best German jazz musicians were rounded up and inducted into a band jauntily dubbed "Charley and his Orchestra" (named after its lead singer Karl "Charley" Schwedler) for this express purpose. Besides these broadcasts, Charley also went to the German front, presenting the same repertory to German troops for morale-boosting purposes. According to the band's drummer, Freddie Brocksieper, these musicians opted to play Nazi propaganda rather than having to take up a gun and go to war. He further contends that they were not Nazis, that Nazism and jazz were opposing ideologies. However, they were handsomely paid at a time when most Germans were living off rations, suggesting that they could just as easily be considered mercenaries and their music "degenerate in the true sense of the word." (Ferguson) The British retaliated by inserting Allied propaganda, sung in German, into typical German sentimental songs to be broadcast by the BBC over airwaves to Germany.

The fact is, swing culture—the culture of resistance and survival—was stronger than Nazism and thrived even in concentration camps, due to the SS desire for swing music and the need to keep up appearances when the Red Cross came to visit. Thus, there existed in the Theresienstadt camp a big band called the Ghetto Swingers, which appeared in a Nazi propaganda film made especially for the Red Cross. (Ackerman, 21)

The Nazi love-hate relationship with the swing aesthetic stands as a high-relief prototype of the ancient attraction-repulsion of Europe (not only Germans, by any means) and Euro-America toward people and creations of African descent. Indeed, schizoid, binary reactions clutter the centuries-old history of the European colonization of Africa, the European relation to African American soldiers and citizens on European lands in the twentieth century, and black-white relations in the United States. In Europe and in white America, with each generation since the minstrel era, black culture has served whites as a subversion of and liberation from their own.

Finale

I was never convinced that the melting pot was an appropriate metaphor for the way in which people ought to come together. . . . Even the talk these days about a mosaic, to me, is still a little bit too static. My ideal of a democratic community is a jazz band. The reason being, of course, because it observes individuality; it allows interplay between the individual and the community without that community gobbling up the individual or the individual somehow seizing center-stage. And one must be always open, listening to the unpredictable—especially given the moods of the musicians at a particular moment—but you always have your eye on something larger than you: the artistic achievement . . . that empowers other ordinary people . . . to enact, not simply allude to, a certain democratic sensibility.

—Cornel West[16]

Racism defined and determined the day-to-day life as well as the long-range aspirations of the black swing era performer. Nevertheless, let us acknowledge and celebrate the fact that this segment of the American populace produced a glowing, effervescent, innovative, and lasting legacy that has affected not only popular culture but also what is known as "art culture," particularly, those movements known as modernism and post-modernism.

Swing text and trope were essential to post–World War I and post–World-War II developments in Europeanist orchestral music and dance as well as on the popular stage. Without it, George Balanchine could not have choreographed *Apollo* (1928), *The Four Temperaments* (1946), and *Agon* (1957), as well as a host of other ballets.[17] Indeed, without this basic ingredient, the Americanization of ballet would not have happened. Without it, Igor Stravinsky could not have composed many of his best-loved works, including the scores for *Apollo* and *Agon;* nor would Paul Hindemith have made the music that Balanchine used to score *The Four Temperaments;* and compositions by scads of others, including Darius Milhaud, Eric Satie, Maurice Ravel, Dimitri Shostakovich, Aaron Copland, Ferde Grofé—to name just a few—would not have come about.[18] Without it, there would be no George Gershwin oeuvre; *West Side Story* and *Fancy Free* would exist neither as a Jerome Robbins choreography nor as a Leonard Bernstein score; Frank Sinatra's song style wouldn't make the heart skip a beat by its impeccable sense of timing, rhythm, and styling. Without it, Jackson Pollock wouldn't have created action painting,[19] and a new school of postwar American visual art would not have developed; jazz buffs Piet Mondrian and Stuart Davis would not have devised the stark motifs that characterized their styles;[20] Henri Matisse would not have originated an inimitable collage series whose sense of style is acknowledged as a resonance of the swing aesthetic by its apt and simple title, "Jazz"; Fernand Léger's mode of painting would be missing one of its definitive characteristics. Without it, basketball wouldn't have developed into the fast-moving, time-sensitive dance that it is today (which was capitalized on decades ago by the magnificent, swinging sportsmanship of the Harlem Globetrotters); T. S. Eliot, John Dos Passos, Ernest Hemingway, Jack Kerouac, Allen Ginsburg, and a host of other poets and novelists would not have developed in the ways that they did.[21]

Without the swing era legacy rooted in the African American experience, there would have developed none of its many white jazz exponents: imagine a world without the sounds of Benny Goodman, the Dorsey Brothers, Jack Teagarden, Bix Beiderbecke, Gene Krupa, Red Nichols, Red Norvo, Stan Kenton, Stan Getz, Chet Baker, Gerry Mulligan, Charlie Barnet, Bill Evans, Gil Evans. Without it white Broadway, after the ephemeral rise and fall of the 1920s black Broadway era, would not have become the swing site that could produce its own version of jazz dance with white exponents like choreographers Matt Mattox, Michael Kidd, Marge and Gower Champion, and Bob Fosse, and legendary dancers like Gwen Verdon and Carole Haney (one could easily do a slowed-down Lindy to the rhythm of her famous solo, *Steam Heat,* from the 1954 Broadway hit musical, *The Pajama Game*). Without it, Hollywood choreographer Hermes

Pan wouldn't have been able to create the Astaire-Rogers routines for their RKO musicals; and dancers like the great Fred Astaire, Gene Kelly, and Donald O'Connor would not have had a repertory.

Without it, white Baptist and Pentecostal Christians probably would not have so easily moved into an African American style of worship, taking on the swinging rhythms of gospel music in their services and the sense of rhythm and timing of black preachers in their sermons. Without it, at least two generations of black and white American youth would not have moved closer together, at least in aesthetic preferences and lifestyles—although black and white worlds still see themselves as separate, and race politics continues to keep them unequal.

Without the black swing era legacy, our world would be diminished. What would we do, if we weren't all so black and blue?

Chronology

Margot Webb's
Professional Career

The data listed below are documented by resources from Margot Webb's private collection and entries from the microfilm archive of African American newspapers at the Schomburg Collection of the New York Public Library, where I carried out a selected search in key publications. Many bookings for artists like Webb were, of course, undocumented. Therefore, the record is incomplete. Gaps in the list of performances do not necessarily indicate that Norton and Margot were not performing but only that documentation was not found for those periods. Yet, this record is useful in providing an overview of the scope and context of Webb's career. In general, specific dates for bookings were found on contracts and programs from the Webb collection; day of the month indicates the beginning day/date entered on the standard, vaudeville week-long contracts in Webb's possession. Documentation is more complete at the beginning of her career with Harold Norton because of the team's initial enthusiasm for what seemed to be a promising future. As the future became the present and their achievement potential stagnated, they revised their expectations, and Webb did not keep her scrapbooks up to date.

(Pre-Professional: 1922–29—Marjorie Smith performed as a semiprofessional on weekends and during the summer with African American chorus lines in white-only clubs and burlesque houses in the greater New York–New Jersey area; 1929—Smith entered Hunter College and continued performing semiprofessionally.)

1932

Smith dropped out of college and entered show business full-time, dancing in the chorus line in:

- The Leonard Harper revue, *Harlem Nights,* at Caton Inn, Brooklyn (12 January)
- Harper's *Sepia Rhythm* revue, at Caton Inn, Brooklyn (8 March)
- Harper's *Creole Revue,* in Montreal, Canada (undated)
- New York State resort areas, including Saratoga Springs

1933

Undocumented. Smith continued as a chorine, with an occasional featured part in front of the line. In one such instance she was assigned a fan dance during the run of a show in Philadelphia. There she met Harold Norton, and the team of "Norton and Margot" was born. Webb recalls that this revue was a touring unit that originated in New York and toured on the black East Coast circuit, playing both theater and club bookings.

Norton and Margot have their first engagement as a team at New York City's Club Harlem (December).

1934

The team of Norton and Margot performed in the following venues:

- A vaudeville tour of the Midwest. Although a *Chicago Defender* clipping asserts that the team toured with the band of Earl Hines, Webb does not remember ever touring with him and cannot recall the dates. This booking is undocumented in her private collection. (January-February?)
- Lincoln Theater, Philadelphia, and Howard Theater, Washington, D.C. (undated)
- Leonard Harper revues with the Earl Hines band at Chicago's Grand Terrace Café (April-December)

1935

The team of Norton and Margot performed in the following venues:

- A Midwest vaudeville tour with the Harriet Calloway unit (January–February)
- Amytis Theater, St. Louis: Webb recalls that this booking was extended for one or, possibly, two additional weeks beyond the original one week specified in the contract, which was a typical practice. (10 March)

- Apollo Theater, New York City (5–12 April)
- (Contract signed for team to tour the Soviet Union. The tour never took place. Contract date: 8 May)
- Lincoln Theater, Philadelphia (17 May)
- Howard Theater, Washington, D.C., with the Louis Armstrong unit. Probably this was the final booking on a unit tour of the East Coast circuit that originated with the 5 April booking at the Apollo (24 May)
- Apollo Theater: Webb asserts that their booking was most likely extended one or even two weeks (14 June)
- *All-Star Creole Review* [*sic*], Starlight Gardens, Philadelphia (1 July)
- Howard Theater (23 August)
- Apollo Theater (30 August)
- Fay's Theater, Philadelphia (6 September)
- Louis Armstrong's Apollo show, after traveling with his unit on the African American East Coast circuit (13 September)
- Grand Terrace, Chicago (mid-September-December)
- Hotel Vendome, Buffalo (27 December–27 January)

1936

- Norton and Margot at the Hotel Vendome, Buffalo (January)
- The team performed on the East Coast, either touring with the units on the theater circuit or in nightclub work. They also performed as paid professionals at black social events (February–June, September–December?)
- Margot taught dance at a Jewish summer camp in the Catskills by passing as a Latina and using the pseudonym "Santana" (July–August)
- Norton and Margot opened their Harlem dance studio

1937

Norton and Margot performed in yet another unit tour of the Midwest. She recalls playing in towns like Muncie and Elkhart, Indiana, and Omaha, Nebraska, on this and other tours (January–February ?).

In early June the *Cotton Club Revue* cast sailed on the *Lafayette* from New York to Le Havre, France. Norton and Margot performed with this unit, under bandleader Teddy Hill's direction, as follows:

- In Paris at the Moulin Rouge, followed by an engagement at the Théâtre des Ambassadeurs (12 June)
- In London at the Palladium, where the original two-week engagement was extended to six weeks (26 July)

When the unit disbanded the team stayed on in Europe and was booked as an independent act on European variety bills, as follows:

- In San Remo, Italy, at the Casino Municipale (September)
- In Paris at the Harlem Montmartre club and the Moulin Rouge (26 September–mid-October)
- In Berlin at the Club Sherbini, as the featured performers on a bill with musicians and a vocalist (October–mid-December)

Norton and Margot were expelled from Germany and sailed from Hamburg for New York (mid-December). At that time they had tentative engagements at the Kit Kat Club in Cairo, Egypt, the Thalia in Bucharest, Rumania, and the Ambassador's Cabaret of the Palace Hotel in Copenhagen, Denmark

1938
- Norton and Margot at Harlem's Plantation Club in a Clarence Robinson revue, *Tan Town Topics,* that was subsequently restaged by Norton in May (February–June)
- Margot participates as a paid professional performer in black New York society functions: fashion shows, beauty contests, etc. (June–September)
- Margot writes a theatrical gossip column for the New York office of the *Chicago Defender,* entitled "Harlem to Broadway" (June–September)
- The team may have toured on the East Coast circuit (September–December?)
- Norton and Margot close their Harlem dance studio
- (Margot resumes academic study at Hunter College)

1939
- Margot performs as a soloist, doing a jazz toe dance at the Apollo theater (June)
- She begins rehearsals for an acting role in a play, *Father Sublime,* by Dennis Donoghue. (The production never got off the ground.)
- She teaches dance and stages a production at a summer camp in Walkill, New York (July–August)
- Margot and Al Moore perform as a team at the Howard Theater (December)

1940
- Margot and Al Moore perform as a team at

Howard Theater, Washington, D.C. (January)

Philadelphia's Cotton Club with Bobby Evans and his orchestra (May)

- (Margot graduates from Hunter College with a B.A. in French)
- Margot works as an actress-dancer in rehearsals of a musical comedy, *Mr. Swing.* (The show never got off the ground.)
- (Margot marries William P. Webb, Jr.)

1941

- Margot performs at the Apollo as actress-dancer in the tabloid version of Abram Hill's play *On Striver's Row* (March)
- Margot and Al Vigal perform as an exotic team in a revue entitled *South Sea Magic* at the Tic Toc Club in Montreal (April)

Norton and Margot perform as a team on the following bookings:

- the Apollo *Club Mimo Revue,* followed by a tour of the East Coast circuit (June–July)
- Dave's Café, Chicago, in a revue entitled *The Show Must Go On* (October–November)
- the Plantation Club, St. Louis (undated)

1942

Mainly undocumented. Norton has married and his wife becomes his dance partner. Bookings are sparse in the wartime period. Webb works occasionally as a soloist and as the ballroom partner of Al Moore.

- Margot and Al Moore perform at a benefit held at the Renaissance Casino in Harlem (May)

1943–1945

Webb retires from show business and begins teaching dance (1944) in the afterschool recreation centers of New York public schools

1946–1947

Norton and Margot stage a comeback, opening in September at Harlem's Club Baron. Again, bookings are irregular, and they break up, definitively, in 1947. (Webb returns to graduate school at Columbia University Teachers College)

Notes

Chapter One

1. For justification of these dates, see the swing section of this chapter.
2. I coined this phrase, fully aware of its contradictory nature, because it matches the deceptions and paradoxes inherent in the American race dilemma, then and now. It is comparable to Michael Dyson's phrase, "ecology of race." (215) Both terms imply a conspiracy of and adherence to written or unwritten codes that kept blacks and whites separate and unequal.
3. On the one hand Josephine Baker, considered too dark, was obliged to wear lighter make-up; on the other, Lena Horne and Billie Holiday were required to "dark down" for particular engagements.
4. Debora Kodish, director, Philadelphia Folklore Project, addressing the issue of the "invisibilized" African American female tap artist. (Njeri, 41)
5. Throughout this work I refer to vaudeville performers as artists and their work as art. I aim to blur the divisions and trespass the boundaries between "high" and "low," "vernacular" and "art." When terminology is utilized in the traditional, divisive way (that privileges "art" over popular performance and reifies the hierarchy), it is placed in quotes.
6. I devised this neologism to indicate a condition or state that is stronger, deeper, and more intense than the meaning carried in the traditional word, invisible, or to make invisible. To be invisibilized, rather than made invisible, is intended to imply racism at work in the process.
7. This phrase is borrowed from the Langston Hughes essay, "The Negro Artist and the Racial Mountain" (1971) which is mentioned in Chapter 5. Hughes uses the phrase to denote in-group rejection of black aesthetics and a concomitant striving to be white; I use it, here, to indicate the accumulated force of racism that obstructs black achievement.
8. Nearly forty hours of interviews that I conducted with Margot Webb (from 1977–80 and, again, 1998–99) form the basis of this documentation and provide firsthand information for this study. I have been unable to uncover information on Harold Norton or his whereabouts.

9. Adagio: Any dance performed to slow music and characterized by grace-ful, sustained movement. In music and dance the opposite of adagio (slow) is allegro (quick).

10. This is not to demean the fine work of these two artists. Indeed, they were extraordinary talents, which is the reason why they were able to squeeze through to crossover fame. However, no one could "cross over" unless, like Fetchit and McDaniel, the performer comfortably fit the stereotype.

11. Two of the preeminent white American ballroom dance teams who played hotels, theaters, cabarets, and had bit parts in films. They were able to draw top salaries (see comparisons in Chapter 4) and their careers spanned several decades.

12. They popularized ballroom dancing in the United States and Europe. Specific dances made famous by them include the Maxixe, Tango, and Hesitation Waltz. (Chujoy and Manchester, 183)

13. American concert dance forms, both what is known as modern dance and ballet, were in their infancy. Virtually all dancers in these genres eked out a living by teaching dance or taking on other types of general work, as an artist's model, typist, or housecleaner. They took on pick-up gigs (book-ings) in vaudeville, Broadway shows, and on cabaret circuits. There was no steady, bills-paying circuit or venue devoted to concert dance. If the situation was serious for whites, it was dire for African Americans. Occa-sionally, white "modern" dance concerts might include a black group or soloist on a shared program, but white companies did not begin to em-ploy token blacks until the 1950s. With few exceptions "modern" dance, to this day, remains racially divided. (But this is only a reflection of the larger culture.) And blacks in ballet were considered an oxymoron until the end of the Civil Rights era (1969), and the advent of African Amer-ican Arthur Mitchell's ballet company, The Dance Theater of Harlem. Although black ballet dancers and ensembles had existed, off and on, since the 1930s, this was the first group to withstand the test of time. For more on blacks in concert dance during this era, see John Perpener, "The Seminal Years of Black Concert Dance" (doctoral dissertation, New York University, 1992).

14. African Americans might be engaged in a medicine show (A form of pop-ular entertainment that thrived during the minstrel and vaudeville eras in which homeopathic remedies were sold along with the entertainment) or carnival but not in a professional capacity that would allow them to draw a substantial salary, make a decent living, and perform in bona-fide theaters. According to Robert Toll (216), "although within a heavily stereotyped framework, black minstrels clearly demonstrated the diverse talents of black people. In the nineteenth century, minstrelsy was their only chance to make a regular living as entertainers, musicians, actors, or composers." Toll

is highly recommended as an excellent sourcebook on African American minstrelsy.

15. For example: "Responding to a racist public policy that condoned segregated and inferior homes and schools, African American clubwomen often formed successful networks devoted to neighborhood improvement. . . . Seemingly frivolous social activities like grand-scale balls worked to circulate money throughout black communities." (Patterson, 226)

16. Goddard, 90, 89.

17. See Dixon Gottschild (1998), especially Chapter 2, 11–19.

18. Ibid., 12 and 19, n. 2: sources for this theory include Thompson, Vogel, and Welsh Asante.

19. Dixon Gottschild, 16–17.

20. All citations from Miller refer to the Preface by Ernie Smith.

21. In fact, Stearns contradicts his own assertion a few pages earlier by claiming that Fletcher Henderson led a "truly swinging band" by the year 1926. (201)

22. See Williams, 1987, 42, quoting Richard Hadlock, and 44, 50 (author's emphasis).

23. Defined in the *Oxford Dictionary and Thesaurus* as "a foreigner admitted to certain rights in his or her adopted country," this word aptly describes the role of the outcasts of medieval Europe and the black vaudevillian traveling in white America in the swing era. (1996, 376)

24. According to Stearns and Stearns (78): "Negro vaudeville had its own chain of theaters, which evolved slowly and late in the day. During the middle teens comedian Sherman Dudley retired to Washington, D.C., where he began to lease and buy theaters. Combining with various white and Negro theater owners in the South, he helped to form the Theater Owners' Booking Association (TOBA), also nicknamed 'Toby' or 'Tough on Black Artists,' which expanded until, by the twenties, it had penetrated most of the South as well as the Southwest and several Northern cities."

25. Interviews that I carried out with Margot Webb and bassist John Williams are listed by date.

26. For descriptions of these dances, see Stearns and Stearns. (196, 324, 98–99, 233, and 41) At the height of white vaudeville, in the teens, "a typical bill in a two-a-day show in a major city could be made up like this, following an overture by the orchestra: 1) an acrobatic or similar 'dumb' act. . . . 2) a song and dance number. . . . 3) a comedy dramatic sketch with special scenery and lots of costumes and lighting effects. . . . 4) a smart comedy talking act . . . as the first big punch of the show. . . . 5) a big musical act. Interval. 6) a strong comedy specialty act. . . . 7) a comedy or

drama with a big name. . . . 8) a top comedian, the headliner. . . . 9) a big sight act such as animals or trapeze artists." (Holland, 4)

27. The customary date marking white vaudeville's demise is given as 1932, the year New York's Palace Theater, the leading variety venue, switched to a movie and stage show format.

28. For a fuller discussion of the aesthetics and sociopolitical implications of the Europeanist dancing body, see Dixon Gottschild. (8)

29. For a full treatment of the relationship between dance and society, see Gerald Jonas, *Dancing* (1992) and companion videotape series of the same name. (WNET-Thirteen, 1992)

30. Webb's description is similar to Lena Horne's account of New York's Cotton Club conditions. (Haskins, 102)

31. It is an irony worth noting that Elkhart, Indiana, was and remains the U. S. center for the manufacture of saxophones, the big band's signature instrument. (Collins, 33)

32. Franklin and Moss (400) explain that the movement to have African Americans employed by the stores where they shopped began in St. Louis, Missouri, and spread to urban centers across the nation, culminating in the Harlem effort, which preceded the Harlem riot of 1935. The movement's motto was taken from the Chicago boycott: "Don't Buy Where You Can't Work."

33. In truth, this was an era when everyone dressed up for department store shopping, just as they did for church.

34. Including Illinois Jacquet, Count Basie, Roy Campanella, Jackie Robinson, writer Roi Ottley, and Margot Webb. For other Queens communities that became home for jazz musicians, see Sengupta. (1, 49)

35. Paralleling the development of the white film industry there had existed, since the teens, a small number of black film companies, some of which were owned by whites. They were low-budget concerns with a low profit margin. Unlike the black vaudeville circuits that provided full-time employment on a large scale, this industry was unable to sustain a steady work force of black actors, directors, or cinematographers on a regular basis. For detailed information about this topic, see Bogle, Cripps, and Leab. These sources also address the careers of the few African Americans who were able to cross over successfully into the white film industry, albeit in stereotyped roles.

36. For a comprehensive examination of African words in American English, see Joseph Holloway and Winifred K. Vass, *The African Heritage of American English* (Bloomington: Indiana University Press, 1993).

37. In this regard, in a literary context, see Morrison.

38. Hellmut Gottschild, in conversation with the author, August 1998.

Chapter Two

1. In an earlier period (1898) the seminal African American vaudeville team of Bert Williams and George Walker lived on 53rd Street. (See Charters, 34) Another church on the same street, St. Mark's, was the site of the emergency meeting by African American leaders following the violent race riot of 1900 that resulted in the formation of the Citizens Protective League, a forerunner of national organizations like the NAACP, founded in 1910.

2. Middle-class apartment buildings had elevators, locked entrances, carpeted halls, and, perhaps, a doorman. Tenements were walk-up buildings that had seen better days. Three to five stories high, they frequently consisted of apartments known as railroad flats: like the cars in a railroad train, it was necessary to go through one room in order to proceed to the next.

3. Webb has been working on her family genealogy for several decades and traces her lineage back to ancestors who fought in the American Revolution.

4. Through the 1980s, three African American orders of nuns existed in the United States: the Oblate Sisters of Providence (Baltimore); the Franciscan Handmaids of the Most Pure Heart of Mary (Harlem); and the Holy Family Sisters of New Orleans (in the French Quarter). (Catholic Board Negro Missions, New York, telephone conversation, 14 July 1980)

5. The most well-known Bouvier was Jacqueline Kennedy.

6. Fredi Washington played Peola, the woman who decides to pass for white, in the original 1934 film version of Fannie Hurst's novel, *Imitation of Life.* She was also a dancer and became a flamboyant figure at home and abroad, allegedly having taught the Black Bottom to the Prince of Wales. Her sister, Isabel, appeared in variety shows such as *Bamboola* and *Harlem,* both in 1929. Spotted by Florenz Ziegfeld, she was offered the role of Julie in *Show Boat,* but turned it down to become the wife of a young minister, Adam Clayton Powell, Jr. (Darden, 98–99,105–106)

7. The time step is a basic 4/4 tap dance phrase that sets the meter for a routine. With a naive chorus line it can become the routine, per se. On the feet of an expert it is the basis upon which a complex battery of sound is created. The Russian dancing was in the Cossack style with fast footwork and kazotskys—feet flying out from under deep knee bends.

8. White and black adolescents routinely lied about their age in order to perform. Hollywood's Ann Miller and cabaret singer Alberta Hunter tell the same story.

9. This figure is verified by Hallie Flanagan, director of the Federal Theatre Project of the Works Progress Administration. (34)

10. Cooper was one of a cadre of multitalented artists who epitomized the Harlem spirit in the swing era. He began as a tap dancer and for a while

was the partner of the legendarily gifted Eddie Rector (see Stearns and Stearns, 288–90); then he became an emcee and, later, an actor in black films; and followed up with a career as a popular radio disc jockey. By the 1960s and '70s he had abandoned show business in favor of a successful career in New York state government.

11. Actually they were a well known family of circus performers.

12. This term was used to denote a routine in which the performers are clothed in evening wear or formal dress and perform with elegance and ease. It stands in contrast to the minstrel stereotype which was still operative during the swing era and involved demeaning or comic costumes (such as oversized and/or tattered farmer's overalls and shoes and, sometimes, blackface) and routines that suggested plantation life and/or tropes of black inferiority.

13. Marjorie and Marion Facey interview, 7 October 1980. As children, these twin sisters began their dance training with Webb at her dance school. They saw the team perform when they were adolescents. They went on to study ballet professionally as students of Aubrey Hitchins (English *danseur* and one of Anna Pavlova's last partners) and made efforts to perform as ballerinas on the white concert stage—with no success. Ultimately, they established the Facey School of Dance in Harlem. For more on the Faceys and the squelching of their ballet aspirations, see Dixon-Stowell, 1981, 699–703.

14. This dance was probably inspired by a Japanese Spear Dance that concert dancer-choreographer Ted Shawn had performed in the 1910s. Norton's version depicted the life of an African male, from his entry into manhood and development into a warrior to his death in battle. Two properties were used: a spear and a huge, specially constructed drum with a head large enough for Norton to mount and dance upon. The dance contained no African dance movements—no torso articulation or rhythmic punctuation—but consisted of a Europeanist ballet and so-called modern dance vocabulary of leg lifts and extensions (*arabesques*—straight-legged lifts, and *attitudes*—bent-legged lifts), deep lunges, jumps, and a variety of turns. For a detailed description, see Dixon-Stowell, 1981, 524–27.

15. For a detailed movement description and documentation of a generic Norton and Margot Waltz interpretation, see Dixon-Stowell, 1981, 438–522.

16. According to Tony De Marco, male lead of one of the stellar white ballroom teams: "The composers always come first. They write it; we dance it. If you dance everything they have in there, you do it right. That goes for ballroom, stage or your own front parlor." (Crichton, 49) This rule was adhered to by Norton and Margot, with the improvisational exceptions already mentioned. However, it does not apply to the call-and-response

improvisatory forms of dance and music that derive from African and African American culture.

17. In interview and conversation with the author (15 August 1980, 7 October 1980, 12 February 1983, and 2 May 1999, rspectively).

Chapter Three

1. This publication was the mouthpiece for the Brotherhood of Sleeping Car Porters and was initiated by A. Philip Randolph, who was its first editor and the head of the organization.
2. Thanks to Neil Hornick, London-based literary consultant and researcher, for this insight. (Correspondence 26 September 1998)
3. Herman Stark was the stage manager and director; both the Berry Brothers and the Nicholas Brothers gained fame as Cotton Club child performers.
4. Chorus girls performed dance routines in precision chorus line work; show girls modeled lavish costumes—and themselves—and decorated the stage with graceful poses and a minimum of danced movement.
5. Tabloid, or "tab," shows date back to early vaudeville and minstrelsy and were shorter, lighter versions of full-length plays made more accessible to audiences who otherwise might not have seen them.
6. See, for example, Morgan S. Jensen, "'On Striver's Row' Draws Crowds to Apollo Theatre," *Pittsburgh Courier*, 13 March 1941; and "'On Striver's Row' Opens Apollo Run," *New York Amsterdam Star-News*, 8 March 1941.
7. The following discussion of the Lindy is drawn, in part, from comments made by Reagon, Manning, Miller, and Smith in the 1992 WNET video, "Dancing." Van Vechten's comments are excerpted from Paul Padgett's volume on the critic's writings. (39–40)
8. Recounted to me in conversation with Robert Farris Thompson, 2 February 1999. Thompson met James in the summer of 1960 through Marshall Stearns.
9. Needless to say, the black-white sexual attraction is a two-way street. It was a hot ticket during the swing era, an underlying reason for perpetuating the segregation of public spaces and entertainment venues. For an account of the sub rosa interracial "intercourse" taking place at Boston's Roseland Ballroom during this period, see *The Autobiography of Malcolm X*, Chapter 3, especially pp. 49 and 66–67. The young Malcolm Little was a fervent Lindy-Hopper in his early life, and, according to this account, "white girls always flocked to the Negro dances—some of them whores whose pimps brought them to mix business and pleasure, others who came with their black boyfriends, and some who came in alone, for a little free-lance lusting among a plentiful availability of enthusiastic Negro men. At

the white dances, of course, nothing black was allowed, and that's where the black whores' pimps showed . . . [me how to slip] . . . a phone number or address to the white Johns who came around the end of the dance looking for 'black chicks.'" (49)

10. This film is listed in Phyllis Rauch Klotman, *Frame By Frame* (Bloomington, IN: Indiana University Press, 1979)

Chapter Four

1. In Christian Blackwood's 1980 film *Tapdancin'*, Coles cites racism as the prime reason for his exclusion from the Hollywood film industry.

2. The fact that Robeson chose to enter the entertainment world only after rejection from the law profession is documented in the Robeson memorabilia that was used as the basis for the biographical play, *Paul Robeson*, by Philip Hayes Dean.

3. For discussion of specific use, quotation, and appropriation of black tap invention by white Hollywood performers see, among other sources, Clover (722–747); Stearns and Stearns (309); and Dixon Gottschild (33–34).

4. Ibid.

5. A manager, or personal manager, works in an individualized, hands-on way with his client and may receive a considerable percentage of the client's salary. This percentage may vary on a scale of "reasonable" to "outrageous." An agent may be sent to a client by an agency and book for only a particular tour. His work is more general, and he receives a smaller percentage of client income. Unlike the bandleaders, most performers and individual band members who were not top-ranked did not have a personal manager.

6. Much of the discussion in this chapter on Glaser, Fox, the Grand Terrace, and Earl Hines is drawn from Dance. (1977, 50, 153, 66, 67)

7. No relation to Cab Calloway. For this booking the team was paid $175 per week, the highest salary they could command.

8. Thanks to Neil Hornick for bringing Payn and Morley's book on Noel Coward to my attention, from which these quotes are drawn. (244, 246–47)

9. According to John Williams, who had been a member of this band, Mills insisted on renaming the Millinder band The Mills Blue Rhythm Band, although he had nothing artistic or creative to contribute to the group. (15 August 1980)

10. Early on the young, already brilliant, but naive Ellington had been compromised in the deal he made to write the show *Chocolate Kiddies* (1925). He completed it in one whirlwind night for a mere $500 advance. According to Ellington, it was the show's producer, Jack Robbins, who profited. He became a millionaire due to its huge success in Berlin, where it

ran for two years. In his typically suave, diplomatic manner, Ellington simply relates the story, allowing the reader to draw her own conclusions. (Ellington, 71)

11. African Americans were not totally excluded from managerial-entrepreneurial endeavor, but their purview had been limited to the least significant markets. There had been a cadre of small, intermediate black booking agents, in the TOBA era of Webb's Aunt Sadie (the teens and early twenties), who acted as middlemen between black performers and white agents, theaters, and managers. Even earlier, James Reese Europe, one of the members of the Memphis Students Band, initiated the first booking agency by and for African American musicians. In 1910 he organized the Clef Club, a chartered organization that bought a house on West 53rd Street that served as both private club and booking office, and furnished bands, small or extended, for private parties and hotel ballrooms to satisfy the tea dance craze that was then sweeping America. These opportunities had died out by the advent of the swing era. (Dixon-Stowell, 1981, 113)

12. However, the racial etiquette of these resorts was heinous, as recounted by Donald Bogle in his book *Dorothy Dandridge* (New York: Amistad Press, 1997). Dandridge was a part of this nightclub circuit before the advent of her film career: "She was frequently booked in clubs where she wasn't allowed to mix with the white patrons; one hotel in Las Vegas threatened to drain the pool rather than let her swim in it. . . ." (Als, 70)

13. Evolving from the tradition of male gospel singing groups, these vocalists were generally four to six in number with one—usually a tenor—designated as the lead singer. They were so named because of the eponymous scat sound of the backup singers.

14. The Rhythm Boys were featured in *The King of Jazz* (1930), Crosby's movie debut; at that time Crosby was regarded as a jazz singer. Thanks to Neil Hornick for this additional information.

15. Remarkably, theirs was a unique example of cultural reciprocity. After the 1929 stock market crash Armstrong left New York to perform in Culver City, California at Frank Sebastian's Cotton Club. There he met Crosby, who came frequently to see him perform and sometimes sat in with the Armstrong band. Briefly Armstrong experimented with Crosby's smoothness of song style, as reflected in recordings from this period, but soon returned to his characteristic raspy delivery. The two became professional friends and appeared together on radio shows and in several Hollywood films, beginning in 1936 with *Pennies From Heaven.* ("Louis Armstrong," 1999)

16. Quoting Nat Shapiro and Nat Hentoff, *Hear Me Talkin' to Ya* (New York: Rinehart & Company, 1955), 235. Information on Goodman in the subsequent paragraph is also drawn from Stearns. (200, 209)

17. See Sudhalter.

18. Billed as a folk opera, it premiered on Broadway because "it had no place else to go," since there was no American musical genre that existed in between opera and the musical. (Bordman, 494)
19. Quoted in *Dance Magazine*, "News of the Century." (January 1999, 77)
20. For more on the creativity and innovation of African American female dancers, see "Plenty of Good Women Dancers: African American Women Hoofers from Philadelphia," video, traveling exhibit and companion booklet produced by the Philadelphia Folklore Project, 1997.
21. Reviewed in "Of Mice and Men" Playbill, 27 December 1937, initialed "J.A.T." ; also in "Fifty Girls to Dance in Robinson Masks," *New York Daily Mirror*, 15 December 1937; and in Haskins, *The Cotton Club*, 129.

Chapter Five

1. Lambert, 23. According to this report, "another paradox was that although Levittown was built for World War II veterans, who had fought tyranny and racism, its doors were opened to at least one former German U-boat sailor, while black American soldiers were turned away." (26)
2. Correspondence with Neil Hornick, 24 April 1999.
3. Franklin Williams, former United States Ambassador to Ghana, told this story in the WNET documentary "I Remember Harlem."
4. In fact, it is occasionally difficult for African Americans to distinguish between light-skinned blacks and whites. See, for example, Lawrence Otis Graham's anecdote in his chapter, "Black Elite in Washington D.C." (213–14)
5. Karl Bissinger, photographer and social activist, recounted to me the effect on him of seeing the original 1927 *Show Boat* production, stating that, "as a young white boy, I was so moved by this that it made me racially conscious for the rest of my life." (Conversation, 20 March 1999).
6. Bayliss, 7.
7. See Bayliss, 14; and Graham, Chapter 16.
8. See Haskins, 73; Darden, 105. Thanks to Karl Bissinger for the Mildred Bailey information. He grew up in Cincinnati before and during the swing era.
9. In their landmark biography, *Having Our Say*, the darker-skinned Delany sister, Bessie, describes the following incident that occurred in New York ca. 1920: "One time, we were waiting on line to get factory work and this white man tried to give me a break. It was always a white guy who was in charge, of course. He said, 'Oh, I see. You are Spanish.' This was supposed to be my cue to nod my head, since they'd hire you if you were 'Spanish.' But this made me furious. I said, 'No, I am not Spanish.

I am an *American Negro!'* I turned and walked out. . . ." (156, author's emphasis)

10. "Nice People," 1933; Calloway, 116. Hall later expatriated to London.

11. Harlem's history is interesting. By the turn of the century, as Manhattan's population expanded, immigrants had begun to move to this erstwhile white, upper middle-class refuge located north of the city's center. By the 1910s African Americans gained entry, due to a politically strategic move initiated by one black realtor who managed to secure several rental properties. (See McKay, 1940) Following World War I the Great Migration of African Americans from the South to the North began, with many settling in Harlem. Invariably, black residency was accompanied by white flight. Well-off whites who had inhabited Harlem's elegant brownstones moved out. Working class white immigrants and a steady flow of blacks from the South and the Caribbean continued to move in. In the swing era there were many white residents in the community. When I was a child in 1950s Harlem, the northern section of the neighborhood (sometimes called Washington Heights—in what may have been an effort of white Harlemites to distinguish themselves and their neighborhood from black Harlem) and the western extreme (namely, two large avenues, Broadway and Riverside Drive) were almost exclusively inhabited by whites, and all the stores that lined Broadway were white owned. The grocery, bakery, and pharmacy that my family patronized were all Jewish-owned and operated; the butcher was German; the fruit vendor was Italian. As in the swing era, some small businesses (tailors, cobblers, carpenters) were black owned. But a significant though dwindling part of Harlem's population remained white well into the 1960s.

12. Other than several nonstereotypical feature roles played by Paul Robeson in British films (that stand apart from the others), there is at least one additional instance of a black actor playing a nonracially defined major role in a European film—"notably, the central role of 'the Negro soldier' played by Dots M. Johnson in a key episode of Roberto Rossellini's *Paisa* (1946)." (Correspondence with Neil Hornick, 24 April 1999)

13. Langston Hughes and Arna Bontemps discuss the situation with cynical sadness in their 1942 letters. (Nichols, 100–103)

14. This contention is borne out by the recollections of choreographer Hellmut Gottschild. Born in Berlin in 1936, he saw a touring American production of *Porgy and Bess* at Berlin's Titania Palace during the 1955–56 theatrical season. He recalls that the image of the African American male "with a big, muscular, rounded back, in overalls, singing spirituals—a sense of physical strength and spiritual, naive belief, mixed with a certain yearning and sadness—all fit into our idea of who 'Negroes' were." (Conversation, 2 March 1999) This image was also disseminated by the popularity

in Germany of Karl May's adventure stories, read by adults and adolescents—Gottschild included—whose black characters fit the same mold. An additional influence in 1950s Germany was the popularity of gospel groups like the Golden Gate Quartet.

15. For a partial listing see Dixon Gottschild, 124.

16. For further discussion of the minstrel image and its significance, see Dixon Gottschild, Chapter 6. According to Englishman Neil Hornick his second cousin, "Harry Gold, now aged 92, a bass sax jazzman, the leader of the Dixieland Band, Harry Gold and His Pieces of Eight" showed Hornick a photo of himself "in a band that played on the roof garden of Selfridge's Department Store way back in 1928—all dressed up in complete minstrel gear—blackface, woolly wigs and all!" (Correspondence, 17 February 1999)

17. This description contrasts sharply with the honorific portrait of the African American bourgeoisie painted recently by one of its own, Lawrence Otis Graham (1999). As an outsider, El-Shabazz' s description may be biased toward the negative. As an insider, Graham's description may be biased on the positive side; it also includes factual inaccuracies. For example, Graham ignores the fact that many members of the social clubs he cites were, indeed, menial workers.

18. According to folklorist Roger Abrahams, the words to this refrain, as sung by the Almanac Singers in the 1940s, did not include the second line, "If you're yellow, you're mellow"; but this group was responsible for spreading the 3-line version of the rhyme in a song frequently performed in northern, leftist labor movement concerts. (Telephone conversation, 1 December 1999) The origin of the saying is unclear, but it seems probable that it is African American. (The Almanac Singers were a group of multiracial folk performers who later became the Weavers and included Pete Seeger, Woodie Guthrie, and Bess Hawes. At times they were joined by African Americans, including Huddie Ledbetter [Leadbelly], Sonny Terry, and Brownie McGhee.)

19. Why African American men could be exempted from the color-caste discrimination code of the entertainment industry is difficult to fathom. It is yet another example of the convoluted ritual of racial etiquette and would be fertile ground for study of racism's relation to sexism.

20. Unlike modern air-conditioned or heated buses equipped with toilets and picture windows, the swing era models were cramped, stuffy, poorly lit, bathroomless vehicles that absorbed every bump in the road and took a toll on the dancing body.

21. According to vocalist Alberta Hunter's biography, the Grand Terrace "welcomed black patrons." (Taylor and Cook, 110). However, Margot Webb counters this contention: "About the Grand Terrace, Chicago: Alberta was there in 1929, I believe. At that time, I believe there were many clubs in

Chicago that featured Afro singers and entertainers—in the Afro-American communities. Norton and Margot—in 1934–35 and later—worked at the Terrace after Alberta [had worked there]—when certain members of the 'mob' owned the club—and I only saw *one* Afro couple in the audience while I worked there—the couple happened to be my aunt from Boston and her new (second) husband who was a wealthy, well-known physician. [Webb's emphasis] I believe Norton got permission from Ed Fox for them to have a table—although I have no written proof of the policy there." (Correspondence, 5 October 1998). Thus, Webb suggests that the management might have changed their policy to conform with that of New York's Cotton Club. In any case, not only were Webb's aunt and uncle wealthy, they were also light enough to pass; the fact that they attended the club as her African American relatives was a matter of principle.

22.   See note 12, Chapter Four, regarding a similar prohibition on Dorothy Dandridge.

23.   Palmer, 70–71; Barney Josephson interview, 19 December 1976; and John Williams interview, 15 August 1980.

24.   Neither from Memphis nor students, these New York-based musicians included James Reese Europe.

25.   But, on the other hand, this is a lesson to show that characteristics that are considered racial are, in fact, culturally programmed responses. Thus, having spent a good deal of time in Germany and having observed and conversed with Afro-Germans of mixed parentage, I find that they are more German than African: their body language is German, with few traces of Africanisms in movement or physical gestures and, certainly, none in their manner of speech. Food preferences, body adornment practices, and other cultural areas also show that race is a state of mind rather than a biological imperative. Likewise, childhood friends of mine who expatriated to France and Belgium and married Europeans raised children who look, act, and consider themselves to be French or Belgian nationals.

26.   Eight individual variety acts (of British or European origin) and an intermission had preceded the Cotton Club Revue.

27.   For an in-depth discussion of rhythm tap and John Bubbles, see Stearns and Stearns, 212–19.

28.   Ibid., 276–82, for an in-depth explanation of flash tap acts, particularly the Berry Brothers and the Nicholas Brothers.

29.   Recounted to me by Karl Bissinger, who spent time in Paris in the 1930s.

30.   Although the bulk of their performance work was in London, African Americans also performed in other centers in Great Britain, particularly Edinburgh, Scotland. Frequently the terms "British" and "English" are used interchangeably—an error that I have attempted to avoid, in order to include those parts of the United Kingdom that are frequently subordi-

nated in favor of England: namely, Scotland, Ireland, and Wales. Thanks to Tricia Henry Young, dance writer-researcher, for pointing this out to me.

31. Besides the authors cited see also Logan and Drake.

32. For a discussion of this syndrome in contemporary Brazil, see Robinson.

33. Back, 186, 191.

34. Muting is a technique used by jazz musicians to modify, transform, and muffle the tones produced by wind or brass instruments through manipulation of a cup- or bowl-like object at the mouth of the horn.

35. Hunter's life was remarkable. Born in Memphis, Tennessee in 1895 she began singing professionally in Chicago in 1911 and expatriated to London in the 1920s. This period was followed by a brief and not very successful return home (1929–30), and a subsequent return to Europe. During World War II, she performed for the troops through the USO. Back in the States after the war, from the late forties through the 1950s she performed on the Camp Show circuit with units that entertained hospitalized war veterans. It may be from this experience that she became a full-time practical nurse (1957), retiring from show business—although she remained in contact with her many friends in the entertainment industry. Through the good graces of Barney Josephson (of Café Society fame who, by the 1970s and long after Café Society was a dusty memory, ran the Cookery Lafayette in Greenwich Village), Hunter made an amazing comeback (1977), singing (at the Cookery) and touring nationwide and abroad (she was a favorite in Brazil). She was forced, for health reasons, to retire in 1984: having given her final performance that summer (she had to leave the stage, unable to continue) she passed away in October of that year, at age 89.

36. A famous American socialite and hostess of celebrity parties.

Chapter Six

1. This is not to imply that cool jazz is or was an exponent of the cold war or conservative politics. Actually, its radical means and product are quite the opposite. However, cultural formations are interactive processes that involve a complex mesh of influences, presences, and interfaces. Art forms emerge as signatures of specific sociocultural contexts—some conscious, some subliminal. The relationship between bebop and the larger, mainstream American context of its era is an area of inquiry that begs further research. Jon Panish's excellent *The Color of Jazz* deals with the cultural dynamic between blacks and whites inside the post–World War II jazz world. However, the larger, mainstream context is not his concern.

2. For example, the original production of the Broadway musical *West Side Story* (1957) had one token African American cast member—vocalist Reri Grist. White Carol Lawrence played the female lead role of Puerto Rican Maria. As an aspiring young dancer in the 1960s, trained in ballet and so-called modern dance, I went along with other black colleagues to Broadway auditions, all of us knowing that we would not be accepted. Yet, we continued to audition regularly so that our existence and our hopes would not easily be invisibilized.

Chapter Seven

1. West, "Race and Otherness."
2. See articles such as Monaghan, Terry. "Swing Shift." *Village Voice*, 7 July 1998, 60, 61, 68; and Williams, Zoe. "Swing's the Thing." *Evening Standard* (London), 23 October 1998, 23.
3. This small oeuvre includes Cheryl Willis's dissertation, *Tap Dance: Memories and Issues of African American Women Who Performed Between 1930–1960.* (Temple University, 1991); a handful of printed articles, such as Itabari Njeri's (*Village Voice*, 28 July 1998, 38–41); and the Debora Kodish-Germaine Ingram-Barry Dornfeld collaboratively produced video (with companion traveling exhibit curated by Kodish), entitled "Plenty of Good Women Dancers: African American Women Hoofers from Philadelphia" (Philadelphia Folklore Project, 1997).
4. This is an interesting concept, and one expressed in a slightly different way about another swing-era giant, Count Basie: legend has it that "he could make one note—struck on the piano in his matchless way—swing." (Giddins, 170)
5. For a treatment of the Africanist presence in modernism and postmodernism see Dixon Gottschild.
6. While the Lindy was read the riot act, the fate of home-grown, German modern dance was cast in a different, although ambiguous, light. Unlike modern music and visual arts, German modern dance was not included in the degenerate category. Well-known modern dancer-choreographers, including Rudolf von Laban, Mary Wigman, and Gret Palucca, had co-operated with the Nazi regime and choreographed and/or performed in the German Dance Festivals of 1934 and 1935 that were organized by Goebbels's Cultural Ministry; these three had participated as choreographers or performers in the movement sections for the 1936 Berlin Olympics. (Manning, 5) Still, their security was not guaranteed. The Third Reich supported them as long as their dances were lyrical, uplifting, and could be interpreted as part of the Nazi ideology and utilized in

the service of its cause. At one point Palucca, whose work was simple and lyrical, was their favorite. Wigman came under increasing suspicion, since her work was somber, introspective, and dissonant—definitely modern in spirit. She may have been able to stay in favor as long as she did because of a reputed romantic involvement with a Nazi. Von Laban (actually Hungarian by birth), who had been appointed director of the Allied State Theaters in Berlin under the Weimar Republic in 1930, left Germany and was living in England by 1938. Palucca's and Wigman's dance schools were later shut down by the Nazis (in 1939 and 1942, respectively). Both women remained in Germany and resumed their careers after the war.

7. For the Africanist presence in Twain, see Fishkin; regarding Melville, see Morrison.

8. See Dixon Gottschild (52–54) for further discussion of this topic.

9. For a full discussion of Africanisms in George Balanchine's Americanization of ballet, see Dixon Gottschild (Chapter 5, 59–79).

10. The Bauhaus institute, established in Weimar, Germany (1919–1933), was devoted to the study of art, design, and architecture and promulgated a theory of functionalism. Bauhaus style was for a time synonymous with modernist perspectives. The same "economy of means" is characteristic of rhythm tap dance.

11. As stated by Smith in "Dancing."

12. *Cab Calloway's Cat-ologue—A Hepster's Dictionary* (1938). Webb private collection.

13. However, the Armstrong reading is not cut and dried. For many African Americans of the baby boom generation and thereafter, he seemed to be, at best, a funny, loveable old man who sang and happened to play the trumpet; at worst, he was an obsequious Uncle Tom. In the swing era he caused a stir in the black community by recording a song called *Shine*. It was a compendium of stereotypes beginning with the opening line, "Oh, Chocolate drop, that's me." (The term, shine, is an epithet.) *When It's Sleepytime Down South* became his signature song through many years of touring with the Louis Armstrong All Stars. It is difficult to reconcile his renditions of these songs with the subversion he inserted into others. He remains the inscrutable trickster.

14. Swing Youth was the subject of a 1993 film, entitled *Swing Kids*, directed by Thomas Carter. Thanks to Neil Hornick for British articles on this topic.

15. Nazi-appointed officials who presided over German provinces, or *gaue*. (In typical Nazi fashion, this antiquated terminology replaced contemporary usage to signal a return to primitive, pure Germanic roots.)

16. West, "Race and Otherness."

17. For an in-depth discussion of the Africanist aesthetic in the Americaniza-
    tion of ballet and in modern and postmodern dance, see Dixon Gottschild
    (Chapters 4 and 5).

18. Regarding Milhaud's link with swing music, see Dixon Gottschild (24,
    43).

19. He regarded jazz and modern art as the only creative arts in America. (See
    Dixon Gottschild 39–40).

20. Smith in Miller, xxix.

21. For a detailed discussion of the Africanist presence in selected examples of
    premodern and modern American literature, see Morrison 1992.

References

Ackerman, Roy. "Dance With Death." *The Listener* (London), 4 October 1990, 20–22.

Als, Hilton. "Dark Star." *The New Yorker,* 18 August 1977, 68–72.

Appel, Alfred Jr. "All That You-Know-What." *New York Times Book Review,* 18 October 1998, 18, 20.

Back, Les. "Nazism and the Call of the Jitterbug." In *Dancing in the City,* edited by Helen Thomas, 175–97. New York: St. Martin's Press, 1997.

Baker, Jean-Claude and Chris Chase. *Josephine.* Holbrook, Mass.: Adams Media Corporation, 1993.

Baraka, Imamu. *The Slave.* New York: William Morrow Company, 1964.

Bayliss, John F. "Novels of Black Americans Passing as Whites." Ph.D. diss., Indiana University, 1976.

"Benefit Directed by Muse Nets $1,147 for NAACP." *Crisis,* September 1935, 277

Bergman, Peter M. *The Chronological History of the Negro in America.* New York: New American Library-Mentor Books, 1969

"Black is White is Not." *Crisis,* September 1932, 294.

"Black Women On: The Light/Dark Thang." Celeste Crenshaw. Schenectady, N.Y.: WMHT-TV, 1997.

Bloom, Steve. "Stayin' Alive." *Soho Weekly News,* 4 May 1980, 22–23.

Bogle, Donald. *Toms, Coons, Mulattoes, Mammies & Bucks.* New York: Viking Press, 1973.

Bordman, Gerald. *American Musical Theatre.* New York: Oxford University Press, 1978.

Brooks, Richard. "When Racial Segregation Was the Law of the Land." *Observer* (London), 26 November 1995, 15.

Buckley, Gail Lumet. *The Hornes.* New York: Knopf, 1986.

Burley, Dan. "Back Door Stuff: A Columnist's File of All-Time Greats." *New York Amsterdam News,* 29 June 1957.

Calloway, Cab. *Of Minnie the Moocher and Me.* New York: Thomas Y. Crowell, 1976.

Chalif, Louis H. *The Chalif Textbook of Dancing.* 5 vols. New York: The Chalif Normal School of Dancing, 1914–1925.

Chambers, Veronica. "The Tragic Mulatto." *New York Times Magazine,* 1 January 1995, 27.

Charters, Ann. *Nobody.* New York: Macmillan, 1970.

Chujoy, Anatole, and P. W. Manchester. *The Dance Encyclopedia.* New York: A. S. Barnes, 1967.

Churchill, Allen. "Meet Willie Bryant." *Magazine Digest,* September 1953, 18.

Clover, Carol J. "Dancin' in the Rain." *Critical Inquiry,* Summer 1995, 722–47.

Collins, Jim. "Horn of Plenty." *Attaché,* February 1999, 30, 33, 35.

Cook, Mercer. "The Race Problem in Paris and the French West Indies." *Journal of Negro Education,* October 1939, 673.

"Cotton Club Puts on 2:30 A.M. Show." *New York Daily Mirror,* 26 October 1938.

Crichton, Kyle. "It Looks So Easy." *Collier's,* 3 January 1948, 19, 49.

Cripps, Thomas. *Slow Fade to Black.* New York: Oxford University Press, 1977.

Cunard, Nancy. *Negro.* London: Wishart & Co., 1934.

Curtis, Constance H. "Lily White 'Walled City.'" *Crisis,* July 1943, 206, 222.

Dance, Stanley. *The World of Earl Hines.* New York: Charles Scribner's Sons, 1977.

"Dancing." New York: WNET-Thirteen, 1992.

Darden, Norma Jean. "Oh, Sister." *Essence,* September 1978.

Dean, Phillip Hayes. *Paul Robeson.* Garden City, N.Y.: Doubleday, 1978.

"Degenerate Art." Los Angeles: KCET-TV, 1993.

Delany, Sarah L., Elizabeth A. Delany, and Amy Hill Hearth. *Having Our Say.* New York: Dell, 1993.

Dixon Gottschild, Brenda. *Digging the Africanist Presence in American Performance.* Westport, Conn.: Greenwood Press, 1998.

Dixon-Stowell, Brenda. "Dancing in the Dark." Ph.D. diss., New York University, 1981.

———. "Interview with Margot Webb." April 1978 typescript. Dance Collection, Lincoln Center Library of the Performing Arts, New York.

———. "Margot Webb's Heyday." *Encore American and Worldwide News,* 24 July 1978, 38–41.

Douglas, Ann. *Terrible Honesty.* New York: Farrar, Straus & Giroux, 1995.

Drake, St. Clair. "A Report on the Brown Britishers." *Crisis,* June 1949, 174, 188–189.

Dunbar, Ernest. *The Black Expatriates.* New York: E. P. Dutton, 1968.

Dyson, Michael Eric. *Race Rules.* Reading, Mass.: Addison-Wesley, 1996.

Ellington, Edward Kennedy. *Music Is My Mistress.* [1973] New York: Da Capo Press, 1976.

Ellison, Ralph. *Invisible Man.* [1952] New York: Vintage Books, 1995.

Facey, Marion and Marjorie. Interview by Brenda Dixon-Stowell. New York: 7 October 1980.

Feldman, Susan. *Band in Berlin.* Philadelphia: American Music Theater Festival, 11–22 March 1997.

Ferguson, Niall. "Nazism and All That Jazz." *Sunday Telegraph* (London), 1 June 1997.

Fisher, Rudolf, "The Caucasian Storms Harlem." In *Voices from the Harlem Renaissance*, edited by Nathan Huggins, 74–82. New York: Oxford University Press, 1976.

Fishkin, Shelley Fisher. *Was Huck Black?* New York: Oxford University Press, 1993.

Flanagan, Hallie. *Arena, The History of the Federal Theatre.* New York: Benjamin Blom, 1965.

Franklin, John Hope. *From Slavery to Freedom.* [1947] 3rd ed. New York: Random House, 1969.

——— and Alfred A Moss. *From Slavery to Freedom.* [1947] 7th ed. New York: Knopf, 1994.

French, Winsor. "Veloz and Yolanda." *Cleveland Ohio Press,* 5 January 1938.

"From Harlem to Broadway." George Melley. BBC Radio, November 1995.

Gates, Henry Louis. "White Like Me." *The New Yorker,* 17 June 1996, 66–81.

Giddins, Gary. *Visions of Jazz.* New York: Oxford University Press, 1998.

Goddard, Chris. *Jazz Away from Home.* New York: Paddington Press, 1979.

Gold, Russell. "Guilty of Syncopation, Joy and Animation: The Closing of Harlem's Savoy Ballroom." In *Of, By, and For the People*, edited by Lynn Garafola, 50–64. Journal of the Society of Dance History Scholars, Studies in Dance History, Spring, 1994.

Gould, Jack. untitled. *New York Times.* 13 March 1938.

Graham, Lawrence Otis. *Our Kind of People.* New York: Harper-Collins, 1999.

Greenberg, Charles. (Letters to the Editor) *New York Times,* 17 January 1999, sec. 2, 4.

Gross, Jane. "Harking Back to the Dance Hall Days," *Long Island Newsday,* 20 May 1975.

Hall, Chatwood. "A Black Woman in Red Russia." *Crisis,* July 1937, 203–204.

Hamill, Pete. "A Dirge for the Lost Soul of Harlem." *New York Daily News,* 4 March 1977.

Hammond, John. "The King of Swing." *Crisis,* April 1937, 110–111, 123–124.

Haskell, Arnold. *Balletomania Then and Now.* [1934]. New York: Knopf, 1977.

Haskins, Jim. *The Cotton Club.* New York: Random House, 1977.

Holland, Charlie. *Strange Feats & Clever Turns.* London: Holland and Palmer, 1998.

Huggins, Nathan. *Harlem Renaissance.* New York: Oxford University Press, 1971.

Hughes, Langston. *The Big Sea.* New York: Knopf, 1940.

———. "Going South in Russia." *Crisis,* June 1934, 62–63.

———. "The Negro and American Entertainment." In *The American Negro Reference Book*, edited by John P. Davis, 826–49. Englewood Cliffs, N.J.: Prentice Hall, 1966.

————. "The Negro Artist and the Racial Mountain." [1926] In *The Black Man and The American Dream*, edited by June Sochen, 117–122. Chicago: Quadrangle Books, 1971.

————, and Milton Meltzer. *Black Magic.* New York: Bonanza Books, 1967.

"I Remember Harlem." William Miles. New York: WNET-Thirteen, 1981.

Isaacs, Edith. *The Negro in the American Theatre.* New York: Theatre Arts, 1947.

Johnson, James Weldon. *Black Manhattan.* [1930] New York: Atheneum, 1968.

Jonas, Gerald. *Dancing.* New York: Harry N. Abrams, 1992.

Josephson, Barney. Interview, Hatch-Billops Collection Research Library, New York. 19 December 1976.

Kellner, Bruce. *Carl Van Vechten and the Irreverent Decades.* Norman: University of Oklahoma Press, 1968.

Kodish, Debora, curator. "Plenty of Good Women Dancers: African American Women Hoofers From Philadelphia." Exhibit and booklet, Philadelphia Folklore Project, 1997.

Kornweibel, Theodore, Jr. *No Crystal Stair.* Westport, Conn: Greenwood Press, 1975.

Lambert, Bruce. "At 50, Levittown Contends with Its Legacy of Bias." *New York Times*, 28 December 1997, Metro Section, 23, 26.

Lautier, Louis. "Jim Crow in the Nation's Capital." *Crisis*, April 1940, 107, 125.

Leab, Daniel. *From Sambo to Superspade.* Boston: Houghton Mifflin, 1975.

Lewis, Harold O. "A General View of the Negro in Europe." In *Negro Year Book, 1941–46.* 10th ed. edited by Jessie Parkhurst Guzman. Tuskegee Institute, Ala: Dept. of Records and Research, 1947.

Lewis, Theophilus. "Round About Harlem." *The Messenger*, May 1926, 150.

————. "Reflections of An Alleged Drama Critic." *The Messenger*, March 1927, 85.

————. "Blackbirds Are Turning Brown." *New York Amsterdam News*, 29 October 1930.

"Louis Armstrong: What a Wonderful World." Harry Connick, Jr. BBC Radio, October–November 1999.

Logan, Rayford. "Great Britain and Race Prejudice." *Crisis*, March 1932, 87–88.

Manning, Susan. *Ecstasy and the Demon.* Berkeley: University of California Press, 1993.

Marsalis, Wynton. "Ellington at 100: Reveling in Life's Majesty." *New York Times*, 17 January 1999, sec. 2, 1, 31.

Martin, Maximilian. "The Pennsylvania Civil Rights Act." *Crisis*, November 1935, 341, 350.

McKay, Claude. *A Long Way From Home.* [1937] New York: Harcourt, Brace and World, 1970.

————. *Harlem: Negro Metropolis.* New York: E. P. Dutton, 1940.

Miller, Norma. *Swingin' at The Savoy.* Philadelphia: Temple University Press, 1996.

Millstein, Gilbert. "Harlem Stompers." *New York World Telegram*, 23 January 1947.

Mitchell, Loften. *Black Drama*. New York: Hawthorn Publishers, 1967.

Monaghan, Terry. "Swing Shift." *Village Voice*, 7 July 1998, 60–61, 68.

———and M. Dodson. "Acceptance and Exclusion—The Case of the Lindy Hop: With Reference to Spike Lee's Film Depiction of the Lindy Hop Scene from Malcolm X's Autobiography." Unpublished ms., 1998.

Morrison, Toni. *Playing in the Dark*. Cambridge: Harvard University Press, 1992.

"Mr. James Crow—And Never The Twain." *Crisis*, April 1933, 90–91.

"The Negro in the United States Army." *Crisis*, February 1942, 47.

"Nice People." *Crisis*, April 1933, 91.

Nichols, Charles H., ed. *Arna Bontemps–Langston Hughes Letters 1925–1967*. New York: Dodd, Mead, 1980.

Njeri, Itaberi. "Shadowed Feats." *Village Voice*, 28 July 1998, 38–41.

O'Connor, Patrick. "Josephine." *Observer* (London), Sunday Magazine, 17 January 1986, 20, 29.

O'Meally, Robert. "The Jazz Singer at A Crossroads." *New York Times*, 3 January 1999, sec. 2, 1, 30.

———. "Reborn, And Going International." *New York Times*, 17 January 1999, sec. 2, 32, 33.

Ostransky, Leroy. *The Anatomy of Jazz*. [1960] Westport, Conn: Greenwood Press, 1973.

Ottley, Roi. *Black Odyssey*. New York: Charles Scribner's Sons, 1948.

———. *No Green Pastures*. New York: Charles Scribner's Sons, 1951.

———and William Weatherby, eds. *The Negro in New York*. New York: Praeger Publishers, 1967.

Padgette, Paul, ed. *The Dance Writings of Carl Van Vechten*. New York: Dance Horizons, 1974.

Palmer, Tony. *All You Need Is Love*. New York: Grossman Publishers, 1976.

Panish, John. *The Color of Jazz*. Jackson: University Press of Mississippi, 1997.

Patterson, Martha. "Recovering the Work of American Clubwomen." *American Quarterly*, March 1999, 221–27.

"Paul Robeson: Here I Stand." *American Masters*. New York: WNET-Thirteen, 1998.

Payn, Graham. and Sheridan Morley. *The Noel Coward Diaries*. London: Weidenfeld and Nicolson, 1982.

Pullen, Glenn. (untitled.) *Plain Dealer* (Cleveland, Ohio), 2 January 1938.

Ratliff, Ben. "The Duke on Disk, Live, Loosened and Otherwise." *New York Times*, 17 January 1999, sec. 2, 31.

Robinson, Eugene. *Coal to Cream*. New York: Free Press, 1999.

Rogers, J. A. "Britain's Black Background." *Crisis*, February 1940, 60.

Roman, Robert C. (obituary) "Hermes Pan." *Dance Magazine*, January 1991, 30, 32.

Rowe, Billy. "Clarence Robinson Dead at 79." *New York Amsterdam News*, 8 September 1979, 43.

Roy, Rob. "Roy is Slipping: He Likes Adagio Dance." *Chicago Defender*, 4 August 1934.

Schiffman, Jack. *Uptown*. New York: Cowles Book Company, 1971.

"The Secret City, An Impression of Colored Washington." *Crisis*, June 1932, 185–87.

Sengupta, Somini. "Where Jazz Put Its Feet Up." *New York Times*, 20 September 1998, Metro Section, 43, 49.

"Skins are High." *Crisis*, June 1932, 193.

Smith, Ernie and Norma Miller. Lindy Hop lecture, Susan Hess Studio. Philadelphia: 2 May 1999.

Spaeth, Sigmund. "Dixie, Harlem and Tin Pan Alley: Who Writes Negro Music and How?" *Scribner's*, January 1938, 23–26.

Spiegl, Fritz. "Did Mr. Punch Have an Aryan Grandmother?" *The Listener* (London), 26 April 1973, 538–41.

Stearns, Marshall. *The Story of Jazz*. [1956] New York: Oxford University Press, 1970.

————, and Jean Stearns. *Jazz Dance*. [1968] New York: Macmillan Company, Schirmer Books, 1979.

Stern, Edith M. "Jim Crow Goes to School in New York." *Crisis*, July 1937, 201–202.

Sudhalter, Richard M. "A Racial Divide That Needn't Be." *New York Times*, 3 January 1999, sec. 2, 1, 31.

Swing Kids. [film] Directed by Thomas Carter, 1993.

"Swingtime for Hitler—Charley and His Orchestra." David Perry. BBC Radio, 1987.

Sylvester, Robert. *No Cover Charge*. New York: Dial Press, 1956.

Tapdancin'. [film] Directed by Christian Blackwell, 1980.

Taylor, Frank and Gerald Cook. *Alberta Hunter*. New York: McGraw-Hill, 1987.

Thompson, Laura. "When You Dance Together, You Can't Fight Each Other." *Sunday Telegraph* (London), 10 June 1993.

Toll, Robert. *Blacking Up*. New York: Oxford University Press, 1974.

Trumbo, Dalton. "Blackface, Hollywood Style." *Crisis*, December 1943, 365–367, 378.

Tucker, Mark. "Uneasiness as Popular Tastes Shift." *New York Times*, 17 January 1999, sec. 2, 32–33.

Vogel, Susan. *Aesthetics of African Art*. New York: Center for African Art, 1986.

Walcott, Rinaldo. *Black Like Who?* Toronto: Insomniac Press, 1997.

Walker, Dan. "Star Dancing Keeps Cotton Club at Top." *New York Daily News*, 26 September 1937.

Waters, Ethel. *His Eye Is on the Sparrow*. Garden City, New York: Doubleday, 1950.

Watrous, Peter. "Catching The Spirit of a Century." *New York Times*, 17 January 1999, sec. 2, 32–33.

Watts, Richard Jr., "The Theater." *New York Herald Tribune,* 1 August 1937.

Webb, Elida, and Garfield Dawson. Interview, Hatch-Billops Collection Research Library, New York. 7 March 1974.

Webb, Margot. "Harlem to Broadway." *Chicago Defender,* New York edition, 17, 24 June; 1, 8, 15, 22, 29 July; 19 August; 2, 9, 16, 23 September 1938.

Webb, Margot. Interviews by Brenda Dixon-Stowell. New York: 19 November, 9 December 1977; 6 March, 17 April, 6 August 1978; 17, 24 April, 22 May, 5, 14, 25 June, 27 August, 10, 17 September, 18 October 1980. Interviews by Brenda Dixon Gottschild. Miami Beach, Fla: 8–15 July 1998; 5 October 1998; 28 January, 16 March, 2, 10 June 1999.

Welsh Asante, Kariamu. "Commonalities in African dance." In *African Culture: The Rhythms of Unity,* edited by Molefi Kete Asante and Kariamu Welsh Asante, 71–82. Westport, Conn.: Greenwood Press, 1986.

West, Cornel. "Race and Otherness," Keynote Address, Twenty-Fifth National Conference of Trinity Institute. New York, 1994.

Williams, John. Interview by Brenda Dixon-Stowell. New York: 15 August 1980.

Williams, Lavinia. "Black News." New York: WNEW-TV, 28 February 1981.

Williams, Martin. *The Smithsonian Collection of Classic Jazz.* Washington, D.C.: Smithsonian Institution, 1987.

Work, Monroe N., ed. *Negro Year Book, 1937–38.* 9th ed. Tuskegee Institute, Ala.: Negro Year Book Publishing Company, 1937.

X, Malcolm, and Alex Haley. *The Autobiography of Malcolm X.* [1964] New York: Grove Press, 1966.

Ziegler, Philip. "Yanks in Limeyland." *The Spectator* (London), 15 April 1995, 38.

Index